A Wife *of* Noble Character

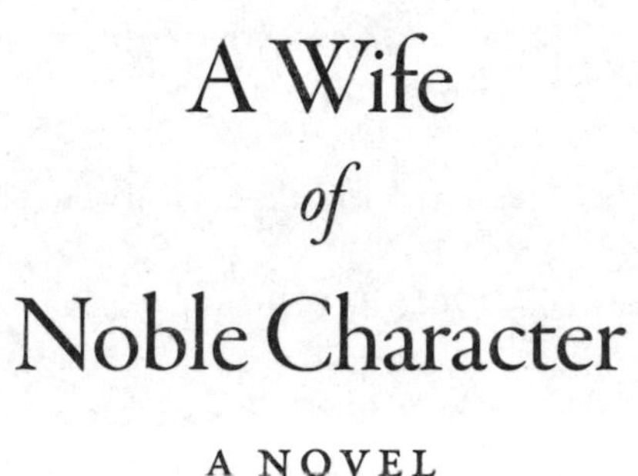

A Wife *of* Noble Character

A NOVEL

Yvonne Georgina Puig

HENRY HOLT AND COMPANY NEW YORK

Henry Holt and Company, LLC
Publishers since 1866
175 Fifth Avenue
New York, New York 10010
www.henryholt.com

Henry Holt® and ® are registered trademarks of Henry Holt and Company, LLC.

Distributed in Canada by Raincoast Book Distribution Limited

Library of Congress Cataloging-in-Publication Data

Names: Puig, Yvonne Georgina.
Title: A wife of noble character : a novel / by Yvonne Georgina Puig.
Description: New York : Henry Holt and Company, 2016.
Identifiers: LCCN 2015036038| ISBN 9781627795555 (hardcover) | ISBN 9781627795562 (electronic book)
Subjects: LCSH: Man-woman relationships—Fiction. | GSAFD: Love stories
Classification: LCC PS3616.U38 W53 2016 | DDC 813/.6—dc23
LC record available at http://lccn.loc.gov/2015036038

First Edition 2016

Designed by Meryl Sussman Levavi

Printed in the United States of America

1 3 5 7 9 10 8 6 4 2

For Toben Seymour

I dearly love the
state of Texas, but
I consider that a
harmless perversion
on my part, and
discuss it only
with consenting
adults.

—MOLLY IVINS

A Wife
of
Noble Character

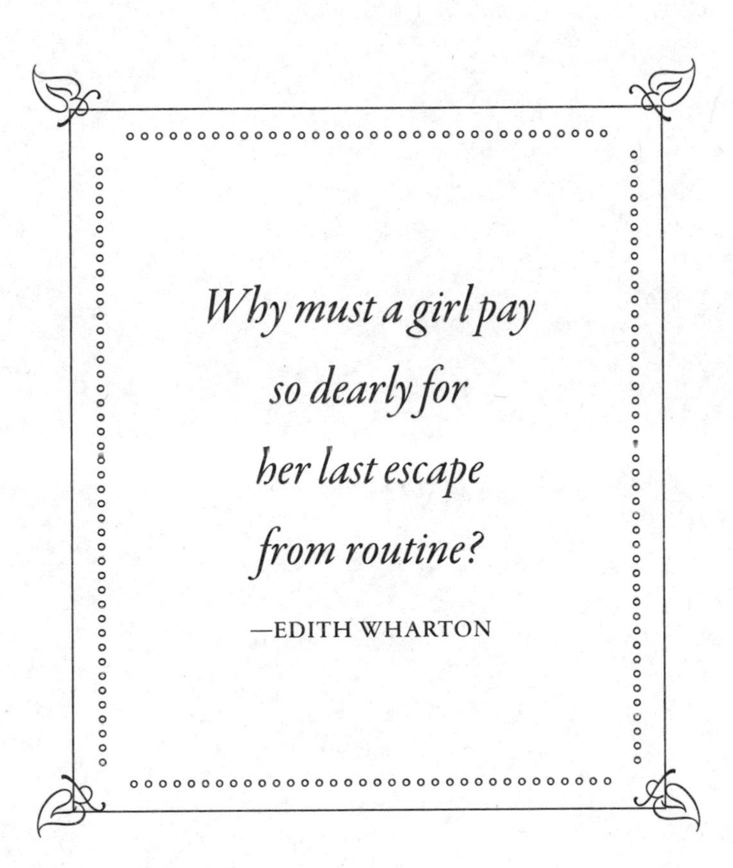

Why must a girl pay
so dearly for
her last escape
from routine?

—EDITH WHARTON

I

PRESTON NOTICED HER IMMEDIATELY. HE ALWAYS DID.

It was a Friday in May, a warm, windy day. Campus was busy. He was going home after a night spent at the studio preparing for his final reviews, but what was Vivienne doing here? She stood in the middle of the path, wearing a long white sundress, as dozens of students rushed past her. The wind played with her skirt, lifted her long, straight hair. She kept glancing around. There was nothing new about her—Preston had known her for years—yet he could not see her without feeling keenly curious.

He decided to approach. If she didn't want to talk, he knew, she would pretend not to see him. If she did, she would be his best friend. He wanted to see which it would be.

"Preston Duffin!"

She smiled and gave him a fragrant half embrace, stirring his senses agreeably after twenty-four hours spent in a room rank with the body odor of future architects. He hoped she couldn't smell him; her height met his shoulders exactly. A few underclassmen brushed by and took a second look, probably wondering who she was and why he got to touch her.

She stepped back and tucked her pale hair behind her ears. She was carrying a substantial and obviously, even to Preston, expensive white leather purse over her shoulder. It was covered in polished hardware and buckles that seemed not to buckle anything, and she slipped her small hand beneath the strap to relieve the weight of it from her shoulder.

He'd seen her only a few weeks ago, but he'd never seen her so radiant, so bright and unblemished. Maybe it was the humidity filling in the grooves of so many late nights spent drinking light beer in West Houston mansions, Preston imagined, calling up his usual distillation of her character. He knew they were the same age, but she didn't look thirty. In the broad collegiate thoroughfare full of earth-toned students and not-getting-any-younger professors, she was a fine beam of light.

"I'm so glad to see you. Thank you for coming to help me." She stood before him at full expectant female attention, her eyes green as spring moss. "You look like you slept with your head on a desk."

He thanked her for the observation—he'd actually been awake most of the night with his head on a desk—and said that he was always happy to appear the moment she needed help.

"I'm looking for the Rothko Chapel. I thought it was on the Rice campus." She interrupted herself to explain that she'd just had breakfast with their mutual friend Bladimir. "I know it's near Blad's, but I can't find it and my phone is dead."

"You're in the area," Preston said. "But the Rothko Chapel isn't on campus; it's a couple miles from here." After some questioning, he figured out where she'd parked and gave her directions.

To his surprise, she suggested they go there together. "Are you busy?"

Preston said that he was never too busy for her, and together they walked to her car through the campus rush and onto Montrose Boulevard, with its wide gravel sidewalks. Traffic passed close. Preston walked nearest to the street. Her car was parked a few feet into a crosshatched red zone. It was a black BMW 325 but an older one, probably late nineties, much older than what Preston assumed she'd drive. Why did he make these assumptions in the first place? The more she intrigued him, the more he was inclined to make assumptions about her.

She pulled a parking ticket from beneath the windshield wiper and frowned—an exaggerated pout, not pretty but endearing. She looked like a little girl.

"How much?" Preston said.

"Sixty dollars."

She was not nearly as bothered as Preston would have been. A parking ticket was cause for a day of mournful thoughts about all the things he could have spent sixty dollars on: a week's worth of modeling supplies, twenty cups of fancy coffee, a supremely minuscule percentage of his massive student debt. But Vivienne seemed to have forgotten about it already.

"Will you drive?" she said. "I don't know where I'm going."

So he drove while she sat beside him, fiddling with the air conditioner. Her car smelled like vanilla bean. He liked how odd and good it felt to be this near to her—he was usually a bystander in her company—but it was no doubt typical of Vivienne to bend a man's will to her need, no matter how small that need, and leave him feeling flattered for it. He remembered Vivienne in high school as a sumptuous vision enjoyed from afar, a sort of impressionist landscape—not someone he'd share friends with one day. But as their twenties narrowed, it seemed their social circles did too. They knew many of the same people; channels crossed. Preston liked seeing her, but sometimes she'd say something and then he'd think that maybe he liked seeing her more than he liked her. And yet, even then, she held his interest. Watching her was like watching a play—every way she spoke, or turned her wrist, suggested design and forethought. Her eyes were so alert. He could never figure them out, and so he could never quite figure out how to handle her.

"So are you an architect now?" she said.

"Almost," Preston said. "Graduating in a couple weeks if all goes well. You just wanted to check out some museums today?"

"I have some time. I told Waverly I'd help her with the seating chart—you know she's getting married? To Clay Fitcherson? I've been putting it off. But I don't have to be there till three."

"I got the save-the-date two months ago," Preston said.

"Oh, good," she said. "It's a huge wedding."

"It must be if I'm invited."

"I'll make sure to seat you next to a pretty girl."

Preston took this as a consolation, meaning she would not be the pretty girl sitting next to him. She was probably dating a guy who drove a big truck. She usually was.

He backed her car into a shaded spot. The morning was spectacularly humid, the neighborhood dewy and alive with the bustle and flap of grackles, the St. Augustine grass underfoot green and shag-thick. They stood before the daunting windowless brick octagon of the Rothko Chapel. It looked nothing like a chapel. There were spots of mossy mold here and there in the mortar. Some crows were perched on the lip of the roof, cawing.

"I always thought this building was an office," she said. "I've passed it a hundred times."

"What do you think about the architecture?"

"I should know better than to talk to you about architecture." So she saw through him. "I like the museum better." She pointed to the Menil Collection next door. "I've always loved that museum. I think my aunt or someone in my family was a patron. I've been to a lot of parties there."

The surrounding homes were all painted in the same soft shade of gray as the Menil. This quiet corridor was oil money at its best. One of Preston's favorite local tales was about Dominique de Menil, who, by way of her family's still-mighty oil-field equipment company, Schlumberger, erected this subtle temple to her art collection in the eighties and in the process gave fusty old Houston a real gift. Preston loved how unexpected it was that behind those gray walls, on the coastal plain of Texas, lay one of the world's most important collections of surrealist art.

He also liked the museum "better" than the chapel, which had always struck him as imposing given the synthesis of the surrounding architecture, a deliberate effort at variety. But he'd usually found a more complicated way of expressing Vivienne's same thought, involving Philip Johnson's intentions and the built environment. She had a point. Why were there so many layers of interpretation? Appreciating, despising, adoring, misunderstanding, not-caring-for. Sometimes you like a thing or you don't.

"The Menil is really a masterpiece of light," Preston said, and thinking he sounded pretentious, added, "I like it better too."

"That's nice," Vivienne said. "A masterpiece of light."

"The chapel is about the absence of light, the muting of it," he said.

"The Menil is about the disbursement of light. Renzo Piano might be my favorite."

"Is that the architect?"

Preston nodded. "Of the Menil."

She poked his arm. "Do you have a penny?"

Preston handed her one from his pocket, which she examined and squeezed tightly. Then she kissed her fist and tossed the penny into the reflecting pond full of pine needles.

Silly, Preston thought. *What does Vivienne Cally have to wish for?* To him, she was the girl who had everything. Though he was always running up against what "everything" meant. He tended to elevate the term above anything money could buy. There was something about Vivienne that seemed bought, as if the men she chose had won her affection with their money—a power he lacked—and so "everything" had to mean something beyond all that, something people with money couldn't hope to attain but that he, who had no oil money or gas pipeline or political legacy, or even a business degree, could. It was a method to convince himself that the tables turned: Vivienne Cally may suppose herself beyond his reach, but, in truth, he was beyond hers.

Inside, she sat on a bench and stared at the twilight-colored canvases while Preston pretended not to stare at her. Her beauty was beyond sexual (though it certainly was sexual). There was nothing angular about her. She was subtly round, her breasts big. He liked her shoulders in particular: strong and soft, but still delicate. Shoulders a man could clutch and feel stronger by. A pale face, a face filled with possibility. If only she didn't know it. But of course she did; she knew it all too well. And when Preston reminded himself of this, that this out-of-context Vivienne, here, was the popular, buoyant rich girl he'd always known, the depths receded. Her beauty was appealing because a man could ascribe any meaning to it he wished. God knows what the men she spent her time with made of her.

"Rothko painted these a few months before he slit his wrists," he said, joining her at the bench.

She frowned. "That's really sad."

A robed ascetic sort of man told them to shush. He was sitting

Indian style on an orange floor pillow. "Should everything make you happy?" Preston whispered.

"No," she replied, like a dart. "But why purposely make yourself sad? I believe happiness is more powerful than sadness."

"That's sweet but naïve," Preston said. "Don't you enjoy feeling sad sometimes?"

She held out a hand for Preston to help her off the bench, despite the fact that she could have stood up on her own. But he obliged the act. "No, I don't enjoy feeling sad," she said. "And I don't go out and make other people look at my sadness when I do feel sad."

Preston felt the back of his neck heat up. This was exactly the kind of ambivalence he couldn't stand. As if artists have an obligation not to upset people's sensitivities.

"Why should his art be dictated by our reactions? Why should he care how we feel?"

Vivienne sighed out her nose. "Who are the paintings for anyway? They're for people to see."

A guard in a baggy security uniform came over—a diminutive man with an impressive gray mustache waxed and twirled at the ends. He had the eager air of a volunteer. "This is a silent area," he said. "Please go outside."

They scooted out into the courtyard, united by a sense of mischief, Preston's budding righteousness diffused. There was something exhilarating about being scolded by an old person—it proved you were still young. You could still break rules without hurting anyone. You could still run away and leave people shaking their heads.

Vivienne blinked her eyes against the light of day and squinted at her slinky wristwatch. "It's still early. Want to take a walk?"

Then, to his bewilderment, she took his arm at the elbow and fixed it into a faux-gentlemanly promenade pose. Of course, he thought, I'm supposed to ask her on the walk that she suggested.

"My place is just down the block. I could make you a cup of coffee."

"*Merci*," she said cutely, in a Texan's impersonation of the French.

The walk to his apartment was five minutes through the neighborhood, shaded with old oaks. The trees were full of brown squirrels, reproaching passersby with tail flicks and terse chirps. The other passersby were harried students and academic mothers pushing strollers or clutching the hands of wobbly toddlers. Vivienne said "Good morning" to each mother they passed and paused to coo at each child, which made Preston uncomfortable, because he rarely greeted strangers and definitely never stopped to admire children. He stood by dumbly as she tickled bellies and complimented diaper bags, wondering if he should be impressed. Still, he liked that the women seemed to think they were a couple. It made him stand straighter, even while thinking over the condition of his studio apartment. He couldn't remember the last time he'd been there for more than a few minutes, and it was possible the garbage smelled or the bed was unmade, or worse. He remembered ejaculating into a sock the other day and had no idea as to the sock's current location.

"The university owns this house," he told her as they walked up the driveway. "It's a scholarship house. I live above the garage in the back." The garage didn't bring to mind anything collegiate. It was a building that spoke for itself: a two-car, two-story rectangle painted over in a peeling shade of beige. The garage door was open, displaying his hubcapless 1996 Civic, his broken LONE STAR BEER sign, his rusty bike fit for a fifteen-year-old, his work desk piled with reams of paper and rulers and eraser shavings. She only noticed the ivy. It covered half the house, forming a sort of structural shawl, softening corners. "It's very East Coast," she said. "I like it."

"Fig ivy," Preston said. "It's native to the Gulf Coast."

Preston started up the steps. Was it rude to walk in front of her? If he walked behind he'd see up her dress, which he wouldn't have minded, but he didn't want to get caught. She stopped midway and slipped her heels off and dropped them into her gigantic purse. He suddenly felt nervous—he was sure nothing would, or could, happen. She'd already told him that he looked like hell, but, still, she was about to be inside his apartment. He'd never been alone with her for so long.

To his relief, he didn't smell anything offensive when he opened the door. There were no socks in sight. The place was in decent order. He loved his habit of underestimating himself. He was always exceeding his own expectations.

"Welcome to my enormous apartment," he said.

Vivienne soft-footed inside and looked around. "This is the tiniest apartment I've ever seen." She set her purse on a brown corduroy armchair draped with a quilt.

Preston busied himself with boiling water and rinsing mugs in the kitchenette. "It's called a bachelor apartment," he said, over his shoulder. "I guess because this is all a man really needs."

"Is it all you need?"

"For now." He turned around and leaned against the counter, drying the mugs. Vivienne was standing at his father's old mahogany shelf, scanning his books. She took one from the shelf, an old Agee first edition, also his father's. She didn't open the book, just held it, admiring its exterior.

"I'd like to have more than one room, though, sooner than later," Preston said.

Vivienne slid the book back in place. "Do architects do well?" she said, turning her focus on him.

Preston smiled. "Territory you haven't thought to explore?"

"That's not what I mean."

He shook his head mirthfully and went back to the coffee. "Then why ask?"

She came over to his corner, arms akimbo. "Just because I asked if architects do well doesn't mean I'm on the hunt for an architect husband. You always needle me."

"Slow down," Preston said. He enjoyed riling her up like this; she was all pink in the cheeks. "Who said anything about hunting for husbands?"

"Never mind," she said.

He laughed. "I'm sorry. I'm not laughing at you," he said, even though he kind of was. He plunged the French press and poured the coffee, gave her the mug with the most crème on the top. She took it without saying anything, immediately closing her hands around it and bringing it to her face as if it were wintertime, and curled up in the armchair. She appeared to be pouting. Preston opened a window to let in some air. He sat at the edge of the bed, holding his mug on his knee.

"Architects can do very well later in their careers," he said. "Entry-level positions in firms are slogs, though. In the beginning you're a draftsman for the principal's designs. It's rare if you get to do your own design work, especially if you're at a bigger firm. It's a trade-off. At a bigger firm you do less design, but the salaries are better. At a smaller firm you get a pittance, but you get to design."

"You'd rather get a pittance and design," Vivienne said.

"I would."

She blew on her coffee. "I don't really drink coffee."

"Said the girl drinking coffee."

She raised her eyes and smiled. It brightened the whole room.

"I survive on coffee," he said. As he said this, he realized how tired he was. His eyes felt dry; his head droned. Vivienne was so pretty that when he looked at her, he woke up a little.

"I'd love to have my own place," Vivienne said. "I'm living with my aunt. The neighborhood is too expensive."

"This neighborhood is pretty cheap," he offered, realizing as the words left him that she was nodding in an over-polite way, probably to conceal her displeasure at the idea of ever moving here.

"Most of my friends live over there," she said. "It's home to me." Over there meaning West—where the money was, where the yards were green and lawnmowers and leaf blowers roared all day long.

"It's too seedy here?"

"It's not seedy here," she said. "It's cute. It's just that—if I lived here, it would be depressing."

Preston laughed. "Why is that?"

"Not for you, for me. If I lived here, people would feel sad for me because I was alone in a studio apartment," she said. "For you, it's a bachelor pad."

"I think that's a convenient exaggeration of reality," he said, testing his coffee with the tip of his free thumb. It was now the perfect too-hot-for-most-people temperature. This was one of Preston's favorite moments in life, right up there with walking the streets of a foreign city at sunrise, reading McMurtry, and completing a difficult design: the first sip. He liked to draw it out.

He wanted to tell her to look on Craigslist for a roommate, like everyone else in the world who wasn't a millionaire, but he checked his tone. "Live with a friend. I lived in a dorm this size with another guy for two years, and it wasn't as bad as it sounds. Assuming the person is sane, you get used to each other's rhythms and manage to avoid each other, or you become better friends."

"I lived in my sorority house with a bunch of girls," Vivienne said. "After college I lived with Karlie and Waverly, but then Karlie got married, and Waverly met Clay. I couldn't afford the apartment on my own."

"There's your answer," he said. "Get married."

"I have a job," she said. "I don't sit around all day getting massages."

"I didn't say you did." Although that wouldn't have surprised him.

"I work at Cotton and Lace," she said. "Cotton for resort and lace for dresses. We do a lot of bridesmaid's gowns and fittings for events."

"The other day I read that this idea that marriage is about soul mates is a modern convention," Preston said. "Historically, it was a practical agreement. The woman committed to the man sexually, and in exchange he provided resources. It wasn't until women had more freedom in deciding who they wanted to marry that it became about romance, generally speaking. But today"—he paused to sip, wondering if the tangent was inappropriate—"women have the same expectation of resources, but they also want love. It seems that without the resources, even with love, what's the incentive for women to marry?"

"Love is the incentive to marry," Vivienne said, as if to say, *What else would it be?*

Preston conceded. "But without resources?"

"I'm not sure I'd fall in love with a man who didn't have a good job," she said, leaning forward to rub the arch of her left foot. He would have rubbed it for her had she asked. "I want to have a family."

He wanted to ask her to define "good job," wanted to pry about numbers. What was the minimum annual income she'd accept? Had it occurred to her that she could be the provider? Why did she want a guy with money if her family was already wealthy? His mind sprung a fount of curiosity for this woman, arm's length away yet beyond him. Maybe that was why he needled her. If he could reach her, he wouldn't have to needle her. The sun shone through the skylight, warming his back, its outlying beams grazing Vivienne's girlishly bony ankles. She sat in his brown corduroy chair as if she'd always been there.

"But is it only about love, then?" he said. "Is it honest to say it's not about resources?"

"What are you trying to get me to say?" Vivienne said. "Whenever I see you, you try to get me to say things."

"I'm not trying to get you to say anything." Was he, though? "I just think for women, marriage is also practical."

"It is for men too," she said. "I know women think about money, but few *only* think about money." She paused. "Are your parents still together?"

"Retired together in Austin. Yours?" The moment he asked, he remembered that her parents had died, recalled the hush surrounding this fact in high school. "Sorry if that was insensitive. I forgot—"

She waved him off. "I couldn't move into a place like this and go on with my life if I was single," she said. "If I did, there'd be repercussions. That's the only way I can explain it." She looked everywhere but at him. When she furrowed her brow, it made her round chin jut out a bit. Her lips pinched up, and he saw a flash of her in middle age. She was more attractive, a woman.

She picked up her gigantic purse and dropped it on the floor, took the quilt from behind her shoulders, and fidgeted it over her legs.

"My grandmother made that quilt." He set his coffee aside and knelt beside her, to show her the embroidery: *To Preston, God Loves You.*

Vivienne narrowed her eyes on him. "I've always liked you," she said.

He wasn't sure whether to be disappointed—knowing such sincere declarations were probably reserved for guys with no chance of getting any—or happy because it was a nice thing to hear. So, this being Vivienne, he felt something like ambivalently flattered. "But I'm not a Republican," he said lightly.

She flicked his shoulder. Preston admired her remarkably soft-seeming arms. And her wrists—such fragile mechanisms they were. It was pleasant to be near a beautiful woman.

"I've always liked you too," he said.

"I like that you don't think I'm trying to, you know, marry you." She squeezed the quilt to her chest.

This prompted Preston to stand and unconsciously dust off his khakis as if they were in urgent need of dusting off. "No, I definitely don't think that." He said it with a smile, but he felt hurt. She liked him because she knew she'd never *like* him.

"You're not the type of guy to get married, or at least not for a long time. People in graduate school"—here she gestured fancily—"think marriage is a joke. They look down on people their age who get married. If a woman really wanted to marry you, you'd run away." She lowered her voice. "My friends think the only thing that can keep me safe is a husband."

"Safe from what?"

She paused, her eyes beyond the room. "I don't know. From being alone?"

Preston disagreed with her on so many fundamental levels that he wished she would keep talking so he could come up with a response. And he felt badly for her. She underestimated herself. It was hard to get sentimental about Vivienne, though, when you thought of the money and all that money could do.

He shouldn't have said anything to begin with. He was in no position to discuss marriage, but it was fun, sometimes, to pretend he was as grown-up as he should be by now. Like Vivienne, he'd always imagined that at thirty he'd already be married. Certainly not living on loans, alone in a garage apartment. But thoughts like these never ruined his day. He could trace the fact that he was single to a cause. He'd made the choice not to get serious with anyone yet. He'd always known he wanted to be an architect and that he'd have to be broke in order to do it. He wondered about Vivienne, though—why hadn't she married yet? Sitting across from him, tugging at a loose thread in the quilt, she looked a little lost.

"Want to share a cigarette?" he said. "I promise I only smoke when I have guests." Vivienne glanced at him with a moment's reluctance in her eyes and then, just as quickly, composed her face into a picture of gladness. The transformation was strange but unsurprising. Wasn't it her job, in a way, to adapt to the various scenarios life presented and, by her loveliness, make those scenarios pleasant for the other people involved? She did it well, but Preston detected a flicker of effort, which he attributed to himself. He'd stuck a fork in her gears.

He found the cigarettes in his kitchenette junk drawer. He kept them to share with girls, but he hadn't brought a girl home in so long that the pack had yet to be opened.

They went to the open window. Vivienne rested her back against the frame and peered down the driveway. Somewhere in the neighborhood a car alarm was going off. Farther away, ambulance sirens. When the car alarm stopped, a pair of mourning doves could be heard cooing in the oaks.

"The Blanks' Memorial Day party is in two weeks," she said, taking the cigarette he offered.

"The annual blowout rivaled only by the GOP convention," Preston said. "I'll bring my rifle in case you forget yours."

Vivienne brought the cigarette to her lips and pulled. "You always tease me," she said, exhaling. She didn't pass the cigarette, but he didn't mind. He didn't even want it. He just wanted to watch her smoke. "You know what's funny? I have no memory of ever talking to each other in high school."

"That was on purpose," he said. "I tried hard to be invisible to pretty girls in high school."

She smiled. "I heard you designed Karlie and Tim's addition."

Preston shrugged. "I didn't design it. I interned for the firm that designed it."

"I don't know why they needed an addition," she said. "Unless Karlie is planning on having a baby soon."

"Because bigger is better. You know that."

"Does it scare you," she said, "not knowing when you'll be able to afford more than an apartment?"

Preston was amused at being put in his place. "Not at all. I'm one of the noble peasants."

"The fact that you'll have to work all the time and find a job—does that worry you? That you won't be able to move around?"

"Well, yeah, with all the parties I'll miss at Waverly's ranch."

She rolled her eyes. "They're honest questions."

"They're also snotty questions," he said.

Vivienne took a final drag and scowled. "Cigarettes are gross." She tossed it out the window.

Preston made a mental note to find it on the driveway later and throw it away.

She leaned forward, gripping the windowsill, hesitating, focused on something above the tree line. "Whenever I see you, I end up wondering what you think of me."

"Probably because you think I'm so wise."

She shook her head and laughed. "Time for me to go."

He stepped aside so she could make her way through the passage between the furniture to the door. "Do you remember how to get back to your car? I can walk you."

"I'm fine on my own."

He felt divided between wanting more time with her—something seemed unresolved—and relief that she was leaving. He let the moment pass and didn't insist. They shared a brief hug at the threshold. She felt small in his arms, her breasts a single, solicitous cushion against his chest.

"You should come to the ranch for Memorial Day," she said over his shoulder.

"Maybe," he said. He knew without a doubt that he would.

He waved goodbye as she made her delicate way down the stairs, watched her from the doorway as she paused on the last step to slip into her heels.

II

I AM INSANE, VIVIENNE THOUGHT. SHE STRAIGHTENED HER shoulders and strode down the driveway, ignoring the blisters burning her heels. It occurred to her that she didn't entirely remember the way back to her car, but she knew it wasn't far. Better to be lost than to slip further into insanity at Preston's. This time she blamed herself; she'd invited it. Just as she was turning the corner—it was a left from the driveway, that much she remembered—a bicycle materialized in the corner of her vision and swept past, nearly catching her dress and pulling her down.

Vivienne whipped around. The bicyclist braked, not to check on her but to park. It was a girl riding with an armful of books. She dropped her kickstand and started up the driveway.

"Excuse me!" Vivienne said.

The girl turned around. She was clearly a student, with her books and frumpy jeans and T-shirt.

"You almost ran me over!" Vivienne felt hot in the face.

"Sorry," the girl said, with obvious apathy.

She gave Vivienne a curious stare and continued on her way. Vivienne watched her. She had pretty hair. It was perfectly straight and shiny, the hair Vivienne longed for. Now she was standing at Preston's door, knocking. Annoyed afresh, Vivienne crossed the street and went to find her car, without turning back. The thought that another girl was coming over to his little apartment seconds after she'd left it, to occupy the same chair, the only chair, and probably to talk about books, which Vivienne wasn't good at talking about, was exceptionally annoying, because it made her feel less special, less set apart from the rest. It was as if all her efforts to charm Preston had been for naught. Surely he found books more charming than her own brand of charm, and the girl had an armful of them.

Her mind felt ablaze. It might have been the cigarette, but it was probably Preston. He was always jabbing her, questioning her, finding fault with her desires. It was the same last time she ran into him, a few weeks ago, at Bladimir's birthday party. They were at a poorly lit bar, sitting around a sticky wooden table with a bunch of people she didn't know. It wasn't her kind of place, and it hadn't been clear to her if it was a gay bar, despite the fact that Blad was gay. She didn't ask Blad or Preston about it, because she was embarrassed that she didn't know.

She and Preston had had a conversational wrangle about reality television, Preston declaring it yet another terrible thing about the world. He'd been a little drunk and was endearing because he got so passionate about his arguments, but Vivienne mainly remembered feeling stomped. She'd only been arguing that reality television was entertaining. Preston had wanted her to *justify her position*. All she could say, over and over, was that she personally found it entertaining. Preston claimed this was *insufficient justification*. She tried to get drunk, but the men weren't offering to buy drinks, and no one had seemed impressed with her, except for Preston, but she never could tell with him.

Preston probably didn't remember that night, which didn't come as a shock, because one of her most firmly held convictions was that men never remember anything, and if they do, they remember very little and always the wrong or unimportant things. Sometimes she felt this worked to her benefit, but mostly it impeded her. If she was in the mood to hear Bucky, whom she was currently dating, tell the story of when they first met, she was forced to ask, "And did you think I was beautiful?" To which he would reply, "Of course I did, baby." All he really remembered was what he ate for dinner that night. It wasn't such a romantic story; Karlie introduced them at a Prayerwood church benefit three months earlier and they exchanged soft conversation over barbecued quail, but she thought he should indulge her in a little exaggeration.

Vivienne's dreams were full of men who remembered. They remembered their eyes falling upon her in bountiful detail; they remembered exactly the words they'd spoken regarding marriage and children, even years out; they remembered in juicy specificity stories about other women they had dated. They even asked Vivienne about things they hoped she remembered, and in her dreams she'd luxuriate in not remembering anything at all.

Preston only seemed to remember the things about her that he disagreed with, which she responded to with her charm, a technique that hardly worked on him, she thought now. This woolly feeling in her brain—was she the one who'd been charmed? The way he looked at her with lifted brows and sideways smiles set her flirting all off course. The apartment with its handmade quilt, and Preston with that curious glint in his eyes and the messy way he rolled up his shirtsleeves. He was the gear around which the whole place worked. It had all been so disarming that she'd had to raise a white flag and leave immediately.

She oriented herself from the Menil and was crossing the museum's lawn barefoot, her heels hanging at her side from two fingers, when she heard an unfamiliar voice call out her name—a man's voice. It was jarring, the sudden sound of her own name. She heard it as if she were underwater. The second time, the voice was louder. She had only a second to breach the surface and to turn and face it with a valiant smile.

Randal Stanley.

"Hello, little lady!" he said. He always used cowboy language, overcompensating for the fact that he wasn't really from Texas.

"Hi, Randal," Vivienne said pleasantly. He was about ten feet away on the path and advancing, which gave her enough time to extend her hand and evade a hug.

"Quite a handshake there," he said, grinning. A woman in a knee-length pencil skirt and silk blouse, both black, and a pair of slim black stilettos, which Vivienne might have selected for herself, was right behind him. Her hair was pulled back in a tight bun, and she held a leather-bound folder to her chest. Out of instinct or habit, Vivienne instantly pictured herself through this elegant woman's eyes—and wilted beneath the image. Her hair was loose and flat, her dress frilly and too white. And, worst of all, she was short. Vivienne dreaded standing before a taller woman. She was five-four, not even very short, but she'd been caught unarmed, flat-footed.

She stepped lightly onto the path and restored herself into her own heels. "My heels were sinking into the ground!" she said. "Isn't it a pretty day?" Sufficiently buoyed, it occurred to her to wonder what was going on, Randal with this woman.

"It is now!" Randal said. He was a midsize man who made no effort to conceal his furriness. A throw rug grew beneath his black-and-floral Rockmount shirt. Yet Vivienne could see he'd taken pains to mask his withdrawing hairline. His hair was sideswept and stuck in place. "Whatter you doin' over here?"

The other woman looked at Vivienne serenely, too serenely. Vivienne had a terrible thought: *Do I look like I've been out all night? Does this woman feel sorry for me?* The idea of being pitied coupled with the prospect of Randal Stanley thinking she was on her way home from a one-night stand was too much. He'd no doubt share his false assumption with as many people as possible. It was too complicated to explain being at Preston's. Why would she be here in heels and a dress before noon? Funny that the actual explanation—that she'd come to the neighborhood to see a museum—was, she felt, the most unbelievable.

Vivienne thought fast. "I came by to check out the space for Waverly's rehearsal dinner." An inspired fiction. She mentally patted herself on the back.

"How about that?" Randal said. "I didn't know this was Bracken's kind of show. He's not a big art guy." Bracken—Waverly's father—was indeed not an art guy. How could she forget that Randal was courting Bracken's friendship? The museum didn't align with the Blanks' ranch tastes whatsoever.

"Oh, it was Waverly's idea," Vivienne said, sweet as pie. "I'm her maid of honor, so I thought I'd take a look for her."

"The museum would be delighted to host the Blanks," the placid woman said.

"This lovely lady works here," Randal said. "I'm gettin' involved and she's showin' me the ropes. She's gonna to teach me about art."

The woman nodded in acknowledgment of his riches. "Mr. Stanley has been very generous."

Vivienne should have guessed that one immediately: Randal Stanley, Museum Donor. There was no other explanation for this sort of giraffe-like woman paying any attention to him.

"She's about to give me the private tour," he said. "Why don't you come along? The place is closed up just for us. Me and two pretty women." He winked lecherously, calling to mind every reason she couldn't stand him. His boots were as slick as his teeth. He was like a snake, always nearing in. That he probably thought she found him handsome was enraging.

"I'd love to, Randal, but I have to go meet Waverly," she said, smiling. "And now that I think about it, you're right. This isn't really the Blanks' taste for a party."

"Aw," he said, "don't turn sour."

Vivienne kept smiling and refused the invitation again. The frustrating thing was that she would have liked to go into the museum, especially when it was empty and she wouldn't have to deal with other people hogging all the space in front of paintings, but Preston had zapped her museum energy with his sad Rothkos, and there was no way she was going in there with Randal Stanley and a giraffe. She could probably get a private tour of her own if she dropped her aunt's name. But if she accepted now and endured his company, she could defuse Randal's hurt feelings. He probably sensed her evasiveness—he was a slippery man but not a dumb man. If she joined him, he'd be so happy he'd forget the way he was looking at her right that very moment, with wet, loutish skepticism. No doubt he was concocting a way to penalize her for not giving him what he wanted.

Vivienne foresaw him dropping it into conversation: *Ran into little Vivienne, and she said the Blanks were having a dinner at the Me-neal, where it just so happens Ima donor!* It would get back to the Blanks, who'd wonder why she said that. Then she'd have to backtrack. She saw the risks before her like items on a shelf. All she had to do was rearrange them a little, play with them, and they'd no longer be risks. She could turn risk into promise.

An hour spent cajoling Randal might reap unforeseen rewards. She didn't want to admit it, but he was up-and-coming. He'd moved to Houston a couple of years ago, from some cold place like Delaware, set on fulfilling vague cowboy dreams by becoming the biggest dermatologist in town. In this short span of time, he'd done just that. At forty, he was the local maestro of blackheads, spider veins, and Botox. His commercials were all over local prime time. Even Vivienne knew his slogan, and not because she'd paid any attention. It was just on so many billboards, on television so often, that she couldn't avoid it. IF YOU HAVE ACNE, CALL THE RANDAL-MAN; HE'LL LEND YOUR FACE A HAND! Vivienne thought it was the worst slogan she'd ever heard. He seemed to pride himself on being shameless, and in this regard he was more Texan than anyone, but Vivienne never said this aloud. There was an odd sincerity to his name-dropping, a genuine avidness Vivienne thought he'd do well to tamp down. He'd lobbed money at beloved Houston institutions and was steadily, inexplicably, moving up. Rudy Tomjanovich had spent the weekend fishing at his house on Lake Conroe. His luxury suite at the football stadium overlooked the fifty-yard line, elbow-rubbing distance from Bob McNair. He'd sponsored the biggest covered wagon at the Rodeo Parade and ridden all the way to the old Astrodome, waving like a Hollywood star. Every time Vivienne heard one of these tales, she'd roll her eyes and imagine Lynn Wyatt reluctantly mingling with Randal. He could buy his company, but he couldn't buy his company's enjoyment.

He'd had his eye on Vivienne for months. She didn't even remember where they'd met, some party or other. He seemed to think she was the cherry on top, the prize that would justify his investment in the state of Texas. He'd made his position so plain that Vivienne often had to get creative in deflecting him. She'd secretly pass gas during their conversations, or feign a sick stomach and escape to the nearest bathroom, anything to reduce his attraction to her. These methods had to be practiced discreetly, of course, maybe too discreetly, but he hadn't been dissuaded by her less discreet approaches either. She'd openly suggest that he ask a certain willing woman to dinner, and suddenly he'd turn clever and whisper that he knew what she was up to.

"Come on, now," he said. "You won't be alone in there with me."

"I wouldn't worry about that," Vivienne said, still pleasant.

Randal tucked his thumbs in his belt loops. He was surveying her tone, deciding whether to be offended. "How'll you know what to say to Waverly," he said, rocking on his boots, "if you don't even go inside? You didn't drive over here just to stand on the lawn, did you?"

The other woman hadn't moved, but her smile was looking a little strained.

He was testing her. "No, I didn't drive all the way out here to stand on the lawn," she said. "I came out here for some time to myself."

It took Randal a few chest-hair-stroking moments to absorb her words. Once he did, he seemed satisfied. "That's what I like about you, Viv," he said. "You don't feel the need to flatter me. I can appreciate quiet time, and I don't want to interfere on you."

Vivienne made sure to preemptively offer him her hand again. Instead of shaking it, he kissed it. She tolerated this but immediately wiped her hand on the back of her dress. He told her not to be a stranger, as he always did, and set off with the woman, who fluttered her fingers at Vivienne. Once they were out of sight, Vivienne practically threw off her heels. She fumed all the way to her car, mostly angry with herself. Not only had she coddled Randal in order to repel him—the easy way out—but he'd taken it as a sign of respect, and in the process she'd humiliated herself. Why didn't she just tell him she was having coffee with a friend and seeing a museum to begin with? Then she wouldn't have had to skirt the fib about Waverly's rehearsal dinner. Now that he'd been coddled he wouldn't punish her, but she didn't feel relieved. He probably thought he held a secret of hers and a reason to seek her confidence. What did it matter whether he thought she was coming from sleeping with a random guy? It was none of his business; she didn't feel entitled to know how and with whom he'd spent his morning, even if she cared.

She sat in the car and pressed at her temples. She missed the feeling she'd had leaving Preston's. That was a more pleasant, flirty sort of confusion. The confusion she felt now pushed her right up against a wall: *Why do you care?*

She drove home, listening to the refrain in her head, unable to answer, blaming Preston. If he hadn't made her feel stupid about her life, she wouldn't currently feel stupid about the way she'd handled Randal. Preston didn't realize how important it was to win people over, to have people on his side. He went around thinking he could analyze and judge everything. He thought success had nothing to do with external expectations, but Vivienne knew how gratifying it was to triumph before her peers, to live up to their standards. Preston seemed to have only himself to live up to, and how could that be enough? The current conflict was a smashup between her desire to exceed the expectations of her world and her desire not to care about those expectations at all. She had no idea where this impulse to not care was even coming from, which was further cause to blame Preston. Not once in all her years of knowing women, of Brownies and Girl Scouts and Junior League and cotillion, or in her sorority, had one girlfriend ever posed to her an alternative on the Way to Be. A few girls had left Texas and gone to New York or elsewhere, but she hadn't known them well. Her own quiet interest in art had never struck her as a path she could realistically follow. The women who went on to careers had always spoken boldly about their interests and their plans in school. Vivienne had come to believe that none of that was for her. Her will was strong but it needed direction, and she didn't like fielding questions about how she might pursue art, because she lacked the confidence to find the answer and she resented how the options posed to her were implicitly postmarriage; she might co-chair an event at the Museum of Fine Arts or take an oil painting course at the Glassell School.

Aunt Katherine, who'd raised her, was least of all a guide to modern womanhood. Vivienne had spent her adolescence avoiding Katherine; in childhood she'd clung to the hope that Katherine would become the mother she'd lost, but by the time she got her period in seventh grade, she'd given it up. She couldn't remember Katherine ever tucking her in or reading her a book. There was no real affection in the house, only politesse and a parade of nannies whose names Vivienne got confused. She hadn't bonded with any of them. Perhaps they'd sensed the unhappiness behind Katherine's bright exterior, or perhaps Katherine hadn't bothered to disguise the unhappiness in the first place, or maybe Katherine's assessment was right: The nannies left because Vivienne was such an awful girl. Just like her mother. Difficult, strong-willed, trouble. Vivienne never actually did anything troublesome that she knew of, but she was the child of her mother, and Katherine considered Vivienne's mother the most troublesome woman in the world. Vivienne only remembered her mother in glimpses, freeze-frames; she didn't know whether she took after her or not. She'd memorized the two photo albums under her bed. Her mother had fairy-tale hair, long and golden and loose. She wore floral dresses. Her smile was bigger in the pictures taken after Vivienne's birth. Her name was May. She named her daughter Vivienne May. The portrait made by the albums differed from the villain Vivienne had come to know through Katherine. *Your mother abandoned my brother—your father! She drove him to his death. She was an atheist. She was never a good wife.* And on it went, till eventually Vivienne stopped hearing it. But the words took shape within Vivienne, a small, sharp shard of shame that her whole identity had to grow around, like a tree trunk over a rope.

Her mother had left the family for a younger man, a mudlogger employee of Cally Petroleum. They were in love. Vivienne knew this because Barbara Grimble, her godsend old-timing, now-deceased neighbor, the woman who invited her over during the holidays for tree-trimming, had told her what she considered the straight facts before Vivienne left Houston for college at Texas Christian. A few months after her mother took up with the mudlogger, her dad drove out to Galveston and smashed his Porsche into the seawall. According to Mrs. Grimble, the wreck had nothing to do with the divorce—her mother hadn't asked for a dime; his gas investments had turned while he was squandering his inheritance playing at being an oilman. According to Katherine, he would never have been so stressed about some investments as to crash into the seawall. He was an heir to the Cally Petroleum fortune; his living didn't depend on his investments. If he'd been worried about money, it was because he'd anticipated how much would be milked from him in the divorce. He was drunk, the police had proved that much. Mrs. Grimble claimed this was often the case; Katherine claimed he rarely drank. The only thing the two agreed on was the wickedness of the media—the whole thing unfolded in the local press as a spectacle. This only caused further invective against Vivienne's mother, who'd then not only privately betrayed the family but publicly humiliated them as well.

All of it meant little to Vivienne. She was three when her father died and four when her mother, who'd moved to Port Aransas with the mudlogger, died too. Turned out all that time she'd been quietly dying of ovarian cancer. "Quiet" was Barbara Grimble's word. The older she grew, the less Vivienne believed that the dying had felt quiet to her mother. On days when she had painful cramps, she thought of her mother. Could she have saved her somehow? Deep inside her, streaming beneath everything, was a second life, the one she might have lived had her mother survived.

There was no custody battle, no need for divorce proceedings, so the divinations of what would have been, the various evils May would have committed against God and Katherine, became speculative myth. Despite the passage of twenty-seven years, it was a subject Katherine and her friends at Gracedale Catholic Church returned to often, and every once in a while Vivienne heard her mother mentioned in passing remarks, usually jokes about the mudlogger himself, a silent figure in the whole tragedy, who'd gotten himself killed in a fire offshore.

That her parents' legacy was this immense unresolved drama full of dead people made Vivienne feel that her life should be the resolution, so that by conceiving her their union hadn't been such a waste. They'd loved each other enough at one point to marry and make a life—her own life—so she couldn't only be the product of loss and collapse. The resolution would be a happy, comfortable married life for herself, with years of love to counteract all the fighting. Vivienne deliberately hadn't mentioned this part of the fantasy to Preston.

Katherine, always determined to convince Vivienne she was unworthy of love, continued to be an obstacle on this point. She kept a slow drip of hurt over Vivienne's head, so slow Vivienne sometimes didn't feel it or, if she did, generously wondered whether Katherine even knew what she was doing. It was part of their private dialogue. Vivienne learned from Katherine that her happiness depended on extricating from her personality any remnants of her mother, that career was secondary to the more important task of getting married—but only after college, and to a reputable man—and that ambitious women were to be avoided: They were usually lesbians. In sinister tones, she reminded Vivienne of what she was set to inherit if things turned out well and what she was set to lose if they didn't, and in the next sentence she'd toss her hands up convivially and exclaim that she *just didn't know what else to say*. Her favorite platitude was that God was like a river—go with his flow and all would be well and right; wrestle against him and drown. Barbara Grimble was probably rolling over in her grave at the injustice this metaphor did to all good Christians everywhere, coming as it did from Katherine Cally's lips, and pretending as it did that faith should be easy. It was Barbara's idea that Vivienne carry a baby picture of herself in the plastic window of her wallet, to remind herself she was lovable. Vivienne laughed off the idea but slid one in front of her driver's license anyway. In the picture she is a toddler, blond as the sun, standing in the muddy Galveston sand in a red toddler bikini, probably a stone's throw from the fatal seawall.

Despite all the reasons she held dear for why she was insufficient, Vivienne was certain of her beauty. Like her insecurities, she held her looks close to her heart and guarded them intensely. To her mind, they were the way out from Katherine and the way into a protected life. If she married well enough, she wouldn't need to worry about the inheritance, she wouldn't need Katherine. It seemed to her that Katherine's threats might be empty. Maybe there weren't so many millions anyway—the company was sold after her father's death, the money scattered amid lawsuits. It eventually made its way to investors, unseen relatives, and Katherine. But Cally remained a name. Vivienne's grandparents had invested grandly in the arts, and the city bore their stamp. Katherine sat on the boards of museums because her parents had purchased the privilege.

Vivienne lived with Katherine in a three-bedroom townhome. It wasn't modest, but it wasn't lavish either. Whether this was because of Katherine's Catholic temperance or because it was all they could afford, Vivienne had no idea. Whatever the estate really amounted to, Katherine had paid for Vivienne's education, and Vivienne got free rent. She used this luxury to amass credit-card debt and spend what money she did earn on trying to maintain a lifestyle appropriate to the oil heiress everyone thought she was. Her name and face were enough to rouse the envy of her peers, even if her home was humble by the neighborhood standard.

Vivienne decided to employ her cure-all mind-clearing ritual. She turned onto Memorial Drive instead of the freeway, opened the sunroof, and unrolled all the windows, even though the sun was getting hot. Each day that month had been slightly hotter than the last, foretelling the blistering summer to come. She stuck her Madonna mix in the CD player, turned up the volume on "Like a Prayer," and sped through Memorial Park. As usual there was roadkill here and there—a couple of possums, an armadillo, and a raccoon—the blood and guts of which interfered with her ritual. The point of it was twofold: to rid her mind of annoying thoughts, and to reinstate her preferred sense of superiority and invincibility. It was hard to feel invincible looking at dead animals, but today she managed to forget the instant she passed them.

At this hour the boulevard had little traffic. Joggers were jogging in packs on either side of the road, weaving in and out of the piney woods. Vivienne felt herself returning. She remembered that an oil heiress by the unfortunate name of Ima Hogg had donated this land to the city. Poor Ima had never married, but her grandfather was the first native-born governor of Texas, and she'd been rich, and look at all she'd left behind. The joggers seemed so glad. The sky above the park was a deep Texas blue. Vivienne wondered whether Ima had been sad about being alone or if she'd been too busy with philanthropy to care. She probably would have married if her name hadn't been Ima Hogg. The thought of people remembering her as rich and magnanimous gave Vivienne the surge she'd been hoping for, and she flattened the pedal out of the park. Her hair lashed around in the warm car wind as she drove the miles-long stretch of mansions leading to her own neighborhood.

A slow song came on next, the one where in the music video Madonna falls in love with a bullfighter who breaks her heart. Vivienne, now fortified, slowed to gaze down the long driveways of the mostly Tuscan, ranch, and Tudor-style mansions. There was even a plantation-style Buddhist temple with a marble elephant playing in a pond full of lily pads in the front yard. Next door an old low ranchburger, set back on several wooded acres, was being read its last rites. Orange tape hugged a couple dozen of the trees, and the house itself was boarded up and stripped. There was a big sign in place of the mailbox: BB DEVELOPMENT.

The sight of Bracken Blank's mark on yet another lot had no effect on Vivienne. It served only as a reminder that she was on her way to the Blanks' house, and she kept on into more-commercial territory, past George Bush's palatial office tower with its synthetic blue lake, past the St. Pius Academy for Girls, to which Katherine had often threatened to send her, and back into another wooded stretch of homes. By the time she'd made a left at Timber Knoll, waved at the Hispanic guy in the security box—whom she always pretended to know, and who always waved back eagerly as if he knew her too—wound down the cul-de-sac to the Blanks' lengthy horseshoe driveway, and parked her car before the big white colonnade of their French Colonial home, she was past the trials of the morning. The day held promise, and the world did too.

III

ON A SATURDAY TWO WEEKS LATER, VIVIENNE'S ALARM rang at nine. She worked five days a week at the store, and in order to make her days off feel full, Vivienne imposed order. Rising by ten was essential to this. From her window draped in gathered floral curtains, she enjoyed the view of an old reaching pin oak. Her most luxurious moments of the day were often spent watching gray squirrels scamper along its limbs; the tree was their on-ramp to the roof. If she slept late, she missed her time looking out the window. But if she kept her eyes open after the first alarm, she had forty-five minutes to lie in the fractured sunlight and snuggle into her duvet—Katherine kept the townhouse at sixty-eight degrees in the spring and even cooler in the summer—and watch the goings-on of the tree. She'd suctioned a hummingbird feeder to the window, but it hadn't attracted any hummingbirds yet. Maybe they'd come in deeper summer.

She could usually guess the weather by how much condensation was dripping from the pane. Today it was sopping wet, but the room was unseasonably cold, so it was possible it was a less humid day than the window let on. Her thoughts wandered around what clothes to pack for the Memorial Day party, her goals being to attract Bucky and to look better than the other girls. She reproached herself a little for this thought. Vivienne was aware, in her heart more than her mind, that she didn't have to try so hard, but this didn't stop her. After all, she'd been an active participant for as long as she could remember. It was a way of giving her mind immediate purpose. Bucky would pick her up in a few hours.

She curled up on her side and hugged her knees. The squirrels were tearing up and down the oak. Katherine seemed to be out. There was no vacuum running, no yard blower blazing outside, and no ring of Katherine's voice directing the hands operating the machines. The house quiet, Vivienne closed her eyes and thought of Bucky. She narrowed her mind hard to clearly see him and the parts of his body she knew best. His rough hands, firm calves. She narrated in her mind the nights to come at the ranch and what she would wear that would lead him to say what she wanted to hear and to touch her how she wanted to be touched. The weekend's outfits came to her as if in a dream.

She nestled her computer in her lap on the bed and checked her email, even though the only people who ever emailed her on Saturdays were the credit-card company, Neiman Marcus, and Waverly. She replied to Waverly's pronouncement that the Memorial Day party was going to be SO FUN. Next, with the usual bad feeling in her stomach, she checked her bank account. Today the balance was three hundred fifty dollars, more than she'd expected but over budget for the month. There was still a week left until June, and she'd already spent more than twelve hundred dollars, four hundred dropped yesterday on a dress for the weekend's party, at a little shop with an unpronounceable name Waverly had discovered near the Galleria.

She sank her chin into her palms and calculated. The boutique would owe her about three hundred dollars next week. She'd probably be fine as long as she avoided expensive dinners and shopping trips—easy enough to do in theory. The dinners were more problematic than shopping, due to the element of group consensus. If six people wanted to get dinner, for example, even at some moderately priced place where drinks just added up, her choices, unless Bucky was there, were to go home for the night, not eat, or pretend she could afford it. Most often she chose the latter. Honesty about her situation was unthinkable. And by the end of these nights, signing her credit-card receipt, she had convinced herself she could afford it.

She knew the only way out of living with Katherine was by saving money, and she promised herself *never again* after every gratuitous expense, but she always managed to forget that promise until after the next gratuitous expense. Somehow living at Katherine's wasn't so bad when she wanted a certain pair of shoes, or a massage at the Houstonian with Waverly, or one more eighteen-dollar pour of pinot noir. And then, once the shoes were home, the massage over, and the glass empty, living at Katherine's was worse than ever.

She set aside her computer and went to the old Sakowitz hatbox tucked away in Katherine's powder-blue closet, where cash awaited. She rarely pocketed more than two hundred dollars at a time, fearing that Katherine might notice, but today she took four hundred. Since September 11, Katherine kept upward of five thousand dollars in there, just in case the terrorists showed up. Occasionally Vivienne permitted herself greater sums, but she couldn't be too careful. She performed her heist in under a minute. If she hesitated, the inner turmoil stopped her: *It's wrong to steal, but Katherine deserves it. That money isn't yours, but isn't it your family's? I'm a bad person, but isn't Katherine a bad person too? Two wrongs don't make a right! Vivienne, you are thirty years old!*

That slippery business done, she packed up her dresses in a garment bag. She brought two extra evening dresses—fun, short-skirted little numbers—and for the car ride wore a gray romper that tied at the shoulders and left her legs almost entirely bare. The drawback with this choice was, as usual, the imposition of her breasts. A strapless bra looked bulky under the fabric. She picked out a purple bra instead, so that the exposed straps could double as a camisole or bikini.

An hour later, Bucky Lawland pulled in the driveway and honked. Vivienne checked her teeth in the entryway mirror and smoothed out her romper. Her bags were cumbersome, so she spent a few moments deciding how to hold them so she didn't walk outside looking awkward and tipped. Bucky tapped the horn again. She greeted him with effort, trying to make her load look light, but he knew enough to help. He took the bags and threw them in the back without a word. He smelled like deodorant and tobacco. Bucky was a handsome guy, built solid, with dark-brown eyes and soft brown hair that curled up around his ears. But his dip habit made his cheeks look fat, and when he hadn't shaved in a few days he developed ingrown hairs in the whiskers on his neck, which Vivienne didn't dare reveal her intense longing to pop.

They'd been on the road twenty minutes when he started worrying about the weekend allotment of beer. "Do you think I brought enough?"

"If you run out, I'm sure the Blanks will have more." She reached over and scratched the back of his neck.

He didn't seem to notice, even though it was the first time she'd ever done anything couplish like that. "Last time that's what I thought too," he said, "but everyone thought the same thing and we ran out."

"Then y'all can just go get more," she said, scratching his neck a little harder.

"That means someone's gotta drive in town," he said. "It's better to have enough when we get there. The town is dry after ten."

Vivienne returned her hand to her lap. "Then we should stop and get some now, to be sure."

"I want to get there before dark." Because she was a woman, he expected her to solve his dilemma by telling him exactly what to do, like his mother, but Vivienne, wanting to be agreeable and lacking experience in mothers, just kept offering suggestions.

"We could call Waverly and ask how much they have," she said.

"Forget it," Bucky said. "Clay's shooting some hogs at dusk. I want to get there in time."

"We're not even out of Houston. There's enough time to stop."

"It's gonna be shitty if we run out," he said harshly, as if that settled the matter.

Vivienne looked out at the flatness. Flat fields, flat parking lots, flat strip centers. Everything in sight was flat, except for the spaghetti bowl of freeways they were passing beneath in Bucky's newly jacked-up Tahoe. She already had to pee but didn't say anything.

Bucky was preparing a plug of tobacco and steering with his knee. She decided not to be nervous about this, because she wanted to trust Bucky. The Tahoe swung a little as he stuck the plug in his gums.

"The weather's going to be nice this weekend," she offered. "Not too hot."

"Yup," he said. He reminded her of a goat when he chewed tobacco. In addition to fattening his cheeks, it gave him an underbite. He took his hands off the wheel again to adjust his cap. Bucky wore a lot of caps, and usually white caps, and most usually this particular white cap from Baylor, his alma mater. It was fraying and soft at the brim.

"Do you like my outfit?" she asked, crossing and uncrossing her legs.

He glanced in her direction. "Sure," he said. "I like how small it is."

Vivienne smiled but couldn't think of anything to say, so she turned back to the flatness outside. In the side-view mirror she saw Karlie Nettle and her husband, Timmy, two cars behind them.

"Don't lose Karlie and Timmy," she said, even though she wouldn't have minded.

"They know the way," Bucky said.

"Maybe this weekend you can teach me how to shoot," Vivienne said, seeing that his attentions needed to be diverted.

"Yeah?"

"Remember, I've never shot a gun before." It was true. With no father and only Katherine at home, she'd never even touched one.

"I'll teach you to shoot, baby."

Gun talk usually sweetened Bucky up. The only thing he loved more than guns was Lawland's, his family's eponymous Texas-wide grocery-store chain, to which his father had recently appointed him vice president. Charles "Bucky" Lawland was a catch. His business degree was being put to respectable use, his personal coffers were ample, and, since turning thirty-one last year, he'd seemed ready to settle down. Vivienne had only known Bucky for a few months, but she'd heard girls talking about him a year before they met. The colossal bonus with him was that, unlike many of his counterparts, he was tall and still in good shape. He'd probably be bald one day, but now he had a head full of hair, and he always tucked in his shirt and wore a belt and had boots for every occasion, in every skin imaginable. His boots were never polished or decorative; he kept them a little dusty and work-worn. He didn't do much boot-wearing work, aside from messing around at his family's or someone else's ranch, but the ranches weren't working. Bucky got his boots worn riding four-wheelers and spinning his truck in the mud.

He was a religious man, but Vivienne tried to avoid the subject with him. Religion seemed to be a thing he kept in a special compartment in his brain for the sake of sometimes acting serious, because that was the way he thought Men should be. In this compartment he also kept his opinions on the way Women should be. There was a time for hunting and a time for Jesus, but as far as Vivienne could tell, Jesus was never available during hunting hours, or work hours, and certainly not during the hours he spent receiving blow jobs from her. In the three months they'd been dating, Vivienne had picked up that he had low expectations and little respect for the women he'd had sex with (and from what Vivienne had heard, there'd been many), but of women he took seriously, he expected angelic behavior and the same compartmentalized devotion to Jesus. In a jolly mood, Bucky wouldn't mind doing a keg stand or two, but in a pious mood, he'd get emphatic and tell her she wasn't "prayerful" enough. She couldn't anticipate his moods, so she tried to behave moderately around him and keep a positive lilt to her voice.

They hadn't had sex yet. They hadn't discussed it either. There was an unspoken agreement that Vivienne would act as though she were a virgin and that Bucky would too. She found this awkward—they were adults; it seemed reasonable to her that they'd talk about sex, even if they decided not to have it—and adding to the confusion was his excessive horniness. Vivienne thought she'd given more blow jobs to Bucky than she had in all her previous years of blow-job giving. He had no problem suggesting anal sex but had only gone down on her once. Vivienne was not sure how to take this. She hadn't taken him up on his offer, partly because hooking up with Bucky was nothing like her fantasies. It was more like sinking into a warm bath, only to be jerked out the minute you feel relaxed, thrown down, and pounded with a dull meat tenderizer. When Bucky got worked up, his tongue turned hard and pointy and he shoved it into her mouth, or he just let it go goopy soft. The three or four minutes she had nuzzling with him, before he turned ornery, were the best part. She liked how he smelled like shaving cream.

She usually went home after a night spent with Bucky sore and dry and swollen from receiving his dry humps, with an ulcer slice forming on her top lip from closing her mouth over her teeth and onto his penis. But she felt lucky to be the recipient of his thrusts and pokes. A lot of girls would have liked to be where she was.

"Your phone is ringing," Bucky said.

It was Karlie, calling from behind. "I'm going to die, I swear," she said. "The fucking AC broke."

"Sorry," Vivienne said. She held the phone off her ear. Karlie sounded like she was in full-blown shrill mode.

"Will y'all pull over? I want to get out and ride with y'all."

"It's not that hot," Vivienne said. "The drive's not that long."

"What is it?" Bucky said, spitting into his red plastic spit cup.

"Their AC broke."

"Put Buck on," Karlie said. Few things were more grating than Karlie calling Bucky "Buck." Vivienne could only imagine the feathers that would fly if she had a pet name for Timmy. But Karlie had introduced them; he was her friend first.

Vivienne overheard Timmy's protests. "It's not broken; it just needs more Freon."

"What the hell is Freon, Timmy! Viv, lemme talk to Buck."

Vivienne glanced out the side-view mirror. Karlie and Timmy were right behind them now, Karlie in a defiant slouch, the phone pinned between her shoulder and her ear. From what Vivienne could tell, she had one heel atop the opposite knee and seemed to be picking at her toenails. Timmy, angled forward with his big forearms draped over the steering wheel, already looked defeated.

Bucky grabbed the phone. "What is it?" he said.

Vivienne watched through the mirror and tried to overhear as Karlie made her plea. Timmy said something about opening the sunroof, Karlie cussed, all the while picking at her toenails, and then both cars were exiting the highway and pulling into the parking lot of a Sonic in Sealy.

It was late afternoon. The sun had been baking the lot all day. A family of five sat in the shade out front of the Sonic. The parents were eating burgers wrapped in foil paper, staring at the highway and the oblivion beyond, while the three small children ran in circles around the tables, flinging Tater Tots at one another. Otherwise, the place was empty. The thought of riding in the car with Karlie for the next two hours made Vivienne want to fling a Tater Tot at someone too, at Bucky in particular.

"I think Karlie is overreacting," Vivienne said.

"You wouldn't like it either," Bucky said. "You'd probably skip out too."

That he made the same assumptions of her as he did of Karlie was yet another reason to fling a Tater Tot at him. She smiled. "Actually, I wouldn't. I'd probably take a nap."

Bucky spit out his cud. "Maybe she isn't tired."

She wanted to remind him that he hadn't even been willing to stop for beer, but there was no point. An argument would only please Karlie. She got out of the car and stretched. It was a sticky afternoon. The heat radiating off the concrete singed her bare legs.

She went to pee. When she returned, Timmy approached with a cardboard carrier holding four huge foam cups. "I got you a green slushy," he said. "I also got orange, red, and purple. But I thought, Vivienne likes green."

Timmy occasionally did these painfully thoughtful things, accompanying them with some painfully thoughtful aside, like this bit about the color green. Vivienne did love green. She loved it even more for the fact that most people usually assumed she liked red. But Timmy looked at her and thought of green. Sometimes he seemed to her the tenderest man she'd ever known. He was a decent soul, Timmy, with a youthful, ruddy face, and a fuzzy hairline. He lacked force, though; his constitution was a gelatinous thing that formed itself according to expectation. He received the world and gave back to it without a lot of analysis, and what remarks he did make, what revelations he did have, he seemed to possess no awareness of. This made his words either really dumb or really profound. He was a bear, floating down the river, with a fat fish caught between his teeth.

Karlie claimed she married him because he was sweet. What she didn't say was what a comfortable life he gave her. Timmy was an associate in oil and gas investment at J. P. Morgan and pretty much let Karlie do whatever she wanted, or maybe that was just how it appeared. It was possible he thought he had her reined. Whatever the case, he was oblivious, and Karlie didn't have to worry about the fact that her party-planning business, NettleBee, had only had two clients that year. She was more interested in posting pictures of parties on her NettleBee blog than in planning parties. Each post was a variation on the theme of ocean chic or sexy Texas, with a tendency toward alliteration involving days of the week. Tuesday was for treats, Wednesday for wish lists.

Vivienne read the blog more than she cared to admit and supposed it was all fine, if only Karlie wasn't so hard on Timmy. She barked at him in front of other people and flirted with men openly. More and more, Timmy's legs appeared shortened beneath his gut, giving him the comportment of a young beardless Santa.

"Green is my favorite," Vivienne said.

Karlie came around and pinched Timmy's gut. "Gimme red," she said.

"I knew Karlie liked red," Timmy said.

"That's 'cause red's the best," Karlie said. This was something she said a lot. Karlie was a bottle redhead, but she'd been on the bottle so long she'd forgotten that she was actually a brunette. She worked to cultivate a personality appropriate to a firecracker. It suited her. She was a taut and freckled woman with a slightly husky voice, shorter than Vivienne, and borderline stout in the legs, a tumbleweed of bumptious female energy that Vivienne had been dodging since high school.

"Vivienne likes green the best," Timmy said.

Vivienne wanted to tell him to let it go. He was just making conversation, but Karlie was liable to be on a mean streak. She was failing at slyly checking herself out in the truck's tinted windows, making a sort of pout and pricking up her eyebrows. She turned back to them and took up her red slushy.

"That's 'cause Viv's weird," she said, "but that's why we love her, right, babe?"

Timmy smiled. How could a man like him possibly answer that question?

Vivienne smiled back at him. Sometimes she tried so hard to treat him genuinely that she worried she came off as false.

"I'm drivin' the ladies," Bucky said. He lifted his cap, ran his hand over his hair, and replaced his cap; this was his signature gesture. Vivienne found it irresistible. His curls were sweaty and peeking out from the brim.

Timmy was still trying. "It's not that hot, Karlie. The sun won't be so high in half an hour."

"Are you seriously still trying to convince me?" Karlie snapped.

Vivienne listened out of one ear. She was watching a Sonic employee cross the lot to a small graveled area with a brown plastic bench and no shade. She looked about eighteen. She sat on the bench and lit a cigarette and took out her phone. Every few seconds she looked up, then back down at the phone in case it had something new to tell her, and smoked the cigarette. Vivienne thought of the cigarette at Preston's. The morning came back to her in an outpouring of images, like a scattered deck of cards, and she tightened all over.

She had to focus on her current options. The only thing she could do to avoid riding the rest of the way with Karlie was to ride with Timmy. This would mean Karlie would ride alone with Bucky, and who knew what she'd say to him. Vivienne wanted to give her friend the benefit of the doubt, but from the beginning Karlie's expression of happiness about her dating Bucky had been insufficient. Not when you compared it with the usual exhilaration with which she greeted things like scented candles and bulldog puppies. There was also the matter of making conversation with Timmy. Lovable as he was, she didn't think she had the energy for it. The back of her neck was damp and ruining her blowout. She pulled her hair up into a loose bun. Maybe it was a little too hot.

They all climbed into the Tahoe and waited while Timmy trudged back to his truck. Karlie took off her sandals and rested her feet on the middle console. Her toenails were cut short and painted yellow, picked raw at the corners.

"Your toes are gross," Vivienne said.

This induced Bucky to turn and evaluate the yellow nubs too. "Ouch," he said. "You're gonna peel 'em off."

Karlie jerked her feet back. "Like y'all don't have any bad habits."

"Just being honest," Vivienne said. "You shouldn't pick at your feet."

"Thanks, Mom," Karlie said. "If you wore the kind of heels I wear, you'd do the same thing. I get blisters."

"Don't wear five-inch heels all the time, then," Vivienne said.

"I wouldn't if I wasn't so fucking short. You don't need to wear five inches."

"I'm short too," Vivienne said, turning to face Karlie, who was scrunched up in the back, fiddling with the hem of her dress.

"But you're taller than me," Karlie said.

"Who gives a shit," Bucky moaned. They were still waiting in the parking lot, because Timmy had forgotten he needed to use the bathroom.

Vivienne looked at Bucky to see if he meant to take her side or Karlie's, but he just busied himself preparing a fresh plug. Karlie had tucked her feet under her weekend bag. She shot a stewy glare at Vivienne.

Vivienne, hot in the face, turned back around and buckled up. Lacking Karlie's penchant for sustaining aggression, she couldn't think of what else to say. No matter how hard she tried to have the last word with Karlie, she lost.

Once they were on the road, Bucky drove faster. It was clear he didn't want to miss out on the hogs. He kept a Texas Trophy Hunters Association sticker on his bumper and looked forward to his hunting weekends the way she looked forward to her pedicures. After twenty minutes of tense driving quiet, Karlie fell asleep, her bag still concealing her feet.

"Do you ever feel bad when you shoot an animal?" Vivienne asked

Bucky, remembering a summer afternoon she'd spent fishing at an expensive Christian sleepaway camp in the hill country. She was twelve, in an algae-stinking rowboat in the Guadalupe River, with two boys and a camp counselor. They hadn't caught anything and offered a line to her as a concession before rowing back to camp. She immediately caught a little carp and pulled the green gleaming fish from the river with a feeling of glory before the boys, but once she really saw it, gill-panting and wide-eyed, she demanded they throw it back. That had been the plan all along—they weren't fishing to eat, and it was just a plain carp—but the hook was big and had lodged in deep. The counselor tugged at it.

"Put it in the water for a minute!"

The counselor, probably seeing her alarm and being the "adult," dipped the carp in the river. The boys were hot and indifferent, absorbed in jealousy that a girl had made the day's catch. With the fish underwater, Vivienne had felt relieved. The drama was over for the moment; the fish was breathing. But once it was pulled back to the surface, the extraction of the hook seemed to go on for hours, the gills opening and closing.

Vivienne thought she would scream but didn't. She became still, like the fish. Finally the hook slid loose, and the carp was free. But a moment later it floated to the surface, flapping on its side, blood threading out from the gills.

Vivienne cried, "Kill it!"

The counselor retrieved the fish with a net, laid it on the bottom of the boat, and pounded it with the flat handle of an oar, much to the delight of the jealous boys. There must have been other words spoken, but Vivienne only remembered the counselor saying, "It was instant," and then tossing the dead fish back into the river.

They all rowed back. By the time they reached the dock, Vivienne felt like a murderer. Less than an hour ago the fish had been alive, living its life. It depressed her, such a pointless death.

Karlie woke up and leaned into Vivienne's ear. "Waverly wants to know why you haven't responded to her text about lilac or fuchsia for the bridesmaid dresses."

"Lilac," Vivienne said.

"I think fuchsia," Karlie said. "Buck, what do you like better?" She fanned the skirt of her strapless paisley-print dress around her knees.

Bucky said, "Lilac sounds like a flower."

"Lilac is a flower," Vivienne said.

"Whatever," Karlie said. "I'm telling her I like fuchsia."

The Tahoe blasted over the low hills of Highway 290. The trees, mainly oaks, passed as blurs in the side of Vivienne's vision. The sun was setting. It was that warm rosy hour.

"You didn't answer my question about hunting," Vivienne said to Bucky. "Don't you ever feel bad about it?"

Bucky adjusted his white cap. "Why would I feel bad about it?"

"Because you're killing something. Do you think about it that way?"

"It's sport," Bucky said. He took his eyes off the road for a moment and gave her a sidelong look. "It's a game."

Vivienne sat on this for a moment. She couldn't decide whether she agreed with him.

"I caught a fish once and felt bad about it," she said.

"Was it a big one?"

"No, it was little," Vivienne said. "It just seemed like it was in pain."

"Fish don't feel pain," Bucky said.

"What are y'all talking about?" Karlie interrupted from the back.

"Vivienne feels bad for catching a fish."

Vivienne sighed. "I was just asking if you think about the fact that you're killing something when you hunt. It's going from alive to dead because of you."

"Isn't that the point of hunting?" Karlie said.

"But it's an animal," Bucky said. "It's not like killing a person."

"I'm not saying it's like killing a person," Vivienne said.

"God made animals for people to use."

She turned to the window. The big Gulf clouds were glowing, underlit by the low sun. "You don't know that."

"People need to eat, Viv," Karlie said. "And there's too many deers, so it's good for them to be hunted."

"Deer," Vivienne said. "And we don't know if God put animals on earth just for us to kill for sport. I don't know if I agree with that."

"You gonna disagree with Scripture?" Bucky said.

She would have liked some sort of response that indicated he'd at least thought about it for one second. But maybe he was braver than she was. He could face his killing, even in his thoughtless way, and she couldn't. "Scripture doesn't say that we're entitled to kill animals for sport," she said. "It talks about how we have animals as a resource—"

"I'm not gonna debate Scripture with you," Bucky said. This sort of holy remark from him meant that he intended to end the conversation.

Timmy was still trailing them. Through the mirror, she watched him tap his hands on the steering wheel and wag his shoulders maladroitly. It was nice to know Timmy danced when he thought no one was watching. She didn't dare betray him to Karlie. She settled back in her seat and crossed her arms tightly, using her fists to lift her breasts, for Bucky.

"Maybe it's healthy to debate Scripture," she said. "Or at least to interpret it in different ways." Except for the occasional event at Prayerwood, the Baptist church most of her friends attended, Vivienne didn't attend any church on Sundays. The extent of her worship was personal, and somehow the big sanctuary at Prayerwood, full of dressy, sociable people, made it less personal, less reverent. Sermons always made Vivienne think of questions she wanted to ask, but she hadn't found anyone she could put those questions to who would answer her meaningfully. The pastor reminded her of a businessman, and she didn't share her questions with him, for fear of what he'd think. She couldn't exactly schedule an appointment with his secretary in order to ask him, in all seriousness, "Did Jesus poop?" So she put the question to Jesus directly; this particular question he hadn't answered yet.

She was baptized a Catholic at Gracedale and brought up in their Sunday school, but she'd always found it boring. This was her secret. Church was boring. In her unspooling dreams of life with Bucky, of the proposal, the wedding, the home, the children, this secret made a snag. More lately, he'd been asking her to go to Prayerwood with him, but he'd slept in on the days she agreed to go. It would never have occurred to him she wasn't a Christian in the way he was. If he'd asked her about her faith, she would've struggled to describe it—she kept it tucked away, an unconscious compensation for the loud blatancy of everyone else's faith. She didn't want anyone else to get their hands on it. Hers was a faith in Jesus the man and the Spirit. She loved him like she might have loved her father, if she'd had one on earth.

"You can't just interpret Scripture any way you damn please," Bucky said. "If God hadn't made animals for us, they wouldn't taste so good." He reached across the middle console and tickled her arm. "You like steak."

She caught his hand but didn't know what to do with it. He waited for her, his eyebrows raised. The hand was pale and somehow frail, even though his palm was wide and rough. She kissed his pinky and pushed his hand back.

"I saw that," Karlie said, scooting forward.

Vivienne smelled Karlie's headache-sweet perfume and turned back to the window. She recognized the country road. The rolling hills were dotted with ash trees and spindly mesquite. At the height of day, these hills were electric green, but in the soft late light they looked like giants tucked in beneath a dark-emerald blanket.

Karlie lifted a chunk of Vivienne's hair and played at braiding it. "You're such a weirdo, Viv," she said.

Bucky laughed from his nose, then made up for it by laying his hand on Vivienne's thigh. Vivienne closed her eyes.

IV

It was blue dusk when they arrived at the gates of the Blank family ranch. A quarter-mile drive down a gravel road to the house and they were in view of Waverly and Clay waiting on the front steps, backlit by warm porch light. It was a three-story ranch house with deep eaves, built of Texas limestone. Vivienne loved the shady porches; Waverly always gave her the room overlooking the backyard and the hills beyond.

She was glad to see Waverly, smiling as wide as she was waving, in a pretty purple strapless cocktail dress and silver heels—she was an overdresser—with Clay at her side, in khakis and a faded green polo, taking a big stance in his shitkickers, ready for the hogs. The girls embraced on the steps. Bucky, Timmy, and Clay carried the bags inside and went off to the garage to get the four-wheelers.

"I love this!" Waverly said, standing back to admire Vivienne's romper. "So cute."

"This is amazing," Karlie said, stroking Waverly's dress.

"Purple looks great on you," Vivienne said.

It did look great on her; Waverly had that effect on things. She was like a beauty queen, or what Vivienne imagined a beauty queen should be. Her flaws only made her more endearing. If she was a contestant in the Miss America pageant, she wouldn't be the most beautiful girl—she was long in the torso—or the most talented—in high school, her cheerleading gymnastics were awkward; she landed her flips in a squat—and she'd probably give a borderline vapid answer to the final question, but she would win. She had a smile like the sun, and her round chestnut eyes looked right at you, and matched her straight, chestnut hair. If Vivienne was the standard by which their friends judged their looks, Waverly was, and had always been, the standard by which their friends judged their goodness. Waverly's very gestures radiated faith that the world was orderly and kind. She possessed no sense of irony and seldom passed judgments. She wanted to be a princess on her coming wedding day, not for the eyes of others or to elevate herself, but because she believed that that's what it meant to be a bride.

Vivienne admired in particular Waverly's ability to love herself. She didn't seem to have an ongoing dialogue in her head. Everything Waverly did, she did absolutely. After college she started an interior design business, and in a year, with the help of her mother's best friends, had a strong client base and her own income. She didn't have any real credentials aside from her parents, but she was a hit because she made every client feel like her best friend. Moneyed middle-aged wives saw in Waverly the young woman they used to be or could have been.

Waverly gave her girlfriends another hug. "So happy y'all are here." Karlie, always eager to shine in Waverly's eyes, held the embrace longer. The four-wheelers sputtered off into the brush.

Inside, they passed beneath the grand buck-antler chandelier. Waverly and her mother, Sissy, had decorated each step of the main staircase with a menagerie of ranch-animal Beanie Babies in a basket.

"Mommy!" Waverly called out. "Kar and Viv are here!"

"In the kitchen!" came Sissy.

They crossed the adjacent vaulted great room to reach the kitchen, where they found Sissy pouring chardonnay at the marble island. "Just in time," she said, handing out the glasses. "To the weekend!"

Vivienne held up her glass with the others.

"Just to let everyone know ahead of time, I'm going to drink too much this weekend," Karlie said, then drank.

"I understand, Karlie," Sissy said. "The wedding planning has me crazed."

Waverly, who always drank less than her mother, sat at a barstool and rolled her eyes. "Mommy, you're not getting married."

"I might as well be," Sissy said, sipping. She was a harried doughball of a woman, no matter how hard she tried to appear otherwise. She bleached her hair monthly, and Vivienne had never seen her without makeup. She was sure Sissy had had work done over the years. The work was good, but her eyes were still quietly frenzied, eyes that took aim. Sissy was in many ways the opposite of her daughter. She had none of Waverly's composure, but she was proud. Her azaleas were the highlight of the azalea trail four years running, and her accent still hailed from the small East Texas town where she was born and raised. At Texas A&M, she met and married the man who became Bracken Blank, Houston's most prominent residential and commercial real estate developer.

"Being the mother of the bride is more work than being the bride!" she said. She was wearing a leopard-print tunic over black leggings. Her chunky silver charm bracelets clanged as she raised and lowered her glass. "It's giving me fluff!" She slapped her thighs.

"Hey, bitches, I've been a bride," Karlie said, raising her glass and laughing.

"We remember," Vivienne said. She and Waverly had been two in Karlie's army of bridesmaids. Reis Hinkle, who'd served Karlie as maid of honor, was somewhere in the dark of Highway 290, en route to the ranch.

"You were beautiful, Kar," Waverly said.

"Thanks, Wavey," Karlie said. "Viv, did you think I was beautiful?"

"Of course," Vivienne said, lying. Karlie just wasn't beautiful, there was no way around it. She was occasionally pretty, but in Vivienne's opinion, a person had to have a much more benevolent disposition to qualify as beautiful.

Karlie lingered on Vivienne for a moment, one arm akimbo. "Anyway," she said, "being a bride was really stressful. Especially if you're marrying Timmy, because he's an idiot about everything."

Sissy circled the island, topping off glasses. "How are you and Bucky going along?" The worst question.

"Fine," Vivienne said. "Things are going well."

"Well, I didn't know whether you'd be sharing a room with him," Sissy drawled, letting the sentence hang open.

Vivienne shrugged. "I spend the night at his place sometimes."

"I think he really likes you," Waverly said, all heart-of-gold.

"Buck's so unpredictable," Karlie said blithely.

"How is he unpredictable?" Vivienne asked. His predictability was one of her main private criticisms of him.

"He's just hard to read. Like you never know what's in his head."

"I don't get that from him at all."

"Aren't all men like that?" Waverly offered.

"Clay was never like that," Karlie said. "He wanted to marry you the day after y'all met."

A small Hispanic woman appeared and pulled a tray of breaded chicken wings from the oven. Sissy, with one jeweled hand on the woman's shoulder, silently pointed to a box of toothpicks on the counter.

"He'll come around, Viv," Sissy said, turning back. "Don't put the pressure on him until you really need to. Men hate that the most. He's gotta get the birds outta his blood. When I met Bracken, he was still paddling pledges. I gave him a little time to realize what he had in me."

Vivienne, not wanting advice, tensed up. "We're just taking it slow."

"Well, don't take it too slow," Sissy said.

"Then he'll take you for granted," Waverly said, nodding. Karlie was listening with her glass suspended before her lips.

"How do you know what's too slow?" Vivienne asked.

"You don't," Sissy said, with a certainty that might've settled the question the world over. "You just *feel* if it's too slow. But don't be too eager. Too fast is even worse than too slow. You have to feel it out." To illustrate feeling, she flapped her wrists up and down her body.

Waverly laughed.

"What I'm sayin' is true! It's not on a timeline for y'all girls, like it was when I was your age—I already had Waverly by now—but y'all still have the same things to think about. Viv, you're gonna be thirty-one around the corner."

All eyes fell on Vivienne, as if she were alone in her fate. "Don't try to scare me."

"Because you could be alone forever and end up an old maid?" Karlie said.

"You don't wanna be working at that store for ten more years!" Sissy said.

"I don't think Vivienne needs to worry about this," Waverly said.

"I'm sitting right here," Vivienne pointed out. She had barely noticed that her glass of wine was almost empty when Sissy promptly refilled it.

"That's not all they look for," Sissy continued. "Bucky needs a mama. Bracken needed a mama too. They all need a mama. If you can find a way to be his mama without driving yourself crazy, you'll be fine."

"Timmy's too dumb to know he needs a mama," Karlie said.

"I'm not pressuring him," Vivienne said. "It's only been a few months. And I don't want to be anyone's mother."

Sissy said, "They can smell it if you're giving yourself a rigmarole in your head. Anyway, that's for career girls. You're not a career girl, Viv. All that aimlessness isn't for you."

"I don't think it has to be one or the other," Vivienne said, reluctant to disagree with Sissy.

"Girls, listen!" Sissy raised her voice to grab the room. She was climbing on her horse. "A career girl would *be* a career girl by now. Viv, if *that* was up your alley, you wouldn't be here. And we're so glad you're here." She lifted her glass.

"But I do have a career—I've worked at the store for three years."

"I mean a career with a capital C," Sissy said. "A woman who doesn't mind earning more than her husband."

"I don't think I would mind that," Vivienne said.

Sissy hooted. "But he would! A man should be a provider."

"Has Bucky mentioned marriage?" Karlie asked, examining her fingernails.

Vivienne lacked the courage to say what she was thinking deep down—that, really, she didn't know if she wanted to be Bucky Lawland's wife at all. She would never concede this to Karlie. "No, but I'm sure he will."

A silence followed. Sissy went with her helper to the bar room to retrieve glasses. Waverly just gazed down into her wine. Karlie lost interest in her nails and took up fingering the petals of a white lily, one stem in a dazzling bouquet of more lilies, yellow roses, and undulant ballet-slipper-pink peonies. Vivienne, feeling the wine, resented their secret judgments. If Bucky had been there, she would have grabbed him and kissed him, to remonstrate with her friends, even Waverly, who wouldn't lift her eyes, who pitied instead of judged.

"What is it, Waverly?" Vivienne said.

She hopped off her barstool. "It's just that I wish—I want it to be easier for you. I don't want you to make things more complicated for yourself when your situation is already complicated." She fished through a kitchen drawer, located an elegant box of long wooden matches, and began lighting the candles scattered throughout the kitchen and great room.

"What does that mean?" Vivienne asked. Waverly regularly spoke in this opaque female nomenclature. The pains Vivienne bore to decipher it often made her feel an inferior member of their gender.

"She means be normal," Karlie said, tearing the petal from the stem.

Waverly was more measured. "I mean that I think Bucky wants someone consistent. I'm not saying that you aren't consistent, but I think that Bucky is very consistent, so he relates to that."

"Has he said anything to y'all?" Vivienne said. "Now you're confusing me."

Both girls shook their heads. Waverly struck a match. "We just know you," she said.

Sissy returned with champagne flutes dangling from between her fingers. The other woman followed, lugging a case of champagne. They all watched as the woman heaved the case onto the counter.

"In case we decide to open some bubbly!" Sissy announced.

"Because you'll always find an excuse to open some bubbly," came a steady male voice, and with it low footsteps and then Bracken Blank the man, freshly shaved, a starched white collared shirt tucked into his jeans.

"Hi, Daddy," Waverly said.

He hugged his daughter, kissed his wife on the cheek, and then stood tall and sturdy in his black crocskin boots, regarding the women in his kitchen.

Karlie became effusive. "Hi, Bracken," she said.

"Hey, sugar," he said. "You and Timmy ready for next season? I got that box in Austin. See if I can't watch those Longhorns lose another season. I'm too old for tailgatin' and I want y'all up there enjoying the view too."

"You know it," Karlie said.

Vivienne waved, but Bracken held his hand open and aloft. He wanted a high five. "Come on, up high!" he said.

Reluctantly she complied, hating him for it. She'd known Waverly's parents most of her life, but navigating adulthood with Bracken wasn't easy. To Vivienne, he was neither a Mr. nor a man she'd name casually. He was someone else's father, and a father was a totem, an authority. Gradually, however, with time and age, the shadows surrounding his persona were receding, and she saw him now in many shades, none of which were definable. She had no name for Bracken, only a certain formal, polished smile. It was Karlie who was carefree with him.

"Brisket smells good," he said, his hand on the small of Sissy's back.

"Don't look at me," Sissy said. "I haven't lifted a finger today."

"Oh, that's right, I smoked the brisket," he said, and gave her a sly wink.

Karlie dropped her lily petal, torn into enough bitty pieces to make a gentle snow upon the countertop. "You know," she said, approaching Vivienne with lowered eyes. Waverly picked up on the frequency and scooted near.

"What?" Vivienne said.

Karlie half-smiled, tucked a few dangling strands of hair behind Vivienne's ears. She loved to play with hair. If she'd been born into another life, Karlie would have been a hairdresser. She had a tender touch with the scalp, and she was an expert sheller of unwanted advice. "Timmy hasn't said anything to me about Bucky getting engaged"—here she made eyes with Waverly, ticking her head to one side—"but he did tell me Bucky thinks you're the most beautiful woman he's ever been with."

"I wish Bucky told me that."

"He's probably shy about it," Waverly said. "That's so cute that he told Timmy."

"I don't think he knows how you feel about him," Karlie said. "Maybe he's nervous."

Bucky came to Vivienne's mind in fragments—facial expressions, gestures, conversations—which she sifted to find a moment of vulnerability. One night caught: They'd had an actual date—not the usual plan-via-text-to-meet-at-a-bar evening but dinner at Brennan's, followed by an earsplitting action flick. Vivienne could barely stand it; Bucky had loved it. Before starting the engine to leave the theater, Bucky had held her face in the dark truck and kissed her. It was the first and only time she'd really felt joined with him.

"Clay and Timmy weren't nervous," Vivienne said, over the laughter of Bracken and Sissy across the kitchen.

"Clay was nervous," Waverly said. "He had to get drunk to tell me he loved me."

Karlie held her wineglass ambivalently aside as she spoke, as if any minute she might toss it over her shoulder. "Timmy has been in love with me since like ninth grade. He didn't need to tell me."

"But guys always say what they mean when they're drunk," Waverly said.

"Or what they only feel because they're drunk," Vivienne said.

"Not about relationship stuff, though," Karlie said firmly. "If a guy confesses when he's drunk, he really means it, especially a guy like Buck. It's hard for him to be sensitive. Why not seduce him a little?"

Vivienne shrugged. She was on the fence, but maybe Karlie was right. Maybe she could be a bit more aggressive.

"Y'all better get ready before everyone gets here," Sissy called out.

"I took the bags up," Bracken said, plopping ice cubes into a glass of whiskey.

"My lord, that must've taken you a while," Sissy said, sliding her arms around his waist.

"I needed the exercise," Bracken replied, and smiled down at her.

The Sunflower Room, as the Blanks called it, was always Vivienne's room. She loved the hotel-like smoothness of the yellow quilt, and the bright sunflower-print wallpaper, the room's overall rightness, its clean, delicate stillness. On the bedside table she found a bud vase holding two illicit bluebonnets and a note: *Don't tell anyone! Sissy xo*

She smiled, imagining Sissy illegally picking bluebonnets, but it was more likely she sent someone else to do it. There weren't many left in May, and these two were weaklings.

Bracken had set her things in the closet. She slipped off her sandals and massaged her toes into the pliant white carpet. Next, she opened the shutters and the French doors to the balcony and sat outside in the rocking chair, listening to the cicada choir. The moon was bright, almost full, the mowed perimeter of the property a black hem, the night muggy and swollen with the aroma of cut St. Augustine. Just then she heard the buzz-sawing of the four-wheelers. Spotlights reared around the brush. The guys kept revving the engines and hollering.

She gathered they were at some kind of game, because they weren't driving any closer. Annoyed, she waited for them to finish, distracting herself with the sight of two early June bugs drowning in the swimming pool, a pair of dark flailing dots casting tiny ripples in the glowing water. Their fate made her a little sad, so she retreated inside, only to find that getting ready had commenced.

She was three rooms away, but she heard it clearly. It was three-layered: the drone of many hair dryers in use at once, country music playing loud enough to be heard over the hair dryers, and a flock of female voices raised over the music *and* the hair dryers. At this hour, the

Blank house was ablaze, its bedrooms charged with laughter, shower-moist and steeped in decadent, purchased aromas. Bracken piped in over the house intercom, "We better not blow a fuse!"

Vivienne pulled out her dresses and draped them on the bed. Then she undressed. The shower water muffled the high-pitched laughter of Waverly's sorority sisters from the University of Texas. Most of these women were from Dallas, some still lived in Austin, a few had married East Coast. The weekend was a reunion for them.

She did a once-over shave on her legs to cover any spots she'd missed that morning. Then she performed a contortionist routine to reach her crotch, jutting her hips and straining her neck to see her progress and to access creases. Vivienne had long been convinced by popular consensus that vaginas were ugly. Men wanted pussies, not vaginas, and pussies were hairless.

She toweled off, imagining future happiness. Marriage would permit her to be a little eccentric; she'd commission paintings for her home and decorate it herself. Not that she wanted to do everything at home herself, definitely not, but the first time that she figured out the washer and dryer—in college—and then folded and put away her own load of laundry, she'd been filled with disproportionate glee at the candle flicker of independence. The fact that she and Katherine paid people to do simple things was now an increasing frustration, born out of a quiet fear that most people did these things on their own and that she may have to do them one day too.

A firm *knock-knock* came at the door. It was Waverly, in a short black dress. "You're not ready?" she said.

Karlie clomped in on five-inch strappy cork wedges, wearing the purple cocktail number Waverly had greeted them in. It was much tighter on her. She opened the balcony door and howled, erupting into drunken laughter. When it occurred to her, mideruption, that Vivienne wasn't dressed, her face abruptly fell. "What the hell, Viv!" she said. "Why aren't you dressed?"

Vivienne withdrew into the closet and emerged a moment later in her new red dress, to the purr of her girlfriends.

"Wow," Karlie said, in a sort of mean purr.

Waverly made a few little *tap-tap-tap* claps. "You look like a model."

"My boobs are too big," Vivienne said, yanking off the price tag.

"At least you're not flat like me," Waverly said.

The three girls went to the mirror and surveyed the reflection. Vivienne's dress was a simple cut, sleeveless and midthigh length, with sheer red mesh over the shoulders that took the emphasis off her chest. Shaped by her form, it became remarkable. Even without makeup, her hair damp, she'd trumped her friends' hour-long effort.

"I hate you," Karlie said, surprising Vivienne with the ultimate compliment, an admission of jealousy. "What do I look like, one to ten? Seriously, what would y'all rate me?"

"Stop," Waverly said.

"We're not answering that," Vivienne said.

"Because you don't want to hurt my feelings. If you're a ten, and Waverly's, like, basically a ten too, then I'm clearly a four. I'm a troll."

In a rare moment, likely prompted by Karlie's choice of the word "basically," Waverly snapped, "Shut up, Kar. We're not rating each other."

Karlie paled. Vivienne began applying mascara. With Karlie's envy she had the upper hand, and she didn't want to lose it now by stooping to base flattery and end up apologizing for the imposition of her own attractiveness upon Karlie's feeble self-esteem.

But Waverly, realizing she'd hurt someone's feelings, chose the only route she knew, that of sweet indulgence. "You're not a troll," she said. Indeed, Karlie's only troll-like quality was her height, but even still she wasn't unusually short, and her physique, if thick, was athletic. In the bathroom's bulb flare, her nose was perkily symmetrical, her long auburn hair lustrous and straight with no visible roots, and her eyes, amid their kohl and sparkle, stood out bright blue and spirited. "Don't be so hard on yourself. You're a bombshell." For confirmation, Waverly turned to Vivienne.

It was Vivienne's unavoidable duty as the impetus of Karlie's minor tantrum to help turn the tide toward agreeability. "You look great," she said. "Nothing troll-like about you."

"Well, compared to y'all . . ." Karlie trailed off, leaning in close to the mirror. She scrutinized her eyes and swabbed her pinky fingertips along the lip of her lower lids. "The humidity in here is messing me up. *Vámonos,* ladies!"

Vivienne stayed back to finish her face and hair. The party was just getting comfortable with itself when she started down the main staircase. Thirty upturned faces watched as she descended. Feeling their eyes, Vivienne held her head high and prayed not to trip on the steep stairs. Sissy, who'd changed into a high-collared zebra-print vest, jangled up to her.

"You look beautiful," she said to Vivienne. "Now go get yourself a drink and something to eat!"

The flames of Waverly's candles warmed the walls of the great room, igniting the glass eyes of Bracken's antlered trophies. The guests were spread among Sissy's crimson couches, their voices drifting up into the wood-beamed cathedral ceiling above. Vivienne wove through the small crowd, giving and receiving many perfunctory hugs. She scanned the room calmly, seeking out Bucky. Waverly was in a corner by some bookcases, fiddling with the stereo. There was Emily, Waverly's sorority sister—a buyer for Neiman's? Vivienne couldn't remember—but she was pregnant.

There was Nicole, another sister, slugging a light beer, and her husband—what was his name? Vivienne waved. He owned a sporting-goods store with his father; that she remembered. She passed a few unfamiliar men—boyfriends and husbands, probably; they wore boat-shoes instead of shitkickers, so she assumed they were from out of town. She slipped through their circle, avoiding eye contact, conscious of their gazes on her back. And there was Bracken, seated on the cushioned arm of a couch, regaling a trio of Sissy's friends, who were giggling and slapping at the air around him. Near Bracken, by the kitchen, was Karlie, talking furtively with—she had to excuse herself around a few people to see—Reis Hinkle, Karlie's best-friend-forever. Karlie signaled her over.

Reis held out an arm, which she draped over Vivienne's shoulders. "Hey, girl."

Vivienne returned the half embrace. "Good to see you."

As usual, Reis smelled like bell peppers. She had a habit of carrying a plastic sandwich bag full of the vegetable wherever she went.

"I know, so good," Reis said, smiling. But her smile was more like a sneer.

This sneer-smile was Reis's defining expression, her upper lip wrinkled up close to the tip of her narrow nose. What Vivienne found discomfiting was the intensely sexual aura she emitted while essentially looking like she smelled shit, but maybe this was part of her appeal. There was something elemental about Reis. She had a slim stature, dark oval eyes, and enviably straight brown hair grown out below her breasts and cut into a blunt set of bangs. Hers was a come-hither sexuality that entreated the most primal butt-sniffing tendencies in men. Vivienne, a more delicate variety, who relied on precisely the opposite tendencies, found Reis repellent. For one thing, tonight she was wearing a black silk tank and jeans—very tight jeans—tucked into a pair of intricately embroidered black cowboy boots, a sartorial strategy intended, Vivienne felt, to alienate other women and make men think she wasn't afraid to get dirty. If the guys took keg stands, Reis would be the first to jump in. If she'd arrived earlier, she'd probably have run off on the hog hunt, all for effect, and all while nibbling bell peppers.

"We were just talking about Buck," Karlie said.

"Do you know where he is?" Vivienne asked.

"I was talking to him a minute ago," Reis said.

"Reis just got a job doing PR for Lawland's," Karlie said. "Buck hooked her up."

Vivienne let this wash over her expertly. "Congrats, Reis!" she said, beaming.

Reis nodded. "Thanks," she said. "A lot of it will be promoting their charity work—"

"They do so much amazing stuff for poor kids," Karlie interrupted. "Reis also got into law school at U of H!"

Vivienne congratulated Reis yet again and excused herself. Most of the men were in the kitchen, talking over the scream of the margarita blender and grazing the platters of fried, barbecued, grilled, and roasted meats orbiting the magnificent brisket, which glowed beneath a heat lamp. She ran into Clay.

He smelled like diesel exhaust, but he gave her the first real hug of the night. Clay was such a nice guy. He was always smiling. Whenever he hugged her, Vivienne thought that if he wasn't marrying her best friend she'd probably fall in love with him, even though he had small teeth and caterpillar eyebrows. She already loved him in a way, because she thought him worthy of Waverly, which gave her hope there was a man out there for her.

"I think Bucky's outside," Clay said, handing her a beer.

Vivienne leaned against the counter, angling her butt on the rounded edge so men wouldn't graze the small of her back. "Could you tell I was wondering?"

"Lucky guess," Clay said. "How are you?"

"Great," she said, nodding. "Really great." She had to talk into his ear to be heard over the blender.

"Still working at the store?"

"Yeah, I'm still there." She sipped her beer. It was a Lone Star, the mother's milk of her college days.

"Bucky got a big hog from pretty far off," Clay said. "They're breeding like rabbits out there. It's not good for the land. They're just munching it down bad."

"Do you have to shoot them? Can't you relocate them?"

"Maybe, but problem is they're tenacious. They've got a short breeding cycle. These hogs are fancy in France. If we got serious about it, we could sell the meat."

"I have an idea." Vivienne clutched her beer high on the neck of the bottle and nudged Clay's shoulder with the base of it. "I'll leave the store and move to France and sell the hog meat from Texas."

"We'll be millionaires," Clay said matter-of-factly.

Clay was already a millionaire, she knew. Or probably would be soon enough, many times over, just like most everyone there. The question mark that was her own future wealth hung over her head unfailingly, a thought bubble brimming with Monopoly money.

"Cally Pork and Petroleum," Vivienne said.

"I'll invest," Clay said. "Hey, you know who I talked to yesterday? Preston Duffin. He told me he ran into you at Rice."

Hearing his name so abruptly beyond the confines of her thoughts gave Vivienne an exposed, embarrassed feeling. She recalled their morning together like a shared secret.

She tried to be casual. "Yeah, he showed me around."

"Rice is designing a library in the fourth ward, and he's on the project," Clay said. "He wants me to come survey the plot. Not sure if it will ever get built, but it's a great project."

Clay, an engineering geologist, loved to talk about groundwater and mineral rights and soil mechanics. His father was a well-known investment banker who'd expected his son to follow in his footsteps, but Clay had an eye for science and forwent his enviable opportunities in finance to "stare at rocks," as his father had put it, and indeed he did this with an artist's passion.

He smiled. "I told him he should come up here this weekend. Doubt he will, though."

Vivienne, though statuesquely composed, felt ripped in two by an intense eagerness to talk about Preston and an equally intense eagerness to pretend that she didn't care.

"Let's take a shot of tequila!" she said suddenly into Clay's ear, and reached over the island for a pair of abandoned shot glasses. She poured the shots full.

"To you and Waverly," she said, holding the glass aloft, her heart brimming with an out-of-the-blue, urgent tenderness. "To love!"

Clay was laughing; he seemed happy. "To love!"

Vivienne swallowed the tequila and closed her eyes against the burn, pressing a wedge of lime to her lips. When she recovered, Clay handed her another. This second shot went down easier; instantly she deepened into the evening's embrace; Preston fell away. There was only the body and voice of the party.

Waverly appeared and nuzzled into Clay's stout, whiskered neck. "Are you getting my man drunk?"

Vivienne tried to slip away, but the kitchen was crowded. She reeled around on her toes. She spotted Bucky playing beer pong with Timmy and a bunch of guys outside. He'd changed into a clean white oxford shirt. Unsurprisingly, Reis was there, leaning one hip against a baluster, cheering the plays.

Waverly snapped her fingers. "One more!"

Vivienne hesitated.

"Come on, Viv!" Waverly protested. "I never take shots."

Clay was nodding.

Finishing it, Vivienne dropped the glass on the counter and watched it roll onto the floor and crack. Three was enough. She threaded her way through the kitchen, toward the great room. The music, a mix of hip-hop, country, and eighties' pop, grew louder.

The demographic had changed. Bracken and Sissy and their friends had moved to other regions of the house. Vivienne passed conspicuously near the window. Bucky noticed her and raised his eyes as if to suggest, *Well, look at you.* She smiled. Nothing compelled her to go to him now. She would make him wait.

The great room teemed with animate shadows. The rack of Bracken's biggest prize, a monster fourteen-point buck he'd bagged in Pecos, loomed over the crowd. She made her way around, feeling loose inside, her heart pumping with self-possession.

Suddenly a song she loved came on. She couldn't remember the name of the song or who sang it, but she was sure it was her favorite song in the world. She closed her eyes and danced. Others joined, and within two songs it was a dance party. A sweaty hour passed, Vivienne half lost in the haze of sweat and twang and half aware that Bucky might be watching. Finally, thirst drove her to the kitchen. She drank a glass of water, holding her hair up with her free arm to cool her neck against the refrigerator door. The kitchen was a wreck of beer bottles, spilled margarita syrup, and finger-food scraps. Specks of chewing tobacco littered the floor like confetti. Leather handbags and silken clutches of various colors and designer labels lay piled on the bar chairs, and in a corner slumbered a small women's shoe department—jeweled high heels, lustrous kidskin heels, stiletto ankle boots.

Bucky came around and pinched her waist. She faced him and pretended not to be elated that he'd showed up.

"You haven't talked to me all night," he said.

"You haven't talked to *me* all night."

His breath was all whiskey and heat. "You look pretty. I like your dress." Somehow his choice of words, compounded by his droll delivery, failed to live up to her expectations, even if the sentiment was exactly what she'd hoped he would express. She checked her annoyance by running her hands over his shoulders and clasping her arms around his neck. She grazed her breasts against his chest, to give him the hint: *Kiss me.*

He went for it. She relaxed against the counter and steadied his lips, holding her hands to his face. A group of girls passed through the kitchen. Karlie, among them, hollered out, "Buck, you want to smoke?" Reis was at Karlie's side, already lighting her cigarette. Vivienne turned around and shot Karlie a why-would-you-ask-him-that-now look, to which Karlie pled ignorance, holding her palms up.

They moved outside. The night was humid and full of stars; thin, stretchy clouds obscured the moon now and then, shifting the pattern of silhouettes over the land.

"Hey, Lawland!" Timmy called from the lounger, where he lay reclined with a Lone Star, like a gorged Bacchus.

People were scattered around in clusters, smoking and talking. The ten or so patio chairs were taken, so Bucky dragged an empty Adirondack near Timmy and instructed Vivienne to sit in his lap. "Come on, baby," he said.

Vivienne was irritated but complied.

"What year were the Texas Rangers formed?" Timmy asked, out of a slurred smile.

"The actual Rangers, not the baseball team," Clay said. He was sitting beside Timmy, leaning forward with his elbows on his knees, looking mirthfully at his friend. "He's on a trivia kick."

Bucky said, "Is it already that point in the night? I don't know—1920?"

"Come on," Timmy said. "Way off."

"1835," Clay said.

Timmy sat up on his elbows. "How'd you know that, man?"

Clay shrugged. "What can I say? I paid attention in Mrs. Lang's Texas history."

The recollection of seventh grade caused a tide of belly laughter from Timmy, the sight of which induced an additional tide of belly laughter from Clay.

In his glee, Timmy rolled full on his back and unfurled himself like a doodlebug. "Holy shit! I remember I forgot the pledge once, and Mrs. Lang told me there was a special place in hell for Texans who forgot the Texas pledge."

Clay feigned serious. "Dude, there is. You don't know that?"

"I have one," Vivienne straightened her back to garner the full attention of the men. "Who was the first female governor of Texas?"

"Jane Long?" Clay said.

"No, man," Bucky said, flicking his cigarette butt at Clay. "Jane Long was, like, Sam Houston's girlfriend."

Timmy shrugged. "That lady who made the flag—Betsy something."

"Miriam Ferguson," Vivienne said, and whispered into Bucky's ear, *"Let's take a walk."*

He scrutinized her for a moment and grinned, realizing her meaning.

"'Scuse me, fellas," he said, standing.

"Don't be a pussy, Lawland," Timmy groaned. When he drank, his talk changed. Vivienne didn't like it. His sweetness went sour.

Vivienne followed Bucky along the flagstone path into the brush beyond the yard. The voices of the party quieted under the hum of night critters. The dry buffalo grass crunched beneath their feet. Vivienne's heart raced. She'd forgotten her drunkenness, forgotten that her feet ached walking on uneven stones in heels, forgotten the need for restraint in dealing with this man. No, she hadn't forgotten; she just didn't care anymore.

"Let's stop here." She squeezed his arm.

They were in a grove of mesquite, romantic by Texas standards. The bare moonlit trees bent in warped directions. A warm breeze blew low, shuddering the high grass, leaving the trees still.

"Watch out for rattlers," Bucky said, pinching her waist, pulling her close. "I was watching you dance. Every guy in there wants you."

While he kissed her neck and squeezed her breasts, she stared skyward. A moving star, a satellite, was sailing over Texas. She lowered her eyes and kissed him; when she looked up again, it had traveled to the far corner of her vision, somewhere over the Gulf, she imagined. Bucky spanked her.

"Hey, space cadet," he whispered.

Now that his groping urge was satiated, he wanted to display his boner. She fiddled with his big belt buckle and within a minute had him standing in the open air, his boxers at his ankles. Drunk as he was, he was steady in this pant leg hold as he guided Vivienne to her knees.

She took him in her mouth. He smelled sweet, like sweat and talcum powder.

In a matter of seconds he was simpering, his knees twitching. She stopped then and glanced up at him. He smiled with clenched teeth. She played with him a little, feigned singing into a microphone, mimed licking a Popsicle—she often performed these little moves as an innocuous means of torturing him and prolonging her own fun—and then she abruptly stood. She wasn't in the mood to give another blow job. She was sick of blow jobs.

"Why did you stop?" He immediately started pleading. "Come on, I'm so close." He pressed on her shoulders to push her back down, but she swatted his hands away.

"Touch me," she said.

He looked like he'd taken a blow. "Wait, no, baby, just one more second—"

"*Touch me*," she commanded him this time, showing his hand the way. He liked this, but when his fingers reached beneath her panties and felt the warmth there, he immediately remembered himself and whimpered, grimacing as if she'd injured him. "Come on, Vivienne, seriously."

She laughed. "Harder."

He obeyed, angrily wiggling his fingers. She reeled back a moment, then ducked into his neck. Abruptly again, she removed his hand and stepped back to regard him fully: naked from the waist down, bound by his own pants, like a man in the stocks, an ample pink boner protruding from beneath his wrinkled shirttail, an expression of dazed surrender on his face.

Vivienne was delighted. For her part, she also looked ridiculous, standing in heels with her dress pulled up at her waist, her thong stretched and askew on her hips. They made a strange pair, facing off in the darkness, half nude. Vivienne put her hands on her hips, both to look prissy and to keep herself from stumbling backward. "Look at you," she said to Bucky.

He smiled at his own image of himself standing there, but whatever beast had seized his body was unwavering in its blow-job objective. "Vivienne," he pled.

Seeing that he couldn't move without tipping over—his boots were too bulky to give him maneuvering room—she scooted back a few wobbly paces.

"What are you doing?" he said.

"Having fun," she replied, and began touching herself. Dark as it was, she could see him flush.

"You're drunk."

"You're drunk too," she murmured.

Bucky had apparently given up being embarrassed and was stroking himself now. "Finish me off," he said.

She smirked. "No."

"Yes," he said.

She smirked wider, stepping close to him. "No."

He blinked at her wildly, like a galled lion. She lifted one leg and rested it in the crux of his elbow.

"Now what are you doing?"

"Shhh," she said, and gripped him. "Lower yourself down."

As she coaxed him inside her, his eyes passed from embarrassed to determined and finally, as he found his stride and she gasped, to something like enraged. It was rage she felt clutching her hips and jamming itself inside her, rage not from Bucky, her boyfriend, to herself, but carnal rage, from man to woman, and she loved it. Bucky grunted. She squealed. He panted. She moaned. For Vivienne, the seconds passed with the gravitas of years. She sought out his eyes, but he'd clenched them shut. Every feature of his face was clenched. His jaw was locked, his nose sniveled up, his brow knotted to folds. Her own face was a foil to his, slack in every place.

"Bucky," she said, out of breath. If he would only open his eyes and look at her.

Suddenly his body buckled, his lips wrinkled up, and, dropping her leg, he expelled a quiet yelp, finishing himself onto the ground.

Vivienne stumbled back and almost fell, disjoined from him with a cruel slurp. They both froze for a moment, Bucky's chest heaving, Vivienne watching him. The whole thing had lasted only a minute, maybe not even that. Bucky's eyes darted around the brush and down to his pants. Perceiving his leg hold anew, he immediately bent over, pulled up his pants, and spent a few—what seemed to Vivienne, who still stood exposed and tingling—long moments situating his belt buckle, even tucking in his shirt. Only when he finished did he finally look at her.

"Why aren't you fixed up?"

She was cold, her whole body tense. The breeze picked up, rattling the mesquite. She pulled down her dress, tiptoed deeper into the brush, and crouched behind a lantana bush, waiting to pee.

Through the thicket, she could make out Bucky in profile. He was kicking at something, a root or a weed, and smoking a cigarette. What was he thinking? Vivienne was deliriously impatient with her body. Seeing Bucky made her want to hurry, but the more she tried to hurry, the more stubbornly her bladder resisted, and she sat there in an anxious squat, miserable and sobering up.

Finally, by dropping her head and fixing her eyes on her toes, she peed. It burned.

Her drunkenness was both ebbing and overwhelming, as if it were just now realizing itself. She felt a sort of clearheaded nausea. When she reached Bucky she wanted to punch him, but instead she mumbled sweetly, "I'm back."

He motioned with a nod toward the house, and she followed. With each step she felt more depressed, as if a hand had come down and was pushing her—literally depressing her—into the earth.

Bucky was a few steps ahead, snapping every twig in his path and silencing the surrounding grasshoppers with the deliberate swoosh of his boots through the grass. He was smart enough to avoid the crowded back patio, cutting around to the garage. Vivienne put one foot in front of the other, one foot in front of the other. He waited for her at the door. Maybe if she invited him to her bed, he'd say yes? She was too scared to ask. The fiery mettle of minutes earlier had gone, pulled from her along with his body.

"I'm gonna go back out with the guys," he said. "Thanks for the treat tonight."

V

VIVIENNE WOKE TO KNOCKING AT HER DOOR. SHE burrowed beneath the covers, imagining that the offender would go away, but instead the door opened: It was the housekeeper, requesting, on behalf of Sissy and Waverly, her presence downstairs.

"Why?" Vivienne groaned, rolling over to look at the alarm clock and knocking over the bluebonnets, which had dropped their petals overnight.

"*Necessita ayuda con la* wedding," the housekeeper said apprehensively, abashed by the state of the woman in bed, still wearing last night's dress.

"*Por favor,* close the door please," Vivienne said. "I'll come in a minute."

It was early—nine-thirty—way too early. Sissy would never bother any other guest at this hour on a Sunday morning after a party. Vivienne often wondered if Sissy's generosity came free. Since Vivienne was the only purely unattached friend in the house, Sissy expected her to be available. At least today the chores would be wedding-related. Sissy usually instructed Vivienne to organize a file drawer or tutor her on using her email account or wrap baby shower presents according to her ruthless specifications.

Vivienne burrowed again, refusing to come to terms with her hangover. Within a minute she was back asleep. She'd been dreaming she was wide awake and already downstairs when she woke half an hour later to sunlight searing her face. The sunlit room could not have provided a more precise antithesis to her state of mind. She was verging on tears, but the pain in her head at the very thought of crying was enough to drive her up to splash cold water on her face. As she stood at the sink, the awfulness migrated to her stomach, so she knelt at the toilet and gagged herself. Nothing came; the alcohol had long soaked into her blood.

Her dress stunk of cigarettes and sweat. She peeled it off, resolved never to wear it again. With effort, she slipped on her cute-casual ensemble: a pair of hip-hugging sweatpants and an artificially faded workout sweatshirt, which hung just so off the shoulder. The outfit had a thrown-together look, appropriate for morning without being too frumpy.

She went out to the balcony for air. The yellow light infused the day with optimism, despite her pulsing head. The hills, cast in the eastern sun, took on a thirstier shade, a rockier texture. She found the spot where she'd gone with Bucky; from her raised view it looked much closer to the house and less private than she'd thought. Had Bucky been more drunk, equally drunk, or less drunk than she was? These details mattered. She hoped that he'd been more drunk. She hoped she and Bucky could keep what happened between them—the drunken night they had sex standing up in a clearing, something to laugh about.

Her flip-flops made a plastic snap against her heels as she made her way down the cool, gray hall, past the many closed bedroom doors, and descended the staircase. At the base of the stairs she froze. There, visible through a half-open door, was Bucky, collapsed on a guest-room sofa. She stepped out of her flip-flops and went to the door. He lay on his side in striped boxers, his pale, hairy legs tucked in close to his body, a cashmere throw blanket covering his chest. Seized by curiosity, and with extreme hesitation, she peeked in further to see his face, smushed against a couch pillow. He looked prepubescent. Some other guy was passed out on the floor.

"What are you doing?" It was Reis, fully dressed, leaving the bathroom. She brushed past Vivienne and went to an empty club chair, carrying her boots.

Vivienne noticed her purse at the base of the chair. "Did you sleep in here?" she asked, whispering.

"Yeah, a few of us were up late talking."

"Talking? About what?"

"Work, spirituality. Lots of stuff."

"Spirituality?"

Reis ticked her head. "Yes—is that okay?"

IN THE GREAT room, a small, silent army of maids was busy wiping surfaces and scrubbing corners. They didn't look at Vivienne as she passed among them into the spotless and glistening kitchen, every trace of the party a memory. The smells of ammonia floor polish, coffee, and bacon filled the room. Vivienne took a few pieces from a platter on the counter.

In Sissy's office, she found Waverly and her mother sitting opposite each other at the big maple desk, which was framed by a stately pair of windows draped in muslin. Sissy's office was in its usual perfectly disheveled state. Papers—it seemed to Vivienne every piece of paper in Sissy's office was pastel-colored or flower-pressed—were set in neat piles on the carpet, on the seat of the tartan armchair, on the built-in shelves covering one full wall.

"Well, good morning," Sissy remarked. "We thought you'd forgotten us."

"Hi, sweetie," Waverly said, sounding tired.

Vivienne wheeled over a chair and joined them. Sissy, fully made up, her hair tucked behind her ears by a leopard-print headband, was in full exasperation over the impossibility of finding fresh-squeezed passion-fruit juice in Texas. The fact that it was so difficult to obtain in large quantities only made her want it more. Laura Bush served fresh passion fruit juice at her luncheons—Sissy saw no reason that she couldn't serve passion-vodka cocktails at her daughter's wedding.

Waverly, always mitigating her mother's desire to impress, rolled her eyes. "Mommy, I doubt the Bushes' juice was even fresh. It was probably from a can. Who would know anyway?"

"*I* would know," Sissy sniffed.

"Please," Waverly said.

"You can order it online," Vivienne said.

"The planner can handle the passion-fruit juice," Waverly said. She stood, shook out her knees, and then bent down to touch the toes of her floppy sheepskin boots. She too was cute-casual, in fitted sweats and a gray T-shirt.

"People have no manners anymore," Sissy said. "I can't even count how many of these wedding vendors take three days to get back to you, and then it's an email." She held up a tense, flattened hand and sliced the air with it. "It's the limit."

Vivienne yawned.

"Princess would rather be sleeping in her bed," Sissy remarked, in the sweet, veiled tone Vivienne dreaded most.

"I'm just a little tired. How can I help?"

"I'd love it if you could stamp these." She handed Vivienne two stacks of envelopes and a roll of stamps printed with a photo of Clay and Waverly smiling, cheek to cheek. The paper was soft as fur. "Those are for the shower thank-you notes." Waverly's shower, thrown by Sissy and sixteen of Sissy's closest friends.

Vivienne felt oppressed by the stamping chore but glad to have her hands busy. "What's the plan today?" she asked.

"I'm never taking shots again," Waverly said. "I feel sick."

Sissy shook her head. "You'd think the world was ending. To answer your question, Vivienne, the plan is to finish these invitations." She paused and narrowed in on a spreadsheet. "Who is Preston Duffin?"

Waverly tugged at the sleep tangles in her hair. "Preston is a friend of Clay's. I think he's coming up today."

Vivienne stopped stamping. "Really?"

"That's what Clay said."

"Is he married or engaged?" Sissy asked.

"I don't think so," Waverly said.

"No he's not," Vivienne said, definitively.

"Then I'm not putting him down for a guest on his invitation," Sissy said. "I don't want my baby's wedding full of strangers who probably don't even write thank-you notes."

"Preston's been here before," Waverly said. "He's an architect. He did Tim and Karlie's addition."

"Huh," Sissy said, fishing a pair of reading glasses from a slim giraffe-print case. She rested the glasses on the bridge of her short nose and began tapping at her laptop. "I don't remember any architects."

"He's tall," Waverly said. "Kind of awkward." Here she paused philosophically and added that she didn't think Sissy had ever met Preston's mother.

"He told Clay he was coming today?" Vivienne said.

"Are you blushing?" Waverly said.

"No, hardly," Vivienne said, too swiftly.

"Well, Karlie will be happy if he comes."

"Why?" Vivienne asked.

Waverly picked up the house phone and dialed an extension. "She's had a crush on him since he did her house. I don't get it. Hang on—Hi, can we have some orange juice and Tylenol in my mom's office? Three glasses." She hung up. "She loves him."

"He doesn't seem like her type," Vivienne said.

"He's not," Waverly said. "I think that's part of the attraction. I wouldn't be surprised if—"

"Poor Timothy," Sissy interrupted. "I think his mother actually believed she married him off for love."

"Surprised if she what?" Vivienne asked.

"Nothing," Waverly said. "Karlie loves Tim."

"Oh, don't be such a powder puff," Sissy said. "Never underestimate Karlie Nettle. I should know."

"What does that mean?" Waverly said.

Vivienne looked at Sissy, grateful to Waverly for asking the question on the tip of her own tongue.

"I mean sneaky girls know sneaky girls," Sissy said, in the same nonchalant tone with which her daughter had called for orange juice. "How do you think I married your father?"

Just then a young housekeeper entered with a pitcher of orange juice, three tall glasses, and a bottle of the requested pills.

"Thanks, dear," Sissy said, clearing space for the tray.

The girl set down the tray and ogled the invitation. "That's so pretty," she said.

Waverly straightened up, rejuvenated by the presence of a person to whom she could be enthusiastic. "Thanks!" she said. "They're going out next week. The paper color is called 'biscuit.' Isn't that cute?" Waverly smiled, a smile full of delight, of confidence in herself and her creative choices.

The girl took the happy smile as her cue to leave and shut the door behind her without a sound.

"I adore her," Sissy said. "You know, she was working at the gas station in town, at that dirty front desk behind the glass, by all the lotto tickets and crap, and I just said, 'You are way too adorable to be working here.' "

Waverly was doodling *WAVERLY <3 CLAY* on a legal pad.

"If you're going to fiddle," Sissy said, "go take a nap or read your book, and, Viv, those envelopes won't stamp themselves."

Vivienne resumed stamping, braced against the over-air-conditioned cold and the very distinct scent of Sissy—a bed of marigolds sprinkled with baby powder. The office here was a distilled version of Sissy's office at home in Houston, comparable in size to a generous studio apartment and—with its candy-striped wallpaper and abundance of frilly pillows on cozy armchairs and fully equipped gift-wrapping station—easily mistakable for a Southern Lifestyle boutique.

"What did you do with Bucky last night?" Waverly said.

"What do you mean?" Vivienne kept stamping.

"You went off with him," Waverly said.

"How do you know I went off with him?"

"So then you didn't go off with him?" Sissy said, with a prosecuting lilt.

"I saw you," Waverly said.

"What does it matter if I did or I didn't?" She handed a stack of envelopes to Sissy. "These are done."

Mother and daughter exchanged glances. Sissy went back to tapping off emails. Waverly took up her book, a paperback of *Emma*. She'd been on a Jane Austen stride ever since her engagement.

Vivienne was too hungover to tolerate the silent third degree. "What is it?"

"I'm just worried about you," Waverly said.

"Why?"

"She's telling you that you made a mistake," Sissy said.

"I know what you did with him."

"How do you know that?" Vivienne demanded.

"Never mind," Waverly said. "I just know."

Vivienne took a tone. "Not never mind. How do you know?"

"Oh, Vivienne, really," Sissy said, pinching off her glasses in an exaggerated gesture of testiness. "Bucky told Clay. Don't act so surprised. What did you think was gonna happen?"

Waverly was somber. "He used the F-word about you," she said. "Clay told me this morning."

"How is this, my daughter," Sissy scoffed. She directed her eyes right at Vivienne. "Sweetie," she said, puffing up, "he told Clay he f-u-c-k-e-d you, and that is never a good sign."

Vivienne felt so humiliated she tried to make light of it. "Maybe I f-u-c-k-e-d him."

"Don't fool yourself," Sissy said. "Men always do the f-u-c-k-i-n-g. Women can try all they want to pretend otherwise, but that's a bunch of baloney."

"I disagree," Vivienne said firmly. If she hardened herself, she wouldn't cry.

"I don't understand why you'd do that," Waverly said.

"Have you been sitting there stewing on this all morning?"

"I was waiting for you to bring it up," Waverly said. "I thought this was something you'd want to share with me."

Vivienne began picking off her nail polish. "Bucky and I have been seeing each other for three months."

"I know," Waverly said. "That's what I mean. Three months isn't very long for a guy like Bucky. Clay and I didn't sleep together until we got engaged, and to be honest, I wish we would have waited till our wedding night."

"Some people aren't naturally prudes," Vivienne said, instantly regretting the comment. It hurt to battle Waverly. "I'm just saying we can't all be so chaste."

Waverly paused, resituating herself. "So then because it's not easy to wait, we should all go off with a marriage-material man and do him against a tree while we're totally wasted?"

Vivienne felt a little consoled that Waverly thought the whole thing took place against a tree. Whatever Bucky had said, he'd at least made it out to be hotter and less clumsy than it actually was.

"Cool it, you both," Sissy said finally. "Viv, you should have known better."

"I don't deserve this," Vivienne said. "I wanted to do it, so I did. That's what couples do." She felt her earnestness welling up like tears. This was how she understood love.

Sissy lolled back in her chair. "That philosophy isn't going to serve you well, especially with a Christian man like Bucky."

Vivienne could hardly stand to hear that from Sissy. Having never had a mother, she didn't take well to mothering. "How do you know, Sissy? Do your philosophies serve you well?"

Waverly sat very still and quiet, folding a page of her book over and over.

"Don't get snippy, Miss Cally," Sissy said, not breaking her lounge. "My philosophies serve me quite well. I'm not sitting right here in spite of my foolishness. You have to make some choices. What kind of woman do you want to be? You want to end up like your mother?"

She could have slammed her fist on the desk. "You didn't know my mother."

"No, I didn't, but I know her *reputation*," Sissy said. "And that's what I mean. Things can get bad if you sashay around, not knowing what you want. You'll end up with a reputation too."

"Mother!" Waverly cried, then turned to Vivienne. "I just don't understand why you'd make yourself into one of those girls," she said imploringly, as if she and her mother had two different, even opposite points to make. But it seemed to Vivienne their points were exactly the same.

"So what am I supposed to do?" Vivienne said. "It's already happened." She brushed the flecks of nail polish off her lap and went to the tartan chair and curled up in a ball.

"All right," Sissy said, in her let's-get-down-to-business tone. "Here's what you need to do. Go to church with Bucky. Take him to the afternoon service. Suggest it offhand, like it's something you're doing anyway. Sweeten him up and he'll probably forget about it, if he even remembers it at all."

"Let's hope I'm that forgettable, right?"

Sissy threw up her hands. Even now, Vivienne loved the sound of her charm bracelets jangling like a man in spurs, following her every move. "If you give yourself away like that, to a drunk good ol' boy like Bucky, you better hope he's forgotten."

Vivienne huddled against the cushions. "Can't anything be about something other than men?"

Waverly looked sad. "I think church is a good idea. Bucky will like that. Clay and I'll go too."

Mother and daughter sat regarding Vivienne with conciliatory faces.

"Don't worry about the rest of the envelopes," Sissy said, waving off the unfinished stack. "Maybe you should rest a bit."

On her way upstairs, Vivienne chanced across Timmy in an ancillary leisure room, reposed on an overstuffed chair, a fat Civil War daguerreotype book on his lap. "You look like you need a hug," he said, setting aside the book and standing with his bear arms extended to Vivienne.

She allowed herself to be hugged by Timmy more than she hugged him. She pressed the side of her face into the flabby pectoral beneath his shirt.

"How are you feeling this morning?" she asked, pulling away.

"About all I can do is flip pages," he said.

She smiled. "Is your wife still in bed?"

He plopped back into his chair. "No, she's up; who knows what she's doing. She got all done up this morning like she was going to another party."

Vivienne knelt to meet Timmy's eyes. She refused to pity him—it was because so many others did that she wanted to fight for his happiness. "How did you know I needed a hug?" she asked.

"You were just wearing a sad face," he said. "You look better now, though."

"Do you think Bucky will want to go to church with me today, if I ask him?"

"What kind of guy wouldn't want to take you to church?" He grinned.

She pinched her cheeks. "No sad face here, right?"

He clutched his book. "If you see Karlie, you can tell her I'm up here reading if she needs me. I might shoot later, but my head needs to take it easy for a while."

Vivienne patted Timmy on the shoulder and stood. "Do you want me to bring you something?"

"No thanks," he said, finding his page.

She wanted to confide in Timmy, to ask him what Bucky was thinking, to edge out Sissy and Waverly with some male perspective, but she couldn't quite find the words, and he'd probably end up telling Karlie. She was such an obstacle to their friendship. If Tim weren't married to Karlie, Vivienne was sure they would be great friends, the kind of friends who called each other on the phone and wrote birthday cards.

"Do you think there's such a thing as too soon for people to sleep together?" she said, deciding a hypothetical situation might suffice. If Bucky had told Clay, Timmy might already know anyway. Maybe Reis knew. And the guy passed out on the floor too. "I mean if they're serious about each other?"

Timmy looked momentarily perplexed by the question. He closed the book and laid his hand flat over Honest Abe's face. "I don't think there has to be rules. But it's better to wait, probably, because then it's more special and there's not so much jealousy and people getting hurt." He made a small shrug and raised his eyes.

The air-conditioning whirred on; cold air grazed Vivienne's neck. Suddenly, apropos of nothing but the fragile expression upon Timmy's round face, she pictured herself dropping the chair to a full recline, pulling aside her panties, and vigorously straddling his head. She felt no sexual desire for him, only the impulse to give her friend a gift she knew he would love. Timmy wanted to give, where guys like Bucky just expected to receive. Timmy probably appreciated a woman's form, but Bucky—he touched her with all the grace of a line cook pounding hamburger patties. Timmy was the one worthy of a walk into the brush. She remembered Bucky leading in the dark—he never once offered his hand.

"You all right?" Timmy asked. He looked ready to get back to his book.

She leaned over and kissed him on the crown of his balding head. "Karlie is lucky to have you," she said, and hurried off, determined to go to church.

She showered, scrubbing her body so hard, amassing such mountains of mango-peach sunrise soap bubbles in her loofah, that when she dried herself off she felt brand-new. *I'm like the kitchen*, she thought; *no trace of last night here.* No trace of the morning, even. She was imagining how to approach Bucky and make her suggestion of church when she remembered Preston. The possibility of finding him downstairs held her back. They wouldn't be leaving for over an hour. She had time for a short nap.

She stretched out on the bed, envisioning life with Bucky Lawland. Church at Prayerwood every Sunday, followed by brunch with the other wives. Tennis three days a week. Autumn tailgating parties in Austin and Dallas, umber leaves scattered on the pavement among rows and rows of tires and barbecue pits. Christmas in the Cayman Islands. Spring skiing in Vail. A ranch of her own. As she dozed off, she imagined him inflating from his center, a balloon floating from a big leather armchair into the sky.

VI

PRESTON CHEWED A TOOTHPICK AND MULLED OVER THE landscape. If he had the cash to build himself a ranch house, he'd design something low, with deep eaves, and nestle it in a shallow valley, make it indistinguishable from a stand of oaks, with a workshop in the back and a wall of glass to the south. Now, with the sun straight overhead and the hills baring themselves, he felt guilty standing there on the enormous terrace, staring at the grandeur. He sank his hands into his pockets and turned his scrutiny on the house, at the Tudor arches framing the terrace, a blight on the already nouveau ranch style. He recalled the pedimented portico jutting out from the front door, with its predicable lunette window. What an imposition. What squandered potential. Gauging by the narrowness of the innermost structure, excluding the extensions and add-ons, it was possible the limestone was original. He examined it on the back wall, traced the ancient shells, poked his pinky into the tiny caves carved by some vanished immensity. If the stones were original, they might have held up the house of an early Texan, a rich one, set as the property was on a high hill, above wildflower meadows and walnut groves, perhaps a descendant of the first Texans, the wild ones, full of haughty pioneer optimism and Comanche bloodlust.

He spit out his toothpick. Originality was irrelevant now—the architecture was too despoiled, the insides gutted to the marrow. The stones had probably been trucked in from some old teardown and used here for effect. To find out he'd have to ask Bracken, and if the house did possess even a brick of original Texas, he was sure to hear Bracken go on about it, as if purchasing proximity to history somehow gave him a role in it. Bracken was the sort of businessman who fancied himself a Texas Ranger in another life, the kind of moneyed man who'd speak smoothly down to Preston's father in high school because he didn't hunt quail or play golf, a man Preston might have to depend on for his livelihood but in his heart disdained. Thinking about it now made him want to leave—but he knew better than to get worked up; it only ruined his day, and he knew why he'd come. Water off a duck's back.

He leaned on the railing and tried to enjoy the sun. School was done, which meant he was really almost an architect. Quite a few tests still needed passing, but the school part was over. The prospect of relaxation felt unlikely. He needed to be looking for a job; with the market so empty, positions were more competitive. But, still, it felt good to get out of town for the day. The pool, preposterously faux-lagoon as it was, looked inviting. He was crouching to examine some surface stonework—not horrible—when he felt a *tap-tap* on his shoulder.

It was Karlie Nettle, in a flouncy green dress, cleavage bulging, her hands pressed on her thighs as if she were about to spring a leap.

"Hello!" Preston said, surprised. He'd expected to see Karlie but not quite so soon, and not quite so alone.

"It's so great to see you!" she said. "You just graduated, right? That's so amazing! Congrats!" She squeezed his forearm, tossed her cinnamon hair.

Preston noted what a shiny package she made in the sunshine. Her skin was dewy, obviously the work of some sort of lotion but nonetheless effective, especially on her visible heaps of breast. The teardrop diamond resting just below her throat refracted the sunlight into his vision. With each movement she launched an industrial-strength wave of floral/vanilla/cupcake aroma in his direction. She was enticing in the way of an expensive advertisement, alluring like blinking lights in the desert. Looking at her gave him the sort of dull headache he often developed after watching too much television.

"You should have come last night," she said. "We could have celebrated your graduation!"

Without remarking on how unpleasant such an evening sounded to him, he thanked her, then took a step back. "Are you and Tim enjoying your game room? Playing a lot of games?"

Karlie laughed. "It's still empty. Timmy is such a bum about it; he hasn't gotten anything for it." She thrust out one hip and rested it on the railing. "He's hardly ever home anyway."

This was exactly the corner he'd wanted to avoid with her, and here he was in it again. Damn this little woman.

"I'm going to walk around now," he said. "Check out the trails before it gets any hotter out."

Karlie inched in. "Yeah, when you dress like it's winter," she said, tugging at his sweater, rolled up to his elbows, and pinching his ribs.

He was inadvertently smiling when Vivienne came through the French doors, bearing the stamps of a nap: pillow-crease depressions forming a sort of town map on her left cheek, her hair tousled and cowlicked in the back. She had a swollen, childlike aspect, as if one foot were still in her dreams.

"I overslept," she said, tugging at wrinkles in her blouse, adjusting her jeans. Then, flatly, "Hi, Preston."

"Hi, Vivienne," he said.

She joined them at the balcony edge. "Where is everyone?"

"Church," Karlie said.

"They left?" She rubbed her forehead, and then, as if suddenly aware of him, angled away from Preston. "Did Bucky go too?"

He noticed that her shoulders were unmarked. She'd slept on her belly, then, but that endearing cowlick on the back of her head . . . Maybe she fell asleep on her back and flipped over midsleep.

"He was rounding everyone up," Karlie said, holding up her hair to fan the back of her neck; Preston saw that the material of her dress under her armpits had turned a darker green. "I told him you were sleeping."

They stood in a triangle, squinting, the sun beating down. If Preston had a tissue, he would have offered it to Karlie. Her glisten was taking on a sopping quality.

"I was up all morning. I was ready to go," she said. "When did they leave?"

"Probably twenty minutes ago," Preston said, trying to be helpful. "I saw them driving out when I got here."

She ignored him. "Why didn't Waverly wake me up? Why didn't you wake me up?"

Karlie shook out her hair, combing it over and over to one side with her fingers. "Waverly went into town earlier," she said, upturning the sentence. "I thought you'd want to sleep off the night you had with Bucky."

Preston understood. His presence there suddenly struck him as ridiculous. He glanced between the girls, intensely curious about the dynamic at work and appalled that he'd willingly inserted himself in it. Vivienne was glaring at Karlie. A small, loud plane soared over.

"I could give you a ride?" Preston offered.

Karlie flicked her eyes back and forth.

Vivienne made a visor with her hand and looked up at the plane flying away. "I'll walk. It's not far. I have enough time to get there for the last part of the service."

"The last part is always the best part," Preston said. He meant it as a joke but it didn't come off, and the girls just looked at him.

Vivienne turned and left.

"Want to go inside?" Karlie asked, resuming her pose against the railing, smiling. "It's cool in there."

"No thanks," he said. "I'm going to catch up with Vivienne."

Karlie blinked as if she'd taken a blow, then squinted hard, throwing her hair to the other shoulder. To his relief, she dropped her pose. The luster fell away, and Preston realized how vitally her demeanor had held it together.

He jogged to reach Vivienne and found her walking fast on the shoulder of the one-lane road. "I'm a little hungry," he said. "Thought I'd grab a communion wafer."

She eyed him, more in curiosity than annoyance.

Preston began power-walking, jutting out his elbows and shifting his hips like a middle-aged woman on a morning walk.

Vivienne laughed. She was sweating at her hairline, causing little curls to form and betray the work of her blow-dryer. The cowlick was weighed down by sweat but still visible. Preston figured she didn't know it was there; otherwise she would have fixed it by now. He liked it—it looked like a miniature continental divide, separating one portion of her scalp from the other. It was the sort of imperfection she probably hated but that actually made her distinct, especially to Preston.

She kept walking, Preston following, crunching the gravel underfoot, both checking the ground to avoid fire-ant beds and bull nettles. For miles ahead the road kept on, rolling with the hills, dilapidated shacks and gilded ranch gates lining its perimeters. At the top of the next hill, they could see the steeple of the church, a simple chapel that the weekend ranch population had pooled money to restore. Sissy had spearheaded this effort, thinking the chapel was the "cutest" she'd ever seen. She'd arranged for her flower deliveryman, who came all the way from Fredericksburg, to bring whatever was fresh to the church every Sunday.

A pickup breached the hill and advanced, too close, causing Vivienne to cringe back to the shoulder. As the truck blazed by, spraying dust, mud flaps snapping, Preston stepped in and blocked her from the road.

"Let's walk on the grass," he said.

"It's better if you don't go to church," she said, her voice flattened by the silence, which felt deeper after the violence of the passing truck. The birds were quiet at this hour, the wind nearly dead. "Thanks for walking me, though." She was politely dismissing him.

"Do you really want to go?" he asked.

She shot him a look. "You're following me like a dog. You're like a lost dog."

He did feel totally out of his element, overdressed, on an empty country road, and so he pictured himself as a dog. Probably Vivienne had a lot of men following her around like dogs. "Let's just go around through the grass," he said. "You can slip in. It'll be like you were there the whole time."

She scuffed her sandals over the ground and pressed her hands to her waist.

Preston waited. "There's more shade on the grass anyway," he said.

Suddenly she stamped off, as if it had been her idea all along.

The road wasn't fenced, so they cut right in and found a narrow deer trail, which wound about a hundred feet from the road. Vivienne stayed on the trail; Preston walked beside her on the open ground, a mix of high, skinny buffalo grass and patchy Bermuda grass, scattered Indian paintbrush and fragments of castaway limestone.

A breeze picked up, almost cool. Vivienne stopped and closed her eyes. "That feels good."

Preston watched her hair lift and flap against her face in gentle honey-colored strands. He didn't know what to make of her. Her attitude was different than it had been two weeks ago. He'd expected she'd be more on than ever, but instead she seemed closed off.

"How've you been?" he asked, when she opened her eyes.

She flitted her wrist, tossing his question into the breeze. "Oh, fine."

"Well, what have you been doing?" he said.

"It's funny, I can't remember." She bent down and plucked a skeleton-weed flower and spun it between her fingers. Her gracefulness drew him in at the same moment it intimidated him. It was such an exact expression of her femininity and revealed itself at the oddest times—now, in what seemed to him a breath of frustration, and here, in this unexpected place. She coalesced with her environment because, by her grace, without knowing it, she coalesced with every environment and improved each, a vivid blossom on a dark bough.

She tucked the flower behind her ear.

"Want to sit in the shade?" he asked.

They hiked a small way up the hill to the shelter of a great black-walnut tree, its limbs forming an umbrella of shade. It was set above the rest of the landscape and patched with dandelions, the grass unscorched, suffused with the magic of an undiscovered place, though certainly it wasn't. Vivienne ran her fingers along the bark, into the carved initials of others who'd taken its sanctuary—lovers, loners, a person called *D.H.*, who *wuz* there in 1998—while Preston dutifully kicked aside the walnut shells at their feet. He made her spot first, then balled his sweater up into a pillow and reclined near her.

Vivienne looked out across the country, thinking it would have been nice if he'd offered the sweater to her. Church definitely wasn't happening. The thought of showing up there with Preston, sweaty and disheveled from the walk, set off all kinds of warning bells; she already had enough strikes against her.

Preston sat up. "Pick a hand," he said, tucking his arms behind his back.

"I don't know," Vivienne said. "I'd rather not play that game."

Preston brought his clasped hands around and together, opening them so it appeared the mini chocolate bar had been in both hands.

"Thanks," Vivienne said, and unwrapped the chocolate. It was melting. Instead of using her fingers, she stuck out her tongue and slid the entire bar into her mouth.

"Exactly what I would have done," Preston said. Actually, he probably would have taken two or three small bites, but he was in an encouraging mood. Usually he preferred to encourage with his own ideas, but in this case Vivienne's method was the better one, so he took it for his own. Something prevented him from just praising her for having a superior idea.

Intoxicated by laziness, his eyes drooping, he sank into the heat. Vivienne, calmed as her body was by the temperature, was swirling with a million thoughts. Preston looked asleep, so she took the opportunity to stare at him. His mouth, even this relaxed, held a slight boyish smile, the upper lip a pale rose line giving way to the fuller lower one, which dipped into a tiny buttonhole in his chin. Auburn stubble grew midway to his Adam's apple, around his mouth, and clear up his sturdy jawline. The light caught a palette of browns and reds on his cheeks; she'd never noticed he had a reddish beard. Indeed, she'd noticed so little about him in all the years he'd lived in her proximity that he felt totally new.

"You're staring at me," he said, his eyes still closed.

"I'm allowed to, because you made me skip church." She squinted to see the mellow, winding Brazos River in the distance.

He opened his eyes. "That's because my only plan was to hang out with you."

She didn't know what to say, so she threw a walnut shell at him. "I thought you came to see Karlie."

He sat up. "Why would you think that?"

"Because she has a crush on you."

Preston dropped on his back again and stared up at the complicated, knotty walnut limbs. He was feeling on a stride because, for the first time, he wasn't nervous around Vivienne Cally. It was bound not to last, though—talk of Karlie made him wonder if he was being led blind without realizing. Women were always doing that.

"Karlie is married," he said. "And I'd never be interested in her even if she was single."

Vivienne watched his eyes searching the tree. He seemed put off, but it made him handsome. With his arms triangulated around his head, his shirt lifted, she could see a path of brown hair beanstalking out from the waistband of his pants to his belly button, a deep inny. She looked away.

"I hope it's okay that I didn't go," she said.

He turned fully on his side and faced her. "You wouldn't have skipped it if you didn't think it would be okay."

He confused her—she felt so happy, but on the other hand she always had to figure out what he was trying to say. "I didn't think the world was going to end, if that's what you mean," she said. "Why do you care anyway?" She plucked a dandelion for herself and blew on the seedpods; a few floated away past Preston. The rest she pulled from the stem and blew off her palm.

He plucked a dandelion and ran his palm over its downy orb. He'd noted the worry on her face when she asked about Bucky earlier, and it wouldn't have surprised him if his company was a temporary bandage for some recent drama. He'd thought about her often the last couple of weeks; she'd come to his mind in the middle of a final, or near dawn, when he was hunched over a model. What he'd enjoyed most about their morning was how she'd kept up with him. He liked the aggressiveness she had no idea she possessed; only he saw it, he figured, because nothing was at stake between them. He tossed the dandelion over his shoulder.

"I forgot to make a wish on the dandelion," Vivienne said. She hugged her knees, trying to forget about the wish. No doubt if she shared her superstition with Preston, he would laugh—he threw out his dandelion as if it were a straw wrapper. Still, it was exactly that response that would dismiss the worry from her mind. She couldn't manage to dismiss it herself; her mind spun worries like silk. She wanted his assurance that to brood over something like that was ridiculous.

Preston watched her fidget, perceiving details: Her second toes were longer than her big toes; there was dry turtle skin around her elbows; her wide mouth went crooked as she concentrated on getting comfortable. He sat up and gave her his sweater. She took it without saying anything and tucked it against the tree behind her back.

"To answer your question," Preston said, "I care because you seem worried, but I don't understand why you care so much what people will think."

"Why do you care whether I care what other people think?"

"Well, it seems exhausting."

"It's not your business." She felt hot emotion rising to her face. "Anyway, caring is better than being alone and broke."

Preston was amazed to hear the word "broke" from her lips. "Quit the store and find something you like," he said. "He'll come along soon enough and rescue you."

"I don't want to be rescued."

"Yes, you do," he said.

"Don't tell me what's going on in my head." She felt defeated—he spoke as if this thought had never occurred to her. He put the words to it and, in doing so, took from her the moment when she might have found them herself. The heat was reddening his cheeks, waking freckles she hadn't noticed, and weighing his sandy hair down into a mop. She tried to think what to say, but thinking was difficult in the hot afternoon with a hangover.

"You can get romantic about it all you want," she said. "But money does provide freedom. I want that freedom, and I don't want to feel bad about it."

"But you think you're entitled to it from a man." He knew he was cutting a little deep, but it was true. To his mind, it was the beating heart of her dilemma. To restrain his frustration, he rose and began a small pace. "Say you end up with all the money in the world." He gesticulated toward the sky, an infinite blue. "What would you do with it? Certainly not buy happiness."

Vivienne got quiet. This was a private subject, even within herself. She knew how much she *wanted*—everything from an open line of credit at Neiman's, to a condo right on the hill in Vail, to a new black convertible Beemer to replace her old, nonconvertible one, to a golden retriever puppy. But she knew this was the wrong answer. "I have ideas," she said. "I've always liked art. Paintings." She took herself way back, to when she cared more about paintings than that open credit line at Neiman's. "Growing up, I used to stare at my aunt's art books. She has these medieval and Renaissance books. I would put myself in scenes from the Bible and mythology. I'd memorize the paintings and then go out to the bayou and try to reenact them."

Preston remembered what an ass he'd been at the Rothko Chapel and how polite she'd been about it. "You didn't mention anything at the museum," he said.

"I'm not familiar with modern art." She paused. "One of my favorites is the painting by Corot of Orpheus leading Euridice out of the underworld. I used to pretend I was Euridice, but I changed it so that when Orpheus turned around, I ducked and didn't have to go back to the underworld. I've always wanted to see that painting in person, but it's in Paris."

Preston imagined Vivienne, a lonely little girl, constructing in her imagination ways that she might save herself from the underworld. "The idea of an underworld has always scared me," he said. "Much more so than hell. I know they're the same thing, but there's something about that word—underworld."

"I used to get scared my parents were in the underworld," she said, picking at the grass. "Sometimes I wonder if all I really want is not to end up like my parents . . ." She trailed off, wondering why she told him this. She hardly knew anything about his family. "I realize what you're trying to say," she said after a moment. "You think I'm more than a trophy wife."

"Isn't that a compliment?" he said. "I wouldn't say that about most of your friends."

"It might be, if you weren't smug about it," she said. "You act like you know everything because you read books."

"I don't know everything, but I do think you're confusing freedom with money," he said. "People compromise their integrity with that kind of thinking all the time."

"Please don't lecture me." She felt the tears welling up, but she held them in. There was nothing to cry about.

Preston noticed. While it wasn't the first time he'd made a woman cry, it was the first time he'd hurt himself by doing it. He stood silently as she tried not to cry and then finally did, very softly. He knelt, unsure whether to touch her. "Vivienne?" he said.

She dropped her hands in a gesture of resignation, and he saw her eyes, patchy red and glistening. He wanted to tuck her hair behind her ears and wipe her cheeks, but instead he placed an awkward hand on her left knee.

"I don't even know why I'm crying," she said. "This is so dumb."

"Maybe I'm an asshole about the things I know I can't give you," he said.

She wiped her eyes. "What, is that your way of telling me you want to be my boyfriend?"

He smiled. He loved her candor. She had no idea how pure it was, how rare. "I probably don't fit the criteria," he said.

"Right, because you know everything about me," she said, and swiped his hand off her knee. She stood, clapping the dirt from her palms.

Preston reached up and grabbed her hand. She let herself drop back to the ground. "Maybe I wish I did fit the criteria."

"Maybe?"

"Yes, maybe," he said. "Because wouldn't I have to be a different person then?"

She tipped her head onto his shoulder. "I'm a terrible reader," she said. "I'd drive you crazy because I never read."

Cautiously, he wrapped his arms around her, and they rested there, he wiping the specks of bark from her back, she watching the day pass in slow seconds from the foreground of his shoulder.

"How'd I get pegged as such a reader?" he said. "Architects don't have time to read."

"You seem like you would be." With her face tucked into the nook cut by his chin and shoulder, she could smell him close; he was earthy, like oats, masculine in a tart hormonal way. His stubble scratched her hairline.

She closed her eyes and exhaled, an audible, blood-soothing exhale, and sank into his body. He sat wide awake, mindful not to let her go or embrace her much tighter, working to suspend the moment. He touched her hair, which spilled over her shoulders like a veil, golden and soft-seeming but between his fingers like straw, chemical-coarse. The skeleton-weed flower dropped to the ground.

He could not have said how much time had passed when her phone chimed. She jerked a little at the noise, and he, anticipating that she wouldn't ignore it, opened his arms before she could pull away. The phone was in her purse, which lay in a lump at the base of the walnut tree. She twisted away from him to grab it.

The text, from Karlie—*where the f are you?*—was like a whiplash rippling all the way from the Blank house.

"I didn't realize it was so late." She stood, shaking dirt from her sandals. Shouldering her purse, she smoothed her hair and tucked it behind her ears, finally regarding Preston from above as if she were surprised to see him sitting there.

"Ready to go?" she said, her tone sharp, not really a question.

He thought of stopping her—but no. He got to his feet and followed her down the path they'd trod, the sun at their backs.

Bucky was waiting for her in the kitchen, grimly eating shards of cold brisket off a napkin. Karlie and Reis were at the table, painting their nails. Bucky asked Vivienne to follow him outside. His truck was already loaded up. Crossing his arms, leaning on the grille, he looked tired and pasty and, worst of all, indifferent. Vivienne felt sick to her stomach and tried to gather herself.

"I think it's better if you go home with one of your friends," he said.

"Why?" She shifted her weight. She knew why.

"Don't make me explain." His tone was shaming, victimized. "Last night—and then today you skip off with that Presley douchebag?"

"I didn't skip off," she said. "I fell asleep. No one woke me—"

"I don't care," he said. "I don't want to know."

She stared at her feet. It was quiet, no four-wheelers, just the cheeping of finches. "I'm sorry," she said.

"What's that?" Bucky asked, tilting his ear, as if he hadn't heard.

She said it again. "I'm sorry."

He pulled his worn white cap from the back pocket of his jeans, slid his free hand over his curls, and slipped it on by the brim. His beloved move. His goodbye gesture. "Yeah, well . . ." he said.

Vivienne didn't watch him drive away. She just kept her head down. *"I'm sorry, I'm sorry, I'm sorry,"* she chanted the words, returning them to herself.

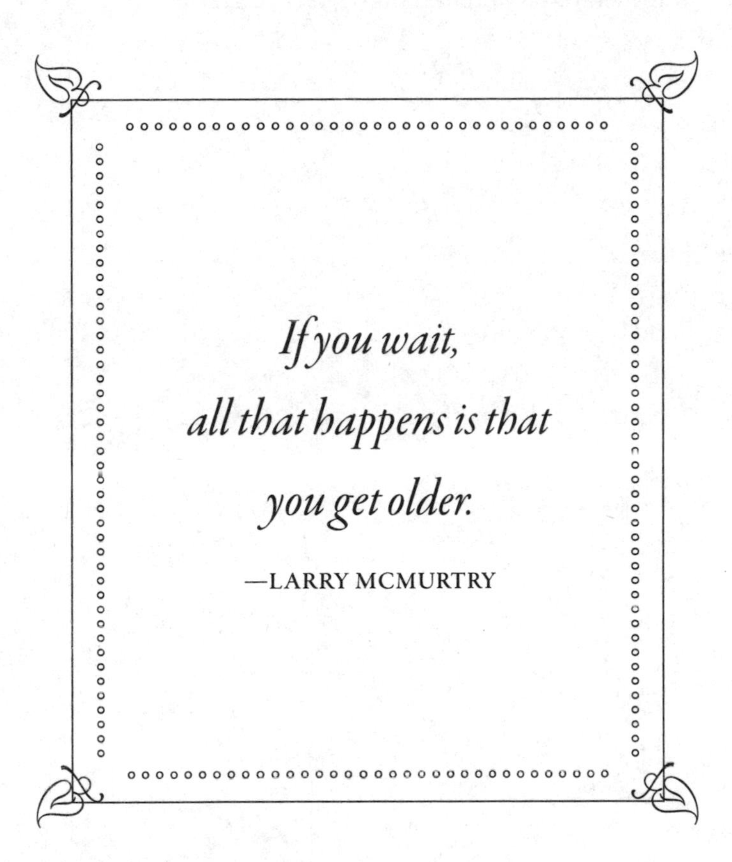

If you wait,
all that happens is that
you get older.

—LARRY MCMURTRY

I

JUNE AND JULY PASSED DREARILY. WITH THE WEDDING approaching and summer in full swing, Vivienne had to increase her hours at the store to six days a week. Bikinis, new sundresses, strappy sandals to replace the previous season's, and gifts for the many imminent showers in celebration of weddings and babies—all insufficient to her salary, even to her less-than-prudent withdrawals from Katherine's hatbox.

Folding designer jeans into flush stacks, fondling cashmere sweater sets, and sitting on a padded stool behind a glass display desk surrounded by lavender travel candles and thirty-five-dollar friendship bracelets provided no comfort from her mounting regret over Bucky. She hadn't heard from him. After he'd left that evening at the ranch, Karlie, bitchy at first, had turned sweet. Then Vivienne really knew she'd blown it—Karlie was sweet when she had no reason to be jealous. Preston had wasted no time in returning to Houston. He'd sent her a couple of text messages asking her to meet for coffee. She wanted to see him, but he was too much a reminder of her mistake. The whole weekend burned in her memory and made her at turns angry, determined to forge ahead with indifference, and hopeless, smiling but on the verge of disintegration, a figurine in despair.

The boutique was located in a fashionable shopping center near Katherine's townhome, a luxury strip center enhanced with light-pink brick, decorative lantern sconces, and long, shady arcades. It was small;

from the register she could see the whole spread. A doorbell admitted customers. She was supposed to play music—something calm and uplifting—but when she was alone she kept the stereo low, or off altogether, so she could zone out into the glint of stainless-steel racks and blended silk. It was like being wrapped in a cotton ball, a cotton ball in a down comforter in a cumulus cloud.

Unless a group of bridesmaids had an appointment to try on dresses, she rarely had more than one or two customers at once, and most only wanted a mini bottle of Pellegrino and to be left alone. But occasionally a talker would come in. Vivienne had two or three talkers, who never, ever asked Vivienne about her own life and seemed utterly unaware of the fact that she was working. She'd recently received a note to her work email from a talker who was in love with her husband's business partner, informing her that she wouldn't be able to come in that day—as if Vivienne had been waiting.

There were also long empty stretches. She eased the boredom by reading blogs, particularly Karlie's blog. Karlie had been blogging a lot since Memorial Day, posting pictures of the weekend—Bucky and Tim on four-wheelers, Waverly and Reis grinning in the kitchen, their cheeks squished together, and pictures from subsequent weekends at barbecues and lunches and shopping dates, Vivienne notably absent from the pictures despite the fact that she'd been there for much of it. Waverly's dress-fitting at Neiman's, for example: Vivienne was there, but only Karlie, Sissy, and Waverly showed up on the blog, with Waverly's gown photoshopped out and replaced with Princess Di's wedding dress. To pretend she didn't care, Vivienne commented, *Ha, love it!*

Bladimir came for lunch. He was assisting the head of an environmental consulting firm part-time, but mostly he did massage at a luxury Thai spa. This job provided an endless well of laughs, as the owner had hired Bladimir—a half Cuban, half Irish American—because he looked "Thai enough." The idea of Blad standing in as a native of Thailand, with his mat of sideswept black hair, china-white complexion, and hazel saucer eyes, was hilarious. A lover of products, Blad had flawless skin. He often brought his latest loot into the boutique to make Vivienne jealous. Vegetable-skin mists. Rosewater masks. Seafoam eye gel. She couldn't understand how these products worked on him but never on her. When she narrowed in on her own magnified face in the scary vanity mirror, she saw faint lines materializing around her eyes.

Blad claimed her wrinkles were stress-related while insisting everything would work out fine. "Just look at me," he'd say, and pose before the triptych of illuminated mirrors in the changing area in one of his two work outfits: a black suit and leather dress boots, or a starched white linen caftan with a mandarin collar, Thai fisherman pants, and flip-flops. He was striking in either ensemble, and he knew it. Vivienne would listen from her perch while he popped around the racks, lamenting his ill-timed birth. He was convinced he should have been a Robert Mapplethorpe model, trolling lower Manhattan in the early eighties, contracting AIDS, and dying in an industrial loft. Vivienne would tell him to shut up, that he shouldn't joke about that, and he'd look at her with sincere, bright-eyed amazement and say, no, really, that should have been his destiny. He was born too late, in the wrong place. Then he'd pull up Mapplethorpe and Avedon photographs online and say, "See what I mean?" She still told him to shut up.

It seemed to her that Bladimir could be a model. He wasn't exactly handsome, but he had an innocence she recognized as special. He was a lanky boy with an unimposing face and gentle eyes but fiery Cuban insides, topped by that wild black hair. Watching him in the mirror, marveling at how he managed to be so confident and sweet all at once, she'd ask why he didn't model now, and he'd laugh.

"Because I'm going to be the first gay governor of Texas," he'd say flatly, and flex his measly biceps.

That was Bladimir. He was the only friend who'd visited her at the store all summer. He'd waltz in with two chicken Caesar salads and two Diet Cokes, demand instant repayment for her half, and give her a kiss on the cheek. If they weren't glamour-posing in the mirrors when the boutique was empty, they were "whisper dancing." This was Blad's term for dancing to in-store music that you couldn't turn up loud. They'd pretend the music—the chosen eighties' hits of their childhoods—was blasting and would go nuts, Bladimir flopping his long arms all over the place, Vivienne getting dreamy and loose, both of them singing quietly along, always in the changing area, out of view of the front door. If the bell rang, they'd freeze, take a breath, straighten each other's clothes, and pad serenely around the corner. Vivienne would smile and open the door, saying, "Good afternoon, ma'am. May I get you anything to drink?"

Only Bladimir knew of her long afternoon with Preston; only Bladimir knew the details of the night with Bucky. Sometimes they'd read Karlie's blog together, side by side on padded stools, Vivienne narrating aloud:

> *June 30: On these hot summer nights, I'm just loving linen for backyard dinners. Nothing whispers light & airy & stylish like natural linen. Wouldn't it be amazing to watch fireworks al fresco, surrounded by shades of beige, complemented by my latest seasonal obsession, blue & white seersucker? Finish the table with seersucker napkins, and blue, white, and red velvet cupcakes—the perfect balance of chic and patriotic! God Bless America, y'all!*

> *July 14: Since one of my besties is preparing for her nuptials on Labor Day weekend, I just can't stop thinking about stationery! I'm feeling inspired to giftie myself some personalized letterpress notecards after seeing all her oh-so-amazing invites. And how much am I loving handmade wrapping paper! Whether it's for a bridal shower or second-baby sprinkle, boutique paper is essential to perfecting your gift. Today I found some super-incredible sheets hand-painted with mini Eiffel Towers! Gush! And of course for that bonus Texas twist, if you squint they kinda look like little oil rigs! Yeehaw! God bless y'all!*

When Vivienne finished, Bladimir would purse his lips, calmly fold his hands in his lap, and with prim equanimity say something terribly vulgar like, "I hope her ass falls on a dildo." And they'd laugh and laugh.

> *August 1: Sometimes a girl just can't decide . . . chicken-fried steak or fried chicken? But seriously, I just want say thank you today. How blessed am I to have the best girls anyone could ask*

> *for . . . heyyy, Wavey and Reis! . . . True ladies! What more could a girl ask for? Devoted readers, what are YOU thankful for today? Let's all remember to count our blessings. I'm not too grateful for this Texas heat, but a week from today I'll be lounging on the beach in Mexico, woohoo!*

This particular entry, coming on the eve of the miserable dog days, when neither Vivienne nor Bladimir had the means to vacation, and which seemed to deliberately exclude Vivienne, resulted in Bladimir slamming the laptop shut.

Vivienne face-palmed into a slump.

"It isn't real! It isn't real! It isn't real!" Blad said, slapping his thighs in quick succession with the words. "Her marriage isn't even real."

"It doesn't matter," Vivienne said. "She still has it."

"Honey," Blad said. "You don't mean that. And there's clearly something wrong with her if she derives happiness from trying to make people jealous on her blog and disguising it with some bullshit about gratitude."

"Well, it works."

"I don't get her," Blad said. "Timmy is such a bear."

"Timmy works ninety-hour weeks so she can blog," Vivienne said.

Blad hopped off his stool and began slipping on all the birthstone rings from the velvet finger display. Blad wasn't effeminate in earnest, but occasionally he'd prance around like a queen to irritate Vivienne, who had to reorganize all the rings after he dropped them on the table during his straight-dude impression. "Whoa, I wasn't wearing jewelry," he'd say in a low drawl. "Rings are for pussies. Man."

The dog days set in. It was too hot to do anything but sit in the air-conditioning and complain. Grackles gathered beneath the shopping center's arcades, cursing. The parking lot was a glimmering desert, the cars like costume jewels. Just the walk to her car was oppressive; the moment she sat in the driver's seat, the backs of her thighs blistered against the black leather.

Blad was particularly grumpy about wearing a suit to the consulting firm and took to bringing along his caftan and changing into it the minute he arrived at the store. In this life-sucking heat and humidity, it was all he could bear to wear. He took one from the spa in Vivienne's size, but she was too embarrassed to wear it. Blad's apartment in Montrose only had an old window unit, and he insisted it was too hot to be there while the sun was still up, so occasionally she'd accompany him back to his neighborhood for a drink. They always went to the same place, a dive bar where Bladimir had developed a reputation of being the guy in the caftan, and they could sit on the patio and drink margaritas while getting spritzed by misters, like lettuce in the produce aisle.

Here, Vivienne thought of Preston. She found herself wishing he'd walk by. Blad, who Vivienne knew saw Preston around the neighborhood, grew impatient with her.

"Did he mention me?" she'd ask him beneath the spritzers.

"No," Blad would reply, pulling at one of the curls at her temples, frizzy from the mist. "But guys don't talk about that kind of stuff. Just go get coffee with him."

At the end of the day, Vivienne tiptoed up Katherine's stairs, crashed onto her bed, and, with self-belying enthusiasm, responded to emails and texts. Pallid as her own situation was in comparison to that of her friends, Vivienne believed in graciousness, believed that by wishing the best for others she would engender the most desirable outcomes for herself, and she tried to be genuinely happy for their rich lives, even for Karlie. But this was mostly a prayer for herself, for the strength to believe her friend was good.

The darkness of her room became the stage for her reenactments of sex with Bucky. She imagined ways she might have tantalized him without sex, how she could have retained him in spite of the sex—*if only I hadn't taken that nap, if only I hadn't walked off with Preston*—tracing the line of thinking that led her to initiating sex, to veering away with Preston, trying to understand why she took such a thorny path. As the summer progressed, she exalted what small passion she could recall. Bucky became a capable lover. She wanted him more, and she blamed Preston but, also most brutally, herself. She fell in love with the idea of herself on Bucky's arm. He would make her visible to herself. She mistook the warmth of this possibility for love.

She would see him at Waverly's wedding next month. This was the source of her scant optimism, the wellspring of her belief that maybe Preston was right, she could find a better job, she could change things up, it was all within her reach. Bladimir would be her date to the wedding.

One uneventful Friday, Waverly stopped by with Reis after their Pilates class and found Vivienne busy marking tags with end-of-summer sale prices. It was late afternoon, the hour Vivienne drank a cup of green tea to keep herself alert. The refrigerated air had been blowing on her all day long. By that point the heat of the tea almost felt cozy, especially today. With her hair wrapped up in a bun, her ears felt like cold rubber.

Waverly came around and gave her a hug. Reis just leaned over the desk for a half hug—and knocked the tea with her purse, a suede bladder with moccasin tassels dangling from the bottom.

"Oh my gosh," Waverly said, and dove in to wipe the liquid off the desk.

The hem of Vivienne's cotton safari dress, which she was wearing off the rack, was soaked. She'd have to steam and iron it now and, if there was a stain, hope her boss wouldn't notice.

Reis examined the damage to her purse. "Ugh," she said.

Vivienne ran to the bathroom for paper towels. She and Waverly daubed up the spill while Reis browsed. "Is your gown finished?" Vivienne asked Waverly. "Sorry I had to miss the last fitting. I couldn't get out of work."

Waverly did a hop and clapped her hands. She had her hair in a messy ponytail, her figure cinched up in purple stretch pants and a white jogging tank. "It's done," she said. "It's amazing."

Reis, nearly naked in tiny black nylon shorts and black sports bra, that enviably straight hair swinging around, impervious to humidity, nodded. "You won't believe it when you see it."

"I picked up my dress yesterday," Vivienne said. The maid-of-honor dress that cost more than she had earned all summer long. Fortunately, she wasn't paying for it, but it made her wonder what would have happened if Waverly had expected her to.

"It feels real now," Waverly said. "Two more weeks!"

Reis was eating a bell pepper from a plastic baggie. "Just remember," she said. "This is your day. Don't worry about pleasing anyone else. It's all about you."

Vivienne was already annoyed that Waverly was hanging out with Reis. Every time she saw Reis she tried to warm to her, but it hadn't worked. There was something about the way she snapped those sliced peppers so deliberately between her teeth that set Vivienne the wrong way. It was as if she'd raised the peppers herself and was munching on her children.

"What about Clay?" Vivienne said, tossing the paper towels in the trash. "It's about him too."

Reis finished off a pepper. "Obviously it's about Clay too, but brides are different. Brides have been thinking about their day their whole lives. Not me, though. Seriously, I never thought about it growing up."

Reis often backed herself up with huskily articulated absolutes: "always" and "never," and an inflated sense of the value of her own personal experience. Vivienne very much doubted that Reis had "never" envisioned her own wedding.

Reis plopped into one of the white leather armchairs and dug the heels of her running shoes into the white carpet the cleaning lady would vacuum later, once the store closed and the parking lot darkened, left to commence its nightlong radiative exhale. "So, who are you bringing to the wedding?" she said.

Waverly interrupted the question with a declaration that Vivienne didn't have to bring anyone if she didn't want to.

"I'm bringing Bladimir," Vivienne said.

"Bladimir Caro!" Waverly said. "You haven't told me that. He's so cute."

Vivienne's girlfriends approved of Bladimir as a sort of lovable object, a stuffed animal of a man whose cheeks they might pinch, a novelty with whom to shop. His gayness was his entirety.

Reis fanned her hair out over the chair back. "Have you talked to Bucky?"

"Why would she talk to him?" Waverly said. "Forget about him."

"He called me a couple of days ago," Reis said. "I haven't called him back, though."

There was a pause. Then Waverly raised her voice. "He's a jerk."

"Is he a jerk, though," Reis said, "like, objectively speaking?"

Waverly frowned. "He was a jerk to Vivienne. He's never called once."

"Totally, I know." She looked at Vivienne. "I'm just saying. That night at the ranch, a bunch of us were up really late and I talked to him for a while, and it was one of those things where you talk to someone for the first time one-on-one and you realize they're different than you thought? I got the sense that he's really confused. Like, I felt bad for him."

"I don't want to talk about this," Vivienne said. "I'm not going to feel bad for Bucky."

Waverly cleared her throat. Vivienne heard a car alarm blaring somewhere in the parking lot. Finally Reis threw up her hands.

"Look, Viv—Buck and I have been talking, okay? Nothing's happened, but we've been talking."

"So you came in here to tell me this?"

"Not at all," Reis said. "There's nothing to tell. I've just been talking to him. But Waverly"—her eyes darted to Waverly, who seemed to be hugging herself—"is looking at me like I should feel guilty. I didn't even know you'd been with him that night when I was talking with him." Her voice picked up. "I found you staring at him while he was sleeping in the morning. You're welcome for not telling him that."

Vivienne scoffed. "Why are you attacking me for this?"

"All right, stop," Waverly said. "It's good Vivienne knows, that's all."

Reis sighed and stood. "I have to get ready for a meeting." She paused at the door. "I love your hair that way, Viv. You look like a ballerina."

They watched Reis stride to her luxury sports utility vehicle, her body so trim and fatless that Vivienne momentarily thought Bucky couldn't be blamed. Reis opened the door, painfully sanguine, and in a moment zipped off.

Waverly offered the only words that could possibly have helped. "Want to get pedicures?"

* * *

Toe beautiful was packed with women just off work. Fey, the middle-aged Vietnamese woman who ran Toe Beautiful like a stern madam, greeted Vivienne and Waverly.

"You want mani-pedi?" she asked.

"Just pedi," Vivienne said.

"No mani?" Fey tapped her own bare fingernails. "Ten dollars more for mani."

"Just pedi," Vivienne said again.

"Mani-pedi for me," Waverly said.

"Okay," Fey said. "Pick a color." Then she yelled something in Vietnamese and a young Vietnamese woman emerged from the hall. "Go there," she said to Vivienne and Waverly, and pointed to the only open pedicure chairs. Vinyl thrones, side by side.

Vivienne disobeyed and went to the bathroom first. She tried to cool her feelings by splashing her face with cold water, but it didn't help. She was so mad, and so hurt, and so humiliated, and so all three at once. In the big vibrating chair, she sat in a kind of stunned reverie, feeling her breasts shake beneath her dress. For her color, she chose a deep, dark red.

"Callus remover?" the woman at her feet asked.

Vivienne leaned forward. "Wouldn't it be great if there was a callus remover for people's hearts?"

The young woman looked up and smiled but said nothing. Vivienne repeated herself, louder, catching the attention of the employees. The young woman smiled the same and pretended to laugh. Vivienne realized she didn't understand. "No callus remover," she said.

"It's not your job to worry whether there are calluses on other people's hearts," Waverly said.

Fey called out something in Vietnamese, and another woman called back, until the women of Toe Beautiful were sharing an animated conversation in Vietnamese. The woman at Vivienne's feet, who'd smiled meekly at her every word, was now speaking fast and forcefully in what sounded like the chiming of mysterious bells. Vivienne wished she and

Waverly could join them. It seemed to her that in their business of providing pleasure that they probably didn't care to give, they were gathered up, bonded close. Vivienne got to have her feet rubbed, but she didn't get to understand that seamless turn from faux-supplicant to woman-among-friends. When Vivienne looked on as if she might understand their secret, they ignored her and said serenely, "Shoulder massage?"

As Waverly paged through a celebrity rag, Vivienne fell under the spell of the footbath. The pleasure soothed her anger, but she kept picturing Reis and Bucky, cuddling and talking. It didn't make sense. She'd been seeing Bucky for three months and was only beginning to feel they'd developed an intimate rapport; how could Reis just happen to be there and connect with him?

Probably because she was a future attorney, she knew how to be convincingly innocent and seductive at the same time. It was near impossible for Vivienne to imagine Bucky turning sensitive and confiding in Reis, unless he was trying to get into Reis's skintight jeans. This possibility called to mind an image much worse, and much more explicit, than the two of them cuddling and talking. But the worst possibility of all was that they'd just clicked, as people do, under the worst circumstances for Vivienne.

"How long did you know?" Vivienne asked.

Waverly folded the magazine on her lap. "Only since today. Reis told me during Pilates."

"Do you really think they haven't done anything?"

Waverly considered this with a compassionate twinkle in her eyes. "Reis didn't tell me," she said. "I don't know."

"So he wants her and not me? And he discovered this only because he had me?"

"Just be glad you hadn't been with him for years. I think this means he's not the guy for you."

Vivienne mused on this while Waverly evaluated her coral toenails. Accepting that he wasn't the guy for her meant accepting that, to Bucky at least, Reis was preferable. This alone would hurt, but its proximity to her nakedness in a field of mesquite made it sickening. Bucky's sweat and juices were still on her while he and Reis were discussing Scripture. It was horrible.

"You look so mad," Waverly said.

"I am."

"Erase it from your mind. It's not worth your energy." She opened her purse and handed Vivienne a small brown paper bag. "Will you bring this by my parents' house? It's a piece of wedding cake. Clay and I had the final tasting this morning. I don't have time to go by there. Date night." She smiled.

"Sure," Vivienne said. Fey came around and gave her a firm tap on her shin. Her toes were done. Time to go.

II

BRACKEN SWUNG OPEN THE WIDE CUT-GLASS DOOR, barefoot in khaki shorts and a maroon Aggies T-shirt, one hand gripping his short glass of Scotch.

"Well, hey, Cally," he said, settling in against the doorjamb.

Vivienne had never liked standing at Sissy and Bracken's door. It made her feel small. She was much more comfortable inside, looking out, with Sissy and Waverly.

"Just dropping this off," she said, handing over the bag. "It's a slice of wedding cake."

He disappeared for a moment, calling to someone in Spanish, and returned empty-handed, wearing loafers. "You want to do me a favor, Cally?"

She hesitated, wanting to decline. But she knew she wouldn't. It was impossible to say no to Bracken. There were men in Houston who would've given up their boots for the chance to do Bracken Blank a favor.

"My car is in the shop," he said, strolling outside past Vivienne, sniffing the air. "Why don't you take me down there to get it. I just got the call it's ready." He was already walking to her car. "It idn't far, down on Westheimer," he said, opening the passenger door for himself and dropping inside.

Traffic was thick, and Bracken was the biggest person who'd ever ridden in her passenger seat, not so much in size as in sheer force of personality. He filled the space with his drawl and Scotch aroma; Vivienne felt choked by it. She unrolled the windows, but then he rolled them back up, blasted the AC, and reclined his seat to a forty-five-degree angle, tucking his free hand behind his head.

"It's been a long time since I spent a lazy afternoon," he said. "Always think it'll do me good, then I remember I'm not the lazy type. It's 'mportant to keep active, keep the hands busy or the brain thinkin'. Otherwise you'll lose it. Ah, you don't need to worry about that yet, but rigor starts young."

Vivienne nodded.

"You might be thinking that's funny coming from a guy with a drink in his hand," he said, holding up his tumbler. "But rigor earns you the right to indulge. Indulgence without rigor is sloth."

"I agree," Vivienne said, changing lanes to keep busy.

"I used to play a game with my kid brother called the blinker game," he said. "We'd try to sync up folks' blinkers on the road. See if anyone's blinker rhythm was the same. Some people got spastic blinkers."

Vivienne clicked up her blinker and made a right onto a short patch of open road. From the corner of her eye she saw Bracken sipping, nodding his head slightly. If she hadn't been familiar with his swagger, she might have thought he was tipsy. He made her uncomfortable because she was always wondering if he was anything like her father; she sensed they had shared a certain posture that made others listen, a persuasive manner of saying things that made you wish you had it too.

But, then again, Bracken came from heartier stock. He grew up in a cowpoke town in the Panhandle, studied his way into A&M, and earned his wealth through a mash-up of brains, charm, and faith. He had the enthusiasm of a former yell leader and the diligence of a wolf—his success had only made him more ambitious. But it was hard to tell when he was back-patting and when he wasn't. He'd always seemed uninterested in her old family name, claiming he was sick of petroleum the minute he was born. "I've seen too many derricks," he liked to say, "too many pumps."

"Just finished that one there," he said, pointing out the window to a sort of French château with a dirt yard and crates of St. Augustine sod piled in the driveway. "So, tell me, Cally, how's life?"

"Great."

"Grand," Bracken said. "What're you doin' with your time?"

"Working at Cotton and Lace," Vivienne said.

"Cotton and lace?" Bracken said. "Which do you like better?"

"No it's one place, not two. The name is Cotton and Lace."

"I'm aware," Bracken said. "I'm asking which do you prefer to wear—cotton or lace?"

Vivienne kept her eyes straight on the road. "Cotton," she said.

"Personally I like lace. Not for myself, though." He laughed and sipped on. "You got a fella?"

Vivienne died a little scrambling for a response. "No fella."

"Well, idn't that an inappropriate question," he said, and laughed again, a sturdy laugh. Perhaps sensing her discomfort, he batted the air and sniffed. "I'm only bringin' it up because I played a round with Randal Stanley not long back, and we got to talkin' about you."

So Randal had succeeded in playing golf with Bracken. He probably thought he was king of the hill now. Vivienne sped up and almost made the next light, but the yellow was too close to call. She stopped hard. "I don't know Randal very well," she said, willing away her fib to him while bracing for it to resurface. No matter how well she tried to cover her ass, it was never enough. And like clockwork:

"He told me somethin' kinda funny," Bracken said, balancing his half-full tumbler in the dashboard's crevice. He stretched his fingers over his hairy knees and straightened his elbows, pausing until a sufficient anticipatory cloud of shame drifted over Vivienne. "Said you were lookin' at some museums for Waverly's rehearsal dinner a while back."

Vivienne tugged at a hangnail till it stung. What the hell was she supposed to say, Randal was lying? The thought landed on her shoulder like a butterfly—blame it on Randal.

The light blinked and went green. "Huh?" she said, pressing the gas, cocking her head sweetly. Bracken either wasn't fooled or wasn't expecting this reaction.

He drawled, "You didn't catch me?"

"No, I heard you," Vivienne said. "I just—" She pressed one hand to her sternum and folded her shoulders inward. "I'm just confused."

"Confused me too," Bracken said, raising a sidelong eyebrow. " 'Cause sayin' that wouldn't be true. Meaning it would be a lie. And a pretty perplexin' lie, because I can't figure out a motive. Why would Cally lie about something like that?"

Vivienne spoke like a gentle narrator. "He must have misunderstood me. I don't know why he'd say that."

Bracken reached for his glass and took a drink. "Bullshit, Cally. I want to know why you told such a funny white lie. I haven't shared this information with anyone, because it piqued"—"*picked*," he said—"my curiosity like it hadn't been piqued in a while. What's Cally up to?"

Suddenly she felt his warm, sandpapery fingertip against her temple, and she barreled her eyes onto the road. She could smell cigar musk in its texture. "What's brewin' in there?" he said, twisting his raised wrist as if uncorking a bottle. She wanted to cry, half from blind fright, half in gratitude to him for calling her out.

"He creeps me out," she blurted. "He invited me to tour the museum with him, and I needed an excuse to get out of it."

Bracken dropped his hand and nodded with relish, as if he'd finally answered life's riddle.

"Now I see that," he said, in a new, avuncular tone. "Sorry I put you on the spot, but it's been biting at me. I'm a sucker for a scoop. Randal idn't subtle, and probably in the extreme with women." He was musing down into his glass. "And he plays things too deliberate with his pimple-poppin', but he's on his way. I'm telling you that now." He sipped. "I respect his ambition. It's showy, but it's tough."

She listened to him as one does without a choice in the matter, wordlessly and with nods, yet she also felt less irritated now that she'd been honest. She'd relinquished something to him, of all people, and it was a relief.

He went on. "Now, I invited him to the wedding. Don't be scared of him. He's a good time, just dudn't have good graces. He'll come around." He focused on her suddenly with a looser, amused expression. "Are you stuck in the mud?" he asked.

Vivienne forced a smile. "What? No, I'm doing fine."

"Well, that's grand," he said. "But the curse of modern youth is choice. When I was growin' up, you didn't have the luxury of choice unless you were willin' to hit the free market and work for it. Kids are interested in plenty, but the question is whether it pays. A lot of you girls didn't include that need in your plans, and a lot still don't have to, but that's how you find yourself stuck in the mud," he said, pausing. "Am I right?"

It was typical of Bracken to employ patronizing friendliness in masking what really were presumptuous, nosy questions. "I'm not stuck in the mud," she said.

"Women are havin' to adapt to a new landscape," he said, ignoring her and indicating the world beyond the car, shifting from large homes with detached four-car garages to manicured townhome communities and, in the coming mile, to expansive commerce. "My feeling is it's the hardest for your generation. There's no tradition anymore, and I lament that. Would you agree?"

Vivienne was feeling nervous again—what was he getting at? "I'm not sure," she said.

"I always felt you fell by the wayside a bit," he said. "Seems to me you didn't get a fair chance." The dealership was on the next block. She accelerated close to the truck in front of her.

"Hold your horses," Bracken said as they turned in. "Stop over here a minute. I got an idea."

Vivienne still didn't have the guts to disobey him, so she pulled into a spot adjacent to the entrance, shifting the car to park without switching off the engine. All around were other, larger lots, concrete prairies lined with Q-tip palm trees and stray shopping carts, stretching out from the banks of enormous shopping centers. Bracken finished the last of his Scotch, washing his mouth with it before swallowing. It made her uneasy how much this man had unwittingly supported her over the years, just by nature of her relationship with his daughter. She felt uncomfortably beholden to him.

"I'm gonna tell you something kinda funny," he said, once the car was still. "I don't like golf. Everyone thinks I love golf, because I play it all the time. They think I'm the golf guy, but I don't care for it. Baseball's my sport. You know why I play golf?" He paused. "I play golf because when I moved to Houston I knew that's what I had to do if I wanted to get where I wanted to go. I plan on playin' with my grandson. And you know something? My grandson's not gonna need to play golf to get where he wants to go. Do you understand me?"

"Yes," she said.

"Now, don't deershit me. You like where you're at?"

Vivienne sat, exhausted, pearling up in sweat. "No," she sighed, and tipped her neck back against the headrest.

Bracken moved his hand to the gearshift, a few inches from her bare thigh. "I want to help you," he said, his Panhandle cadence like drawn butter poured from a glazed spout.

Vivienne began fiddling with the hem of her dress—Reis's spill had left a water spot.

"Are you interested in that kind of thing—art museums?" Bracken asked.

"Yes," Vivienne said, fiddling hard. "If you mean art, yes, that interests me."

"You've never been easy for conversation, have you?" He scrutinized her straight on. "You're no Karlie."

Embarrassed, Vivienne blushed. "No, I'm not."

"Well, I like that about you. Always have. There's something to be said for being tough to figure out." He withdrew his hand and settled back in his seat, satisfied that he was the one who'd finally figured her out.

Seeing he wasn't looking at her, Vivienne looked at him. As Waverly's father, he was revolting. But, still, she acknowledged that he looked good, definitely not sixty. The delineation of his hairline was a dark stronghold sprouting from his forehead; the hair flowed back in a sort of undulation. Even his legs had a youthful sturdiness. He was a man who grew more rugged as he grayed, tighter in the jaw, and more vehement in the eyes. And yet glad. Bracken was free to take his time in conversation. He carried himself with an enviable self-possession. He warranted his arrogance. "If you mystify people, they'll listen to you.

But you can't force it. Some people just don't have that quality." He paused. "Look how hot it is out there. This city's a pancake in a frying pan."

Bright heat glinted off the steel and metal of new Porsches. The sun, just finishing for the day, hung low on the horizon.

"Here's what I'm thinking," he said. "We're movin' to a new building next month. Big tower near the Galleria. And we had an idea to make an art collection there. I'm partnering up with a guy from Midland. He's got a gas pipeline and wants to get into development. So we got the wall space and the money; we just need somebody to choose the pictures. How'd you like to do it?"

"That's a curator position," Vivienne said, facing him. "People study for that."

Bracken shrugged. The crow's-feet fanning his eyes aged him in reverse, made him spry and cunning. "They go to school for it because they don't have someone like me sittin' here offering it to them."

"That doesn't seem . . ." she faltered.

"Easy does it," Bracken said. "We'll have a meeting and get it all straight. Figure what kind of pictures we want. Look, if we've got the budget, all the doors are open."

Vivienne didn't say anything.

"You want it or not?" Bracken said. "I keep hearing Waverly talking about how you need an angle. Well, here's opportunity pullin' over and openin' the door for you." He delivered the last sentence with such conviction that she snapped out of her bewilderment. Bracken was offering her a job.

"An angle?" she said.

"An angle in," Bracken said. "You'll meet a lot of people doin' this. There'll be travel. We'll be on the fortieth floor. I'll set you up with a nice view."

Her mind spun. She saw men. Freshly shaven men in suits with loosened ties, popping into this office of hers to say goodbye at the end of the day. And hotels.

"Forty-five K to start," he said. "I know that's pennies take-home, but there's gonna be tidbits. And room for more if this works out."

The sum, low as it was by her peers' standards, sounded massive, considerably above the fourteen dollars an hour she earned now. "Why me?" she said. "You could get anyone."

Bracken nodded in acknowledgment that, yes, he could get anyone. "But you're part of the family. I don't like the idea of you stuck workin' as a shopgirl, Cally."

"Does Waverly think it's a good idea?" she said. The mention of his daughter's name seemed to puncture their new, unnameable dynamic. "She hasn't mentioned anything about me needing an angle."

"She will," Bracken said.

Vivienne pulled up her hair, limp from sweat, and bit her lip. The car felt tight. The small of her back was damp. "I wonder why she hasn't said anything—"

"I hope she let you try some of that cake," he said, opening the car door and climbing out. "I'm paying for it."

He shut the door and knuckled the window. As Vivienne lowered it, he reached in and deposited his empty tumbler in her glove compartment. "Doesn't fit in my pocket," he said, leaning over, fixing on her. "You let me know first thing Monday. Sometimes the bus only pulls over and opens the door once, Cally."

Vivienne didn't watch Bracken stride into the Porsche dealership. She'd set her eyes on a skyscraper glistening in the near distance: Bucky's office. If she could parlay her circumstance into a job opportunity—which she may have just accomplished without even trying—why couldn't she confront Bucky?

Ten minutes later she was pulling into the parking garage, sailing on a forty-five-thousand-dollar wind. She went through her trunk for a better dress, as the current one was now stained in front and sweat-drenched in back. In the passenger seat, still sunken with Bracken's weight, she writhed out of the safari dress into a short black jersey dress—wrinkled, but it worked. Bucky liked to work late. The office would probably be quiet. She would suggest a drink.

Her sandals snapped against the marble lobby floor. People were trailing out, but it was mostly empty. It felt strange to be there—she knew it from once before. The occasion had been a rare romantic gesture on Bucky's part; he'd told her to meet him in the lobby for a surprise. And he'd emerged cheerful, pulling on his tie. Then he'd taken her to the Waterwall, where they closed their eyes against the spray and took pictures of each other's silhouettes on the bright vertical water. Months ago, Vivienne realized.

She went to the bathroom to check herself. She tried to see a change in the mirror, but there was only Vivienne, the same, maybe worse. She'd been doing her own highlights for half the summer and it showed. Uneven roots, brassiness. Her eyes blinked at her from what felt like a wad of rosy putty. Her face. Taking a slow breath, she reminded herself to be more confident. Her breasts and her lips were in full bloom, her stomach flat, her skin clear, and she now had the power to move on from the store.

She waited for the elevator. An older man in a gray suit, carrying an armload of brown file folders, waited beside her, his eyes drilled to the floor. Her reflection in the door parted, and she stepped aside to let the passengers out. But the man beside her hesitated. "You going out, Mr. Lawland?" she heard him say, in a submissive baritone.

Vivienne raised her eyes to the figure in the elevator. Bucky, his tie even looser than she expected, did not look happy to see her. He stepped out of the elevator slowly, holding the door open with an outstretched arm as the man with the folders passed inside.

Vivienne felt unprepared; she hadn't expected to see him for three more minutes, which at that moment seemed like the precise quantity of time she required to know what to say.

"Hi," he said finally. His voice was kind enough, but his posture was impatient all over. In one fist he held a leather briefcase, and his shoulders slanted slightly on that side. Every few seconds he switched his weight to a different foot, like an edgy child. "What are you doing here?"

"I was hoping to talk to you," Vivienne said.

"My office?"

"I was in the area."

"Well, you can walk me to my car," he said.

Sarcasm? She couldn't tell. There was a brick in her stomach. An angry brick.

She walked beside him. In profile she watched him slip off his black single-breasted jacket and drape it over his free arm, his chin raised. He took the stairs down to the garage, sparing them both the tension of standing in the elevator together, but Vivienne fell behind, descending in sandals. When she rounded the corner out of the stairwell, he was waiting for her, leaning against his truck in a slice of orange sunset, rolling up his white shirtsleeves, his space marked with a white reflective sign: RESERVED FOR CHARLES B. LAWLAND, JR.

"What did you want to talk about?"

Now, beyond the yawning echo chamber of the lobby, she recognized him, the way he crossed and uncrossed his forearms. The old attraction remained, burned. Her intentions in talking to him revealed themselves as totally nebulous.

She stopped short, pulling her purse close to her shoulder. "Want to go somewhere? Are you hungry?"

"I'm volunteering at Young Life tonight. I gotta head out soon."

Vivienne remembered her own high school Young Life leaders. They had been just like Bucky. They moved from enthusiastic buddy to spiritual confidant with movie-star ease, and she'd fallen for all of them. They'd all seemed so fun, like they had a permission slip from God to make worship a party. In her home, religion was say-your-prayers-or-go-to-hell; at Young Life it was cute guys playing acoustic guitars and performing morality skits in hula skirts. She remembered one of them swallowing a goldfish.

"I want to talk about what happened. I never heard from you after . . ."

He sighed and ran his hands over his head, scruffing up his hair. "Oh, man, Viv." He tapped his boot on the concrete—only Bucky could pull off shitkickers with black suit slacks—and puffed out a breath. "I've been workin' and travelin' all summer. What do you want me to say?"

"We left it so abruptly—"

He tipped forward and caught her waist. "I've been meaning to call."

In his hands, she curdled. "Wait—"

"You look great," he said.

Vivienne stared at his sun-grazed Adam's apple the way she might have a warm chocolate chip cookie, her signals crossing all over the place. She wanted to tell him that Bracken had offered her a job, but the jumble of anger and desire prevented it. Suddenly his lips were over hers and they were kissing. As if the hand of time had plucked them from the ranch and placed them in the parking garage, they stood pawing each other again.

Bucky slid his hand under her shirt.

"There are people around," she said, through their busy lips. He kissed her harder.

Vivienne gave up. It felt too good. It felt so much better than being mad. Her anger became a hungry mouth. Okay, fine, she thought, he's gonna get it. She was going to screw him till he couldn't see out the windows of his own truck. She would ride him till the truck snapped on its struts and he realized his mistake in ignoring her. Reis would love to hear all about that.

He swung her around and opened the door. "Hop in," he said.

Vivienne hoisted herself up and, midstep, tried to catch his eye. She saw he was cradling his phone outside his pocket, typing a text. All at once her focus shifted, and the present clarified itself. She noticed a trough of sweat beading at his upper lip, red splotches on his neck, his quivering, attenuated tongue wetting his lips. Her crossing signals collapsed as if unplugged from a wall, and she stepped back out of the truck.

Bucky slipped the phone inside his pocket and grinned. "Get back in there," he said, lowering his voice to a mischievous quiet.

"Were you just texting with Reis?"

He froze. "I don't need you questioning me," he said.

Vivienne grabbed his arm, involuntarily digging her nails into his biceps. "Answer me," she said.

He jerked away, got into the truck.

She stepped between him and the door. "It was Reis, right?"

He twisted around and grabbed a tobacco tin from his middle

console, began shaping a plug. "You come here like some psycho—I'm not telling you anything."

Vivienne's entire musculature seized up. He was so blithe. He looked down at her from his jacked-up throne like her existence was just another thing he had to deal with. He used to make her feel like a woman; or maybe the idea of what he could become, what she might mold of him, made her feel like a woman. And now he sat there like a king shitting on all that precious validation, completely oblivious.

"Look at me," Vivienne said, her voice wavering.

He tucked the plug into his lower lip. He wouldn't look at her. "When I met you, this is just not how I imagined things panning out with us."

Just then a small group of office workers who looked ready to take off their shoes exited the stairwell. Bucky wished them a good night, his voice altogether beneficent, almost unrecognizable.

Once they were gone, he shook his head. "You kinda ruined things for us."

Vivienne didn't move. Either she was frozen in place for the rest of time or she was going to explode into a thousand pieces.

"It doesn't happen like that with the girl you stick with," he said. "I thought you were different, at least with me." With that he glanced at the door.

She was standing in his way.

"Don't be crazy," he said. He butted the back of his head against the headrest, then spit onto the pavement, narrowly missing her foot. "It was your idea to take that walk."

"I thought it was mutual. We were dating."

Bucky pressed his hands on his knees. "Like I said, it wasn't the way I imagined things panning out, and it isn't what I want."

"So you were just going to toss me into your truck, even though this isn't what you want?"

"We can do it again right now if you want to have a good time," he said. "But I thought we were waiting, and things might go somewhere."

"You wanted to have anal sex. How is that waiting?"

"Lower your voice," he snapped. "I didn't think you were some girl who—" His words tripped over the dip, and he spit, this time into a foam cup he retrieved from a holder cantilevered over a vent. "—Some girl who wants me to rail her out in the woods drunk. And then the next day you go off with that Presley douche—and while we were supposed to be at *church.*"

"His name is *Preston,*" she said loudly.

"Lower your voice," he said again, watching her the way he might watch a criminal or a bum, her nearness an offense to his soul. "Look, you don't realize this was hard for me. I had a lot of guilt over that night. Don't come in here guns blazing when you don't know half the story. I don't feel forgiven for that."

"Forgiven? You'll sleep with any random girl without feeling anything about it, and then if you have sex with a woman you're actually dating you feel guilty? That makes no sense."

"It makes perfect sense, 'cause I separate those things, and God knows my intentions." He shifted in his seat, his face eager and pained. "You weren't a random girl, and then we soiled it. I have a lot of guilt about that. And you should too. That was nothing but lust."

"So just now—what was that?"

"That's why you're not good for me, pulling me back into lust. I want a Christian relationship."

Her interior voice screamed at her to step aside and let him drive away, not to say another word. But fury covered her reason. "You want a Christian relationship?" she said, stepping close, so that his knee depressed her stomach. "Is that what you were texting Reis about? To tell her you want a Christian relationship?"

He drew back, but she leaned in with his angle. "Because no doubt that's why you're interested in Reis. That's the only reason. It can't possibly be anything else." She smelled his snuff breath, noticed how the pores below his lower lip dilated over the lump of tobacco beneath. "Does she know that part of a Christian relationship with you means blowing you day and night? Do you think Reis will be up for that?"

He sneered. "She already is up for that."

"You're so disgusting. I can't believe I apologized to you."

His face rose to the shade of a boiled beet. Mumbling "Crazy" under his breath, he reached for the door handle. "Move," he said.

She didn't.

"Move," he said again, meaner.

Quick as a lizard's tongue, she lunged across his lap and snatched the cup full of dip spit. "Fucker," she howled, and flicked the cup.

At impact, all she registered was his face: grimacing tight, eyes wrinkled shut, brown juices dripping over his brow line, off the tip of his sharp nose, down his pinched-up lips. Vivienne put a hand over her mouth and backed up. He was spitting it off his tongue and scrambling to wipe his eyes, finally using his shirttail, but before he could speak, she turned and ran, nimble as a hurdler, out of the garage, past the potted ficus trees in the organized office green, through a blinking DON'T WALK crosswalk, down three blocks, and into a mixed neighborhood of lofts and crummy row houses, finally stopping in an abandoned overgrown driveway, her chest heaving explosively. Dip spit streamed down her arm. It was late dusk, the sky a spectrum of blue from its crown to the horizon, the street alive with blackbirds ringing on and off the power lines. Over the street rose Bucky's building, its mirrored windows reflecting a shining, distorted sky.

III

THE PASTOR BOWED HIS HEAD. "THERE IS NO FEAR IN love. But perfect love drives out fear, because fear has to do with punishment. The one who fears is not made perfect in love." He paused. "The Word of the Lord."

"Thanks be to God."

Vivienne raised her eyes. The pastor nodded. It was time for her reading. Her hands trembled as she approached the podium and unfolded the paper on which she'd written her chosen verse, the Scripture to bless the union of her friends Waverly Blank and Clay Fitcherson.

"Proverbs thirty-one," she said, to the fluttering of pages. "Verses ten through thirty."

"A wife of noble character who can find?" she read. *"She is worth far more than rubies. Her husband has full confidence in her and lacks nothing of value. She brings him good, not harm, all the days of her life."* She paused to catch the quiver in her throat and looked up, the shock of her own amplified voice hanging in her ears. The Prayerwood sanctuary rustled, over three hundred full. There was Karlie, second in the line of dutiful bridesmaids, clutching her calla lilies. Alongside Clay was Bucky, a groomsman, whom she hadn't seen since the parking garage, with his eyes on the carpet. In the back, wearing a fire-engine-red blazer, Blad. And standing in the vestibule, directly behind Bucky in her sight line, half a football field from where she stood—Preston. She cleared her throat. *"She selects wool and flax and works with eager hands. She is like the merchant*

ships, bringing her food from afar. She gets up while it is still night; she provides food for her family and portions for her female servants. She considers a field and buys it; out of her earnings she plants a vineyard. She sets about her work vigorously; her arms are strong for her tasks. She sees that her trading is profitable, and her lamp does not go out at night. In her hand she holds the distaff and grasps the spindle with her fingers. She opens her arms to the poor and extends her hands to the needy. When it snows, she has no fear for her household; for all of them are clothed in scarlet. She makes coverings for her bed; she is clothed in fine linen and purple. Her husband is respected at the city gate, where he takes his seat among the elders of the land. She makes linen garments and sells them, and supplies the merchants with sashes. She is clothed with strength and dignity; she can laugh at the days to come. She speaks with wisdom, and faithful instruction is on her tongue. She watches over the affairs of her household and does not eat the bread of idleness. Her children arise and call her blessed; her husband also, and he praises her: 'Many women do noble things, but you surpass them all.' Charm is deceptive and beauty is fleeting, but a woman who fears the Lord is to be praised."

She smiled, and returned to her standing place beside the bride. Waverly reached out and squeezed her hand.

With two flames, the couple lit one candle. Sissy wept. Bracken wrapped his arm around his wife's shoulders and looked on with a proud square face. Sunlight fell through the gilded stained-glass dome above, splashing a rainbow of jagged color across the bridal party, particularly upon Waverly's ivory semi-cathedral train, which Vivienne occasionally knelt to adjust, gently tugging out creases.

As maid of honor, she held the bride's bouquet for the ceremony and stood at the head of the line of maids, all tucked up in Waverly's dress of choice: a boat-necked floor-length fuchsia silk gown with a low gathered bustle. Their hair swept up into subtle bouffants, Vivienne and her team were a picture of exactly what the bride intended them to be: herself.

Waverly wept through her vows. Clay wiped a tear from her cheek as he said, *I do*. Vivienne watched with a pierced heart. Bucky hadn't made eye contact. She scanned the pews to see if Preston was really there and found him beside Blad. Was he wearing a tie? The idea of

Preston selecting a tie touched that tender gummy spot inside Vivienne that believed wedded felicity was possible for all but her.

The declaration of man and wife made, Clay scooped Waverly up and kissed her, over and over until she pulled away, giggling. Mendelssohn's march bellowed from the organ's shining stacks as the newlyweds led the procession down the aisle, reaching out and wiggling fingertips with the many joyful faces affirming their love. Vivienne trailed over a cushion of pink rose petals and waved at Blad as she passed. He was clapping; Preston was smirking. Once the couple had crossed the threshold out of the church and into the day, Vivienne returned the abundant bouquet to the bride and, at the curb, lifted the outpourings of her gown into the waiting black limousine, folding in the train before waving them off with a kiss.

THE BALLROOM AT the Bayouside Club rang with happy atonal chatter, drowning out the string quartet playing beside the bar. Drained from the photo session in which she was asked to jump up in the air in unison with the other maids, lie sprawled on the manicured club lawn with her chin cradled in her adjoined fingers, and pose with invisible guns like Charlie's Angels, Vivienne, permitted finally to detach her bustle for the party, took a seat at a cocktail table to scope out the men before the newlyweds made their grand entrance. Blad brought her a drink.

"It's a passion-fruit cocktail," he said, toasting up his own. "Tastes like Hawaii."

"Thanks, I'm thirsty," Vivienne said.

He pressed a finger to his cheek. "Is it just me or do I stand out here?"

Vivienne laughed. "Thanks for coming."

"Are you kidding? This is incredible." He popped his red collar. "It's like Disneyland, except everyone's mean to me."

"Not everyone's mean to you," Vivienne said, swallowing the cocktail a little greedily.

"Please," he said, leaning an elbow on the table. "I'm a kitty at the dog show. Look at that guy . . ."

She turned to Blad's sight line and found a chubby-cheeked guy staring deadpan at Blad. "That's Bucky's old roommate. He's not staring at you. He just looks like that."

Blad cringed. "He looks like a boar."

"Bucky hunts boars."

"Oh, I know that guy," Blad said, pointing out a striking forty-something man in a gray suit.

Vivienne recognized him, and the woman on his arm, from photos in the *Chronicle*'s "Out and About" column.

"How do you know him?"

"The Korean spa," Blad said, still looking at him.

Now they were both staring at the man. "I thought you worked at a Thai spa."

Blad laughed. "You're so innocent. This was at the *Korean* spa. Very different sort of spa. We jerked each other off." He shrugged. "I doubt he'd recognize me. The context is too different."

Vivienne examined this man and the immaculately coiffed woman at his side. The context was in fact so different that she had trouble believing such a thing was possible. "I wonder what he'd do if he did recognize you."

"Nothing," Blad said. "It's a mutual understanding; we both pretend."

Vivienne shook her head. "I wonder if she knows."

Blad laughed again. "Of course she doesn't know. And if she does, she's also pretending."

"I would know if the guy I was dating was gay," Vivienne said.

Blad pursed his lips. "Everyone has their own blinders." He lifted his finger again, subtly, toward a tubby guy with a head of sandy curls waiting in line at the bar. "Remember him? I had sex with him in high school."

Vivienne's jaw dropped. "Greg Garfield?" She leaned into Blad's ear; it was too loud to whisper. "You had sex with him?"

"In the bed of his truck. After a field party."

"You're lying."

"I promised him I'd never tell. And I actually never did until just now, so don't say anything."

The image of Greg Garfield, nose tackle for the football team, who sat next to her in chemistry and always cheated off her work, and who, last she heard, was a manager on Governor Perry's presidential campaign, giving it to—or taking it from—Blad gave the ballroom and all its glisten a deeper, contorted dimension.

She reached out and squeezed Blad's forearm, feeling guilty that she'd fallen asleep worried that bringing him as a date would be alienating—and here he was enlightening her, and she loved just sitting next to him. "I hope you're not uncomfortable. You can leave whenever."

"I'm enjoying myself fine," he shushed. "But thanks for the get-out-of-jail-free card."

In his high lilt she detected a deliberate diminishing of how he really felt, but he was valiant in that way. As he often said, he didn't grow up queer in Texas for nothing.

"What did you talk about with Preston?" Vivienne asked.

"I knew you were going to ask me that," he said. "We talked about how old-man-hot Bracken is."

"Come on," Vivienne pleaded.

"He said the dress looked like a melting cupcake, and I laughed," he said. "Now I'm going to find the bathroom."

Blad gone in the crowd, Vivienne cupped the stem of her empty glass and admired the centerpiece she had helped design: a bundle of white hydrangeas in a low rectangular vase, a dark palm leaf wrapped around the perimeter of the glass. It was as dazzling as she'd envisioned, but for all she'd given to create it, it only conspired to remind her it wasn't her own. Beside the bandstand, a pocket of guests danced to the background music, *Way down yonder on the Chattahoochee.* The room was crowded and growing loud. Vivienne wanted another drink, but a long line had formed at the bar. She settled into her stool, nudging away an encroaching sense of disappointment. This party was supposed to have been fun, liberating, the day she shed her sodden summer skin and met someone new, so that she could put the trauma of Bucky fully in the past. But unfortunately, because she knew both the bride and groom, there were scant new faces, and those new ones she caught had perspiring, receding hairlines. She found herself looking around for Preston.

"Who are you looking for?" It was Karlie, coming around Vivienne's back and taking a seat.

"Blad," Vivienne lied.

"How beautiful was the ceremony? The only thing that kept me from losing it was the fact that this mascara isn't waterproof." She laughed and began mining her swan-shaped rhinestone clutch for something, which turned out to be lip gloss. "I can't believe Wavey is married. You're next, Viv. You better fucking catch the bouquet tonight."

Vivienne trod carefully with Karlie. When Karlie behaved as if nothing were amiss, it usually meant she was wont for gossip. Vivienne's only choice was to respond by feigning indifference to whether she knew anything or not.

"I'm so ready to take off this dress," Karlie said, tugging at the bunchy skirt.

Vivienne nodded. She thought the dress was most flattering on Karlie's smaller frame, but the fuchsia clashed with her hair. She withheld this commentary.

Karlie pressed her hand over Vivienne's. "Did you see Buck is here with Reis?"

Vivienne gently withdrew her hand. "I did see that."

"Well, I wanted you to know that I fixed up the seating arrangements," Karlie said, daubing gloss onto her lips from the little disk of goo. "So you won't be next to Bucky. I figured that would be a disaster."

Vivienne felt her stomach drop. Of course she knew she was next to Bucky; she'd helped with the seating chart, and she'd placed herself beside him—at a table with the rest of the wedding party. And she intended to keep that seat.

"I'm not switching seats," she said.

Karlie wiped her finger on the tablecloth. "Sissy had a few last-minute invites, so I had to tinker with it anyway."

A woman in a tuxedo came by and offered them champagne. "Yummers," Karlie said, taking two flutes and handing one to Vivienne. "I feel like Reis could have waited a little longer with Buck, though. It's only been a few months."

Vivienne's reaction at the moment was no reaction at all; her purpose was only to deprive Karlie of the satisfaction of upsetting her. "They could be good together," she said casually. "But I'm not moving seats. I'm the maid of honor, and I'm sitting at the table with the wedding party."

Karlie looked at her with eyes like a cranial drill. Whatever lingered at the tip of her tongue went unsaid as Reis appeared, in a paisley bias-cut cocktail dress, her waist trim as a stick, her hair rolled up into a sort of croissant. Vivienne thought she looked like a go-go dancer at a fraternity costume party. But all her silent slander could not change the fact that she would never have a fit, upturned butt like Reis, or ballerina arms like Reis, or a thirty-four-inch inseam like Reis.

"Hi, Vivienne," Reis said. Neither made a move. "I liked your Scripture."

"Thanks. I didn't see you."

With her piano fingers, Reis brushed aside her bangs—as blunt and straight as freshly milled paper—and said, "I slipped in late, traffic. I started class this week."

"I am dying about this outfit," Karlie said. "Only you could pull that off."

Karlie was right, only Reis could pull it off. Vivienne wondered how many corners she'd slithered out of simply because her style deviated a shade from the norm, as if eating bell peppers and wearing vintage defined originality.

"Where are your peppers?" Vivienne asked dryly.

Reis smiled. "In Buck's coat pocket."

"So Bucky doesn't mind," Vivienne said, "you going to law school?"

"Why would he mind?"

Karlie was quiet, waiting for the drama to unfold. But Vivienne hesitated. As much as she wanted to rip that infuriating croissant right off Reis's head, she felt some small respect for her. In some ways, Reis struck her as the most compatible match imaginable for Bucky. But, more deeply, she knew that it probably wouldn't work between them in the long run. Bucky couldn't handle a woman with ambition. And maybe, like Vivienne, Reis would get hurt. The difference was, Reis wouldn't be broken by it. She'd have ground to stand on. Reis would never need to throw snuff juice in Bucky's face.

Vivienne softened her tone. "He's threatened by strong women. He'd never admit it."

Reis and Karlie glanced at each other. "This doesn't need to be an issue between us, Viv," Reis said. "Y'all have both moved on, and it's all in the past. We're at Waverly's wedding."

There was an irritating aspect to her voice that was either kindness in keeping the dip-spit secret or patronizing in pretending that she didn't know. Vivienne picked up the tea candle on the table and blew it out. "I only brought it up because I don't think Bucky is the kind of guy who knows how to have a partnership with a woman."

A tense silence followed, during which Vivienne knew they were thinking that, actually, Bucky just didn't want to have a partnership with her.

The room got quiet, startling Vivienne, who'd sunken comfortably into the noise. The lights dimmed, and over the speakers a velvety voice wished the ladies and gentlemen a good evening.

"I hope everyone's having a good time out there. But we can't get the party started without our newlyweds. Ladies and gentlemen, please welcome *Missssterrrr and Mrsss. Claaaaaaay Fitcherson!*"

The band lit up, horns blazing into "Fly Me to the Moon." A spotlight swung over to a double doorway, where Clay and Waverly stood, holding hands. Waverly had let her hair down under a floral tiara and changed into a short, lacy dress with a bustier bodice—a dress Vivienne had turned her on to in an email. Reis and Karlie were gone; the crowd parted to make way for the couple. From her seat, Vivienne had an unobstructed view of the first dance.

The father-daughter dance came next. It gave her the same feeling she had watching Bracken walk Waverly down the aisle. Vivienne wondered who would dance with her. *Me me me*, went her mind; she closed her eyes and let the horns ring against her eardrums till she couldn't hear herself. The band took up a slow tune, a brassier version of an Alan Jackson country ballad. The ballroom was all moody purples and pinks, the crowd, when Vivienne stood on her toes, a swarm of black and bare peach shoulders. It was hot, and she couldn't make anyone out—where was Blad? Suddenly Bucky and Reis were at her elbow.

His hair was slicked into a little visor. He looked like a mean kid posing for his school picture, childish in the very clothes that should make him into a man. He looked right at her, both of them replaying the path of dip spit sailing through the air and onto that now soft, groomed face. Vivienne wanted to say something, anything, so that he would make a face other than the blank, braced expression he wore now and the one she saw in her mind, dripping with brown juice, but he gave her nothing. Reis wrapped her sinuous arms over Bucky's shoulders and they fell back into the crowd.

She ducked off to the courtyard. No Blad. No Preston either. So she sat on a stone bench and swished around the skirt of her dress to air her legs. The evening was mild, the first in months below eighty degrees. The patio was full of people cornered off in groups, smoking and laughing.

"Jus' the gal I've been lookin' for." Randal. He was sitting a few feet away on another bench, smoking a cigar and drinking a bottle of Shiner. "Been a while."

"Hi, Randal," she said.

He came over unsolicited and sat at her side. He was actually wearing a bolo tie with a Texas tux—jeans and boots on the bottom, formal tux on the top, and, to her amazement, a Texas-flag cummerbund.

"A Texas flag?" she said. "Really?"

"Pride does funny things to a man," he said. "Cigar?"

"No thanks," she said. "Cigars make me dizzy."

Randal nodded. She tipped her eyes to the sky, to signal him away. It was a dark muddy gray, the stars erased by city glow. The walled courtyard was cut by pebbled concrete footpaths, like a quilt, in each square a sweet blooming mimosa tree, a ring of monkey grass, and a bed of white periwinkles. There was the tinkling of a grotto fountain with a trio of cherubs, built into the far wall.

"I hear you're workin' for Bracken," Randal said.

The evening had beaten her into submission enough that she was willing to tolerate him sitting beside her, smoking a cigar, but not enough to answer his questions.

"I start next week, but I'd rather not talk about work," she said, and smiled.

"I'm not one for chitchat either," he said.

He'd grown a beard. Facial hair suited him, at least when his chest was concealed. In his usual Western costume, the beard and the chest hair joined up in one contiguous mat.

"*But,*" he added, "I heard I had a hand in that job of yours."

She maintained her smile. "Then thank you."

He groaned. "Don't be so glued on. I happen to think you're a very engaging woman."

So Randal wanted to be real. She rolled her eyes.

"That's more like it," he said. "Roll those eyes, roll 'em."

More smokers spilled out into the courtyard, among them Bracken, in search of a light. "Randal Stanley!" He sailed over, his bow tie undone, an uproarious grin across his face. "Hey, I got a boil on my back; think you can take a look?" He pretended to lift his jacket and laughed, then spread his arms wide. "And Cally!"

Vivienne stood and joined in this awful three-way hug. The two men stunk like donkeys dipped in liquor and aftershave. She pulled away, but Bracken had caught her at the waist. "Cally, can you believe our girl is married? I gotta tell you, I thought it would happen years ago but it doesn't make me any less a sad daddy."

"Clay is a great guy," she said.

"Oh, Clay is top notch, top notch," he said. He tucked her into the crux of his shoulder. "And I'm proud of you. Stanley, you know this girl's gonna be running circles 'round my office? Givin' everyone a run for their money. She's turnin' the place into a museum. The biggest collection of Texas art in the state of Texas."

She felt ten years old standing there, underneath Bracken. Maybe this was how it felt to be embarrassed by your father.

Randal tipped up his beer. "I heard as much."

Vivienne shuffled her feet, looked past Randal to see if she could spot Blad, not that he'd intervene. She angled her head away from Bracken's shoulder, to see better, and there was Preston, twenty or so feet away, cupping a drink and regarding her with that characteristic strange amusement: half disappointment, half delight. She looked away.

"You gave me the idea, Stanley," Bracken said. "I tell you, I got the art bug. And it makes sense—you build houses, you gotta have an appreciation for beauty. But the thing is, it gets muddled up, 'cause one person thinks one thing's beautiful, and another's got a whole 'nother opinion on it. And I see this beautiful girl here, and I want myself some beautiful art, and it's a perfect picture.

"You excited, Cally?" he said, in a lower tone, looking down at her. Vivienne glanced up; Preston was gone.

"Definitely," she said, and even though she was saying it while standing in Bracken's shoulder hold, she meant it. The prospect of money made men matter a little less.

Bracken gave her one last squeeze. "That's right," he said. "Hopefully you won't be workin' for too long, though, right? We gotta throw you a party like this one." He lit his cigar with Randal's lighter and puffed up clouds of cozy smoke. "I'm gonna go dance with my wife."

Vivienne sat down. Randal sat right down next to her. She needed to be a good maid of honor and go inside, be a good date and find Blad, but her back ached; she wanted to be alone for a minute. She looked out at the golf-course trees on the other side of the wall, trimmed to lollipops, and thought about Preston seeing her folded up with Bracken and Randal. Just imagining his judgments tilted her off her axis.

"Did you see what I got 'em on the gift table?" Randal said. "A truck. Framed a picture of it. Bracken told me Clay's ranch truck was run down, so I got him a new F150 to play around with out there."

Vivienne didn't tell him she thought his gift was overkill, because she pitied him for thinking this detail would impress her. There was something naïve in his excessiveness. "Have a good night, Randal," she said.

Inside, three hundred people were in the midst of finding their assigned dinner seats. Waverly and Clay were nuzzling at their table, a white Parisian-style café table, at the very head of the ballroom. Vivienne weaved around, passing through pockets of perfume and conversation, smiling graciously at the faces that lingered on her, to table number two, in the innermost layer of tables, where she had placed herself in the arrangement. Sissy was already in her seat at the family table, her face framed in a high-collared plum bolero gown, an emerald brooch in the shape of a bow over her heart, her hair freshly blond and swept away into two mirror images of the letter S over her ears.

"Sweetie," she said, waving Vivienne over. She held a glass of white wine—always chardonnay for Sissy—high over the table. Vivienne could tell she was drunk. Her glance didn't exactly stick. "Sweetie, you know Mzzz. Nettle moved you to number four. I didn't know till it was too late, but you can't blame her. You really want to sit by Charles the Second all night? I just had to talk to his father for ten minutes and I almost fell asleep flat on my face."

Vivienne knew exactly which table number four was—she knew the entire layout: still in front but farther from the bride. The ballroom was getting more coherent as people sat down; Vivienne skirted around to table four. There, among the expected friends of Sissy, were Blad and, unbelievably, Randal, sitting on either side of an empty seat. Blad saw her and shot up his arm.

"I see you," Vivienne said, squeezing through the white chairs.

"Fancy this," Randal said.

Vivienne turned to Blad, widening her eyes.

"The *der-ma-tol-o-gist,*" Blad mouthed.

Vivienne nodded. "Randal, this is my friend Bladimir."

Blad reached over. "I recognize you from your billboards," he said, vigorously shaking Randal's hand. "I work at a spa, so we both work in skin."

Randal crossed his arms and sat back in his chair, chuckling. "Then you understand the importance of exfoliation. No one gets it but girls and gays—'scuse me. You tell a man to exfoliate and he'll think yer light in the loafers."

Blad looked exultant. "You're an exfoliating cowboy!"

"Best compliment I got in a while," Randal said, and held up his beer. "Exfoliation's not just for the face either."

Vivienne noticed Preston then, caught among a parade of waiters.

He looked around—*For me?* Vivienne wondered. No, he was locating an exit. She followed his progress—deeper into the onion he came, stopping to shake hands with someone. Vivienne was sure she hadn't sat him this close; she clearly remembered placing him near the back (*not* beside a pretty girl, despite her promise). Finally he stopped in front of Timmy, who stood and bear-hugged him. Then he pulled out a chair—Vivienne raised her chin to see over the heads in her view—and sat down between Karlie and Bucky, in just the seat she had reserved for herself.

She seized Blad's hand. "Get up. Follow me."

With Blad behind, she strode back to table two, her eyes burning into Karlie's shimmering shoulders. She felt the eyes of every man track her as she advanced. When she got there, she gave those shoulders a little squeeze. Karlie turned around and, seeing Vivienne there, curled her lip.

Vivienne waved at Preston. "Can you scoot down a little for Blad and me?" she said to him. Preston looked jubilant, his expression countering Karlie's in every aspect. "We can fit in two more." She signaled to the waiter to make two more settings.

"Wait a second, Viv," Karlie said.

But Preston was scooting, nudging Bucky, and soon Reis was scooting too, everyone making room. Vivienne sat beside Preston, and Blad beside Karlie. Vivienne took a sip of wine and smiled, right into the faces of her friends. Blad squeezed her knee under the table.

Dinner was served: bacon-wrapped filet mignon, red potatoes au gratin with smoked Swiss, and brussels sprouts in a venison-butter glaze. Timmy suggested an after-party at his and Karlie's house, in their new game room.

"This guy made it for us," he said, toasting Preston.

"To Preston!" Blad said loudly, like a queen. Vivienne knew he did it on purpose and loved him for it.

Everyone held up their glasses halfheartedly, except Bucky. "This table is for the wedding party," he said to Preston.

"He's my date," Vivienne said.

"I'm just here for the water," Preston said, toasting up his water glass and drinking. Blad and Timmy laughed.

"Then who's this guy?" Bucky said at Blad.

"He's my date too," Vivienne said. "I have two dates."

Blad thrust his hand over the table to introduce himself. "I'm Bladimir Caro."

Bucky looked at Blad's manicured hand, like a dog unsure what to do with a ball, and then took it as he might a woman's, squeezing Blad's fingers.

Reis rested her hand on Bucky's shoulder. "It's fine, babe."

During the toasts, Vivienne took the microphone beside Waverly and Clay and spoke right to them, offering a brief, sincere toast to their happiness. Karlie followed with a ten-minute tearful declaration of love for her besties, the Fitchersons. Bucky came next, looking ruffled under the lights. He told Clay that his taste in women was just as exact as his quail shot.

The cakes were cut. German chocolate in the shape of an igneous rock with grass sprouting around its recesses for Clay, and a teetering four-story lemon cake with iced yellow rose of Texas petals cascading from its peak for Waverly. A reporter from the *Chronicle* tapped Vivienne's shoulder and asked for her comments on the wedding. "A fairy tale," she said. Then she drank the teacup of coffee placed before her and listened as Karlie told the reporter about her blog. She only exchanged pleasantries with Preston but felt him beside her as a grand tree, sheltering her from a cold wind.

After cake, the lights dimmed and the band returned. Vivienne lost track of Preston but danced with Blad to a sing-along of "Friends in Low Places," and then Waverly rolled the lace garter down her firm satiny leg and tossed it back, into the eager clutch of Greg Garfield. To her surprise, Vivienne caught the bouquet. She felt like a pageant queen; the other single girls, even Reis, surrounded her in congratulations, as if she'd accomplished something. She took part in the clamor, accepted their hugs, and pressed the flowers to her nose, drunk with their fragrance and the occasion they afforded her to shine. As the novelty faded, Vivienne was left standing there, wondering what to do with a bouquet the size of a basketball. She noticed Preston watching her from the table, drinking coffee, and ducked away down a hall into the restroom.

How embarrasing that he'd seen her shameless relish of the bouquet. She ran her fingers over the petals, calla lilies and hydrangeas, all sweetly wilted, and felt a tremendous warmth for them, that they represented beauty and love, the things she wished to build her life around.

A soft knock came at the door.

"Just a sec!" She flushed the toilet with her shoe, dabbed the oil off her face with a monogrammed hand towel, and opened the door with an aim to appear refreshed.

It was Preston, his face in a sort of limbo, as if he had a thought but couldn't form the words.

Vivienne overcompensated, immediately hugged him. "Hi," she said, smiling.

He cocked an eyebrow at her. "Hello," he said, his tone three notches lower.

Her face was heating up. The charge between them felt like a million twiddling fingers beneath the surface of her skin. His hair was longer than it had been on Memorial Day, just at his ears, parted to one side and at the top smoothed over but very imperfectly, as if he didn't know how to use hair gel. She was taken aback by how cute he was. He'd taken off his tie, its bright tail peeking out of his pants pocket, and rolled up his shirtsleeves. She wanted him to smile, wished he'd returned her hug with enthusiasm, but his eyes, while warm, shone with that reticence she could never place.

"Did you follow me to the bathroom?" she asked.

"I guess I did. I wanted to talk to you," he said. "I felt strange talking at the table. It was a weird dynamic."

"Are you having fun?" she asked.

He jangled some change in his pocket. "I'm not not having fun," he said. "Think the clock has struck, though. Bracken and Blad just did the 'Boot Scootin' Boogie.'" He crossed his arms, a gesture of evaluation. "Thanks for moving in back there. I was mad at you for a minute, because I thought you'd put me there on purpose."

"Karlie put you there," Vivienne said. "That was my seat. She moved me and put you next to her."

"That Bucky guy . . ." He paused. "He's not your boyfriend anymore?"

"No," Vivienne said.

She watched him mull on this, noticed the little razor spots on his neck. He was looking down at her hands.

"You seemed happy about that bouquet," he said.

"I had a feeling you were going to tease me about that. I saw you looking at me."

"I thought maybe you were happy because there's a guy in the picture, that you'll be engaged soon."

It killed her, his power to see through her girlish notions while at the same time holding her to them. He trapped her into seeing things in a new light, without letting her step out of the old one. And she loved it too. But she couldn't bring herself to give him the satisfaction of knowing this, wouldn't. "Did it seem like I'm with Bucky? He's with Reis now."

"I wasn't sure if I was getting in the middle of something. Last time I saw you—"

"It's over," she said. "I threw dip spit in his face."

Preston looked delighted. "Not your own, I hope."

From the ballroom came a spectacular chorus of applause and whistles: the departure of the bride and groom. She should have been there, but Waverly was too happy to notice.

"There they go," Vivienne said, toward the noise. Then she rolled her head along the wall and faced him.

He reached out and cradled her chin, and kissed her. Gentle, individual kisses, each kiss in amazement of itself. She let her body slacken and kissed him back, harder. He wrapped his arms around her waist. Into her ear he whispered, "I've been wanting to do that for so long."

Vivienne didn't know what to do. Nothing in her experience had prepared her for being kissed by a man with whom she couldn't see her life spelled out, should she choose to spend her life with him. His kiss opened a door in her mind, as most kisses did, except she couldn't see past the door into the next month and year and decade. She couldn't even see the next day—not even, she realized, the next hour.

And yet she felt alive with thirsty force, her hands weak, her bones loose.

The clacking of heels came around the corner and behind it a group of girls, arm in arm.

She signaled him back a little. "*Hiiii, Vivienne,*" they cooed down the corridor as they passed. Their high collective voice carried with it all the prescriptions Vivienne knew for how to live well.

Preston was calm, his eyes two quiet blue pools, but he held her firmly. "Come with me," he said. He took her by the wrist and started away through the turns of long marble hallways. Each looked the same to Vivienne, with skinny side tables pressed against the beige walls, supporting bouquets of bird-of-paradise and fern in ceramic vases, and nothing else, never anything else. She knew these halls well.

She took off her heels, scrutinizing Preston, wondering whether she should trust him. "How do you know your way around?"

He smiled. "I used to sneak in here and play basketball. Come on."

Barefoot now, Vivienne felt lighter, freer. She followed him faster. They turned onto a carpeted hallway, beyond a Pilates room visible through a plate-glass window, and past a vestibule dividing the locker rooms. Vivienne smelled the chlorine and eucalyptus and stopped. "No way," she said. "We can't go to the pool."

"Yes, we can."

She laughed. "You're crazy. I'm the maid of honor." She said this while he kissed at her, between pecks on her cheeks, her neck, her left ear. She pulled back.

"The wedding's over," he said, and kept going, out the double doors to the pool.

Vivienne fully wanted to go with him, but she couldn't admit this, or recognize it, so she told herself she had no choice but to follow him: She had to convince him that swimming wasn't a good idea. She trailed behind, out the double doors and down the pebbled footpath lined with monkey grass, to the wrought-iron pool gate, where he waited. The pool was dark.

"It's locked," he said, then hoisted himself up and over it. Vivienne noticed his shoulders beneath his shirt. Something in her flinched, receded, like an arrow drawing back before release.

Fear rose up and rolled over in her stomach. "I think there are cameras out here. Let's go back. I'm sure someone will look for me."

"Of course there are cameras out here," he said. "There's security all over this place."

"I can't climb over in my dress. It'll tear. It's worth more than my car."

"I'll help you."

She hoisted herself up and he took her under her arms, to ease her over. But on the way down she tried to find the ground as he backed up, and the hem of the dress caught the rails and they both stumbled. Vivienne hit the gravel on her hip. Preston was on his bottom, leaning to one side, trying not to laugh. He stood up first, rubbing his tailbone, and helped her up.

"Is this dress really worth more than your car?" His eyes were sheepish, but he sounded charmed by his own mistake.

Unnerved, Vivienne shook her head, fiddling with the torn hem, frowning. "You're probably secretly happy the dress tore."

He laughed. "I am not. Why would you say that?"

"Because it represents everything about my life that you find annoying."

He went around to the open pool house and grabbed two towels from a polished metal cart.

"Those towels are for wiping sweat off the sun chairs," Vivienne said.

He was unbuttoning his shirt and then his pants, until he stood skinny in his plaid boxers at the pool's edge. She liked his body; it was lean without being too lanky. It had an innocence about it that belied his whole persona in her life. "Are you getting in?" he asked.

It seemed he deliberately put her in these places where he knew she would struggle to make a decision, for which he would ultimately judge her either way. There was a right and a wrong answer; the trouble was, Vivienne's mind was masterful at the gray areas, worn deep with the angles by which her actions might be interpreted. Each option—to swim or not—involved risk and sacrifice. Either was a gamble.

The water looked like black glass, but in the dim halo of the perimeter lights she could make out the colors of the tropical landscaping—blue plumbago hedges, yellow coleus beds, and, beyond, the dark jungled bayou. The evening being particularly humid, the toads were busy holding a celebratory concert. Clouds were passing over fast, cutting over the half-moon. There was the noise of the city, the freeway hum, but a sticky breeze was picking up in the direction of the wedding, rustling away the sound. In this quiet, the party and all its regalia felt like a recollection, a story from another time in her life. That it was actually happening then and there, while Preston waited by the long rectangular pool in his underwear, didn't quite make sense.

"Here," he said, tossing her his undershirt. "You can wear this." She caught it as he cannonballed in, breaking the water in two and sliding beneath. He surfaced with a grin. "Jump in!"

Vivienne felt something like an interior smile, which conveyed her to the shadows, where she climbed out of the apparatus of her dress and strapless bra and stretched the undershirt over her hair. His shirt was big enough to cover her rear end and tummy-flattening underwear. She felt like a kid swallowed up in a grown-up's T-shirt.

Preston looked at her as if she were a goddess emerging from the clouds.

"I'm only doing this if my hair stays dry, and only for a few minutes." She stepped in and pushed off; the water was warm and smelled like chemicals that reminded her of summertime. His shirt ballooned off her body like a life jacket. She swam to the side and draped one arm over the tiled lip of the pool. The way he swam toward her, she knew he was going to kiss her again. She braced herself a little. All her thoughts directed toward him, what he was thinking, what he was feeling; her experience of the moment instantly formed to her perceptions of him.

But then this shifted, and she came into her body. She felt her bones light in the water, the resistance of the water between her fingers, the spread of her treading legs, her muscles animating her legs. She swam to the deep end and he followed, bobbing up with a grin, circling her like a cartoon shark. He chased her back to the edge and swam close, gripping the edge on either side of her shoulders. She felt beautiful. She felt in love with being Vivienne.

His neck smelled like sweet, late-nineties' cologne, which made

Vivienne want to keep kissing him. He'd probably dug through his tiny bathroom for cologne he hadn't worn in a decade. His breath was all warm coffee, which also made her want to keep kissing him, because he drank coffee like a detective in a movie, and she'd never met a man who drank coffee like that. She wanted to kiss him because he didn't smell like beer. She wanted to kiss him because of the dimple in his chin, which reminded her of a childhood book she loved about a teddy bear who lost a button. The dimple looked like a dot where a button should be. She brought her finger to it—it was soft like cookie dough, and she discovered he was sensitive there.

He laughed and splashed her hand away. "When I was a kid I used to think if I squeezed it, it would turn inside out."

The pool was shallow enough for him to stand but was too deep for Vivienne. He reached under the water and held her up by her bottom.

"What is this underwear you're wearing?"

She smiled. "It keeps things in place."

"Everything looks in place to me."

"It's too dark for you to tell," she said.

He lifted the T-shirt from her body and ducked beneath it. From the window of the shirt pulling away from her neck, she watched him nibble on her breasts, floating like buoys. "I can't believe I'm getting to kiss your boobs," he said.

She laughed and tucked one thumb beneath her underwear and rolled it off her hips. He dipped beneath the water and surfaced with it between his teeth. Snatching it, she kissed him through their laughter.

Spreading her arms wide, holding the pool's edge, Vivienne leaned her head back and listened to the lap of the water as he kissed her body—it felt good, but not so good that it seemed bad—and angled herself so he could ease inside her. Preston was gentle yet eager, his eyes disbelieving. She brought her forehead close to his, to calm him, but suddenly he hesitated.

"Should we?" he said.

She hadn't even thought of that word—should. "You don't want to?"

"No, I do want to," he said. "That's why I'm not sure if we should."

He was so close she could feel his heavy breath on her lips, his body grazing hers. They hung there in the dark water. He ran his fingers along her cheeks. "What if we were together?" he said quietly, almost rhetorically. "Do you think that's possible?"

His voice was so endearing and assured, his eyelashes so long, the sensation of his arms around her body so intensely warm, it was as if his question burned her. He'd changed into a man she'd never seen—the same man, in a different, closer light. When she imagined saying yes, an abyss opened beneath her feet and instantly she dropped. "No," she said, startling herself.

His smile froze a moment, then fell. "Why not?"

"Because we just can't."

"That's not a reason."

She wiggled her hips out of his grasp. "You and I can't be together. Think about it. How could we be together?" She tried to laugh, but she couldn't make light of the words.

He moved his arms to either side of her shoulders. "What are you talking about? We'd be together by being together."

"No, I mean practically," she said, her voice quickening. She felt trapped, but she couldn't dunk her head underwater to swim away because of her hair. "You have different priorities. Don't bring me into it."

"Bring you into what?" His voice took on a special intensity.

They countenanced each other. The shadows on his face drifted with the water. She felt stupid and helpless and guilty. It made her uneasy the way he was always trying to find her eyes. So many men do that, she thought, and they all probably think they're the only ones who do.

She was cold now; the tile on her back felt like a sheet of ice. "Into your plans," she said. "We have different plans. It wouldn't work." Knowing he was appraising her words, she resented his being such a good listener. She wanted him to forget every word she'd ever said. But she didn't know which parts she'd meant and which parts she hadn't.

"It's that I don't have money, right?"

"Don't reduce it to that."

"What is it, then?" He sounded impatient, as if he'd expected this would come up but had convinced himself otherwise.

In Vivienne's mind, she and Preston were walking together through a hill-country landscape like the Blanks' ranch, except it wasn't the Blanks' ranch; she was barefoot, wearing a loose dress. This scene was her answer to his question, yet she felt compelled to disagree with him in spite of it, or maybe because of it.

She pushed his arm away and swam to the steps. "I'm not after money."

"But it's not guaranteed with me," he said. "You think it's too uncertain."

She sat on the steps and planted her elbows on her knees. His words pissed her off, but she held it in. "Don't pretend to know me so well," she said, "and then make me out to be some gold digger."

He replied coolly, "If you were a gold digger, you would have played your cards a lot better with Mr. Buckshot."

"Can we not talk about this?"

He stared her down. "Look, I don't care what happened with him. It doesn't matter to me. I'm not looking for a girl who'll throw rodeo parties and eat Adderall every morning so she doesn't get fat on the chicken-fried steak she fries for me."

"Stop it!" She pressed her hands over her eyes. "I know it doesn't matter to you what happened with him." She dropped her hands, feeling beyond the conversation; it seemed so sad that she and Preston were even talking like this. A sense of time wasted, wasting, yet held down catatonically by something outside her range of understanding. She played his words over and imagined herself preparing chicken-fried steak and burning her hands on skittering oil.

Her mind wheeled around against him. "What kind of girl are you looking for? A girl who will agree with everything you say? You'll judge her if she cooks for you, yet you constantly need to be reading her mind?" She got out of the water, crossing her arms over her body and turning her back so he wouldn't see the shirt suctioned to her sagging breasts.

He sighed. "You're misunderstanding me."

"How?" she shot back over her shoulder.

"Vivienne, stop—" She heard him slosh out of the water and turned around, her arms still folded. He was dripping wet and covered in goosebumps, his hair flattened over his forehead.

She laughed suddenly, almost deliriously. "We look like wet cats."

He smiled and wiped his hair back.

"Do I have mascara all over my eyes?" she asked.

He ticked his head. "I'm looking way past that," he said, then gently slipped one hand behind her neck—it was cold, but she could feel his pulse in his fingertips. "I'm saying I want you to be yourself." He grabbed a towel and wrapped it around her shoulders. "I have a crazy idea, but I think it's a great idea."

She waited for him to keep talking, her jaw clenched by nerves and cold.

"I have an opportunity to intern at a firm in Paris," he said. "I just found out the other day. I want you to come with me. It'll only be for a few months. Come with me. Have you ever been to Paris?" He smiled.

"You can't be serious," she said.

"I'm serious. Don't overthink it. Let's just do it."

"What? I'm starting a job."

"What job? You said you wanted to leave the store."

She pulled out of his arms. "Bracken hired me to help him develop his art collection. For his company."

"Develop his art collection?"

"Yes," Vivienne said. "Please don't judge it."

"I'm not judging it, I'm surprised. And I don't know what that means."

"You are judging it. And you shouldn't be surprised, you should be happy for me."

"Well, put it on hold." He rubbed the top of his head. He didn't look happy. "Tell him you can't start for six months."

"I need to dry off," she said, and went off to the dark behind a magnolia tree. She peeled off the sopping shirt and wiped her eyes with it, covering it in mascara. Her body trembled even wrapped in the towel. The tummy-flattening underwear was floating in the pool, so she put on the dress without it. The bra felt sealed to her body, but the dress drooped off her chest even more. The torn hem was probably noticeable, but this fact hardly registered. When she came back around to the pool, he was dressed, drying his feet.

"I can't drop everything and leave," she said. Her voice in her ears sounded like the voice of a woman she didn't recognize.

"Why not?" he said. "Don't tell me it's because you're scared. That doesn't count. Everyone is scared all the time. I already know you're scared."

"It's too sudden," was all she could rally in reply. "It's not what people do."

"It's not what people do," he repeated. He paused to absorb her words and then, in no rush, put on and tied his shoes. Vivienne stood there silently rupturing, galled by his diligence with the shoes of all things after what he'd asked her. She closed her eyes; there was the scent of magnolia mingled with chlorine, the cry of a car alarm, and the distant bellow of an eighties' dance anthem, now inextricable from this moment. When he finished with his shoes, he knelt at the pool's edge and grabbed her underwear. He wrung it out and handed it back to her. "And working for Bracken is what people do?"

"Just throw it away," she said.

He went to the fence line and pitched it into the bayou. He helped her back over the gate; they walked in together, through the labyrinth, which seemed a very different set of halls than the ones they'd walked an hour before. She wanted to look at him but he kept looking straight ahead, maybe waiting for her to say something, she didn't know. At the foyer leading to the ballroom, he stopped.

"I'm parked out here," he said. Still so calm.

"Preston—" she said.

He held up his hands. "I'm not going to argue with you, Vivienne Cally. You know the answer. You have your plan." He stood beneath the brushed-copper chandelier—an ornate latticed star, afire at its tips—and said to her, "I believe in you."

IV

VIVIENNE WENT STRAIGHT TO THE BATHROOM TO CHECK herself in the light. Within a few minutes she restored herself to the sweetly disheveled maid of honor who'd danced her bouffant away. By now everyone was drunk enough not to notice that her dress was torn, or they chalked it up to her own drunkenness. To this crowd, there was nothing more hilarious than debauched indifference to extravagance.

When she returned to the ballroom, the crowd had dispersed. She took a seat to settle into the scene as if she'd been there all along. She waved to guests, stood to kiss their cheeks goodbye, made half-hearted assurances of lunch to former sorority sisters, while behind her twinkling eyes there budded the certainty that she had to see Preston tomorrow. Her response to him already felt reactionary, and she didn't like having answered without taking time to think.

A woman approached her, a housekeeper in a black uniform dress. "Miss?" she said, and handed Vivienne a folded sheet of yellow legal paper.

Vivienne took it. "What's this?"

The woman shook her head. She was a little out of breath. "By the pool."

Vivienne opened the paper and beheld the words *Dear Preston*. Instantly, she recognized Karlie's bubbly writing and skipped to the signature: *xo, k*

The blood fell from her face. She folded up the paper. "Right, thank you."

But the woman wouldn't go away. "It was on the ground," she said. "I saw you leaving."

"Thank you," Vivienne said again. "I really appreciate it."

"Someone else could have—"

She wanted a tip. Cash, the Bayouside Club's heartbeat, upon which everything depended but which no one ever saw or spoke of by name.

Vivienne didn't have her purse. She had no idea where her purse was. For a moment she felt indignant—she didn't care whether this woman told anyone or where a note from Karlie ended up—but then, Preston.

"What's your name?" Vivienne said. "I'll leave something at the front desk."

"June." June didn't look convinced. She'd probably heard this before. The club's hard devotion to money left little belief in generosity, especially toward staff.

"Thank you," she said. "I will leave something."

She was too nervous to read it. She went looking for Blad and her purse but found Sissy and Bracken instead, en route to their town car. Sissy hung on her husband's arm like an easy prom date. "Viv, Viv, Viv!" she called, raising her jeweled hand. "Where have you been? We were looking for you!"

Vivienne beamed, using her own intense sobriety to undermine Sissy. "Well, here I am!"

Sissy lurched to embrace her, and Bracken caught her by the waist. "Thatta girl!"

"I just want to tell you, Viv, that I am so grateful my little girl has you for her best friend," Sissy said. "I know you come from brokenness, but so do I. And I don't know if I've even ever properly told you that. My dad was drunk all the time. And we were poor!" She burst out laughing, a cackle that Sissy, with her wide-open smile, pulled off. It was the sort of quality that, while abrasive now, would make her adorable in old age. "You think it's bad dealin' with that stuff—imagine dealin' with it on an empty piggy bank." She pointed her thumb at her face. "I should know. And Wavey—bless her heart—she dudn't know anything about that business. And I think it's good for her to have a friend outside of prayer to talk to, someone who's experienced pain." She checked in with Bracken, towering behind her, his hands planted on her shoulders and his eyes on Vivienne. "Brack and I worry about you. I know you don't wanna get into it, but life idn't easy. I make it look easy"—she laughed, as Bracken interjected, "Yes, you do sweetie"—then continued, "And it's a hell of a lot harder if you go at it alone. Forget women's lib and man's lib and dog's lib, whoever's lib, all that nonsense; it's tough goin' at it alone. You need a partner. I am so relieved that my baby has a good partner, and I want that for you, Viv, 'cause you don't have your mommy to want that for you." She sighed; her eyes drifted off to the left and reeled back to Vivienne.

Sissy was hardest to dismiss when drunk, because she was most sincere when drunk, and her drunken words rang true in Vivienne's heart at the moment she needed least to be reminded of the perils of solitude.

"What if I told you I enjoy being alone?" Vivienne asked, with a coy tilt of her head.

"I'd believe you!" Bracken hooted.

Sissy pursed her lips and straightened her high silk collar. She looked Elizabethan via Houston. "I'd tell you I enjoy being alone too, m'dear, but it's not my job to enjoy it, and that is *why* I enjoy it. Viv, where is your date?"

"The little fella, right?" Bracken said, smirking. "I thought I saw him leave with one of the busboys."

Sissy swatted at him. "I thought he was cute, but I don't think you'll get far with him, honey."

"If he did leave with a busboy, then good for him for not being alone, right?"

"Don't get snippy, Viv. You're the snippiest snip in this town." Sissy tripped back. Catching herself against Bracken, she brought the back of her hand to her forehead and feigned fainting. "Time for me to go." She started away, then, remembering Vivienne, swayed back. "I also want to tell you not to worry about that Karlie. She's a chili pepper and you're a peach. Love you, love you, love you." In Sissy's embrace, Vivienne caught a soft bouquet of aromas, the subtleties of which she knew by rote—face powder, golden sweet wine, French perfume.

Sissy let her arms down and whispered to Vivienne with dropped eyes, "You smell like chlorine, honey. I mean, you *really* smell like chlorine."

The heat rose to Vivienne's cheeks, but she knew how to play it off by appealing to Sissy's saucy East Texas slant. Sissy wouldn't suspect it was true if Vivienne suggested it actually was true. What was important was the womanly chumminess—if Vivienne back-patted Sissy a little, it didn't matter what was true. That they were conspirators erased any offense on Vivienne's part. She had long ago learned that the women of her world were bothered less by actual offenses than they were by not being privy to them. She drew near to Sissy's ear, out of Bracken's range. "Maybe I took a swim," she whispered, lubricating her voice and pulling the smile that felt irresistible, even to her, across her own face.

Sissy held a slightly baffled grin and then burst out in a cackling laugh. Within a moment, she'd forgotten about the smell of chlorine. "My baby got married tonight!" she cried, and threw up one arm, wiggling her fingers toward a group of incoming women, who promptly wrapped her up in a squealing circle. The ease of their laughter, the clarity of their joy, made Vivienne see that they'd all attended one another's weddings and would attend the weddings of one another's grandchildren. A desolate feeling passed over her, a sort of scrim. She felt much older than these women, already more tired.

She needed to find her purse. Last she remembered, it was on a chair—during cocktail hour? The overhead cleanup lights were blazing over the ballroom. A teenager in a baggy waiter's vest told her to check the lost-and-found pile. Suit coats, pashmina scarves, a snakeskin clutch, heels, and a gold cuff bracelet—piled atop a corner table. She rummaged futilely. The teenage waiter said that was everything he'd found; he didn't know where else it could be. As he answered, Vivienne realized she'd been awake for eighteen hours.

Finally, in the bridal dressing room, strewn with blow-dryers and low-fat granola-bar wrappers and uncapped lipstick, she found her purse. She sat on the floor amid the wreckage, with her bag on her lap, and stared at the folded note. She very nearly opened it, but a sense of violation prevailed over her curiosity. Preston wouldn't want her to read this. The paper was fresh. She looked around the room. There, on a vanity, beside Karlie's things, was a yellow legal pad.

She hid the note away, in a side pocket of her wallet. Her curiosity screamed. But she wouldn't listen. If she read it, she would become the girl that Preston suspected she too easily became. She wanted to be the better girl, the one he believed in. She wanted to believe in that girl too. The temptation burned—*xo k xo k xo k xo k*—but she fought it back.

With a drunken groan, Karlie appeared in the doorway. "Where were you earlier?" she said. She'd taken her hair down. It hung straight, little bobby-pin tangles here and there.

"I was here," Vivienne replied.

"I didn't see you for, like, hours."

"I didn't see you either."

"I didn't see you *or* Preston."

Vivienne pulled her bag close, crossed her arms. "Why were you looking for Preston?"

Karlie slagged over to the vanity and began piling things into her bag. "I wasn't. I just noticed I didn't see either of you at the send-off. Which I thought was odd."

"I missed it," Vivienne said. "I was in the bathroom."

"Yeah, I found your bouquet in there." She exhaled dramatically. "Don't take this the wrong way, but if you *were* hanging out with Preston, you should probably do yourself a favor and *stop* hanging out with him."

Now the letter felt like a bomb in her purse. "Why?"

"*Because*—while he was working on the game room, he would totally come on to me. I don't think you want to get involved with a guy like that." Karlie was wrapping the cord around a straightening iron. She kept wrapping and wrapping. "I saw how he was looking at you," she said, without losing her focus on the cord. "Didn't you notice?"

"Yes," Vivienne said. "So?"

"Nothing." Karlie dropped the iron into a big monogrammed leather bag and heaved the bag over her shoulder. "Did I tell you that tomorrow afternoon I'm going on the news to talk about fall-event inspiration? The station likes my blog." She gave Vivienne a one-armed hug. "Gotta go. Tim's waiting."

Vivienne went to the front desk and left ten dollars in an envelope for June. It was all the cash she had. Back in the bridal room, alone, she sat before the glowing vanity. Things had the feeling of swirling over her too quickly. In the quiet, she tried to find something small and still within. She slid forward, bowing her head into the crux of her arm; her hair draped forward and enclosed her. She looked out with one eye, imagining herself peering through the fold of a circus tent. On the other side was the circus. A noisy, lurid circus, full of shouting masters and sad animals. She shut her eye; everything softened. She prayed: *What do I do?*

Her phone buzzed.

It was a message from Preston. *Can I see you tomorrow?*

V

PRESTON STOOD AT THE CURB, WONDERING WHAT THE hell had just happened. He went searching for Blad.

Back inside, he passed the ballroom and caught sight of Vivienne talking to Bracken and Sissy. She was all put together again, as if nothing had happened, which bothered him. He hastened to the courtyard and found Blad chatting with a pair of older men. To Preston, they looked like the contented fathers of girls who'd rejected him over the years. Heavy-lidded, half-smiling, waiting for you to cut to the chase. Preston could hear Blad explaining the merits of high-density building in a city like Houston, where sprawl was out of control, and dangerous, and no longer economically sound, and they appeared on the verge of interrupting. Preston called his name.

They got two beers from the bar and walked to Preston's car, parked along Memorial Drive to avoid the twenty-dollar valet charge. The bored, oversize men in the security box watched as they passed. Blad waved. The wooded recesses of the Bayouside Club seemed miles away in the empty concrete street flooded with buzzing streetlights.

"So this must be the VIP parking," Blad said.

Preston twisted open his beer and flicked the cap into the street.

"Don't mess with Texas," Blad said.

"I just asked Vivienne to go to Paris with me," Preston said.

"Really?"

"She said no."

Blad sat on the trunk of Preston's old Civic. "I didn't know you felt that way about her."

Preston felt relieved of an emotional burden he hadn't realized he'd been carrying, but dread crept in to fill the space. Blad's phrasing made him fumble his good feeling. "Should I not have asked?"

"I have no idea," Blad said. "Are you really going?"

"I found out yesterday." He drank his beer with the slow force of lament. "Maybe I shouldn't even go—I don't know. I didn't realize that I wanted her to go until I asked. Obviously I hadn't spent a lot of time thinking about it."

He stared at the cursive metalwork sign—THE BAYOUSIDE CLUB—staring back at him from across the street. "I think I freaked her out. I think I blew it."

Suddenly Blad pulled the beer from his coat pocket and catapulted it into a swan dive. It spun and dropped onto the club drive, shattering.

They were both quiet for a moment. Then Preston said, "Why did you do that?"

Blad shrugged. "Oops."

Preston knew Blad wished he could leave Houston too. Maybe it was insensitive of him to go on about moving to Paris. "I'm sorry—I didn't mean to be flippant about leaving."

"No, I'm happy for you. It's amazing." Blad nodded hastily, exhaled a little burp, then pressed one hand to his chest.

"Are you okay?" Preston asked.

"Of course. I'm fine."

Preston turned his back on the street and went over to Blad. He leaned his elbows on the trunk. "Did you know she's working for Bracken Blank? That's why she said she can't go."

"She told me," Blad said.

"Is that a good idea?" The memory of Vivienne encompassed by Bracken and the big bolo-tie guy made him push off the trunk and brood. "Is that what she wants? Do you think that's the life she wants?"

Blad hopped off the trunk. "It sounds to me like you're talking yourself out of it."

"I'm like a dog chasing a squirrel, and when I catch the squirrel—"

"You don't know what to do with it. And Vivienne is the squirrel."

Preston felt sweat beading at his temples. He was tiring his friend's patience, but he needed momentum. "I'm going to ask her again."

Blad was looking toward the 610 Loop in the near distance, a long gray beast asleep at the horizon. Beyond it, the tree line of Memorial Park looked torn from the brown sky. "She isn't like her friends," he said.

The plainness of Blad's voice struck Preston, and he felt ashamed. He had doubted himself and ensnared Blad in his insecurity. Was he worthy of the leap of faith required of him? Was he capable? It seemed to him then that he wasn't. He fell too easily to his own enemy forces.

Blad took off his coat and hung it over one arm. "Can I get a ride? I have work in the morning."

Preston nodded. He fumbled in his pockets for his keys and felt something missing. The note from Karlie. The dreaded, awful note from Karlie. The note detailing his worst mistake. Not there. "I think I dropped something," he said.

Blad needed to grab his bag inside, so Preston parked illegally along the drive and ran to the pool area. He jumped the fence again and circled around. It was nowhere. He stood in the dark, rubbing his forehead. Someone had already cleaned up; the towels were gone. It was probably thrown away. He hated Karlie for writing it and hated himself for not responding to her emails, which caused her to write it in the first place.

The pool was calm and black and empty. He already missed Vivienne. He took out his phone and typed her a message: *Can I see you tomorrow?*

Back in the car, waiting for Blad, he noticed Bucky and Bracken and the big bolo-tie guy standing in a circle. He half-listened to their small talk, something about the pheasant hunting down in King Ranch, and was checking his phone when he heard the bolo-tie guy say, "That Cally girl, she's a hard nut to crack."

To which Bucky laughed, replying, "Nah, she's easy to get inside, she's just a nut."

Bracken nodded with gravity. "Watch out for her. Little Lolita, if you catch my drift. And she knows it."

At this, Bucky looked amused. "She can't keep playing that card forever," he said. "I feel bad for her. If she was smart, she'd take it while she has it. Where's she gonna end up?"

Bolo-tie's eyes lit up, but he spoke gravely. "Could be she needs a guy like me."

VI

Blad was washing his face when Vivienne came knocking near two A.M. She was still wearing her dress, but the skirt was rumpled, the bodice slumping over her boobs. He was annoyed—she was interrupting his bedtime ritual, and he had work in the morning. She looked like she'd been crying. Blad knew her crying face—it was duckish and, after the tears, swollen like a ripe tomato. She went straight to his little bedroom and face-planted on the bed, her dress making an elaborate rustle as she collapsed.

"I would have blown up the air mattress for you," he said, standing over her. "What happened?" Her eyes were open, her mouth smushed into his royal-blue sham. She rolled onto her back.

"Can you help me out of this dress?"

She sat up and flopped her head forward. He unzipped her, then she flopped flat again and began sliding out of it, kicking it into a heap on the carpet.

"I just want you to know that I am abashed by the sight of a three-thousand-dollar dress crumpled on my cheap apartment carpeting," Blad said. "And I'm not interested in seeing you pantyless or knowing why you're pantyless." He picked up the dress.

To hang it up, he had to shove the entire length of his own clothing down a foot, and still it bulged out, like a pink dog tongue. "Your dress looks like a John Hughes movie in my closet," he said, trying to cheer her up. He found her a pair of polka-dot boxer shorts—the castaway garment of a guy he went on three dates with—and his favorite extra-soft blue T-shirt.

"You know I only share this T-shirt with special people," he said, handing it to her.

She folded his blankets over her legs and made a sort of closed-mouth smile-frown and sat up. Then she reached behind her back with one arm and did something, because suddenly her lacy peach bra fell and with it her breasts. They swung a little, seemed to exhale; in color and size her nipples were like small buttermilk pancakes. Blad went to the kitchen to get her water.

"As entertaining as I find boobs as a concept, I really don't need to see them in my bedroom," he called out.

She called back, "Sorry, Blad!"

He washed out a glass, turning the water on hot—he liked to warm his hands under hot water. "It's two o'clock," he said. "I have to be walking up some guy's hairy spine in six hours." He filled the glass and grabbed a vitamin for Vivienne, returning to the bedroom to find her a new girl, in the polka-dot boxers and T-shirt, hugging her knees.

"Drink some water," he said. "And take this."

She finished the glass in a few long sips and smiled. "I'm so glad to be out of that dress."

Blad sat at the foot of the bed. She wiped mascara from beneath her eyes and then wiped her fingers on his clean sheets. "I just washed those," he said.

"Where did you go tonight?" she said. "You left without me."

"Preston gave me a ride home," he said. "Were we supposed to leave together? I thought you were busy with wedding-party stuff."

Suddenly she was fighting tears.

"What happened?"

"Nothing," she said.

"Then why are you crying?"

She pressed her palms over her eyes. "Do you think Preston would ever sleep with Karlie Nettle?"

Blad shrugged. "Preston is one of the horniest guys I know."

"So you do think he would sleep with Karlie Nettle?"

"I doubt it. She's married to that bear. Why are you asking me this?"

"But you think he might?"

"I don't know why you should be surprised if he did," he said, a little petulantly. "He's a man with a penis."

"But *Karlie*?"

"Maybe she seduced him with her blog," he said. "If he did, I don't know why you should be upset about it. You've hooked up with people; so have I. Not married people, but still. Don't act scandalized."

Vivienne grazed her fingertips over her toenails. "I wish you wouldn't be such a devil's advocate."

"I'm not going to sit here and talk about hypotheticals with you," he said. "I'm tired. It's the middle of the night. Is something actually wrong?"

"We almost had sex tonight, in the pool." She broke down. "But then he didn't want to. And then—" She grabbed his pillow and dropped her head into it. "He asked me to go to Paris with him. I didn't know what to say, because I was overwhelmed. I'm starting that job. I'd have to give it up. I didn't know what to do."

"He told me," Blad said. "Not the sex part, the Paris part."

"He did? What did he say?"

"He told me he asked you. Don't tell him I told you."

"What do you think I should do?"

"This is not a bad problem to have," he said. There was so much that Vivienne didn't see. She had this pure way about her that made beautiful places more beautiful and brought ugly places into uglier relief. She didn't realize that she looked like she didn't belong in this apartment, with its low cottage-cheese ceilings, in a bedroom with plastic vertical blinds concealing an alley where bums relieved themselves behind sticky shit-brown trash bins. Or in a bathroom with a shower door caked in utterly irremovable soap scum from old unknown tenants, or in a kitchen with warped beige linoleum flooring and fake-wood cabinetry. She didn't know that she made all his attempts to spruce the place up—the blond matching Ikea bed frame and side tables, his splurge on a black sabre-leg coffee table from West Elm, the votive candles in their ninety-nine-cent glass holders placed here and there on bamboo corner stands—seem pathetic. "You're like the heroine in the latest French novel Preston read, and now he's going to save you in Paris." He paused. "Your *problems* are the things I daydream about."

Upstairs, his neighbor's toilet flushed. They were both quiet as the water rushed and rumbled down the pipes. Blad sighed. "I really resent how every time I hear that it makes me visualize a shit sliding behind my bed."

"I'm sorry," Vivienne said. "I didn't mean to ignore your feelings."

Blad crawled over her legs and slid under the covers on the side of the bed he never slept on. "Forget it," he said.

"Whenever I talk to Preston he hassles me," she said. "I always leave him feeling like I'm doing something wrong. He didn't want to have sex with me."

"Why do you want to have sex with a guy who makes you feel like you're doing something wrong?"

She hugged herself. "I don't know."

Blad sat up on his elbow. "I think you're confused because you can't wrap up your entire existence in him. You didn't love Bucky; you just loved that you could wrap up your entire existence in him."

Vivienne went over to the mirrored closet door and despaired at her reflection. "What if you're right?"

"I am right," Blad said, plopping back down. "If you like Preston, you can't hide from yourself."

She whipped around. "Why have you never told me this before?"

"Because it didn't come up. Lots of people are fine living their lives that way."

She turned back and stared at herself with a wrought, self-condemning expression. "At least your life is yours, Blad. I know you think it's dingy here, but it's yours."

She rubbed her hands over her face and returned to the bed, nuzzling under the blankets, facing him. "The only thing I really know how to dream about is men."

"Welcome to the club."

She smiled, wiping her eyes. "He doesn't take me seriously."

Blad shook his head. "He's just critical. That's how he is. I doubt he'd invite you to Paris if he didn't take you seriously. Actually, he probably takes you *too* seriously."

"I'm scared he wants me in Paris because he's trying to prove something to himself. It's a victory for him."

"Are you worried Preston feels about you how you felt about Bucky?"

She buried her face in the pillow again.

"Preston doesn't play games," Blad said.

"I told him no," she said, "when he asked me if I thought we could be together. Would he believe me if I told him we could try?" She looked up and folded her brows into a tender, unpretty expression of insecurity. She blinked at him, at the ceiling, then down into his sheets, her face contracting with a fierce resistance.

Blad pulled the comforter up to his chin. "Sometimes I look at you and I see all this potential that no one else I know has. But you don't believe it because you always feel like you're doing something wrong for being yourself. The world is a bully. I know all about it too."

Vivienne whispered, "What should I do?"

"Stop asking me that," he said, his eyes growing heavy. "I can't answer that for you. You shouldn't want me to."

VII

VIVIENNE ARRIVED HOME WEARING BLAD'S T-SHIRT AND flannel pajama pants, her dress bundled into his suit bag. Katherine had gone to church. The house was quiet and spotless, the white shutters closed, darkening the den and the kitchen to an hourless gray. The grandfather clock chimed ten times. The long, empty countertop glowed like ice. She grabbed the Sunday *Chronicle* and went upstairs to her room, where the shutters would be open, the morning light streaming in.

She took a quick shower and went right to bed. Her sheets smelled like rosewater. It was a green day; the breeze picked up the leaves on her tree. She thumbed through the paper till she found what she was looking for: the celebrations, and a color quarter-page portrait of Waverly, doe-eyed, hair in a tight bun beneath her raised veil, in profile at an angle to highlight her bustle and train, holding her bouquet before her like a prize.

Waverly had agonized over this photo shoot, gone through three different photographers and locations. Vivienne hadn't quite seen the difference in any of the resulting photos. In this one, she was standing in a gazebo, but you could hardly tell. It just looked as if the photo was taken outside, azaleas blurred into magenta dots in the background. Waverly was pretty, though, and that was the point. The only bride in color, and the only bride who looked like she'd be pretty even without the gown and the makeup.

Waverly Blank Weds Clay Fitcherson, Jr.

Miss Waverly Madelyn Blank and Mr. Clay Tanner Fitcherson were united in marriage on September 4 at four o'clock in the afternoon at Prayerwood Baptist Church. The double-ring ceremony was officiated by the Reverend Stratton Johns of Houston. Following the ceremony, the parents of the bride hosted a reception at the Bayouside Country Club, with entertainment provided by the Dazzle Orchestra. On the eve of the wedding, the parents of the groom hosted a rehearsal dinner at the Petroleum Club of Houston. On Friday, a bridal luncheon was hosted at Houston Country Club by the groom's mother, Mrs. David Fitcherson. The bride is the daughter of Mr. and Mrs. Bracken Blank of Houston. The groom is the son of Mr. and Mrs. David Fitcherson, Sr., of Houston. Escorted by her father and given in marriage by her parents, the bride wore a couture gown of ivory silk accented by a crystal-embroidered sash and a semi-cathedral-length veil of ivory silk illusion. The fitted gown, with a sweetheart neckline and multiple draped pleats, flared into a trumpet skirt. The bride carried a bouquet of calla lilies and white hydrangeas, tied with the handkerchief carried by her maternal grandmother on her wedding day in 1948. Serving as her maid of honor was Miss Vivienne May Cally of Houston. Following their honeymoon in Cabo San Lucas, Mr. and Mrs. Fitcherson will reside in Houston.

Maid of honor. Miss Vivienne May Cally of Houston. It all had such a decisive ring to it. The announcement summed up everything anyone else needed to know, but the satisfaction was short-lived, like a rich dessert that sickens the stomach. She sat imagining what Waverly was doing, wishing she could call her and discuss. The newlyweds were already in Mexico. Bracken had chartered them an early plane. She imagined the palm trees, an infinity pool disappearing into an electric-blue ocean. Waverly was married. It was done and, knowing Waverly, for good. Her best friend had begun her life. Vivienne felt left out, eddied by a cruel tide.

The memory of Preston's voice struck her hard. *"I want you to come with me. . . . Have you ever been to Paris?"* She'd never been to Paris. What would everyone think if she flew off to Paris with Preston? What would it be like, walking the streets of Paris with Preston? He was a different man to her now. The vulnerability in his voice, the assurance of it, the strength of his kiss. The more she thought about it, the more impossible the whole thing seemed. And the more impossible it seemed, the more appealing it became. It was so typical of Preston to encourage her ambition, only to undercut it with his own romantic whim. He'd ridiculed her for being the very kind of helplessly romantic woman he now expected her to be with this invitation.

She picked up her phone and stared at Preston's message: *Can I see you tomorrow?* It wasn't a friendly message—no friend would phrase a text with that urgency. Its assumption of intimacy had to be a direct reference to his invitation. Or her rejection. She planned to return Karlie's note to him today. She didn't want it, and as much as she was dying to know what it said, she also didn't want to know at all. If she read it, she'd have to return the note to Preston and confess that she had read it, or return the note to Preston and lie that she hadn't read it, or not return it at all, which was also a sort of lie. That it was written by Karlie meant that it could say anything and that anything it said could be untrue.

She wrote him back: *What time?* And he responded within seconds: *6:30?* She replied, *Where should we meet?*

To which, a moment later, he asked, *Can I come there?* Katherine would be at her bridge group. *Sure,* she replied, and gave him the address. *Okay,* he returned, no smiley face, or *xo,* or even an exclamation point. *Okay*—period.

As the day went on, Vivienne's initial unease dwindled. An outfit would have to be selected, a mood adopted. She would be charming but reserved and then wing it from there, depending on what he had to say. Her mind took on romantic scenarios she wasn't even sure she wanted, but the thought of them pleased her anyway because of the chance they gave her to live out various fantasies. Preston would come over with a bouquet of flowers and reiterate his feelings. Her smile would undo him. But then what would she do? That was the problem with Preston—

knowing how to react. What if he'd changed his mind about Paris? And why did this idea devastate her?

The afternoon was long. She heard Katherine come home and leave again. She ate avocado on toast for lunch, standing at the island, mindlessly petting the pages of *Garden & Gun*. She gave in and read Karlie's blog. It had been a few weeks since she'd checked it, but there were sure to be wedding photos. The entry today was the "Sunday Special," highlighting a special event in Karlie's life. Wedding pictures were there, as Vivienne predicted, and she was conspicuously absent from all of them. There was Preston, though, at the dinner table, looking handsome and serious, his elbow balanced among a gallery of champagne glasses, and Bucky beside him, a beer to his lips. They looked in opposite directions. Blad was there in profile, mid-turn to Preston, grinning.

> *Last night I was so blessed to serve as a bridesmaid in one of my besties' wedding! It was absolutely dripping in love and so many amazing thoughtful details, from her bouquet to the embossed menu cards to the hand-embroidered napkins to the dark-chocolate fountain. I always obsess over weddings, but there's nothing like the bliss of a girlfriend's wedding, a girl you truly know and love. I was swooning, y'all! As a bridesmaid, I had the opportunity to help the bride select her palette for the bridal party. We went with fuchsia because it's the bride's favorite color, and it has a pop to it that works for any season! For shoes we decided matching heels were best because we didn't want our feet distracting from the full silhouette of the gowns. So we had the heels custom-dyed to match the dresses and it was perfect! Check out the snaps below for more of the look—it was storybook!*

Vivienne clicked on the "mood board," a collection of pictures she and Karlie had found online for inspiration, which Karlie had assembled into a single image to unite the "look" of the bridal party. Scrolling down, Vivienne noticed banner ads for an online boutique flanking the text and, to her surprise, saw that the post had thirty-eight comments, mostly women exclaiming, *Gorg!* Other posts down the page had a few dozen comments too. So people read Karlie's blog. Vivienne wasn't sure what to make of this. There was an out-of-order aspect to it. Karlie already had everything she wanted.

It was four-thirty. The blog had slumped her mood, so she took to puttering in her closet, trying on outfits. What would Preston like? A pair of three-inch red peep-toe heels. He would hate those. Black ballet flats. Unlikely they'd make any impression on him. All the lovely shoes in view—piled on the carpet, hanging in gauzy shoe bags from decorative hooks among dried roses, stacked in built-in cedar shoe cubbies—were unsuited to Preston. A pair of strappy red and orange espadrilles. Too popcorn. Kidskin riding boots. Too formal, too deliberate. She stood in the little universe of her closet as if everything there belonged to a stranger.

Reaching on her toes, the tips of her fingers grasping, she pulled out a canvas bin of old shoes from an upper shelf. Mostly it was full of heels she'd outgrown but still loved or beloved damaged heels she intended to have repaired. At the bottom she spotted a pair of worn-out white sneakers that she'd kept in hiding for years. She'd bought them in college to wear to morning classes, as a cute sneaker to accompany the planned pajama look most of her sorority sisters adopted for eight-A.M. lectures. But now they seemed right to actually wear. They still fit, and her big toe peeped out from a hole on the top. They felt like warm hands around her feet. She grabbed her cutoff jean shorts and a soft white T-shirt she liked to wear to sleep. Standing before the mirror, she felt giddy, and laughed at herself for feeling giddy, then had a moment of extreme self-consciousness—she could *not* wear this—but came back around to the fact that she felt comfortable. And that was the thing about Preston: He was always at ease.

Without knowing quite how or why, she suddenly reminded herself of herself. An idea came: She wouldn't straighten her hair.

The time was approaching. She dallied around downstairs, opening the French doors to the sunken living room, spreading the curtains for light, so the place didn't look so untouched. She sat on the couch, feeling like a visitor in a museum of sixties-era furniture and color schemes. Placards detailing the name and date of each piece seemed appropriate. The room was rarely entered. It was the kind of space where one felt compelled to sit on the edge of things with a straight spine. The couch was salmon colored and stitched with white Oriental koi fish, a relic from Katherine's travels. The springs were coiled tight. Sunlight hit the lush pistachio carpet and gave the room a greenness.

What would Preston say about it when he arrived? He'd probably make a joke that would defuse all its dark insinuation. Here was the chamber in which the shadowy pathology of her family slept, which held the frozen objects acquired by fortune, and she wanted to open it to him, so he would see it and want her anyway. She needed to see him in this room. Preston judged from the outside and thought it was all so black and white, rich girls and their rich husbands, but it was tradition. It was people marrying the people they lived among, as people do, creating a thread over time.

She sat as her mom must have, on the same couch, clumsy with the thread yet centered by an interior glimmer, a pinhole of light. The thing Karlie called weird. The thing Bucky called easy. The light Katherine darkened. The thing Preston wanted. He wanted in her what she most disdained in herself. Hitting this conclusion was brief; it bounced off the walls of her brain and landed in Paris, on the bank of a wide old river, with Preston.

She waited.

The time came and the house was quiet. The couch springs creaked. The longer she waited, the more she regretted how she'd acted the night before. He was right—she was scared. Of course she was scared. Much as she resented all this stuff, it was safe. It was what she knew. That Preston stood for the unknown was both terrifying and sublime—it was his willingness to take a chance, a deep yet simple sense of how much she liked talking to him.

Waiting here felt wrong. She moved to the big leather chair in the den and obsessively checked her phone, forgetting when she checked it that she'd just checked it two minutes earlier. Twenty minutes later, its silence was like a scream. She typed a message to him—*Are you lost?*—and instantly regretted it. He'd know she was waiting and wondering. Ten minutes later she was at the window, peering down the street. She walked the footpath to the curb and opened the mailbox, even though she knew it would be empty. Funny the idea that going outside would somehow make him appear.

Her phone pulled her back. The brief distance from it made her feel saner, but there were still no messages. It was too soon to be angry, so she grew worried and surer of what she would say—if only he would get there. That's all he needed to do. Her house wasn't difficult to find. If he was lost, he would have called. She imagined his mangled car on I-59; it would be her fault if he died. If she'd only given them a moment last night, he wouldn't have needed to text her and come here. Maybe he would already have been here. Outside, a thunderstorm gathered, but no rain fell, just wind spinning through oaks. The clouds were dark with sunset and storm. *Seven-thirty.* Katherine would be home in half an hour.

She ran upstairs and checked the traffic reports online. This felt like an insane thing to do, but she had to do something. The maps were confusing, red and purple lines over green lines crosscutting a map that was apparently Houston. She didn't have the patience for it. There were no flashing banners reading: THE MAN YOU MIGHT GO TO PARIS WITH IS DEAD.

Call Blad! Her energy spiked.

He picked up, his voice tired. "Hi, sweetie. How are you feeling today?"

"Fine. Do you know where Preston is?"

His tone changed. "No, I'm at work. Some wifey wants a candlelight massage, which technically could happen anytime during the day, because the room is dark, but she insists it actually has to be nighttime. What's up?"

"Have you talked to him today?"

"No, why? I don't talk to Preston every day. Is everything okay?"

"He was supposed to come over at six-thirty, but he never showed."

Blad cleared his throat. "Well, he's probably at the studio, or studying. This is how architects are. They work all hours and forget about everything else."

He was right. His voice shifted her world back into perspective. Time, which had wrapped itself into a knot in her belly, stretched free again. But then the minutes kept passing, and passing. The house got heavy with quiet. She recognized the whir of the Cadillac pulling into the driveway—Katherine. She began to hate her phone, the way it baited her to look, to worry, and, worst of all, to hope. Finally, she flung it across her room. It smacked the old bulletin board and hit the carpet, taking a handful of tacks with it. As it set in that Preston may not show up at all, that he wouldn't be there to listen, that the words would need to be swallowed, she curled up on the bed and blinked at the moon rising behind her tree.

THE NEXT WEEK marked the arrival of the first hurricane of the season. Vivienne spent it in a haze of willing Preston to call and willing herself not to call him. Her mood charged up, empowered against him, or withered, helpless before him. All she felt in those days was in reaction to what he might be feeling. And still she expected he would call. Though their time together at the wedding had been short, the events in her memory evolved to magnificence, more radiant for the fact of their brevity and their blossoming, as the days passed, in proportion to the bitter realization of her desires.

His disappearance produced wretched swings from anger to regret. In romantic moods, Vivienne felt as if she were reassembling her heart from a pile of dust. All along, she'd taken for granted that she held the power in their flirtation. And all along it was Preston who had held her. She felt used to no purpose but his own amusement, foolish for thinking she was anything more. Somehow she'd assumed that by critiquing her he'd invited her into the safety of his confidence. Without realizing it, she'd come to trust him totally.

Vivienne watched the rain, and listened to the television blare about the imminence of Hurricane Henry, wondering whose job it was to name hurricanes, and unable to decide whether she should thank Preston for shattering her pride so much that her heart had opened or hate him for revealing to her the splendor of her heart, only to turn his back and disappear. She felt like a little creature scratching at a wall, believing in a door that didn't exist.

The lawn crew crossed the windows with tape. Rain fell from the watercolor green-and-gray sky. Bracken's secretary called to postpone her start date at the firm by ten days, in case Henry was earnest. Blad refused her invitation to stay over and drove to Austin to stay with friends. The three-hour drive took him seven hours, but he insisted the traffic was enjoyable compared to being under the same roof as Katherine during a hurricane. Karlie called to fret and complain about Timmy's general lousiness in stressful situations, without uttering a word of the wedding. In her state, Vivienne both resented and appreciated Karlie's silence. It was the hindrance to any authentic intimacy and thus the source of her distrust, as well as the necessary element that kept their friendship afloat on the peppy surface of things. Sissy pressed Vivienne to come to the ranch, but she refused. To Sissy's eyes, Vivienne had taken on an unpleasant willfulness in remaining at home, but Katherine herself agreed with her niece's decision to remain in Houston instead of fleeing with the masses. It hadn't even occurred to Vivienne to leave. Preston might call, might still arrive. She felt him like the storm itself—invisible, yet leaving its mark on everything in sight. The empty roads and green calm reflected her mind and gave her impressions a dark unreality. Despite the determined fluttering of Katherine, and the troop of workmen slicing bad branches from the trees, she felt alone. She thought of her mother. If only it was May. May, when the crepe myrtles awakened and brightened the streets with their pink and white popcorn flowers. She threw her old white sneakers in the trash.

Houston, her roads relieved of so many cars, seemed to sigh and flatten herself more deeply against the Gulf. The city took on a feverish, hyper dread. The probability of destruction produced stories from every person Vivienne encountered; those who stayed became comrades. Would Henry join the ranks of Carla and Alicia, or would he be a big anticlimax like Gilbert and Andrew? Most every hurricane in Vivienne's life had failed to live up to its anticipation, except for Ike, and she'd missed Ike. She was in Colorado with the Blanks. She wanted this one to be the real thing. She wanted the distraction, even the chaos.

The stillness of the afternoon prophesied the storm; the sun pierced through the clouds hanging heavy over the city. Vivienne was restless. In her heart's self-absorption, she believed her private waiting to be far more agonizing than the collective waiting beyond her window. Eight hundred miles off their shared coast, barreling toward them, was a grinding, unstoppable storm—surely Preston would call.

Sunset lit the sky a fiery, unsettled orange. The trees stood still. Katherine came upstairs and told Vivienne she was going to bed early. If the storm was bad, they'd meet in the hallway while it passed. Night fell without wind or rain. Around nine, the doorbell announced itself through the house. Vivienne put on her robe and rushed downstairs, calling to Katherine it was for her. She discovered Randal Stanley, bearing a large cardboard box. Her disappointment wasn't lost on him.

"Surprised to see me?" he said. "Can I come in? Special delivery here."

He walked in like the UPS man, dropping the box in the foyer, looking up and around, down the hallway leading to the kitchen. "Something tells me if you'da decorated this place, it'd look different," he said.

"This is my aunt's house," Vivienne replied, enclosing herself in the full collar of her robe.

Randal nodded. "I figure your house would be all white with lotsa flowers. I think it would smell good."

As usual, Vivienne was repelled. It occurred to her that Randal might have felt permitted to come over by the same thinking that permitted her to think Preston might still turn up: The usual rules didn't apply when disaster was impending. Didn't this make Preston's silence even worse?

"How did you know where I live?"

"Oh, we know enough of the same people, don't we? I brought you some supplies in case this guy turns out to be a doozy." He knelt over the box and, with a paternal air, explained the function of each thing, even though it was obvious. A hefty flashlight. Two cartons of canned tuna. Band-Aids. Batteries. Three gallons of water.

Vivienne couldn't help noting the kindness of the gesture. In the midst of her indignation, she realized it was probably the nicest thing a man had ever done for her.

"In Delaware, we got some hurricanes too," Randal said, pushing off his knees and standing. He was sweaty, in a black T-shirt, jeans, and old boots. His beard was trimmed, uncovering a landscape of old pockmarks, a sort of connect-the-dots game over his cheeks. Somehow, the scars made him seem less deserving of her attitude. "Back east, they're usually pretty weak by the time they hit the coast, because the Atlantic's not as warm. But, hell, with this humidity in the Gulf . . ." He signaled toward the open door. "You're gonna get misquitas in here."

Vivienne held herself in her robe, not sure what to say. She didn't want to be mean anymore, but she didn't want to be too friendly either. "The storms are never as bad as the news says. I think everyone just wants something to talk about."

"It's good to be prepared anyhow, right?" He ran his palm over his greasy hair and smiled like a black Labrador. Vivienne felt a little bad for him. Preston was rejecting her, and she was rejecting Randal. Everyone was having a hard time. There was nothing easy about anything.

"My aunt is sleeping, so . . . thanks for all this. It was thoughtful of you to stop by." She turned to the door. He took the hint and went outside but stopped at the landing.

"Look, you make this hard for a guy," he said, rubbing his brow. "I'm not saying I came here under the guise of dropping off supplies just to ask, but I gotta ask: I want to take you to dinner. I want to take you out and discuss how I can help you out."

The wind flurried up and sent the treetops swirling, taking the entirety of her budding goodwill with it. "What do you mean, 'help me out'?"

"Come on. This is what I mean, how you make things hard. I know you're in a tough spot, and I want to—I want to take care of you. I don't like thinking you might be in—any uncomfortable positions. Let me take you out for a good time."

"I'm not in any uncomfortable positions," she said.

"I think I've caught you in a couple," he said. "I'm happy for you that job is coming through. I want all that to work out, but maybe it's not a stable situation, and you don't wanna invest yourself in an unstable situation."

"What does that mean?" The words left her mouth without passing through her head. "If I don't go out with you, you'll find a way to mess up my job with Bracken?"

He paused. "Let's not go slinging mud. Let's level. I'm new to all this. I'm trying to fit in. And I think in your own way you're trying to fit in too. We both want to make friends—"

"I have friends."

"You do, but you don't. Because you got a situation that makes life feel like trying to fit a circle in a square. I can tell by the way you are. That's why I noticed you. That's what makes you a cut above. You have real things on your mind. I know we're not on the same page now, but I see you, and I see movement. I see things happening. I think you and I can be"—he hesitated on the word—"powerful together. The cream of the crop. Just give me a chance to take you out. That's all I'm asking."

Vivienne took a delicate tone. "Let's talk about this another time, when a hurricane isn't coming."

"But you catch my drift? We can help each other?"

The wind stilled as lightning illuminated the sky and bled into the fat gray clouds. Thunder followed close, loud and low. Randal took a loose toothpick from his pocket and began chewing it between his front teeth. Sweat beaded on his forearms, flattening the hair there. His small eyes waited for her with a satisfied patience, gleamed with the suggestion of a shared goal. She lost patience.

"So you think," Vivienne said, leaning against the doorjamb, "that we can help each other because we both want to fit in? You want me to help you make the right friends, and in exchange I won't have to worry about money?"

"That's one way to put it."

She shook her head. "That's gross."

"The higher you climb, the farther you fall, ain't that right? What strikes me as unfair these days is that women have to climb two ladders"—here he mimed climbing a ladder—"but you can't climb two ladders at once. Some point you're gonna fall. One of 'em's gonna tip back, and then you'll be stuck"—here he mimed a frozen fallen body—"but if there was just the set one, things'd be easier."

He thought a moment before tapping his temple and shaking a finger at her. "Thing is, I like women with opinions. So my only winning strategy is the exact kinda strategy that'd probably never work on the kinda woman I want. But you—you're some other kinda woman. You're like a whirlpool spinning around."

Even though she didn't really know what he was talking about, this made Vivienne smile. "Why do you want to be friends with the Blanks so much?"

He answered without hesitation. "I like being at the top of whatever heap is in sight. I don't settle for less. Settling is a bunny slope. You're going downhill, but you don't hardly realize it because you're going so slow. Then suddenly you're stuck at the bottom."

Lightning lit the sky silver. Now the thunder was immediate, a crack. "None of that will matter if we all die in a hurricane tonight," Vivienne said.

"That's the spirit," Randal said. "But I'm not gonna die in this storm, and you're not either."

"Did you come to Texas to get away from something?"

The deeper she pried, the fuller his confidence grew. "You bet I did. You wanna leave Texas to get away from something?"

"No," she said.

"Well, good. The key to unhappiness—always wantin' to be somewhere else instead of where you are. See, right here at your doorstep, this is where I want to be. No place else."

"Please go home, Randal."

Nodding, he tipped her his figurative hat. "Fair enough," he said. "I'll take this conversation as a maybe."

Vivienne fell asleep to the streaming of the wind. She dreamed she missed a bullet train to a European city she'd never heard of. Randal was the conductor, wearing overalls and a floppy striped hat. Reis and Bucky were there, laying pennies on the tracks and collecting the pressed ones after the trains passed. Vivienne missed the train because she was looking for her luggage, only to remember right before she awoke that she hadn't brought any.

Morning heralded the passing of Hurricane Henry, a storm for the book of disappointments. She woke to the sight of skinny tree limbs strewn over the street.

And still he did not call.

Walk as children of light.
—EPHESIANS 5:8

I

ONE YEAR LATER

PRESTON FOUND A BENCH IN THE SQUARE AND SAT, ROLLING a cigarette on his knee. People passed, shuttered in their light coats, eyes toward home. He hunched forward and licked the paper, cradled a match, and leaned back as he exhaled. His head felt thick, out of time. It was a Thursday afternoon, but the crowds swarming around his bench seemed of a different, busier world. They were retreating to their own warm apartments, and he was emerging, his brain full of sludge, into their midst. He needed a shower, but it was a long walk home, and he wasn't quite ready for it. He wanted to beam himself to his own shower, just be there instantly. The other possibilities available to him—the Metro or a cab—would also have to wait. No decision would be made until he finished this cigarette.

He sniffed his shoulder. Grease and perfume and smoke.

In his attempt to avoid recollecting the evening prior and feeling anything about it, his mood darted among various animal urges: eat, piss, call someone—that girl Celine? Every desire that surfaced he wanted gratified immediately. If only he could piss right there without anyone thinking it inappropriate. Why couldn't a pepper steak *avec haricots verts* just materialize on his lap?

He smoked and thought of the girls he'd been seeing lately—their wide-set eyes, their tentative English, all starstruck with vague artistic ambitions, little Jane Birkin wannabes who needed tutoring in how to give head—and continued to feel nothing about them, aware of his feeling nothing, aware of the coldness of this deliberate choice to feel nothing, which was exactly how he wanted it, despite it filling him with terrible feelings. The minutes were ticking toward his favorite time of day, when the lights of the cars cast colors across the faces of the gray buildings. In their narrowness, the streets looked to him like tunnels of light, winding alleys charged with mystery. Having grown up in Houston, a city with streets as wide as the Seine with none of the grandeur, he appreciated the power of attenuated spaces. There was history in it, the old proportion of things, a sense of romance, all the things he tried not to buy into about old Paris but, in truth, did completely.

Paris seemed to human scale. He thought of the freeways in Houston, of driving across a twelve-laner, one in a four-story pile of other freeways, beneath towering billboards, all of that, and it made him feel anxious, like an insect in a gargantuan world. Here—this was good. This triangular cobblestone park, with two benches, three mature plane trees preparing for autumn, little cars honking in disorganized traffic, and the dome of the Panthéon rounding out the near distance.

These scenes reminded him why he came to Paris and stayed; when he was otherwise steeped in aimlessness, soaked in the film of meaningless sex, tired of redesigning toilet closets—*this*—this air, this view, pushed him on.

An elderly man with a small dog came and sat on the bench across from him. He was wearing a brown suit and holding the dog under his arm. His face was long, his eyes kindly sagging. He moved the dog to his lap and sat watching the traffic. He looked loved but lonely.

The dog kept glancing up at the man.

Preston wondered where the man had come from and where he was going. The thought made him antsy. He wanted somewhere to be, someone to be waiting for him. There were places he could go; he saw his friends scattered around the city, faces that would smile on seeing him, women who wanted a call. Yet this awareness just clenched him up where he wanted to open, folded him inward when he wanted expansion—joy, simplicity, a widening circle. The apartment anticipating him was empty and quiet, making its dark sounds without him, dripping and ticking.

He reached for his phone to text a friend but resisted. Company would only drag him down when he was already out of sorts. The thing about this familiar sickness was that its sole cure was solitude, a return to himself, only achieved by wading through gloom. Once again he would have to wade. The aspect he most deplored in men was greed, men who gorged and boasted. And yet here he was, a gorged man, taking in the show of Paris's lights flickering on, as if he was so special, as if hundreds of men hadn't sat in that very spot, full of ennui, smoking and thinking of women and getting old. A sudden ardor pulled him to his feet and he left the park, watching the little dog's black marble eyes follow him away.

He wound around like he always did, taking the darkest streets possible, making the city a labyrinth. The sky was still dusk blue, but in the narrowest lanes, named after accomplished dead men, full night had already fallen. He listened to his shoes scuff the cobblestones. Each step carried him away from his mood. When he reached the river, the beauty slowed him down. Notre Dame—underlit, tremendous, its gargoyles charging in early moonlight. He'd never tire of the place, no matter how many tourists clogged its archways.

Tonight he paused to take his hundredth picture of it with his phone, but he didn't linger. He crossed the bridge, the river sparkling and split by boats, a floating party shining a spotlight into the luxury riverside flats. He crossed off the island and came upon a pudgy man wearing a worn black tuxedo and playing a violin; nearby, a group of teenagers performed break-dancing tricks. The world smelled like melting ice cream and wet dog, and down on the quay, where he descended to take the long way home, like old water and urine. He raised his head to get a better sense of the sky, and a gust of wind rose and took off his hat. This beloved straw hat, made custom for his head, a Parisian splurge that he'd purchased when he first moved to the city, flew into the Seine and landed upright on the water's surface, as if it had found itself a new head.

Preston nearly jumped in after it.

Hatless, he went home. Back to his own neighborhood, where his apartment window provided a view of a McDonald's golden arch and teenagers spray-painted the sidewalks and spoke not-easily-identifiable languages. He was feeling sorry for himself. Why did that have to happen? The universe had swiped his hat as punishment. But for what? The familiar wheels turned. Nothing he had done was exactly wrong, it was only . . . not right. And it was only not right because it wasn't . . . fulfilling. But according to whose standard did every experience need to be fulfilling? And were there not multiple ways in which experiences could be fulfilling? He thought he'd finish some drawings or go north for the weekend to see some of the country he hadn't seen. These thoughts occupied him as he climbed his stairs, wonderful creaking old stairs with mahogany banisters smooth as baby skin, and found his pretty neighbor struggling with some groceries in the narrow hallway. He loved how often he found himself in situations he could take pleasure in without deliberately pursuing them; it made him feel less culpable. His intentions were harmless, making his actions excusable. He would be the gentleman from Texas.

That night he neglected his drawings and made no plans to leave town. She came over and they shared a bottle of wine on empty stomachs. Preston only had cheese and crackers, and she didn't offer to share her groceries. Usually he let these things happen naturally—the night getting late, the reluctance to take a cab, the use of his couch, *But, oh, you don't have to sleep on the couch*—but she lived across the hall, so he didn't bullshit. As his body rose to the occasion, his mind went mute to the voice inside, wondering what this woman would think if she knew he hadn't showered from the woman the night before, and how awful that was, and what did he think about that, and what did he even want, and did he really want her? The words cut out, and he did the work of his body.

She wanted to sleep in her own bed—a great relief, which also doubled her attractiveness. He watched her dress. This wasn't a girl from the Rice library. He was still amazed that he could actually get hot women in Paris in a way he rarely could at home. It had taken him a few months to realize women here thought it was exotic that he was from Texas and said "y'all." This girl wore shoes like—Vivienne.

He stayed up late on the computer, developing a headache in a wormhole of useless social media and pretentious architecture blogs. At three A.M. the screen's blue glow made him feel his brain was suspended in a tank. The world online was one where everyone made more money, worked more productively, got more credit, and looked better doing it. Though he knew it was mostly a farce, the calculated perfection of it all got to him, and he circled back: *Well, that guy may be designing a gallery and have a beautiful wife and two Eames chairs, but he was probably changing a shit diaper while I was kissing the breasts of a woman who smelled like fresh coconut.*

The thought made him groan at his own lowness. But the fact of his living in Paris shored his ego up again. He imagined all the millions of people, staying up late, holding warm mugs to their hearts like amulets, scrolling through websites that presented the world as a place where no one should require warm liquid for existential comfort. At least he was living through it in Paris.

Finally he went to bed. As he rested on his foamy rented mattress, the bad feelings crept in. Out of his mind's file came the recollection of a proverb, something about how a fool returns to his folly like a dog returns to his vomit.

II

"CONGRATS!"

The three women lifted their arms, a spectrum of fingernails in shades of fire, and gently clinked flute against flute. Vivienne made sure to touch each woman's glass. It was back luck to miss one.

"*L'addition, s'il vous plaît,*" Karlie called in twangy French, after taking her sip.

Waverly pretended to sip. "You are so impressive. I don't know how you speak French without being embarrassed. I can't even say hello."

Karlie reached one hand over the table to rub Waverly's belly. "You impress me. Most gorgeous pregnant woman."

Waverly beamed. "This is such a special time in our lives." She brought both hands to her mouth to contain her voice. The surrounding patrons cast them shushing glares. "This is the time you look back on when you're old, sitting around with your girlfriends." She blinked back tears. "I know, I know. But this is the time I dreamt of growing up. Being a wife, seeing my girlfriends become wives and mothers, beginning our lives. I'm so blessed to share it with y'all—in Paris!" She smiled, then sighed as though she never needed to sigh again. "I also want to make a toast to Vivienne. This is totally your moment. I bet a year from now you're engaged and moving into the cutest house in West U."

Vivienne blew Waverly a kiss across the table. She sat back in her chair, nestling the flute to her cheek. It all felt so good. Even though the restaurant, a minimalist place on the roof of a contemporary art museum, had turned out to be the wrong choice—her friends were too big a presence for its austerity—Vivienne loved it. Its glass walls revealed the grand, rambling city below.

Karlie thrust her chair back, hitting the back of a stranger's. "Maybe I'm next," she said.

Waverly's eyes went big. "Are you—Kar?"

"No," she said. "But we might start trying. Maybe his sperm has some personality."

"Whenever you say things like that, I wonder what Timmy would say if he heard you," Waverly said.

Vivienne nipped the last bite of her salad. "This means you'll need to sleep with him."

"Thanks for that valuable information, Viv," Karlie said. "Timmy and I have a great relationship. And you don't know—none of you girls really know—what goes on. So y'all shouldn't pretend that you do."

Waverly cradled her chin. "Do you think they'll have a big wedding?" she asked, changing the subject. Bucky and Reis were engaged, Bucky having proposed on a tubing trip down the Guadalupe River. To her surprise, Vivienne had felt glad for them, albeit a somewhat disdainful gladness. Reis, ever diplomatic, seemed to hold no grudge toward Vivienne for having once had sex with her fiancé. And Vivienne—as the woman who'd made the past "mistake"—knew better than to begrudge Reis for being loved by the man she'd once desired. Typically in such cases, Vivienne would be the one who had a right to be mad, but there was no fighting the established consensus: She'd botched it with Bucky. Now it was all water under the bridge, thanks to time and, in particular, Vivienne's willingness to deprecate herself in support of their union. Everyone admired how gracefully she'd admitted her fault and given her blessing. The events would have played on without her, but with her repentant, they played on with friendships intact. Secretly, Vivienne felt grateful. She couldn't imagine wearing the ring on Reis's finger. The thought of marriage to Bucky now felt like a pillow to her face.

Waverly circled her hand over her belly. Waverly's happiness was never circumstantial; it just was. If the world took it all away, she would still find a way. For all her easy shelter, she was the most steadfast person Vivienne knew. Faith was the fiber of her heart. "Being pregnant feels so right," she said.

"It's good you're having a baby first, because I have to learn from you," Karlie said. "I might be the cool mom who lets her kids drink at home so they're not out drunk-driving." She adjusted the flouncy sleeves of her dress, which were supposed to rest just off her shoulders but kept rolling too low and accentuating what she called her "arm pudge." She looked exceptionally healthful surrounded by skinny French women, like a freckled pinup, glowing "America."

She began taking pictures of the champagne bottle in its drippy ice bucket. "Do you think our waiter would pose for my blog?" she said. "He's so hot."

Hearing this, Waverly mustered herself up and said, "Have you ever cheated on Tim?"

This was a shocking question from Waverly. Vivienne knew Karlie wouldn't answer, but hearing it made her think of Preston, and she didn't want to think about Preston. That he was still in Paris was not something she wanted to bother herself about. He'd written once, a few months after leaving, a brief, way-too-friendly email to *say hello,* totally ignoring his disappearance. She didn't respond. She was over his games, his insecurity, his arrogance. She wanted to forget him.

Karlie popped a sugar cube in her mouth. "Everyone cheats in France."

"That doesn't make it right," Waverly said.

"I believe marriage is a vow," Karlie said. "But my marriage also represents me in a practical sense. It's part of how I present my life on my blog. It's part of my identity."

"The things you say on your blog aren't what you say in real life, though," Vivienne said.

Karlie turned instantly and held the camera inches from Vivienne's face. The shutter clicked. "In case you want to know what you look like when you're being bitchy." She stirred her champagne with her pinky. "The face you wear matters. I don't care if people say it's shallow, but the way you look and how you represent yourself online can determine your success."

The waiter appeared, slid the check on the table, and curtly departed. "I'm getting this," Waverly said. "Clay is spoiling me on this trip."

Vivienne snatched it from Waverly's hand. "I'm treating."

"Power lunch!" Waverly said. "Anyway, for me, there's no difference. What I'd say about Clay here and what I'd say about him online is the same. I don't see why there has to be a difference."

Karlie swallowed the rest of her champagne. "Then you haven't cultivated your ideal self. We all have one." She rested her elbows on the table and slit her eyes. "If you could be anything, what would you be? I don't mean, like, a certain job, but, like, a whole way of being and living."

"So you're saying my ideal self would cheat on my husband?" Waverly looked hurt.

Karlie said, "What I'm saying is that I don't think we have to choose one way. I personally believe you can have it all."

"So you mean cheat and be married," Vivienne said.

Karlie shrugged. "I mean have multiple, equally valid selves that don't betray one another."

"Sounds like multiple personality disorder," Vivienne said.

"What have you been reading, Kar?" Waverly asked, digging through her bag. "Do y'all want to go shopping at La Samaritaine today?"

"Everyone's standards in a relationship are different," Karlie said. "Every couple is different."

"Maybe if you live in Paris," Waverly said. "But I don't think Timmy would agree with you."

Vivienne could tell Karlie was trying to keep her voice down, because a little vein running over her forehead inflated.

"I'm sorry, Wavey," Karlie said, "but when was the last time you talked to Timmy about his relationship standards?"

Vivienne watched Karlie, surprised at her confidence, at her unusual lack of deference toward Waverly.

Waverly persisted. "But don't you ever want to feel safe and at peace with Timmy? How can you sleep next to him at night knowing that hypothetically you might—"

"Let's talk about something else," Vivienne said.

Karlie tickled Vivienne's arm. "I know you agree with me, Viv. Isn't it tempting to imagine that you can have it all?"

Have it all—a string of words so familiar to Vivienne that she could hardly find a meaning for it.

"I do have it all," she said to Karlie.

Waverly smiled wide. "So do I."

Karlie lingered on Vivienne with an impish look, then peeled back, flipping her hair over her other ear. "Let's definitely go shopping today," she said.

III

Preston ran into the Houstonians in the sort of gorgeous *fin de siècle* gilded-wainscoting café he pretended to avoid. A tourist trap—haunted, according to every Parisian tour guide ever written, by the ghosts of glamorous drunk literati, and most frequented, it seemed, by American tourists who gave off the impression of never having read a book in their lives. And yet the café had really good ice cream. Creamy ice cream that reminded Preston of home, served in generous portions that also reminded him of home.

So occasionally he went there, to his own chagrin, and spent the equivalent of nine American dollars on a bowl of chocolate ice cream. He ate in a single seat at a tiny round table in the corner, the café cast before him, and listened to people speak English. Why he enjoyed this, he didn't care to know. He wasn't consciously homesick. What led him weekly to this café was a quiet feeling, so gentle he obeyed it without question.

He was doodling ideas for a remodel when he heard a female voice—a voice out of place. So impossibly out of place that he didn't look up from his drawing, until he heard a man call his name with low incredulity: "Preston?" It was Clay. And so it was true—it had been Karlie Nettle asking the girl behind the counter if they had rainbow sprinkles. Clay approached. "Are you kidding me, man?"

Preston's very first thought was of Vivienne. *Was she with them?* Clay looked exactly the same—khaki pants, an untucked white button-down, Top-Siders—a man who knew what the day would bring tomorrow.

Preston stood, feeling embarrassed and stunned by this sudden intrusion into his personal space. But it was good to see Clay; he looked eager and alive. The two slapped each other's back, and Clay stepped away to evaluate.

"Man! This is crazy. Did you get my email?"

He had gotten the email, but he'd also gotten an email from Karlie. He'd chosen to ignore both, as making plans with Clay in Paris meant making plans with Karlie in Paris. Of course, when he got the emails he'd wondered about Vivienne, but she'd never responded to his email. Admittedly, it was a lame email, maybe the lamest email he'd ever written, given everything he wanted to say, but somehow that enormity, coupled with all the passing months and the fact that he knew he was in the wrong, made him feel that the right approach, the only approach of which he felt capable, was to be brief and friendly. His eyes dashed to the counter and the tables—looking for her. "I did, sorry about that," he said. "Work's been busy."

Clay pulled at Preston's knit vest. "You look good. Lookin' sophisticated."

Preston shrugged. "It rubs off on you, this French stuff."

A moment passed in which the men just looked at each other, the scenery so beyond the context of their normal range that neither seemed to know what to say next. Preston punctured it. "So—what are you doing here? You guys on vacation?"

Clay nodded vigorously. "Yeah, yeah. We're having a baby, and we figured we wouldn't be able to travel for a while after that—it's a girl." He raised his eyebrows and pretended to brace himself.

"Congratulations."

"Yeah, so the girls put this trip together. A last hurrah kinda thing. The Blanks are also here on business, so we figured we'd just make it a big trip."

"Right," Preston said. He shifted his weight. "So the whole group is here?" Through the window, at a far table, Preston saw a blond Karlie Nettle and a pregnant Waverly Blank—no Vivienne.

"Come say hi," Clay said, clutching his shoulder.

Karlie spotted him first. "No way!" she cried.

He joined them at the wobbly table set over old bricks. Karlie wanted to finish her story about how she thought every Metro station was called *sortie*.

"We're trying to go shopping. We all get off the Metro and we're staring at the map. And I keep saying, this one is called *sor-tie*, that's where we are—"

"And I keep saying, it's not on the map, Kar!" Waverly said.

"Till finally this nice lady stops and she's, like, it means 'exit.' How was I supposed to know? That's what the effing sign said!"

Just then, the bells of Saint-Germain-des-Prés rang out the four o'clock hour. Karlie put a hand to Waverly's bump and murmured, "Do you hear the bells, little lady?"

Preston caught Waverly giving him a sort of stink eye, though she wasn't the type of woman to make a face like that. He'd hardly said anything but hello and goodbye to Waverly Blank in all the years of their acquaintance.

"My back hurts," she said. "I think I want to go to the room and take a bath."

Karlie stood and came around to Preston, pinching his arm. "Come to dinner with us tomorrow night. We're staying at the Ritz. Meet us there and we'll all go together."

Karlie had gained a few pounds, which suited her. She struck him as more brazen than he remembered and now she was blond. The effect was garish. He thought of Timmy and wondered if he was around; good, hapless Timmy—he hadn't thought about him in a long time. A heat gathered at the back of his neck. It was all very weird, too heavy with reminders. By shades each of them had changed, but broadly they were the same. That they seemed so delighted by this, or unaware of it, was strange to Preston. He exhausted so much life force pushing himself both literally and psychologically, all in an effort to create change. The fact that these people could exist without this exertion was unsettling—he lost respect for them, yet at the same time he envied them.

The sweat was making him cold. "I'm working tomorrow night," he said.

"Come on," Karlie chided.

"I'm working," Preston repeated.

"No, you're not," Karlie said. "You're coming to dinner."

Clay hung back. "Want to grab a quick beer?" he said. His eyes went wide, as if to say, "*Please* grab a beer with me."

Both men walked with their hands in their pockets, toward the river, Preston feeling unsure of his body language in Clay's company. He found it hard to believe it was really Clay, of Houston, of beer-drinking in fields, of rocks. They jogged down a flight of stone stairs, past hand-painted flood markers, to the quay. Clay went close to the water's edge and waved at a group of young people floating by on a long tour boat.

"How do you like Paris?" Preston asked.

"Incredible." Clay raised his eyes, took a deep breath.

"How long are you guys staying?"

"A couple more days. Thanks for stepping away. I needed a break." Just then his phone buzzed. "She keeps close tabs."

Preston felt a rising anxiousness over what to say. He fought himself not to steer the conversation toward Vivienne. "So what business are the Blanks doing here?"

Clay picked up a rock and skipped it into the river. "Art stuff. You know Vivienne is working for Bracken? They've got a whole thing going on. Some big collector of Texas paintings is out here, so they're trying to buy up a bunch of this stuff, woo the collector."

"French people love Texas," Preston said.

Clay grinned. " 'Cause it's the best."

Preston lit a cigarette and offered one to Clay.

"No thanks," Clay said. He was looking out at the river and the wooden boats grazing its concrete banks and the sky winding down to evening. Behind them, noisy cars passed in packs. During the periods of silence, Preston heard the lapping of the water.

"Almost makes me want to say a prayer," Clay said.

Preston noticed his eyes were closed. Maybe he really was praying.

"Is Vivienne here?" Preston said.

Clay nodded. "She went to another museum today. She's been doing the museum rounds." The breeze was picking up the loose strands of hair over his forehead, exposing his hairline in retreat. His nose was pink in the wind.

They stopped at a street vendor and bought dark German beers and sat in a pair of rickety metal chairs under some poplar trees. Clay drank his beer with heart, giving himself a foamy mustache with each sip. They talked about work for a while. Clay was in awe of the Roman ruins beneath Notre Dame, more for the visible layers of earth they revealed than for the ruins. Preston found he enjoyed the conversation. His French was lacking, and even in the best English-speakers the accents were thick. It was nice to just talk.

But Vivienne remained in the front of his mind. "So Vivienne is working with a collector here?"

"A lady from Texas who lives here," Clay said.

"How's she doing?" For as often as he'd thought about her, he'd also told himself he was lucky. He'd escaped unscathed. But now that he knew she was somewhere in the city, the realization of a wound was growing on him.

"She's great. Do y'all stay in touch?" Clay let the question hang there.

Preston traced his thumb along his perspiring beer mug. "No."

"Bracken didn't want to bring in a hoity-toity art-world chick," Clay said. "Vivienne has a good eye and she's good on the eyes. I don't say that against her, it's just—it's just obvious." Here he cleared his throat.

Preston swirled his beer around the bottom of the mug. "Is it obvious to her?"

Clay swallowed a full gulp. "I don't know. She doesn't really have anyone looking out for her. I look out for her, but I'm her best friend's husband and Bracken's son-in-law. I mean someone looking out for her who has something to lose, if that makes sense."

Now Preston cleared his throat. "Is Timmy here?"

"He's been hanging out at the hotel bar and checking the markets. I'm too pumped with protective juices to let Waverly go anywhere on her own—" He paused. "Karlie's probably fooling around on him. Not that he'd do anything about it. He probably wouldn't. But sometimes I wish he'd just face it, you know."

Preston didn't answer. He looked away from Clay toward a crowd of pigeons fighting over a baguette.

"She's an intense girl," Clay said.

"Vivienne?" Preston said.

"No, Karlie."

The sky was in full orange now; the sun had set, but its effulgence warmed the whole riverbank, even the faces of the vintage postcards in the street vendor's spinning stand. Preston was a little cold, increasingly troubled, and didn't want to put off the long Metro ride home after Clay jumped into a cab on Bracken's dime.

Clay sighed. "Sorry if I unloaded on you, man. Guess you kinda caught the brunt of me after hanging around my in-laws and three women all week." He laughed. "Come to dinner tomorrow. I think the painting lady will be there too." He said this as if Preston should be relieved.

They made their way back to the street and shook hands by the Metro station. Clay smacked Preston's shoulder with manly solidarity and said, "You better not bring that vest back to Texas."

IV

PARIS MADE VIVIENNE FEEL LIKE A SLOW-BUDDING FLOWER. Each successive morning she woke imperceptibly blossomed, breathing more deeply, seeing more vividly, filled with energy. The effect was so granular that she hadn't perceived the change until today, when, through a part in the damask curtains, in the quiet of the vaulted room, she watched the morning sun cross over the empty arena of the Place Vendôme. Napoleon's old bronze column seemed to her a sort of sundial, or the gear at the center of a clock, a guide.

Karlie was asleep in the next room, without Timmy, a long lump beneath the duvet, crowned with a blond flame. The beauty of the morning swelled into a moment of tenderness. If a place like this existed in the world, then Vivienne could love Karlie despite her many, many flaws. There was no one else like her, after all. The traits that made her suspect were the very traits that made her endearing: the tartness, the cunning, the spontaneity.

Today Vivienne was finally meeting Kitty Crawford—seventy-something expat collector of Raleigh Wester's original watercolors, great-great-niece of one of the original Spindletop guys. Vivienne had tracked her down after discovering a replica of Wester's *Band of Charging Comanches* in an antiques store in Fredericksburg. Finding the painting's owner had taken weeks and happened only by chance, when Vivienne came across a picture, in an old catalog, of Kitty in a silk robe, with the caption *Collector of Texas* beneath her name. She looked her up online and clicked through the history of a woman who moved to Paris and took Texas with her. The walls of her apartment in the Latin Quarter were supposedly hung with early paintings of the Big Bend, the antlers of a buck shot by Sam Houston himself, and two of the first Texas flags ever sewn, one by the mother of Texas, Jane Long. When Vivienne had reached Kitty by phone, Kitty told her to come on over and take a look, as if it were a matter of a walk around the block.

The Wester painting suited Bracken's tastes, but it had something extra that kept Vivienne looking into it: the Comanches charging over the barren Edwards Plateau, wrenching back atop their naked horses as the Texas Rangers neared, the sunset behind them all a deep summer red—and, among them, Cynthia Ann Parker, the Texan girl captured by Comanches as a child, tearing back her buffalo skins to reveal her pale breast. The watercolor blurred their faces, but their bodies were tense and alive. She kept the reproduction by her desk. It was the only picture she had up in her office. She glanced at it probably a dozen times a day, and it never lost force for her.

Bracken's associates—all of them men—teased her for it. They couldn't understand why a girl like Vivienne would hang an Indian war picture in her office. Vivienne tried explaining it was Cynthia Ann's last moment of freedom before the Texans captured her, the moment she revealed herself to save her children. After this, the white men took her to the piney woods of East Texas and made her live with her white relatives. They were strangers to her, and she ran away as often as she could. They found her praying and sobbing in the forest, singing Comanche songs.

The associates didn't like this story. It wasn't so much the story, Vivienne thought, as the fact that she was telling it. They looked at her as though she wasn't doing her job. Her official title was vague: "Junior Consultant." She liked her office—just as Bracken promised, she had a view—and she liked dressing up and having somewhere to go every morning that felt legitimate and professional, but for a year, all she'd done was conduct light research and send suggestions to Bracken. When he actually made a purchase, he did it through a nonprofit he'd set up in his company's name and worked with an art brokerage or, depending on the scale of the piece, an auction house. This process could take several weeks or months and involved tax attorneys and financial managers.

Occasionally he sent Vivienne out to meet with a gallery owner, to collect information, and, as he put it, to "make an impression." Indeed, "making an impression" was Vivienne's strength. She tried to think of herself as the face of Bracken's endeavor, and she did her best to look the part. The guys loved her, and, true to her fantasy, they all wore suits. Bracken requested that she "take care of them." Vivienne took this to mean she should act as a sort of female confidante. She was expected to join them once or twice a week for drinks after work, to boost morale around projects, to unite the team. She had dinner with the guys she thought were cute, but most of them were married. There was one single attorney, but he was leaving the firm. After the goodbye party they went out to his truck and he kissed her. He was tall, from Fort Worth, and he'd recently bought a small ranch outside Dripping Springs. He was so good-natured and fun, she thought they'd connected, that he would open new doors. But it fizzled. Vivienne cried for a night and thought of Preston.

Bracken would saunter into her office on Friday afternoons, clutching his Scotch, and tell her how pretty she was and how much they all liked having her around. If any of the guys heard him, they'd come in and tell her too, until they blocked the doorway. A big chunk of twangy men telling her how pretty she was. To her surprise, she didn't like it at all; she hated them for it. Sometimes, when she had it in her, she'd laugh and shout, "Sexual harassment!" and push them all out. She worked up the nerve to ask Bracken about Paris on one of those Friday afternoons. He was just lubricated enough to think it was a wild idea. She sold him on the fact that Kitty Crawford was notoriously private and reluctant to sell, yet here she was—eager to meet. Bracken announced that they were on their way to Paris, that Vivienne had a done a superb job making an impression—and would she mind escorting a couple of the boys out tonight?

To meet Kitty today, Vivienne put on a simple red knee-length wrap dress, a gold cuff bracelet, black heels, and Waverly's knee-length camel trench. Then, without waking Karlie, she slipped out. It was half past eight. The hotel was quiet. She strode over the long Persian carpets, past display windows selling luxuries one could buy anywhere luxuries were sold, past a few women already smoking cigarettes and staring into their phones in the lounge, beneath teardrop chandeliers. She loved the sweet energy of consensus: They were all delighted, intoxicated, pretending to belong. She bore it with confidence, while inside she trembled in amazement that life had brought her here.

Waiting at the valet for a cab, she ran into Timmy. He exited the hotel as if expelled from it, looking disheveled and totally American. France had the effect of making Timmy look more overweight than he was, tubby where at home he was normal. No one had mentioned this aloud, but Vivienne was certain Timmy noticed; he'd taken on a rosy self-consciousness since they'd arrived and had kept to the hotel bar, apparently in awe of the fact that it was named after Ernest Hemingway.

He gave her a big hug. "You look so beautiful," he said, as if it made him sad.

"Have you been up all night, Tim?"

"No, no, no," he said defensively. "I got up early and walked around."

"You should go crawl into bed with your wife," she said. "She's still sleeping."

He sagged his fists in the pockets of his seersucker pants. "Yeah . . ." he said noncommittally. "I'll probably do that. Where you going all dressed up?"

"I have a meeting." She watched his eyes pitch back a little. He was drunk. "Why don't you go sleep for a while, Tim? And we can take a walk later. I'll text you."

His eyes faltered, then brightened. "Sure," he said.

A TAXI TOOK her to Kitty's address in the 5th arrondissement, across the river. The building was on a cobbled street—a passage, really, just barely wide enough for the cab to fit—behind a stone wall with a royal-blue doorway. After the noise of the taxi's muffler drained from the cavern of the buildings, Vivienne noticed a swarthy old man peering out a window across the street, his dark and plentiful chest hair exposed by his loose white undershirt. He was listening to an opera, a passionate song, and looking at her with no interest whatsoever. When she turned away to knock, he said to her, in a thick accent, "You want to see Kitty? She never hears the door." Then all of a sudden he thundered, "Kitty! Kitty! Kitty!" It was a beautiful baritone call, uncannily like the voice singing opera in the background.

There was a clang from behind the door, the fiddling of a lock, and then the door opened. "Thanks, Eddie!" the woman said, in a soft singsong. Eddie just nodded and remained peering out the window, up and down the street. She turned to Vivienne. "I'm Kitty Crawford."

Kitty nudged the door shut with all her weight, then slid a long rusty bolt across it. "*His* name is really *Eduard*." She said the name in flawless French but made fun of herself with a flourish of her wrist. "But I just call him Eddie. And he still doesn't realize that 'kitty, kitty, kitty' is actually the way everyone else in the whole stinkin' world calls real felines. You'd think this would be universal knowledge, but Eddie missed the boat on that one. I think the neighbors believe he has a cat that he loves very much. He just stands at that window all day, like he's waiting for someone, and no one ever comes, except sometimes to see me. It's become that he stands there waiting for people to come see me. Then he cries—'Kitty! Kitty! Kitty!'—from the depths of his old French soul. I suspect I share a name with the woman who broke his heart when he was a young man."

They hadn't taken a single step into the courtyard, and already Vivienne loved Kitty. She looked smaller, less glamorous than in pictures, and older, more endearing. She was a round woman, inflated by a ruddy fullness that seemed to carry her lightly on her feet. Lines split off from the corners of her eyes, which were bright and hazel and wondering. Loose gray curls formed a crown around her head. Her nails were a shade of Easter yellow, and she wore an unshapely red silk jacket with a mandarin collar and dainty black toggles, unfastened, over a beige linen dress. It followed flowingly in her shadow as she crossed the gravel courtyard, a pair of black velvet house slippers snapping against her heels.

Suddenly she stopped. "You can't be comfortable," she said, staring down at Vivienne's shoes. Vivienne was a few steps behind, sinking into the soil beneath the gravel. "They make my feet hurt just looking. I don't want you rolling down my stairs. Put 'em here." She pointed to a lopsided teak table set. A tuxedo cat slept in a perfect circle on one of the chairs. "That's Ulysses. The irony is, he ignores Eddie. I'm the kitty around here."

Vivienne took off her heels and put them side by side beneath Ulysses's chair. Kitty noticed the care she took and smiled. "Don't worry, they'll be fine."

She followed Kitty to the open archway of an unassuming townhouse. The style was recognizable to Vivienne as classically Parisian: gray slate roof, cream stone and stucco, ivy creeping along the windows. Two old poplars, just turning to color for the season, framed the arch under which they passed inside to a small foyer. It had the look of a place with happy ghosts: faded striped wallpaper, a warm stained-glass lantern hanging from above, little black-and-white-checkered mosaic tiles, cool and dusty underfoot—a place where many people had embraced.

"I know it's dirty in here," Kitty said. "Truth is, I only clean it twice a year. I like how you can see all four seasons of the year blowing around. Leaves from fall, mud from melted snow, dried-up flower petals and pollen. Come summer, I clean it up. Filth is bad, but this obsession with cleanliness, I don't buy it. Follow me. I live up top and rent out the bottom floors."

Up they went, ascending the sort of fragile spiraling staircase that made Vivienne marvel it had ever been new. A wooden sign hung on the front door: UNLESS YOU'RE GOD OR GEORGE STRAIT, TAKE OFF YOUR BOOTS! The apartment was a series of rambling rooms filled with the aromas of cinnamon and rose, stacked with hard-bound books and yellowing canvases, paved underfoot with richly patterned, faded rugs. In what of the floor the rugs exposed, Vivienne saw scuffed white-washed slats. Framed Texas flags, some worn, some bright, lined the main corridor. Kitty wound about her furniture as if navigating a maze she knew by heart. Vivienne followed, held by the pleasure of being led. They came to the main room; a stand of tall, slender windows opened to the garden below. Vivienne could see over the wall to Eddie's window, still occupied by Eddie.

Kitty opened her arms and said, "Here they are." Vivienne turned and beheld a wall like the walls she'd seen in the Louvre, climbing to heaven with paintings. But here, the pictures captured something different—Texas. Vivienne gazed at this tower of watercolors, quietly awed. The landscapes were too good for Bracken, she thought; they didn't have the sentiment he wanted, no cowboys, campfires, not even a bareback Comanche. Simply the land, shining out. The paintings hung by geography, creating the true color of Texas, spanning from the deep grass green of the coastal plains to the burnt mountains and orange sky of the Big Bend.

Vivienne looked at Kitty. "Don't sell them."

Kitty belted out a laugh. "Long way to go to tell me that."

Realizing what she'd said, Vivienne covered her mouth. "I'm sorry."

Kitty winked. "Come have a cup of coffee."

Her galley kitchen was simple and unadorned—white walls with white tile and coffee-stained grout. A small round table, laid with a patchwork tablecloth, overlooked the garden through a window of old warped glass. Kitty already had a pot going in a big American coffeemaker. She directed Vivienne to the table and a moment later placed before her a steaming mug. "I like to drink coffee in big portions. I had to order this machine online because I couldn't find one like it here. Everyone's too dainty. This coffee is roasted in the Panhandle; I order it."

The memory of sharing coffee in Preston's apartment brought the present moment alive. She hadn't let herself think of that cup of coffee in . . . she couldn't remember how long. The feeling she had that day with him was similar to what she felt now. Everything a first. Everything revealing itself.

Kitty joined her at the table, adjusting her backside onto the chair like a nesting bird. Then she raised her blue tin camping mug. "To your venture!" she said. Her yellow nails stuck out like paint drips on the blue of the mug. "Tell me more about it. I want to know everything."

Vivienne had the answer. "Well, Bracken Blank—BB Development—is the largest residential real estate development company in the greater Houston area. To pay homage to the state he loves and has helped develop, Bracken is creating a collection entirely of Texas art for his new building. And much of the collection will be on rotating view to the public, in the main lobby, so the city can share in this project."

She finished, feeling proud of her peppy delivery.

"You already told me that part on the phone. Why do you like my watercolors?"

"I love Wester's work. It's my favorite of Texas that I've seen. It's not so . . . macho. I've done a lot of research on this, and so much Texas art is macho."

"Macho? What makes art macho?"

"Cowboys everywhere all the time," Vivienne said. "Longhorns. The Alamo."

"And why don't you like macho artwork?"

"I guess . . ." She tried to articulate her reason, and only feelings came up—taut, wiry feelings. "I guess I think Texas isn't only a macho place. I think it's feminine too."

"What do you think is feminine about it?" Kitty sipped her coffee casually, as if she'd just asked Vivienne her favorite color.

"It's beautiful," Vivienne said uncertainly.

Kitty tucked her wisps of curls behind her ears; they drifted back up immediately. She settled for resting both hands flat atop her head. Vivienne thought the pose was macho, the pose of a man after a long day. "That's true," she said, and looked out the window.

Vivienne watched her watching the garden. White clouds lurked low and smooth across the sky, brightening Kitty's skin to photographic evenness; a cool draft seeped in from the window seam. "I'm watching Ulysses," Kitty said quietly, as though he could hear. "He's never going to catch that bird."

They watched as Ulysses, down in the garden, skulked along in his furry tuxedo and pounced at a sparrow. His effort was so overconceived that he landed past the bird and scattered the gravel, scaring a whole flock of sparrows out of some boxwood bushes. He stared with wide eyes as the sparrows flew off, then, realizing there was nothing left to pounce after, sprawled out in the very spot where he landed and began licking his belly.

Kitty chuckled. "He's got no talent for it, but he never gives up. I'm rooting for the guy. It's all he wants. He thinks he's a lion, so he can't understand why he hasn't gotten one yet. Maybe he'll get a fledgling in the spring."

Listening to her, Vivienne wished that Kitty was her aunt, and that she was Kitty's niece, and that this was how she'd spent every morning of her life. That bird would have a name. And Ulysses's ineptitude at hunting would be a running joke they shared. And Eddie would have watched her grow up and given her advice on men while they drank bottles of wine together after her bad dates. And she would know by heart the jagged line of rooftops on the horizon.

"Growing up in Beaumont, I had a pet duck," Kitty said. "I couldn't wait to get home from school so I could go outside and play with him. We'd look for bugs and root around under bricks together. Have you ever really known a duck?"

"No," Vivienne said. "But my ex-boyfriend hunted ducks."

"Well, there's that," Kitty said. "I eat plenty of duck living here. But they've got personality. Never underestimate a duck. Did you have pets growing up?"

"No," Vivienne said.

"Not even a fish?"

"Not even a fish."

Kitty's brow sank. "That's not good for a child. I'm sorry to hear that." She finished her coffee in a hurried, transitional way. "So you want to buy some watercolors for a big building in Houston? I haven't been to Houston in twenty years."

"Did you know Raleigh Wester?" Vivienne asked.

Kitty set aside her mug and rested her chin in her right palm. "First let me ask you: Why'd you tell me not to sell them?"

"I didn't mean that."

"Yes, you did," Kitty said. "I could tell you meant it."

"I don't know. I probably spoke too fast." She paused. "It's just that I don't think my boss would appreciate them. He doesn't get to know paintings or take the time to let himself feel anything about them. He just wants to see something that makes him feel Texan when he's leaving the bathroom."

Kitty smiled. "Your boss, the big real estate developer. Isn't the whole idea for the art to be shared in the lobby, and he gets a load of tax breaks in the meantime?"

Vivienne looked over her shoulder to the next room, at the paintings. "I think he wants the public to respect him as an art collector. He wants to be more than a guy who builds big houses."

"There are worse things, right? He wants to be better than he is. We all want that."

Bracken took shape in her mind like a person she knew once, a long time ago. "I'm not sure if he is anything more than a guy who builds big houses."

Kitty's face opened with delight. "So you've come here to tell me that you want my art, but you're not going to let me sell it."

"Not exactly, but kind of, yes."

Kitty pulled herself up and retrieved the pot of coffee. Her clothes made a soft rustle as she moved, reminding Vivienne of ballerinas in costume, passing one another in the electric hush of a dark theater wing.

"Well, this is all working out for the best," Kitty said, returning to her seat. "I would never sell them in a million years. I had no intention of selling them. I just wanted to meet you."

Vivienne's heart nearly stopped. "Me?"

"Don't be nervous," Kitty said, reaching out. "You sounded lovely and curious and a bit confused on the phone, and I think you reminded me of myself. Old people get selfish like that. A young woman from Houston reading a pleasant little script? You didn't pull off the script, so you made me curious. I never pulled off the script."

"We flew to Paris to buy the paintings."

"People always have other reasons for coming to Paris," Kitty said. "You didn't come to Paris to buy my paintings."

"I wrote that script."

"Do you believe it?"

Vivienne turned her eyes to the garden. Ulysses and Eddie were out of sight. "I believed it when I wrote it. Bracken is coming here tomorrow if this meeting goes well."

"I have plenty for him to see. I have a collection of flags. Some great cowboy prints. I have way too much. He won't miss any paintings."

"Are you still coming to dinner tonight?"

"Am I still invited?"

Vivienne nodded. "Bracken will probably like old Texas flags better anyway."

Kitty said, "You know, I was pretty like you. I personally think being born pretty in Texas is a burden you have to climb out from under. Look at you"—she took up a section of Vivienne's hair—"a woman, but still young, right in that place when you don't realize what you know. I was like that. Beaumont is a lot smaller than Houston, so you can imagine. You think you're working for the real estate developer, because that's what you're supposed to do, but you're really working for yourself. I used to need permission to do everything."

"I am doing this for myself."

Kitty smiled. "Put your hands here," she said, placing her hands over her own belly below her navel. "Don't press, just rest your hands here."

Vivienne followed. Her body felt warm and taut and small.

"Make your plans from here," Kitty said. "I realized at some point that I could leave Beaumont and survive. But it was only by the grace of God that I figured it out and did what I needed to do. If you're born into a world where you don't belong, you don't have a choice. You have to find a way out. In my case, I could paint."

"Is that why you decided to collect?"

"These are my paintings," Kitty said, almost as an aside. "I paint under a false name. It keeps my life simple."

Vivienne thought she'd misheard. "These are your paintings?"

"Yep."

Vivienne stood and went to the paintings. "You're Raleigh Wester? I thought you inherited oil money and became a collector."

Kitty followed after. "When people think you're enigmatic, they invent stories about you. I inherited some money from my grampa, but there wasn't much left. It kept me on my feet in Texas, but I drank a lot of it away, so I was mostly off my feet. I knew I had to get better, so I took what was left and came here and made my way."

"You painted all these?"

Kitty smiled. "Wisdom is a woman."

"Why do you keep it a secret?"

"An open secret. I'm fine with people knowing, but I don't broadcast it." She went close to one of the paintings, a green picture of the lazy Frio River, a fluffy bald cypress in the foreground. "I didn't keep it secret at first, but once people started liking my paintings, I realized I wanted more privacy. In France, artists are still celebrities. People weren't stopping me in the street over watercolor pictures, but it was still too much hoopla in the art circles. Interviews, galas, parties, dresses. I didn't care, and I didn't want them calling me. I remember thinking at first how flattering it was. But then it sucked all the life out of me, and I couldn't paint. You can't be a reactionary and cut off the people who care about what you do, but there are ways of skirting around it peaceably. And the people who knew me before I changed my working name—they respected that." She paused. "This is a really old one. I painted it when I first got here. I was so homesick."

"Do you have *Band of Charging Comanches*? I keep a copy of it by my desk."

"Oh, Cynthia Ann Parker," Kitty said. "The Comanches called her 'Naduah,' meaning 'someone found.' I gave that painting to Anthony's sister a few years back. I don't know even know how it ended up in the catalogs. Some photographer must have come over and taken pictures."

"Who's Anthony?" Vivienne asked.

Kitty's lips edged up, coaxing two dimples to her cheeks. "Anthony is my husband." She hurried over to an old wall piano and picked a frame off the top. "This is Anthony."

Vivienne saw a youngish Kitty, her hair tied up in a bandanna, sitting in a sailboat beside a shaggy-haired man wearing round glasses. Kitty was red-lipped and smiling, holding the rudder; both were wearing shorts and white shirts, Kitty's tied up around her midriff. The picture had that muddy, faded sixties color palette, which seemed to Vivienne the way everything must have looked back then. He was smiling, holding Kitty firmly around the shoulder. They looked giddy and dorky, delighted by the novelty of a boat, and pure.

"I always prayed I'd go before him."

Vivienne didn't know what to say. What Kitty said frightened her.

Kitty saw her face and said, "There's nothing to be scared about. I'm alone, but I don't feel so alone. We were fortunate. It's scary to be that in love. It's a tightrope, loving yourself and another at the same time. But we did it. I'm still proud of us." She set the frame back on the piano.

It was too hard to pretend he wasn't in Paris. Even the splendor of the Ritz couldn't diminish the acuity of Preston, out there in the city somewhere. After all the silent self-assurances that she had a million other reasons for coming here, her heart looked straight upon the fact that she ached to see him and that here, in Kitty's sitting room, in his mysterious proximity, she felt so strong and glad and yet hurt afresh. She was still so mad at him.

Kitty went to the window and whistled for Ulysses. In a moment he was galloping upstairs, announcing himself with a series of unruly meows. "Hush," Kitty said, picking him up and handing him to Vivienne. "He's not the real thing, but he gives the best hugs."

He had some weight. Vivienne propped him up on her shoulder and squeezed. He smelled like rock dust and felt like a very small, soft water bed.

Kitty was petting his long black back; he had his purr turned up high. He rubbed his cheek against Vivienne's. "This guy used to squirm like all hell whenever I tried to give him love," Kitty said. "And now look at him."

V

VIVIENNE TOOK TIMMY TO SEE COROT'S PAINTING OF Orpheus leading Eurydice out of the underworld. It was the second time she'd gone to see it. She remembered her young self as Eurydice, escaping from Orpheus's gaze, but realized she now related most to Orpheus, holding his lute high. Not Eurydice, who seemed shy and dazed, but Orpheus, fighting to look ahead.

Timmy was a great museum companion. In her short time in the far periphery of the "art world," Vivienne had learned that people had a tendency to be pretentious about art. But Timmy wasn't pretentious about anything, especially art, so when he commented on a picture, he commented with the curious perspective of a child. He made up a story for each painting he liked, invented funny names for the sitters in portraits, and bought postcards of all his favorites at the gift shop. They split the cost of a "Baby's First French" CD set for Waverly and Clay and stopped at a boulangerie on their way back to the hotel. They agreed not to tell anyone they'd stopped for sweets before dinner. Vivienne told Timmy about her new favorite person in the world, Kitty Crawford.

The sun was setting over the Tuileries. Vivienne's eyes followed the garden, the geometry of dark hedges, the bronze statues of coy women hiding among them. They came into the great octagon of the Place de la Concorde, late light pouring across crowds and cars and tour buses, Cleopatra's obelisk cutting a long blade of shadow through the scene.

"This was where they chopped all the rich people's heads off," Timmy said. He ran his finger across his throat matter-of-factly.

"How do you know that?" Vivienne said.

"I read it," Timmy said. "In a biography of Ben Franklin."

"I've never met anyone who loves the founding fathers as much as you."

Timmy's eyes glazed over a little. His cheeks pinked in the light. Maybe he looked like a young Ben Franklin.

"Let's take a picture," Vivienne said. She held out her phone, Timmy tipped his head down and sideways so that his face was perpendicular to hers, and they both made big toothy smiles.

They kept walking. The wind hit their faces straight on.

Just as they were crossing out, Vivienne glanced over her shoulder and noticed Karlie, sitting beside Bracken on the lip of the tiered fountain about fifty feet away. She was hugging a furry vest over her chest. Certain they had seen her, Vivienne was raising her arm to wave when Karlie suddenly stood and turned her back to them.

Timmy was musing on the unfortunate fact that Ernest Hemingway and Ben Franklin never had the chance to meet, because they would have made great friends.

Vivienne interrupted him. "Did you see—" But something in the deliberateness of Karlie's body language stopped her. Maybe Karlie didn't want to talk to Timmy? That happened often. Or were they planning a surprise for Waverly? Could they be talking about her?

Before they turned off to the hotel, Vivienne glanced back again. The wind whipped her hair over her eyes. Through its soft screen, she saw Bracken, walking away from the fountain, and Karlie, looking directly at her.

Later, in the room, Vivienne was sitting on a silk ottoman, listening to Karlie and turning a gold bracelet around her wrist.

"The marketing people at Bloomie's are giving me new baking supplies, a cute mixer and everything, if I promote their line of baking products on my blog," Karlie said. She was leaning in close to the mirror, painting her eyes with wet black liner. She stepped back and blinked at herself. "Isn't that amazing?"

"That's great," Vivienne said. "But you don't bake."

"It doesn't matter. It shows that my blog is, like, a vehicle. I'll get more ads now." She grabbed a tissue and defiantly blotted her lipstick. "I want to look good tonight."

"Why?" Vivienne scooted back on the ottoman and stretched to touch her toes.

"Because Preston is coming."

In an effort to conceal her reaction from Karlie, she got up and went into the toilet closet and pretended to go to the bathroom. "Preston?" she called out, realizing it had been a long time since she'd said his name. "I thought you didn't like him. Didn't you tell me to stay away from him at Waverly's wedding?"

"I still think it's fun," Karlie said. "Tim's been such a drag. And now it's like I have an audience. It's no fun dressing up if you don't have an audience."

Vivienne folded over and pressed her forehead to her knees. She would get through this, she had to. A few moments later, when she emerged, Karlie told her about running into him, until Vivienne had the impression that they'd all talked for hours over ice cream and tiny espressos.

"What were you doing with Bracken earlier?" Vivienne said. She didn't want to hear about Preston anymore, not from Karlie. "I was walking with Tim, and I saw you sitting by the fountain."

Karlie was squeezed tight into a red sequined dress, like a fifties-era secretary, her hair wound up into a high bun, which she held atop her head in the way of a villager carrying water. "Why didn't y'all come say hi?"

"I was about to wave," Vivienne said, "but then you turned around. I thought you saw me."

"Huh," she said, and whirled back to the mirror.

Vivienne was beginning to feel self-conscious under Karlie's strange confidence. She went to the mirror and smoothed her hands over her black gown. The neckline plunged, narrowly enough to remain elegant, and the dress held her hips firmly, loosening around her legs so she could move comfortably. It was an old dress, but it still fit like new.

Vivienne turned her back to the mirror and adjusted the cross straps over her shoulders.

Karlie watched, expressionless. Then her phone buzzed. A text from Waverly: Everyone was waiting in the lobby. Patting at her bun, she snapped into the mirror, "Ready?"

VI

PRESTON WORE A SUIT AND TIE—THE ONLY SUIT HE owned, the one he wore to Waverly and Clay's wedding, which he hadn't had dry-cleaned since. As he dressed, he caught a whiff of chlorine on the jacket collar.

He was brimming with a sense of alignment; it all made sense, Vivienne being in Paris now. He'd slept fitfully, playing things over. He wanted another chance, but his stomach lurched at the thought of Karlie and Vivienne at the same table. How would he get Vivienne alone?

When he set the time to visit Vivienne the day after the wedding, to pitch Paris to her again, he'd intended to keep it. But as the hour neared, he decided he'd been wrong. He kept thinking of that trio of men and the easy and terrible certainty with which they'd spoken of her and presumed her needs. Maybe they did know her better. They spent more time with her. There was so much he didn't know about Vivienne, an entire dimension of her life, a much larger dimension. She couldn't say yes because she'd promised her life to another, altogether different idea; the fact that she'd even accepted the job from Bracken said it all. Maybe she really did need a man in a bolo tie. And he didn't want to be some random adventure, her experiment in independence. Better to cut it off. So he'd followed his injured ego, and he left for Paris.

But time had worn away the pride, and over the last twelve months he'd very gradually realized his huge error. All the girls, all the work, all the brainy explanations for why he shouldn't want her, did little to dampen what was now striking him as his actual feelings. By leaving, he'd made her into the girl those men imagined she was. But her character couldn't be decided by them or by him or by anyone but her, and so in leaving he'd cut out Vivienne the real person, who'd wrapped herself in his grandmother's quilt, and who'd slept on his shoulder in the sun, and who'd braved the swimming pool in her underwear. Shame was the dark hand over his eyes all these months. And now shame made him stand still a moment in the street. A year was a real span of time—people change in a year. Would she be the same? Was he the same? The chlorine on his collar—it smelled just the same.

The restaurant was intimate and candlelit, tinkling with the chime of silver on porcelain and thick with muted French talk, a place where leaders of nations dined in dark corners. He was the first person there, so he went to the bar and ordered a sixteen-euro beer and waited. A few minutes later, he heard them. A big, crowd-parting loud. The hearty noise of Texans arriving. Preston swallowed his beer in anticipation. The moment he saw them he felt their full impact. The restaurant raised its eyes; it was not accustomed to gleaming bands of Texans.

Sissy and Bracken led the way—Sissy wrapped in white fur, and Bracken clean shaven and barrel-chested in a navy-blue suit and bright white shirt, no tie. Then came Clay and Waverly, the prom king and queen, holding hands. Behind them, Karlie in lipstick red, her cleavage a superabundance of flesh and shine, and Timmy, dressed for a fraternity party, in khaki slacks and pastel-pink button-down and plaid tie. They made a blaring, powerful ensemble. He waited for Vivienne.

She came in last, in a black wrap coat, her long hair straight and loose. She untied the coat and tranquilly handed it to the host. The host thanked her, as if her beauty alone justified service. Preston now beheld her in full. She wore a long black dress that, for a moment, made him forget his own name. He recalled instantly the warm shape of her body under his hands, and his blood surged with deep, nervous life.

She saw him and approached, her face a little raised and suspended, as if she was holding her breath. She said hello and gave him a very formal hug. Her body was hard, just perceptibly shaking.

She smelled as he remembered—floral and dulcet, yet organic, suffused with something that couldn't have come from a bottle. Then she walked away without him, before he'd said a word. Preston was dumbfounded.

A hostess roused his attention. "Monsieur—the party ez here?"

The dinner was in a private room, lit with dim medieval wall sconces. A line of tall candles flickered down the length of the table. The scene was dark and cellarish, despite the presence of a large window affording a view of the Seine and the Île Saint-Louis.

They overwhelmed him, calling his name, slapping his back. Clay clearly wanted to make him comfortable and directed him to sit at his side, diagonally across from Vivienne, in spite of Karlie's insistence that he sit beside her. Timmy came around the table and gave him a hug, so painful to Preston that he hugged Timmy too hard in return, like a brother. He felt shot through with the dread of having made a mistake; he had no business being here. Vivienne watched it all unfold and turned her eyes away the instant he tried to meet hers.

He observed her. She laughed at every turn in the conversation that called for laughter, smiled along to the telling of stories she must have already heard. When he sensed the others were engrossed, he leaned across the table and said, "How are you?"

She received the question as one might an interrogative from a stranger at a crowded party, an overture neither solicited nor unexpected. "Great," she said. "It's so beautiful here. How are you?"

Preston responded in kind. "I'm great too."

And she kept talking with Waverly.

He noted the seamlessness of her participation with the group. She hadn't changed; if anything she looked younger, and this only added to the sense of ease she projected by her gentle mannerisms and polished exterior. The overall impression was pride. She was proud, and she was Vivienne in every way he recalled except for some abstraction he struggled to articulate, a fine patina over her surface. Was she glossing over the effort more than usual? Or had she just hardened to him? He tried to reconcile her with his vision of the woman who might have been here with him all along.

He dulled his nerves with many glasses of wine and downed several oysters drizzled in lime juice and sprinkled with fresh mint, which he selected from a three-tiered silver tray adorned with mini-gargoyle ice sculptures and endive garnish.

"They say Michael Dukakis lost the '88 election because he suggested American farmers grow endive," he remarked. "The public thought it was too French."

This got a laugh from Clay and a smirk from Bracken, who raised one arm and snapped his fingers. "Can we get some of those French cheeses over here?"

Bracken seemed to be listening to everyone's conversations at once, his eyes narrowed in satisfaction. Who would he be without his money? Preston wondered.

Preston's father always told him that millionaires forget who they were without money, or they grow up never knowing. Everything is easy; the ego expands like bacteria in a petri dish. "Those are things broke people tell themselves to feel better," Preston usually replied. Yet there was something to it, he thought now. Bracken was horribly magnetic. He was like a smooth pillar, reinforced by so many layers of cement and plaster that it was hard to know what the pillar contained. But he had nerve. Maybe if I had nerve, Preston thought, I'd have Vivienne.

An older woman came in then—whooshed in—her silky caftan following on its own time. Her hair was a mess of short curls, and she held a black embroidered wrap around her shoulders. Preston took her to be the "artist."

Bracken stood bigly, chin high.

"You must be the big guns," Kitty said.

He thrust out his hand. "I guess you could say that."

"Well, don't be greasy with me," she said to him. "I'm from Beaumont."

Sissy barked out a laugh the likes of which probably hadn't been heard in Paris since Ann Richards toured the city in the early nineties. And then they all were best friends—this, Preston noticed, to the bewilderment of the waitstaff, who slunk in and out like lab assistants. Vivienne lit up when the whooshy older woman entered, hugging her, leading her to the seat at her side, smiling. Preston could hardly pry his eyes off her. By the time he'd finished his filet of grouper, he was having fun, Vivienne's smile his anchor. She'd hardly acknowledged him, but he wasn't thinking about that now. He didn't need or even want her attention. It was seeing her happy: It made him happy to see her happy. He could feel Karlie's eyes on him, but he pretended not to notice. Then he inadvertently caught a glimpse of her cleavage, and she noticed. He immediately glanced at Vivienne to make sure she hadn't seen, and she was looking right at him.

The waiters delivered several trays of pungent cheese. Bracken smeared some Roquefort on an apple slice and turned the conversation to Kitty. Preston liked Kitty. She was real, no bullshit.

"How many paintings you got?" Bracken asked her, lighting a cigar. "Boys, who else wants a cigar?"

"I'll take one," Kitty said.

"Damn right," Bracken said. "Now, how many you got?"

Kitty took a cigar; both began biting and lighting at the things. "I have hundreds," she said.

"Did you ever meet this Wester painter? What was he like? A real cowboy? A son of a gun? Is he still alive? I wanna be proud to have these pictures on my walls. They're gonna represent the company."

Sissy was nodding. "What kind of investment will they be? Will they go up in value? I think they should be something that draws people in, makes them want to be better Texans."

Kitty puffed her cigar. "Better Texans," she echoed. "That's an abstract goal."

Preston, rather drunk, was deeply enjoying this exchange. He felt privy to the sort of conversations that occurred within rooms he typically didn't enter.

Bracken continued: "This whole art thing is new to me. What I want is a collection of pictures that will reflect the majesty of Texas and leave a legacy of grit and might for BB Development." He made a fist; maybe he was rather drunk too. "I want a collection that's gonna make a statement that Texas is the best place in the world and that BB Development is the best company in Houston."

"How funny that that intention took you to France!" Kitty exclaimed.

Bracken leaned in, straight-faced. "Not funny at all—I'd go to Timbuktu. And people all over the world love Texas. You're one of them. Name your price."

"Well, I'm a Texan," Kitty said. "Loving Texas if you're born there is more complex than if you love it from afar, with all the notions about riding horses to school."

"That's true," Preston said. Everyone turned and looked at him. Kitty nodded and pointed at him slyly.

Bracken said, "I often rode horses to school. I rode 'em so my kids wouldn't have to."

Sissy rolled her eyes. "Here we go with the horses to school."

"Riding a horse to school sounds fun," Waverly said. "We should have done that."

"It's not fun if it's the only option," Bracken said.

"Well, we're all Texans here!" Sissy said. "Here's to that!"

Karlie raised her glass. "Hell yeah!"

Kitty seemed not to hear this toast and continued: "You say you'd go to Timbuktu, but you haven't even come to the fifth arrondissement. And you've got to keep in mind that they're watercolors. In terms of leaving a big fancy legacy, watercolors don't pack the same punch as oil."

"I don't need to see 'em as much as I need an expert opinion. My opinion on them doesn't matter so much as the artist's reputation and the market."

"But that's always changing," Kitty said. "You have to connect with the painting above all."

"What did you think of them, Vivienne?" Bracken said.

Vivienne looked startled. "To be honest, I thought they were beautiful but not for you." Now everyone looked at her. "They photograph well, but they're too soft. I think you'd love her memorabilia, though. She has original Alamo-era flags. We should also look into that gallery in the sixth with the horse photography before we leave."

Bracken bit the end of his cigar. He turned a leery eye on Kitty. "So what am I winin'-and-dinin' you for?"

"Actually the question is, what am *I* doing winin'-and-dinin' *with* you?"

Bracken reached over and patted Kitty on the back. "We're gonna be good friends. I'll take the flags." He sat back, satisfied with his performance—he seemed to be high off making a deal. How many artists had paid the rent because of men who got high off making deals? But the high had a brief flowering, for Bracken's eyes were already glazed with a lost wine-look, as if he didn't know what to do now that the business was concluded and there was still dinner to finish.

A lull fell upon the table, and Preston heard Sissy say to Kitty, "Tell me how you got the name Kitty, and I'll tell you how I got the name Sissy."

Chatter resumed. Karlie got up and instructed Clay to trade chairs with her.

In the many months that had elapsed since his Great Mistake, it had become clear to Preston that he'd had sex with Karlie Nettle not only because his horniness had damaged his reason (his first explanation to himself) but also to punish her for the fact that she embodied everything he looked down upon as tedious and inferior and had been forced to endure his entire young life. But this rationale had only poisoned him and turned his resentment inward. So then he had sex with her one more time, to punish himself. He'd given all his anger to Karlie, and she'd loved it. She wanted more. They were both so bent on self-destruction that the sex, those two times it happened, was brief and ferocious.

But where Preston knew he was being self-destructive and couldn't stand it, Karlie was either impervious or oblivious. She was getting off on deceiving her husband, or not thinking of her husband at all, while Preston battled a monster of guilt. He felt as if he'd stepped onto the road where a man goes after plumbing too deeply into the potential darkness of his own psyche. He'd seen it, acknowledged it, and he chose to turn around. He wanted to be better. Awareness had snapped him back, and it lashed at him now, in warning, as Karlie discreetly squeezed his thigh under the table.

"What is it like living here? Do you step in dog shit every day?" she whispered into his shoulder.

He refused to look at her cleavage. "Every day," he said.

She leaned in; her breasts were like two huge warm buttered rolls. "What are you up to tomorrow?"

Preston caught Bracken's eye—a strange eye. Preston had a thought: If he fell for the warm buttered rolls, then surely Bracken Blank could too. Bracken was one of those guys who always had to uphold. Upholders crumble quickest and into smaller pieces. Preston had the whole novel written in his mind when it occurred to him that maybe everyone knew about Karlie and him.

Suddenly he felt shame hot on his face, a guttural sense of exposure.

Karlie cleared her throat. "Viv took my husband to a museum today. Maybe you and I could go somewhere tomorrow?"

Preston blended his voice into the surrounding prattle. "Stop," he said.

Karlie glared at him a moment, then slipped back to her seat, tapping Clay to move. Immediately, she picked up her phone and began thumbing it close to her face.

Preston noticed Kitty watching him. Concerned, discouraged—whatever she had seen from the bleachers, she didn't like it.

"Bring on some of those French pastries," Bracken yelled at one of the waiters, a man of seemingly infinite patience. "I flew all the way from Texas; I want some real French pastries."

Kitty flattened her palms on the table and stood. "No sugar for me. I'm off."

Bracken put up a hand. "You're not leavin' before we eat some French pastries."

Sissy nodded. "You can't leave before dessert."

"Sorry, but it's late for me," she said. "I've gotta go home and feed my cat."

Vivienne rose. Kitty hugged her tight around the shoulders.

"Kitty's gotta go feed her kitty cat," Bracken hooted.

"Yes I do, sir," Kitty said, almost gravely. "Thank you very much for dinner."

All the while, Karlie sat plugging at her phone, Timmy at her side.

Preston felt exhausted. Too much to keep track of. Too many feelings. Too many motives.

Once Kitty had gone, Vivienne seemed less relaxed. They still hadn't spoken. He just needed to get up and sit beside her and talk to her, but he couldn't muster it.

He went outside to smoke a cigarette and get some air, but his hands were cold and the smoke made him queasy. He didn't want to smoke anymore. Smoking hadn't made him feel even a little French, it just made him feel dumb that he'd allowed himself to start. Rain was moving in. The air was heavy and damp. He lingered under the red awning. The river moved slowly; the cobblestones shone. Suddenly Karlie pushed out the door.

"What was that back there?" she said, catching his arm. She pulled him around the corner onto a darker side street. Her eyes were way too wide. " 'Stop'?"

"You know what I mean," he said. "Don't point your boobs at me."

She laughed meanly. "Why, do you like them?"

"No," he said. "I don't."

She paused, curling her lip. "Really, Preston?"

"I'm not going to touch you again, ever," he said. He could hardly believe the words coming out of his mouth. He'd never been so blunt with her.

She stepped closer. He felt physically cornered against the stone wall; her cleavage was within an inch of pressing against his chest. "Well," she said, "you're not going to *get* to touch me again, ever."

"Good," he said. "Now please back off."

She withdrew, wobbling on her stilettos. "I hate you," she said.

"That's fine."

"I really hate you."

"That's fine too," he said. "I'm going inside."

And in an instant, tears flooded her eyes and she drooped, pressing her hands over her face. Her bare arms were freckled and covered in goosebumps.

"Karlie," Preston said, entreatingly but also impatiently. "Come on."

"Everything is so messed up," she cried. "I'm so unhappy. I can't leave Timmy. I'm so trapped."

Preston scratched the back of his neck. This was not good. "Please stop, Karlie. There are a lot of people inside."

She didn't seem to hear and kept sobbing and wiping her eyes. "I thought you'd still want me."

"I don't think I ever wanted you," he said. "You're married."

"But Timmy is so boring."

"Then leave him. If that's how you feel about him, he'd probably appreciate it."

Suddenly her entire voice lifted and lunged at him. "Why do you think I came on this trip? I don't give a shit about Paris."

Preston raised his hands. "I'm not going to answer that. Because there's no way it was because of me."

Her eyes flashed with rage. "Well, I wasn't gonna let *Vivienne*"—she mocked her name—"come out here on her own and see you."

The dark street seemed to have a heartbeat: a red, furious throb. "You're telling me you flew across the world to keep Vivienne from being alone with me? That's beyond fucked up."

She dropped her head. "I don't know why I'm here." Her voice collapsed into a suppressed wail. "I could sleep with Bracken if I wanted to."

Preston didn't want to know any of this. He was aware of the divide between the painted world of wine and oysters and the thorny, moonless life beneath, but when confronted with it, he couldn't believe how stark the divide really was. "Karlie, that would be an insane thing to do. Don't do that. Don't even think about that."

"You're no better than Bracken," she cried. "I'm sure Bracken would prefer Vivienne too."

"You need to stop."

"I want you to make me stop," she said, reaching for him.

He stepped back. He couldn't stand to watch a woman cry, but he didn't move. She wiped mascara off her cheeks and fell against the wall at her back; her white figure in the red dress was like the bright center of a flame.

"We need to go back inside," he said.

She rubbed her eyes, sniffled. "Do you love Vivienne?"

"Stop, Karlie," he said.

"You do, don't you?" she said. "I know you do."

"You don't know much about anything."

"I told her to stay away from you. I know you went off with her at Waverly and Clay's wedding, and I told her when I saw her that you're a creep who sleeps with married women."

Preston howled a laugh of desperation at the universe, envisioning Vivienne hearing this warning only minutes after they'd been together. But Karlie seemed to have no idea anything had happened between them. Vivienne, he realized, hadn't told.

"It's not Vivienne's fault that I don't want to be with you," he said. "I never wanted to be with you. I regret what we did."

"I don't want to be with you either," she said. "You're a spineless coward."

"We're both spineless cowards, Karlie," he said. "Let's just leave it at that."

Her eyes went somewhere far away again, somewhere Preston didn't envy. She pressed her palms to her eye sockets. "Timmy is content with sitting in the same chair and drinking the same gross piss beer every night of his useless life."

"Then why did you marry him?"

He'd grazed the ineffable: To answer this question, Karlie would need to stare into the sun. "I don't remember. I thought I had to," she muttered.

He took her by the shoulders and she went limp. Her eyes were puffy, but her face looked alive, washed of all that stuff now staining the backs of her hands. Her small glittery silver purse hung still from her shoulder. He wanted to coax the frightened animal out of her, wanted to help her see, but the certainty that he could not accomplish this for Karlie rendered him helpless.

"I'll go first," he said.

Inside, Vivienne was standing, slipping her arms into her coat. He helped her with it, mumbling something about the wine. He knew his eyes were pleading, asking for a break, a crack in the door, just enough to say anything that wasn't a banality.

She thanked him.

"Do you want to take a walk?" he said. "Walk off some of the food?"

If she was surprised, she concealed it. "No thanks."

"Just a short walk?"

She turned away.

As Bracken and Sissy settled the bill, the rest of the group went outside and made a loose, full-bellied circle. Karlie emerged renewed, chin up, any trace of emotion chillingly erased, and snuggled up to Timmy. "I think we should all go to the hot-air balloon tomorrow," she said.

"Or Chart-res," Waverly said, tracing her budding belly. "It's supposed to be the most beautiful church in France."

"Unless Vivienne has plans already?" Karlie said. "Who are you running around with tomorrow?"

"The hot-air balloon or Chartres sounds great," Vivienne replied—to Preston's ears, too earnestly.

"But I mean," Karlie said, "today it was Tim, tomorrow Clay?"

Clay came to the rescue with his usual levity. "Yeah, Viv and I have a whole day planned." He turned to Waverly. "We were going to invite you, babe, but we thought you'd rather not walk all day."

Waverly smiled. "My ankles are fat."

"Seriously, though," Karlie said. With those words—"seriously, though"—all went quiet, as if everything prior had been unserious. "I'm not comfortable with the way you've been hanging out with my husband without even telling me what you're doing. I saw y'all today taking pictures together. I think it's totally inappropriate." She tucked the hood of her white coat over her head and crossed her arms. Timmy paled.

Preston stood, suppressing the urge to push Karlie into the river, shake Timmy by the collar, give Clay a high five, toss Vivienne in the air in an elaborate bit of ballet, and then skip off down the quay, singing in the rain.

"Oh, please, Kar," Waverly said.

Karlie persisted, slitting Waverly's effort with razor precision. "I mean, I woke up this morning and you both weren't there. And then I see you hugging in the square. Are you really that girl, Vivienne?"

Clay caught Preston's eye.

"I know you and Tim have always been friends or whatever"—she spoke as if he wasn't there—"but you're crossing the line." Timmy had slowly migrated behind Karlie. It started to drizzle. Everyone shrank.

Vivienne looked sternly at Karlie, still listening.

"You need to get your own room," Karlie said, her voice a gavel. "I don't trust you."

Clay raised his voice a notch. "Come on, Karlie—you're drunk."

Vivienne kept her eyes on Karlie but raised a hand to quiet Clay. She looked shocked but upright, as if the blow had made her stand taller. "No, it's okay," she said finally. "You're right, I should have told you. I didn't want to wake you this morning, but I should have. Actually, I was thinking of going to Kitty's tonight anyway. I still have more to see at her apartment. Preston was going to walk me to the Metro."

"What?" Waverly said. "What about your things?"

"I'll get them tomorrow."

"If you were thinking of going back with Kitty, then why didn't you leave with her?" Karlie said. "You're telling us you're going to show up at her door right now and stay there? I highly doubt that's where you're staying. To be honest, I'm still confused how you ever got this job collecting art to begin with." She paused, then added with viperous emphasis, "I wouldn't put anything past you, Vivienne. Let's be real, you're like the office escort at Bracken's, and now you're going home with Preston."

Vivienne blinked at Karlie, disbelieving. The color drained from her cheeks, and the first thing she did, Preston noticed, was look to him—not at him, but *to* him.

"What's going on here?" Waverly said. "Why would you say that, Kar? That's not true—"

Vivienne turned calmly to Waverly. "It's better if I stay at Kitty's. There's still a lot to see there. This works out better."

"That's right," Bracken said, just then pushing out the door to join the circle, Sissy on his arm. "Dig through the place and bring me back every flag she's got."

Vivienne went to hug Waverly. Uncomfortable good nights began all around. Bracken spoke in oblivious, overcompensatory tones about the success of the evening, while Karlie and Timmy hung back. Promises of text messages were made for the following day, and then Vivienne said, "I'm going this way," and walked in the opposite direction from the hotel. Preston followed.

Around the next corner, she abruptly ducked out of the drizzle into a dim vestibule. "Where does Kitty live?" Preston asked.

"The fifth."

"That's the other way," he said, realizing as he spoke that it was a fiction. "I have a couch at my apartment." Horns beeped somewhere. French-sounding laughter. Vivienne was running her hands over her hair, slicking the mist over her scalp, breathing from her mouth.

"My face is hot," she said, tapping at her cheeks

"Are you okay?" Preston asked.

She looked right at him. "I feel like none of this is mine," she said, and stepped out from the corner. The others were nearing the far end of the street, beneath a canopy of black umbrellas. She walked off. Preston followed again.

"Wait!" Vivienne called.

Preston saw Karlie's eyes draw to a foul impatience. A confused pall took over as everyone waited for Vivienne to justify herself.

She faced Bracken. "I need to quit this job. I can't do it."

Bracken coughed. "What's that?"

"I need to quit."

"We've all had a lot to drink," Bracken said. "Whatever drama's going on here, we can talk about it in Houston."

"What are you doing, Viv?" Waverly said.

Karlie sighed. "This is really disrespectful to the Blanks."

For a moment, Vivienne was silent, everyone watching her.

Then Clay blurted, "Shut up, Karlie," his normally melodic voice a thunderbolt. "I don't want to hear you anymore." He pointed at her, his hand poised to launch a dart. "Remember that I've always seen through you. Always."

And then everything seemed to sink. Timmy continued to say nothing, while Karlie, silenced, absorbed Clay's words. A couple wove by, arm in arm, quickening their step. Sissy went to her daughter, her eyes charging round. "Good Lord," she mumbled, as the two huddled beneath her umbrella.

By now Vivienne's coat was damp, the wool heavy on her shoulders. Her hair frizzed up in small tendrils from her part. She looked very young and tired. Preston loved her, loved her with a humbling wordless intensity.

Waverly persisted, "What's going on? Is this because of him?" She threw Preston a vicious glare, catching him by surprise.

"No," Vivienne said. "I needed to tell you now, so there wasn't confusion at home."

Amid the group, Bracken stood like a tent pole, still and encircled, his eyes calm, his mouth hung in a chiseled, deliberating frown. "And do you wanna provide any reason for this sudden change?" he said evenly. "I don't see why we hafta stand here in the rain for your vanity show. You want to quit the job I gave you, you tell me in my office like a professional, not like a goddamn rodeo queen."

"If she wants to quit the job, let her quit the job," Clay said, speaking over Bracken. "Everyone leave her alone. Let's go."

"I don't feel like I can stay in this job and respect myself at the same time," Vivienne said, as evenly as Bracken. "That's my reason."

Bracken laughed. "Cally the women's libber! Convenient she realizes this on the free trip to France!"

Sissy balked. "Have you lost your mind, Vivienne?"

Vivienne just looked at her with a fierce and sad sincerity. Waverly's eyes cut between her two friends, landing sharply on Karlie.

Bracken shook the change in his pockets. "Plentya other girls who want it."

Suddenly an angry French voice, a woman's, rang from the windows above. "PEOPLE ARE SLEEPING, AMERICANS!"

Bracken spit. "Let's go, everybody," he said, then hollered up to the window, "God bless Texas!"

* * *

SHE WALKED FAST. Preston kept following her without knowing where they were going, until after two blocks she whipped around and put up her hand. "Stop following me."

He spoke gently. "I want to make sure you get to where you're going."

"What time is it?"

He glanced at his phone. "Ten to midnight."

"I need to pick up my stuff from the hotel in the morning," she said.

"You can stay with me."

"Please don't be accommodating," she said. "I don't know why you followed me."

"You told them I was walking you to the Metro."

"I didn't mean it," she said. "What was I supposed to say?"

"I didn't want you to run off alone."

"Don't talk to me like that," she said. "So meek and sympathetic. Why were you even there tonight? You just show up here, at Bracken's dinner party? Are you insane?"

"Clay invited me. I wanted to—"

"Don't say you wanted to see me, if that's what you were going to say; do not say it."

Preston froze. That was exactly what he was going to say. "I'm sorry," he said. She didn't respond. She started walking again, faster.

He was on her heels. "I should have called you. I think about it all the time."

"Okay, so now we're going to talk about this," she said.

She spoke with such a curt finality that Preston felt squelched. "You said no, Vivienne," he said. "You said you didn't want to go to Paris."

She stopped, breathing hard. "You said you were coming over and you never showed up. I waited for you."

He looked down the long street, cross-lit by cozy, dark intersections. By its narrowness, he could tell this was an old neighborhood—quiet, the streets clean, the sort of neighborhood that power-washed its buildings. He didn't say anything. He stood feeling and looking very serious.

She opened her purse and took a small piece of folded yellow paper from her wallet. Preston noticed a faded picture of a little girl in the plastic window—Vivienne? But he didn't say anything. "The housekeeper found it by the pool. I meant to give it to you when you came over . . ."

They faced each other in silence. That awful note, this whole time.

"Take it," she said. "I don't want it. I never wanted it."

He took it. "It was a horrible mistake," he said.

He watched as her eyes fought, and lost, a gentle march of tears. "So you were with her," she said, wiping her eyes. "I never read it. I only saw the signature and then I never opened it again. I kept thinking I should give you benefit of the doubt."

He hung his head. If it had happened to him, he would have read it. "It had nothing to do with you. It was months before the wedding."

"It didn't occur to you to tell me?"

"It's not something I want to remember." He tried to touch her arm, but she pulled away. "It's not relevant to how I feel about you."

"How you feel about me? I haven't seen you in so long. It's actually amazing to me that you have feelings. You didn't tell me because you knew it would be relevant to how I felt about *you*."

Trust seemed to him like a filament, a most delicate fiber, the structure of which could be destroyed before one even knows its necessity. "You're right," he said. "I'm not proud of it. I didn't want you to know."

She turned to him. "I want to know why. Why did you disappear? No sermon—tell me why."

"I thought it was for the best," he said.

"Couldn't you have guessed I needed a night to think about it? You completely sideswiped me. Why did you make plans to see me if you were already so certain I wasn't going?"

"I sideswiped myself," he said. "I was overwhelmed."

"So you never meant it? It was just some passing feeling?" She drew back.

Preston was cornered by that feminine talent for making a man feel every word he says is the wrong thing to say. The words he wanted wouldn't emerge. The emotion wouldn't form into anything coherent beyond frustration and yearning and an inarticulate certainty that what drove him away was the fact that his feeling *wasn't* fleeting.

"I guess I don't know women very well," he said. The words had the ring of a cop-out, but he believed they were true. He didn't need to tell her about the men in the valet line, but he did anyway, as a sort of private repentance. "I heard Bracken and Bucky and some other guy talking about you when I was outside after we went to the pool," he started. "They were talking about you like you were part of their world, in this way that made the idea that I could be a part of it seem impossible or just unrealistic. I thought I was an idiot for thinking I could be with you. I assumed the worst."

"What other guy?" she said.

"A big guy with one of those cowboy neckties."

Her voice leapt. "Randal Stanley? So you assumed if a guy like Randal was talking about me, then I must be below you?"

"No, not below me. Just not mine to hope for."

"You're satisfied with yourself, right? That everything you thought about me was true? You made it true in your own head by running away."

She assumed the best in me, Preston thought. Suddenly he longed to be somewhere regular—not so historic and beautiful, just some place like the places he begrudgingly frequented growing up, eating two tacos for ninety-nine cents at the Jack in the Box on Gayner Drive, tromping through the pine needles at the arboretum, stirring up mosquito nests and listening to toads and the dripping of water from all the hundreds of big Texas trees after a rain, installing stereo wires at old Mrs. Menger's down the street. All the years he helped her with things like stereo wires, up until he graduated high school, she always told him that she prayed for him. The idea of Mrs. Menger praying for him, alone in her house, with its dusty figurines and plastic-covered velveteen sofa, made him feel abstract and uncomfortable. Years later, his mom mailed him envelopes with blank floral notecards inside, stamped and addressed to Mrs. Menger's nursing home, which he never wrote or sent. Strange how clearly he remembered the act of forgetting them.

"Who am I to think I can make you happy?" he said. "I don't have a million bucks. I can't give you the life you want. I want to, and I keep thinking that if I tell you how I feel it'll be enough. But it's not enough."

"I don't want you to give me my life," she said. "You have no idea what makes me happy. You look down on everyone who has money and then feel sorry for yourself because you don't. You belittle people because they have what you don't have."

"You belittle yourself by the way you live," he said.

"So according to your high and mighty bullshit I'm shallow? Is Karlie shallow? Was she shallow when you were with her? You're not sorry, you're the same as you've always been."

"Vivienne, you just ran out on your job and your whole life," he said. "You just admitted you were belittling yourself."

She gave him the straightest look he'd ever seen. "That's not for you to say. I trusted you. You said you believed in me. You treated my life like a toy for your analysis."

"That was never my intention. I do believe in you."

Her voice grew hot. "I actually told myself I had an important job, that I had a career. I'm tired of taking the girly high road with you. I'm not afraid of what you think."

"I don't know why you were ever afraid of what I think."

"You wanted me to be impressed with you," she said. "I'm not. I see you, and you're not as profound as you think. You're no better. And you're insecure because you know it deep down."

Preston looked at Vivienne and couldn't stand her—for being right about him, for knowing how to tear him up, for being what he wanted. They stood apart, looking at each other. In Houston, the hum of freeways filled the night; in Paris, it was distant, rattling mufflers. "That's true," he said.

"You told me once that being scared isn't a good excuse for anything."

"It isn't," he said, and he recalled that day in his apartment, how she burst into it like the sun through clouds, like a flower against the rain, like every metaphor of bloom, her coy eyes and sweet questions, that high feminine air, confident in its indifference but filled with secret wonder. He remembered how, after she left, a classmate had stopped by to drop off some books, how she'd said something like, "Who was that girl?" And he'd replied, "An old friend." He remembered this vividly because it was such a strange answer to unconsciously pop off. Strictly speaking, she wasn't an old friend at all, yet she felt like one. If only she would let him love her, but it was his own doing that prevented it.

"I'm sorry," he said, closing his eyes: And there she was, laughing in his apartment. How flitty she'd seemed to him then, like a thing one might blow away with a breath. He'd been blind to the meaning of his curiosity. By tossing her off as entertainment, or folly, or fun, he'd failed to grasp the chance he'd been given. When he should have loved her, he made light of her. And now he could not go back in time and change anything; you lose what you love when you don't love it enough.

It had been a sort of game to him, hadn't it? Because he'd only considered himself, the possibility never earnestly crossed his mind that she might be affected, that he had the ability to hurt her—or that he might be loved in return. He pictured himself, the skinny boy in Houston, Texas, shaking in his boots, reactive, lonely, excluded.

When he opened his eyes, he reached over and gently tugged a curl over her ear. The smallest, rebellious, beautiful curl.

She recoiled. "Please don't touch me."

She tucked her coat tightly over her chest. Even in the low light, he could see her cheeks were flushed. He was cold too.

"I'm walking away now," she said. "And I don't want you to follow me. I'm not saying that, secretly hoping that you will follow me. I mean it. Do not follow me, Preston."

The sound of his name on her lips hung in his ears; he wanted to fight back, just to keep her close.

But her voice was too strong and too disparate from any voice he'd heard or even imagined in her. "I won't follow you," he said quietly, after a few moments.

She paused, glancing around to choose the way. She took the brightest direction, toward the river. Preston watched her figure recede under the orange lamp glow and listened to her steps against old, wet stone. He watched until she turned a far corner and was gone.

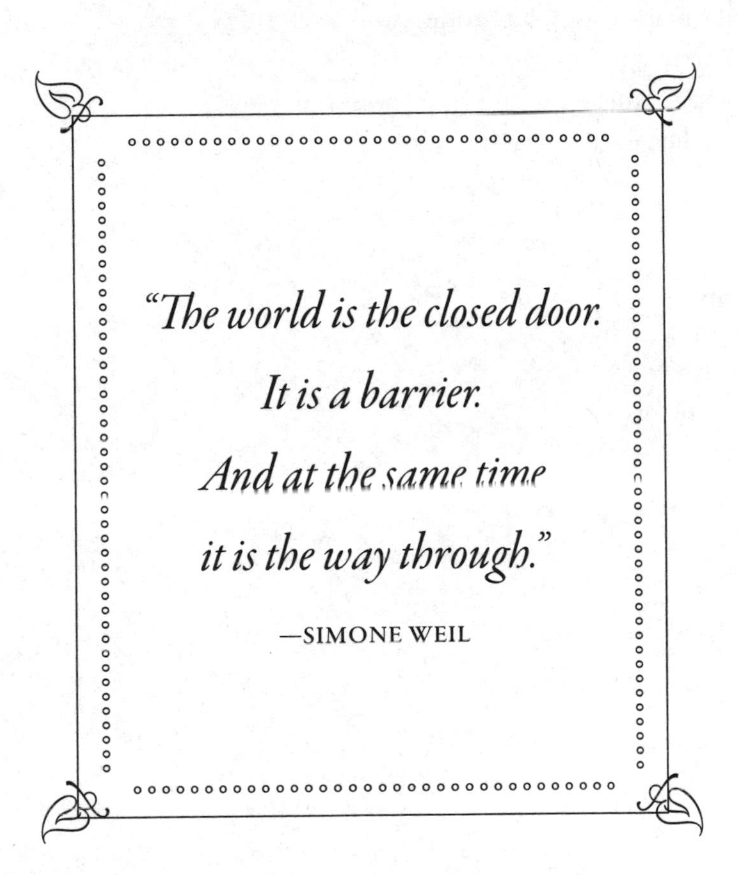

"The world is the closed door.

It is a barrier.

And at the same time

it is the way through."

—SIMONE WEIL

I

"WOULD YOU LIKE A DRINK?" THE FLIGHT ATTENDANT asked.

"Ginger ale," Vivienne said, and returned her head to its cubby between her sweatshirt and the window. Beside her, a middle-aged man was listening to music so loud she could hear the treble through his headphones. She plugged her ears with the airline headset, but it did little else than collect every sound into a cloudy white noise. The big screen at the front of coach read: 7 HOURS, 14 MINUTES, TO HOUSTON.

The ginger ale would settle her stomach. She tried to think what to do for the next seven hours, and every option gave her anxiety. Movies would hurt—they were either too happy or too sad. A book required attention span. Her laptop was dead. A crossword puzzle seemed okay, but when she paged to the back of the airline magazine, she found that someone else had already finished it. Sleep evaded her cruelly; her eyes closed and she saw Katherine, standing at the kitchen island in a beige silk button-down and tweed slacks, instructing her, as she waited by the door for the airport taxi, to beware of pickpockets on crowded trains in Paris.

Vivienne played this scene over and over in her mind, trying to remember if she had responded. All she remembered was feeling impatient to leave. This inability to remember whether she'd even said goodbye flooded her with an implacable dread. No amount of mental exertion could conjure anything but the certainty of her indifference in that final, mundane moment. She got the news from a lawyer in an email three weeks after leaving Paris, subject line, *Important*. Katherine was found collapsed in her bedroom, a stroke. Her friends discovered her after she didn't show up for bridge.

The night she left Preston, she went to a little inn near Kitty's apartment and lay awake in a small, sparse room, wondering what to do and where to go, so wrought with fear that she couldn't cry, so pulsing with determination that she didn't want to.

She'd decided she would travel for a few weeks and stay with Blad awhile. Katherine already couldn't stand that she was working for Bracken Blank. Just the thought of returning to her distant I-told-you-so energy, everything in the house so plush and comfortable, made Vivienne feel she would disappear. She sent Blad an email to ask, then tried to sleep.

The next morning, she returned to the Ritz as if to an alien place. It was incomprehensible that only yesterday morning she strode through it as though she belonged. At the front desk she found her orphaned suitcase. She went to the bathroom to wash her face and brush her teeth, and to change into jeans and a sweatshirt, and saw her things had been packed with care, everything folded neatly, nothing missing. In the front flap, where Waverly must have known Vivienne would look for her phone charger, she found a note. A heart, and inside the heart, in Waverly's cursive, *Thinking of you*. Vivienne knelt beside her open suitcase and let her face fall into her hands.

She spent the afternoon petting Ulysses in the garden while Kitty told stories and drank Panhandle coffee from the tin camping mug. Kitty admitted she'd had a sour sense about Karlie from the beginning of the meal. Preston she liked. "He has something to him," she said. But Vivienne didn't want to talk about Preston.

Kitty gave her a small, framed watercolor of the flat green marshes along the Texas coast near Matagorda Bay. The gray sky blended into the gray and green water; the skinny brown reeds stood upright and still. Kitty had painted it from memory. It was a muted landscape, not claiming to be much else than what it humbly was and, in that way, very true to the real place. "To keep you grounded," Kitty said. When

Vivienne told Kitty she wanted to travel, Kitty replied, "Switzerland," and gave her the address of her old friend Tom.

She took the night train to Zurich. The train tore through station after station, wiping the brightly lit platforms into darkness like a hand over wet paint; as the sun rose, mountains cut a shadow into the horizon. Her heart beat hard. At dawn, the train slowed into a gaping skylit station.

She rode three more trains that day, each one older and slower. The final train wound up and through the most immense mountains she'd ever seen. She'd skied the Rockies on trips with the Blanks; the mountains before her now seemed like their great-grandparents, though she knew they were millions of years younger. More vital, stronger. The train took her to a red gabled station that looked like a wooden toy she might have played with as a little girl. A yellow sign above the tracks read, WILKOMME TO THE TOP OF EUROPE!

The town was one short pedestrian street, with gabled cottages dotting the surrounding hills. It was late afternoon, and the sun was setting. The air smelled intensely of pine and autumn, that crisp scent of change she loved. She walked down the street: on one side, wooden chalets with white shutters housing gift and specialty shops, on the other, an empty playground and a panoramic view. The mountains were inconceivable. Snow and sharp granite became green meadow and forest. Narrow waterfalls poured down wide valleys into dark-green depths. She stopped in the middle of the street and stared, trying to make sense of it. The quiet enveloped everything. She only heard the wind. It bit her nose and seeped beneath her cotton sweatshirt. It howled through the passes like an animal and then settled, leaving the rusty playground swings creaking. She felt bewilderingly alone.

She found Kitty's friend Tom by asking the receptionist at the hostel. He made a call, and within a few minutes she was squeezing the waist of a stranger on the backseat of an electric scooter. He drove up a hill to a three-story house with warmly lit windows and deep eaves. Overgrown flower boxes hung from the sills; smoked curled from the stone chimney. The house had a bright-blue pitched roof.

Tom was waiting on the front step. Vivienne figured Kitty had called him, because he hugged her like an old friend, but then he laughed, "And who are you?"

When he heard she was Kitty's friend, he jumped up and down. Tom was tall and lean, with a mop of gray curls; he wore a pair of baggy striped pants and a linty fleece sweatshirt. Vivienne thought he must be in his seventies, but he smiled with his entire face. He showed her upstairs to a cozy room with a twin bed, gave her a parka to borrow, and took her on a tour of the property by lantern light. There was a barn in the back, where a donkey and a goat were sleeping, and a cabin art studio.

In the main room of the house, a man about Tom's age sat at a chess table beside the fire. A pair of clear round glasses rested low on his round cheeks. He wore a black knit hat and a set of plaid pajamas. This was Charlie, visiting from Austin. Tom poured Vivienne a cup of peppermint tea and invited her to watch the conclusion of the game. Vivienne learned Charlie was a retired high school history teacher with early Parkinson's. Charlie had come to Switzerland to paint. He'd always wanted to paint, and now for the first time in his life he had the time. Tom was originally from El Paso. He'd bought the house with money he made on a patent in 1989. Now he lived off cash work—handyman jobs, renting extra rooms. He rarely left the mountains, except to cope with visa troubles. "Twenty years here and still not a citizen," he said. "One of these days they'll send me back to El Paso." Both Charlie and Tom had known Kitty for thirty years, since Texas.

"One of us was her lover for a while," Tom said, his voice thick and mischievous. "But I'm not going to tell you who."

Vivienne sat in a folding chair and watched the men play chess, a game no one had ever taught her to play. Her impulse was to feel suspicious of the ease with which Tom and Charlie integrated her into the house. Why were they so nice? They regarded her with delight, but not so much delight that the evening changed course or that they asked her a bunch of questions. They were happy to have another Texan around and glad that Kitty was doing well, but these sentiments were expressed with a complete lack of nosiness. They asked what brought her to Switzerland and she said, "I wanted to see the mountains." This response was accepted without further inquiry. Tom said she'd come at the most beautiful time of year, right before the first snow.

The silences that fell as the men played were silences that felt like being alone. She'd expected to have to explain herself, but the only thing expected of her was that she drink her peppermint tea—made with leaves foraged by Charlie. The firelight flickered over things laid about the room. Stacks of *National Geographic* along the baseboards, a row of rusty hand-churn coffee grinders atop the kitchen cabinets, an overstuffed brown corduroy couch. Mobiles constructed with pencils and forks hung from the exposed beams, refracting bits of light on the knotty-pine walls. Vivienne recognized one of Kitty's paintings, the sunrise desert, probably somewhere in the Big Bend.

"You know she paints those herself, right?" Charlie asked.

"She told me," Vivienne said.

"Then she likes you," Tom said.

That night Vivienne slept for fourteen hours. She woke to birdsong. Outside, the mountains were bathed in white sun, the sky pure, empty blue.

For the next three weeks, Vivienne walked. She walked through meadows, on trails over loose rock or spongy green moss, alongside herds of brown cattle wearing big brass bells around their necks. She plucked the grass and tied it in knots. She hiked as high as she could in her tennis shoes and sat on hard tracts of last winter's snow. She tore up her ankle in the stems of an alpine thistle and got to know a family of busy marmots. One day she saw an ibex fifty feet away, grazing on a steep incline. Another day she met a little girl near the playground who told her dandelion fuzz was made of fairies. You blow on the dandelion and the fairies go flying off to grant your wish. She ate chocolate every day.

Water came from a spring adjacent to the house. This amazed Vivienne almost as much as the fact that no one pried into her life. For the first few days, she worried they didn't like her. She didn't know where she was or how to be, but each day she realized more that she didn't have to be any particular way. Neither Tom nor Charlie ever complimented her at all, which, to her surprise, she appreciated. She found a book about alpine plants on Tom's shelf and taught herself how to identify the wildflowers growing on the hillsides.

Charlie painted in the cabin behind the house, whistling, using many colors. Vivienne loved his paintings. They were close-ups of the human body, of organs sliced apart and enlarged, out of tenderness, not violence. A broken human heart magnified and peeled open, or a human brain fallen in love at first sight, butterflied. They looked as if they could be folded back together again safely. He was working on a pair of hands. Charlie wanted to paint his hands before they would no longer sit still. When Vivienne asked him about his work, he was modest.

"I'm just trying to imagine what a feeling looks like in the body," he said.

Tom and Charlie played chess almost every night. Tom usually won, then carried his cup of tea off to bed. He never went to bed without his cup of tea. He told Vivienne the story of how, ten years ago, after his brother died, he began to keep a cup of tea beside his bed to ward off nightmares. If he woke and sipped the tea, the nightmare broke. It comforted him just to know it was there. Before she died, his wife used to make the tea for him.

By twilight, the stars were electric and infinite. She saw the Milky Way for the first time and discovered she didn't know any constellations. Charlie showed her the Big Dipper, the Little Dipper, Orion's Belt. She felt the sky pulled into relief, as if she'd been staring at a painting her entire life and only just now saw that the image had dimension.

From her bed, she could see a corner of the black sky. Migrating birds clipped through her view like ghosts. Frogs chirped high-pitched songs along the spring. An owl hooted—not the sweet hoots of the screech owls from home, but a deep, shadowy hoot. The owl spooked her sometimes, and the foreignness of it all became too much. She switched on the light and wrote Blad a postcard or scrolled through her phone looking at pictures from Paris. Other times, she lay awake listening, thinking about Preston. Where was he? What was he doing? Moments passed in which she felt him there, listening with her. Or she thought of Waverly; memories came to her, games they played as young girls, schemes they'd planned, notes they'd written in class. Instead of forcing the thoughts away, she lay with them till she fell asleep. In the morning, she usually woke with a sharp pain in her heart. Had it all really happened? Yes, it had. And now this—the autumn world outside, Tom's hot pot of coffee in the kitchen—was happening too.

She didn't read or listen to music. Her phone hadn't had service since Zurich. She wore the same clothes every day. There were days when she felt the feeling in her body had risen to the surface of her skin, amplifying every emotion. The uncertainty of home, of the future, buckled her spirit in fear, but the joy she felt in the mountains was something altogether new and whole. On her walks she felt healed, from what she wasn't sure.

When she finally got the email, at the hostel's big tourist computer, Katherine had been dead three days. Vivienne left Switzerland on the morning of the first snow; the sky was white, and she caught the first flakes in her open palms.

II

THE HUMIDITY IN THE JETWAY AT GEORGE BUSH Intercontinental Airport was a thick and insolent thing. Baggage claim was loud and inexplicably organized, everyone moving, no one touching. Vivienne stood on the curb outside, exhaust trapping her breath. Families hugged, couples kissed. No one was coming to pick her up.

Two hours later, a shuttle bus dropped her off to a house filled with people.

Lawyers. Bridge friends. Neighbors she'd never seen, bearing casseroles, lingering at the door. Would there be an estate sale? Cousins she'd never met or heard of calling the house—everyone asking for things. The *Chronicle* calling to fact-check a prewritten obituary. Such a stream of voices, in a house that had always been so hushed. What surprised Vivienne in the topsy-turvy days after death was how urgent the concerns of other people became, as if their grief over Katherine's death granted them permission to admit need for various pieces of furniture and glassware. Blad checked in but avoided the scene. Waverly left a message, which Vivienne didn't return.

A trio of church and bridge friends came to talk among themselves and pack boxes. They regarded Vivienne with scolding eyes, as if she were a naughty child. Everyone expected her to feel guilty, but secretly Vivienne was relieved she hadn't been home to find Katherine. The chilling thought was that it might have taken Vivienne longer than a few hours to find her; she never looked for Katherine at home. The women spoke of their friendships with Katherine with ardent tenderness, reiterating that she died peacefully, that her faith kept her strong, that this sort of quick exit was exactly what Katherine would have wanted. They told Vivienne, "She loved you," as if to defend their friend. At moments, in the whirlwind of so many strangers, Vivienne felt she wasn't even a Cally. But she was actually the only Cally.

Katherine had named her priest as executor. Father Bennison was about seventy and bald, a man who embodied the expectations of his profession: He listened, spoke carefully, maintained eye contact, and nodded a lot. Vivienne liked him. God only knew what he'd heard from Katherine over the years, but still he treated her with kindness. He also didn't ask for anything, only the occasional glass of water.

He told Vivienne that Katherine had bequeathed her estate to the Diocese of Harris County, all assets totaling 2.8 million dollars. The great surprise—to everyone but Vivienne—was not Katherine's beneficiary but the comparatively small estate for a Cally. The *Chronicle* ran a story full of anonymous quotes about the lost Cally fortune. Vivienne didn't read it but figured everyone else did. Waverly called and left another message:

"Vivienne, it's me. I'm so sorry about Katherine. Please call me back. I'm confused. I want to come to the funeral, but I don't know if you want to talk to me? I won't go unless you call. I hope you're okay. Please call me."

Vivienne didn't call.

In a binding trust, Katherine left Vivienne's future children one hundred thousand dollars each, to be distributed for medical and education purposes only and to be liquidated upon the youngest, or only, child turning thirty. She left Vivienne nothing.

"But there's a stipulation here specifying that you are entitled to medical distribution," Father Bennison told her. They were sitting in the green room, that old haunted room. She looked around at the trifles, or the places where trifles used to be, and at the boxes in which those trifles were now wrapped up, amazed that none of it really meant anything to her—a good thing, because none of it was intended for her from the beginning.

"So in the event of a medical event or illness, you may use the trust for expenses."

"What happens if I don't have children?" This was a possibility she'd never imagined voicing.

"Then the money will go to the diocese." The priest put his hand lightly on Vivienne's shoulder. "I may be speaking out of turn, but I believe it is harsh too. You've always seemed like a very nice girl. But we should bear in mind that Katherine's decision reflects her state of mind more than your own character or anything you have or haven't done."

He paused and cleared his throat. "Let us pray that where Katherine is now, she is freed from the . . . the pride and the anger that too often held her heart and kept her from loving in the way she was capable of loving."

Vivienne closed her eyes, his hand still on her shoulder.

"Let us honor this trust and this medical stipulation as a remembrance of loving kindness above all pettiness and malice. Lord, we ask that you hold these things in Vivienne's heart as acts of love from her aunt, so that her own life may become an act of love in the fullness of your spirit."

When he finished, he handed Vivienne an envelope bearing her name. "I found this with her papers. Read it later, when all this is done."

Once the will was read, the church would come to collect valuables, and the lawyers had already set a date for the rest to be packed and moved. Father Bennison had pushed it back a month, to give Vivienne a little time. What he didn't ask was where she would go and what she planned to do about money. She sat on her bed and looked at the things she'd bought thanks to the Bracken job: so many pretty dresses, several never worn, shoes she couldn't walk anywhere in, worn once, to dinners that cost as much as a deposit on an apartment. Hair appointments! And now her hair was just brassy and dark at the roots, fighting to return to itself. And all those manicures, when now her fingernails struck her as fine—why did she always paint them before? The long spa days with Karlie and Waverly. What had they even talked about?

She'd spent money for no other reason than to spend money, because it was what every woman she knew did. Weren't there so many other things to do? If nothing else, she could have walked through Memorial Park. That was free. She calculated that she could have saved some real money, and then maybe she'd be moving into an apartment now instead of onto Blad's air mattress. The hatbox in Katherine's closet was gone. She needed to find a job.

The church women planned the wake, an event equal parts solemn and social. Vivienne sat alongside Katherine's friends in the front pew, mere feet from Katherine herself, lying in a bed of white lilies in her shining open casket, wearing her best suit, her face painted. Vivienne could hardly stand to look.

The sanctuary was full, and fragrant with perfume and incense. Older women Vivienne had never seen wore elaborate black hats adorned with silk ribbons and flowers. They held the arms of tall, serious men in tailored suits and python boots, the kind of stately men other men hung near. Parishioners read Scripture and told stories of an aunt Vivienne never knew. Her devotion to the food bank ministry, her kindness to grieving parishioners, her unbeatable bridge game. Someone recalled a story about the glamour of Katherine's gowns in the 1970s. But the stories had the ring of leaving out what everyone was really thinking, a particular sort of over-polite energy Vivienne could pin in an instant. They were thinking about the money. They were pitying the family. They were nosy.

Before closing, Father Bennison asked if anyone else would like to say a few words. Vivienne stood and went to the pulpit, tuning out the whispers at her back.

"As you all know," she began, "I'm Katherine's niece, Vivienne. Thank you for coming today. I'm touched by the stories about Katherine. It's nice to see her through your eyes. I feel like I got to know my aunt a little better today. As y'all also know, for a long time now it was just Katherine and me. I want to say that I'm proud of the way Katherine kept her head high during hard times. She loved our family, and she had a strong sense of who she was as a person. Some of her best traits were also her worst traits, but she was a complex and intelligent woman.

She was a woman with high expectations, and she was hardest on herself. We're all trying to be braver and more compassionate people than we are, and when this is too much to ask of ourselves, at least we're trying. I think it means something to try, and I think Katherine tried all her life."

After the service, Vivienne toiled in the narthex, shaking hands. When the sanctuary had finally emptied out, she sat to rest her feet. An elderly woman holding a cane joined her on the bench. She was regal in spite of her posture, wearing a classic pink shoulder-padded suit, with black hose and black pumps. Her silver hair shone like the coat of a Persian cat. Her makeup was precise—too precise for her own hand—her eyes just perceptibly lifted.

"I think what you said was lovely," she said. "I'm Louise." She had a tough, smoky voice.

"Thank you," Vivienne said. "How did you know Katherine?"

Louise shrugged, mostly with her drawn brows. "Church and parties, I suppose," she said. "I didn't know her all that well, really. But I knew your mother, honey."

Vivienne turned her whole body to face Louise. "You knew my mom?"

"I did," Louise said. "Now, I didn't know her all that well, but I wanted to tell you that I saw you up there today, and you are the spitting image of your mother. I didn't know if you knew that, because you lost her so young."

"How did you know her?"

"I saw her in church. You were just a baby." Louise said. "She was a glowing mommy, sun pouring out round her head. One of those women born to be a mom." She laughed and then coughed sharply. "You were a real joy to her. I remember that."

Vivienne said, "What was her voice like?"

Louise smiled. "I'm too old to remember her voice. But she was like you. That's what she was like. Don't think about it too hard; just know that you have the spirit of your mother and that your mother was lovely."

"Did you know her when . . ." Vivienne hesitated.

Louise frowned. "She moved away. I always thought all that was a shame. There was such a natural joy to her. You know how people get jealous of that." She coughed again. Above them, the afternoon sun streamed through the stained glass of Mary, her open, luminous hands warming the narthex to gold.

"It ain't worth a tinker, other people's talk," Louise said. "Your mom was strong, but she learned that the hard way."

Vivienne had so many questions. She wanted to crawl out of her motherless life and into Louise's life, a life that had known her mother.

"Took me a long time, but after I lost my mother—and this was before people talked so bluntly about their feelings—I learned that she wasn't really gone, because she's in heaven, but also because I'm carrying her in me," Louise said. "I'm not gone, so she idn't gone. The thing to do is listen for her, and you'll find her, and she'll tell you what to do. She told me to come up and talk to you."

"Your mom told you to talk to me?"

"It doesn't make sense," Louise said. "But most of what's true doesn't make sense. You just hafta learn how to separate the true stuff that doesn't make sense from the false stuff that does make sense." She tapped Vivienne's knee. "My ride is leaving."

Vivienne helped her up and out the door. "Thank you," she said.

"Goodbye, honey," Louise said. She made her way to a white van with a picture of two smiling senior citizens bannered to the side: COME HOME TO PALMHILL SENIOR LIVING. Grackles cawed around the oaks. Bands of cirrus clouds were crossing the sky. Vivienne heard a man call her name.

There was Timmy, approaching submissively. His appearance was so startling that without thinking she walked toward him, if only to avoid having to watch him get closer.

"Hi, Vivienne, do you have a minute to talk?" He was redder than usual, sweaty at the hairline. "Just five minutes. Three minutes." He was all buttoned up in a suit and tie.

"What are you doing here, Tim?"

"I don't know how to tell you how sorry I am," he said.

Vivienne wanted to run, but she tempered herself. It was Timmy, after all.

He was nodding, almost talking to himself. “I should have stuck up for you.”

“I can’t stand here and jump into this.”

“I didn’t know how else to find you,” he said. “I drove by your house yesterday and there were a bunch of cars there. I knew you’d be here.”

“You drove by my house?” she said.

“To make it right,” he said. “I feel awful. I think about it every day. It wasn’t fair to you what happened.”

She was trying to stay focused on Louise, but she’d never heard Timmy so articulate. He looked clammy and fat, but he sounded uncharacteristically vigorous.

“I’d rather leave it behind, Timmy.”

He withdrew, his face twisted cruelly. “Shit,” he said, then lowered his voice, as if God might have heard. “I knew you wouldn’t have held a grudge.”

This embarrassed her. “Don’t make me into some noble victim.”

He was squeezing the skin on his forehead. He did this when he was upset. Timmy was a person so rarely upset that when he was, there was no doubting it. “Things are terrible with Karlie and me,” he said.

The sun dipped behind the oak grove, instantly darkening the courtyard. “I’m not your audience for this. This is my aunt’s funeral.”

Timmy nodded. “I know, but I think I can make it better.”

“Make what better?”

“Everything,” he said.

“What are you saying?”

“Everything for you,” he said. “I want to make everything better for both of us.”

Suddenly Vivienne felt unnerved by the picture of effort Timmy presented. He came into focus as the friend she knew, and she understood the monumental effort he was summoning. He had something important to say. “I don’t need anyone to make anything better for me.”

“I didn’t know she was lying. When we got home, I looked in her email and I found—” He stopped, wiping his eyes. “Do you know she cheated on me two months after we got married?”

She’d always known this moment would come with Timmy, but

she'd imagined it differently, that it would require a delicate balance considering her friendship with Karlie. With that loyalty removed, she felt even more uncomfortable than she'd imagined.

"Did you know?" Timmy said. "Did everyone know?"

Pain had softened Vivienne, and her heart contracted for Timmy. Of all the people helpless to deal with such a scenario, Timmy seemed like the most pathetic case.

"Why didn't anyone tell me?" he said. "Why didn't you tell me?"

"I thought you knew and didn't want us talking about it."

"Maybe I did know. I don't know," he said, his eyes in a daze. "She's jealous of you. She's always been jealous of people, but especially you. That's why she always had it out for you. I knew she did, but I didn't say anything, because she always wants to fight too. She wants to fight all the time. The worst part is, I love her. I don't want to leave her, because I don't know what she would do without me. She doesn't earn enough money from her blog to support the way she lives."

"Timmy—I want to be here for you, but with everything that happened I really can't. I'm sure there's someone else you can confide in."

"But you're the only person who knows." He slumped, a miserable creature.

"Knows what?"

A cool wind rustled the oak and chased dry leaves about their feet. Timmy turned to her. "Everything. How unhappy I am. I can't talk to anyone, because they all pretend like it's not real. They don't want to acknowledge it or say anything. You understand."

Vivienne stiffened. "Maybe you can talk to Clay."

"I'm stuck," he said. "Do you know how much a divorce will cost? Karlie has no idea what the numbers are. She has no idea what it takes. I'm gonna buckle supporting everything while she's off doing what she's doing."

Suddenly his tone turned pleading. "You can help me if you just say what you know. It wouldn't have to be public. Your lawyer could write a letter to the judge. Then I could get out of it in decent shape. Then she couldn't take everything I have. I don't even have that much, that's the thing. She just makes it look like I do because she spends every last dime. She berates me for my job like it's not good enough, but it's the reason she lives how she does. If I lose my job, she might try to go for my family's money—she's making me donate all this money to the Bayou Society so that they'll throw her luncheons or ice cream socials or some stupid shit that's costing me a fortune—"

"Please stop," Vivienne said.

"Will you help me?" he said. "I know you know something." Sweat had gathered at his collar, dampening its edge.

She averted her eyes.

"Will you?" he said again.

The vision of Timmy's appeal unfolded in her imagination. This broken man dangled before her everything she needed to exact a clean revenge on Karlie. And certainly in the luster of revelation, sympathy would turn its eager eye to her. She would be tucked back under that downy wing. By way of connections, a convenient new job opportunity would probably come her way. Karlie would be the one cut out. And what would she blog about then? What would her mood boards look like when she couldn't pay rent and had to find a new man to foot the bill? Oh, the prospect of Karlie crying over her keyboard, torn from curating her life into perfection for the jealous eyes she craved, too broke to afford her dye job, it was delicious—too delicious.

"No," she said abruptly.

Timmy's eyes fell. "Why not? Don't you want to get back at her?"

"I want to be left out of this."

"Please," Timmy said. "She deserves it. I think she was with Preston—can you believe that? We can make him talk. She is going to destroy my life. She already has." He hung his head, scratched his cheeks. "Bracken will give you your job back if you apologize. You could have your job back."

"You want me to help you smear Karlie so that you can divorce her—that's what you're saying right now."

He cleared his throat. The terms, put crudely, were not words he was willing to speak.

"Please, Timmy, I want you to go away."

He shut his mouth and stared at his shoes. He looked shattered. Vivienne fought her urge to save him. He was so savable. Nothing more to say, the sun sinking, he left her to the oaks and the leaves and Katherine lying still in the narthex.

It wasn't until the next day, when the burial service was over and everyone was returning to their cars, that Vivienne really perceived the shiny wooden box anchored over the dark hole in the ground. And beside it, her father, and her grandparents. She stood at the head of the casket, surrounded by the bones of her family. Katherine rotting in this box, the whole thing decomposing into bones that would never move from this place. Her mother had been cremated, her ashes scattered into the Gulf. Vivienne preferred that, because she felt she could imagine her mother was everywhere. She didn't want anyone she loved, or would have loved, or who loved her, to end up a pile of bones. She pulled a few lilies from the wreath on the casket and went around to her father. She laid the lilies over his grave. Katherine was finally with her little brother again.

That night, after everyone had come and gone, Vivienne sat alone in the green room and opened the envelope from Father Bennison. It was a handwritten note from Katherine, dated two years ago:

Dear Vivienne,

I know I am not the aunt you deserved. Please take comfort in knowing I was aware of this deficiency and that I found it painful. As I write this, I realize that forgiveness is my struggle, and I'm afraid I'm still not up to the task. In the attic you'll find a box of your mother's things. I've kept them without knowing why. Perhaps this note is the best explanation. You are a strong young woman. I hope that in a small way I helped make you that way, but I admit this hope knowing it's probably false. You are strong because you are you. Do not take after me, but do forgive me.

Your aunt, Katherine

Vivienne went hunting in the attic for this vestige of love. She slid a bunch of identical brown boxes down the attic stairs. Most were filled with vintage kitchen appliances, moldy books, handbags from the eighties. But she found a photo album sticky with yellow glue and roach droppings. Black-and-white photos of unsmiling, unfamiliar Cally people in gowns and tuxedos. She rummaged awhile before she saw faces she recognized. Young Katherine with her brother at the beach. Katherine at the altar on her wedding day, smiling. In the wedding picture that Katherine had kept hanging in the hall, she wasn't smiling. But in this group picture she looked gleeful, victorious, her bouquet raised, Vivienne's young parents grinning at her side. Vivienne looked so much like her mother, it was like staring at herself in a dream.

Katherine had had pain, after all. She'd had secrets. The ice between them had been crushing to her too. Maybe every time Katherine saw her, she thought of her brother, and maybe that hurt too much.

Vivienne tossed the album aside. Loose pictures spilled out. But that wasn't enough: She wanted to ruin it. She grabbed it and battered it against the floor. The binder rings popped, pages scattered. The anger rose to her eyes, and she tore a handful of photos to pieces. This made her feel better, and sort of silly, but only for a moment. Then, finally, she cried. Her body gave way to the floor, and she cried for the arms of her parents around her, for knowing that she would never, ever know how that felt. She cried into the room's dumb perfection, the pristine, color-coordinated stupidity of it.

She lay down and pressed her cheek against the parquet, as if somewhere deep beneath it she might discern a heartbeat. The hard cool felt nice on her hot cheek. She listened to her breath. It sounded full and familiar, like the mountains. Then she heard something, a voice within her own voice, and saw herself curled there on the floor. *Get up*, it said. *Get up, Vivienne.*

Slowly, she gathered herself, wiping her cheeks, sitting for a while in the quiet of herself in the empty house. She packed the boxes and pushed them into a corner, climbed the attic stairs to switch off the light. There was a box she hadn't noticed. An X was written in black marker on the top. She slid it downstairs. It was sealed shut with layers of packing tape, which she had to break with her teeth. The inside was piled with loose photos of her mother's life as a Cally, every one with an

X on the back. At the bottom of the pile, beneath the photos, was a bundle wrapped in tissue. She exhumed it and sneezed, then gently broke the Scotch tape. The tissue fell open and Vivienne recognized it instantly—her mother's wedding dress. In teary awe, she climbed to her feet, holding the dress out before her.

She'd always thought it was gone, but all this time it was right above her head. The dress was long and embroidered, with gauzy sleeves that buttoned at the wrist, a floral panel draping off the low neckline, the skirt full and loose. The veil was folded up in the bottom of the box, the tulle wrinkled and moth-nibbled but intact, a headpiece of crispy brown roses stitched to the crown. Vivienne didn't dare try them on, but she held them close. There wasn't much else she needed or wanted here, but these things she would take with her.

III

Vivienne,

Today is a cold day in Paris. Maybe it's a cold day in Texas too. Sometimes it's romantic here, but mostly it's just gray. You are every color I see in this gray city. Women pass me on the sidewalk wearing bright red scarves. An orange cat has been coming around my building lately. He's an old tomcat, kind of beat up from the street. He's got a round head and nicks all over his ears, green eyes, and a crooked tail. It seems like a lot of people have written him off over the years, but he'd never write himself off. That's what I like about him. Something about that reminds me of you. Your beauty, great as it is, is the least interesting thing about you. If I had the chance to make you another cup of coffee, I wouldn't talk so much. Did you know you're a little knock-kneed?

HE STOPPED. TOO MUCH. COMPARING HER TO A TOMCAT? Bad idea. He went to his window—sad Sunday sky and damp street. Winter was already over in Texas. Maybe there would still be a cold front or two, but the grass was green and the sky was blue. He wondered if he'd even seen the color blue in months, except on painted doorways and the street sweepers' coats. April would come, with its promise of poplars blossoming along the boulevards and tulips filling the esplanades. It would probably be very beautiful. But he had a melancholy feeling about it, because he knew it would all make him wish for Vivienne.

Since her visit, he hadn't seen any more girls. He'd been too busy working, in the office every morning by seven, out past seven, after midnight on deadlines. His co-workers teased him for being a crazy American workaholic, and they were probably right, but he liked his schedule. He rode the Metro before the crowds. He practiced his French with the old lady in the bakery where he bought his coffee. She lived in the back and had a habit of resting her elbow on the counter and cradling her chin while talking.

The city felt so alive in the morning, teeming with possibility. He never put the possibility too far in the future, though; he put it into the day, and that was how he was able to work so hard and for so long. This felt much better than his old schedule working the minimum, drinking the fourth glass of wine, screwing the girl. He still wanted to quit smoking and get more exercise, but he felt healthier, and sad in a clean, simple way. Before he felt sad in a dirty, philosophical way. Working distracted him from thinking too much about Vivienne and gave him something to accomplish. Lately he'd been feeling good about his designs.

But he was at a crossroads, and whenever Preston was at a crossroads he doubted and contradicted himself. Stay in Paris, or return to Texas? His contract ended in March. His current firm didn't have the budget to renew him, but he'd made contacts in Paris, and his French was decent now. If he stayed, he could renew his visa and maybe even start the long process toward citizenship. But the thing was, he missed Texas. For as much as he loved Paris, sometimes he felt that he loved the idea of it more. It was only since Vivienne had left him there in the street that he'd slowly come to realize this, that it was tough living without Texas, even in a place as great as Paris. Still, he was reluctant. It was Texas, after all, and again. He felt very paradoxical and grumpy when he thought about it, remembering vividly all the things he couldn't stand about it (he ran through his top three: guns, humidity, mosquitos) and how puffy and grand he'd felt in leaving it, and yet—and yet what? Well, he just missed it. He just didn't know if he missed it enough to go back.

He could always find another city, but he'd still have to go back to Texas for a while and regroup. For all his work, he was still pretty broke because he'd been paying off student loans while getting by. The prospect of returning poor to his apartment, where he'd have to boot his subletter, a raggedy biology postdoc, wasn't appealing. Better to let it all go? The guy could take what he wanted and pack the important things in boxes to ship to him, wherever he ended up.

Ended up. Somehow that prospect seemed dull. He didn't want to end up; he wanted to choose. Any place in the world was an option, in theory, but not without a whole lot of effort. It was curious, how the loss of Vivienne, the drag of money, the decade of thirty, had pacified his romantic ideas about wandering. He didn't exactly want to settle either—it was more that he was done with moving around without purpose. Wherever he went, he wanted to go for a reason, not simply for the sake of going.

He picked up the letter and read it again. He'd written it and rewritten it, and he never got it right. He wanted to be understood, and in trying to make himself understood he sounded dumb, or too airy. Vivienne wouldn't like airy. It would make her think he was idealizing her, and she hated to be idealized. He didn't assume he could change her mind, but in time maybe she would accept his apology. It was the thought that she'd forget about him that he hated.

He sat on the edge of the bed and folded the letter in half. On a day like this, when his mood was too contemplative, he needed to get outside, see a movie in English, or go grocery shopping, but it was just so cold and wet. People from Houston only have clothes for warm and wet, which made him wonder: *Why haven't I gotten myself the right coat?* He'd spent the last three months bundled up in fleece from the late nineties, and it hadn't occurred to him to buy a new coat. He answered his own question with the thought that he must not have considered Paris a place he would stay.

The building across the street cast a long gloomy shadow into his room. It might have been 1723, or 1845, or 1926. That was the thing about Paris. The radiator rattled and thunked, sending an echo down the pipe—the portly French super working the boiler. That was another thing about Paris. There were ancient boiler rooms that held wine before boiler rooms existed, where all kinds of secret things may have happened. Plots against the Nazis, or Napoleon, or King Louis XVI. This he enjoyed, that around any corner something terrible or marvelous might have unfolded. He recalled the plaque on the porch steps of his childhood home: ON THIS SITE IN 1897, NOTHING HAPPENED.

One image kept intruding into his thoughts over what to do. A treehouse. A treehouse made from reclaimed wood, joinery-fastened, with old, warped windows, nooks and crannies for books, maybe even a ventilation system that would safely allow for a potbellied stove. Big enough for two people, and cradled by the limbs of two grand old trees. On the back of the letter to Vivienne, he made a rough sketch. He rounded the roof and drew the door arched and short, a door for a hobbit. Spanish moss dangling from the boughs. A blue jay perched atop the flagpole. A flagpole for a handmade flag. A place to read and tell stories and make love. He added a few details. A porthole window, a flower box. He kept going. A bungalow below the treehouse, with a porch and a brick chimney. Grass growing around the stepping stones, and a secret hole beneath one of the stones for storing secret things.

The cathedral bells rang a few blocks away, filling the streets. There was a time during his stay in Paris when the bells caused him to brood, but lately they gave him rest and a reassuring sense of order and mystery coexisting. He sat back and listened. He could stay here in Paris, where bells sang out in the streets. Or he could go home and build a tree house for Vivienne—but maybe it was true that he could only love her by keeping his distance. No one could give him the answer. He would have to rely on something very foreign and uncomfortable to him: faith.

IV

SHE REMEMBERED A TIME WHEN SHE WANTED EVERYTHING to be easy, but now she wanted everything to be hard. She wasn't happy, but at least she felt alive. While Blad was at work, she sat on the couch in sweatpants, her hair tied in a knot, selling her designer clothes online and applying for jobs. The most basic entry-level jobs required a list of experience and demanded: DO NOT REPLY IF YOU DO NOT MEET ALL REQUIREMENTS. Even the retail jobs asked for a specific set of qualities: Did any person in the world love teamwork, crave a fast-paced work environment, possess a passion for sales, plus minimum two years' experience and open weekends, all while earning nine-fifty an hour? The extensive requirements of the curatorial jobs—master's degrees, assistantships, French and German language proficiency, references from the field—reinforced the real absurdity of her position with Bracken.

Her experience researching Texas art on the Internet for BB Development wasn't going to cut anything. Even the internships at galleries required a bachelor's degree in art history, or fine arts, and that applicants be within one year of graduation, not to mention that they were unpaid. Everyplace she went, she regarded employees curiously, with a new eye. Where she hadn't noticed them before—or had, but only in the context of her own job folding soft sweaters—she now saw them as people who were better at life, people with *skills*. The baristas were so good at making coffee. The postman was so efficient at delivering mail.

Even lawn crews—whom she used to regard with pity or, if any of the guys whistled at her, total contempt—struck her as having the right idea. They knew how to work.

Blad went to the spa six days a week, and three of those days he worked all morning at the consulting firm. He'd been hoping for a promotion for months. In the morning, he listened to NPR while making coffee—mostly bad news about the economy and violence in the Middle East. Every day she thought about calling the store and returning to folding soft sweaters, but she didn't want to run into anyone, and something stubborn and deeper made going back unbearable. To return was to forget the early-morning light in the Place Vendôme. Whatever it was she would do, it would be something she hadn't done before.

Blad seemed to understand, even more than Vivienne, that she needed time. He gave her space, and didn't ask her for help with the rent, and didn't bring up Preston. Sometimes she imagined that her life would be different, less chaotic, if she'd never gone back to his apartment for coffee. That morning felt like a hinge on which her life had turned. He lingered with her in a way she'd gotten used to. She didn't miss him like before, or pretend not to miss him like before, but she heard him all the time, a sounding board in her head.

Though Blad never complained, she still felt like a strain on him. The bathroom situation alone was untenable. He was impeccably clean, all his many products organized according to brand, and Vivienne, unaccustomed to cleaning up, had to forcibly remind herself, with notes taped on the mirror, to wipe down the sink and return the cap to the toothpaste. He tried to get her a job at the spa, but the owner only wanted people who looked like they could be Thai, or from somewhere in Asia, or, at the very least, brunette. Blad told Vivienne they could probably sue the owner, but then they both forgot about it. It was awkward for him to bring dates home, and lately, exasperated, he'd been telling her to take a job at McDonald's. And when she'd tell him they probably wouldn't hire her, Blad would retort, "I can't believe you'd take me seriously. Vivienne, you cannot work at McDonald's. You have a college degree!" To which Vivienne would reply, "In communications!" And then Blad would roll his eyes.

These conversations did get her wondering: Was she really too proud to work at a fast-food restaurant? Yes, she was. But wasn't that the problem? What good had her sense of entitlement ever done her? What was the difference between folding soft sweaters and dipping potatoes in a fryer? At least people at McDonald's didn't have to suck up to the customers or contend with pretension. Was that the trade-off in life? Either you get material comfort, as long as you can smile for people with more money than you, or you can be yourself, but covered in fryer grease?

There were times when the silence she received in return for so many overtures to the world made her feel crazy. Dreams came in which Karlie posted salacious lies about her on her blog and the entire city read them. Drowning dreams. Drowning in a lake. Drowning in a pool. Then birth dreams: delivering another woman's baby, losing a pregnancy, giving birth to a worm—she couldn't shake that one. She'd awaken, sweating, and find she'd sunk into the leaky air mattress. Most days she had to roll onto the floor to get out of her body's own vinyl depression. She'd pull up Karlie's blog—nothing but the usual party pictures and fashion and design trends, and then one day the launch of a professional redesign, which Vivienne could tell was expensive. Another day there were pictures announcing Karlie's new role as an auntie. Waverly had delivered her healthy baby girl, and her name was Grace. In the pictures, Karlie, Tim, Clay, Reis, and Bucky were leaning in around the hospital bed, with smiles that created a bright rainbow around Waverly, her hair tousled, eyes aglow, Grace at her breast. Vivienne knew she should call, but didn't.

The week of Christmas, she and Blad found a squat tree at the corner lot for half off and threw themselves an ornament-making party, with sugary cider from the dollar store and Bing Crosby carols. They cut snowflake ornaments out of newspaper and hung them from the branches with red pipe cleaners. Blad cut the star, but he accidentally gave it six points, so atop their tree they hung the Star of David, covered in green glitter and Elmer's glue. They wandered the nicer part of the neighborhood, collecting pecans from front yards, and made a pie. Vivienne spent Christmas with Blad's family and recited "To Jesus on His Birthday" as her gift.

To celebrate the New Year, they went barhopping on Montrose, but Vivienne walked home before midnight. The bars were loud, and they stunk. She felt less alone by herself. It was a mild, sticky night. She sat on the steps of the apartment, swatting mosquitos from her legs and thinking of people. She thought of Katherine, then Kitty, then Tom and Charlie, and Waverly and her baby, and finally Preston. She tried to imagine each one and what they were doing at that moment, even Katherine. The next day she drove to Katherine's, just to see what was going on, and found a family moving in. They must have thought she was a neighbor, because they waved as she drove by.

January brought news that BB Development was under investigation for misappropriating funds.

Blad was sitting on the couch, scrolling through his phone, when suddenly he thrust the screen in Vivienne's face so she could read the headline herself. She had to read it a few times. He was giddy with delight.

"I knew it," he said. "Knew it. Knew it. Knew it."

"I didn't," Vivienne said, pushing the phone away.

"Denial," he said. "You just didn't want to see it. No one can be that big of an asshole and not be doing something illegal. I bet all his friends are involved. What are they going to do if they lose everything? Imagine if the Blanks moved into our apartment complex. Can you imagine? I would be so nice to them, to make them feel bad for not being nice to me."

"Waverly was always nice to you."

Blad desisted, but later, while they were maneuvering around each other fixing sandwiches, he said, "Do you think they know you're poor now?"

She hated the way he dropped bombs like that. "I never had as much money as them. I only looked like I did." She threw a flap of plastic cheese at him.

He opened a can of Dr Pepper and sulked over to the table. "Do you think we're going to live in here forever? Do you think I'll ever have health insurance?"

Vivienne sat across from him. "I don't know if you'll ever have health insurance, but we won't be in here forever."

"How do you know?" he said.

"Because we both don't want to be," Vivienne said. "I'm trying to believe that if we try our best and believe that we won't be, then we won't be."

Blad stared out the window with a wistful look. It was easy for Blad to look wistful, with those dark lashes. "It's hard not knowing what's going to happen."

Vivienne nodded. "I think I lived my whole life so that I'd always know what would happen, but that didn't work at all. At least we know that we don't know. It's better than thinking you know when you don't."

Blad said, "Remember last year when you had a big fancy dinner with bottle service for your birthday?" They both laughed.

WINTER WAS GONE so fast, and returned so little in the way of answered emails, that by the time March arrived, Vivienne could barely remember if she'd even done anything, except exchange her old smart phone for a used flip phone and learn some basic cooking skills. She loved when Blad didn't work at the spa in the evenings. She'd make buttered noodles or baked potatoes with a microwaved frozen veggie medley, and they'd sprawl out and watch a DVD from Blad's collection that they'd both seen a dozen times.

In early April, when her old friends were returning from spring break in Vail, Vivienne interviewed for an administrative position at the front desk of a gallery. She drove there early and waited in the parking lot, breathing through the fact that she'd never been on a real job interview. It didn't go well. The gallery owner, a small, quivery woman with curly hair, who seemed as if she might spring loose at any moment, told Vivienne that she liked her look but didn't like that Vivienne said she'd talk to the artists. The front-desk girl was not supposed to talk to the artists. It was best if the front-desk girl wasn't interested in art at all. Vivienne lied, insisting that she wasn't interested in art, but the gallerist shrugged. "It won't work," she told Vivienne, "the artists will be interested in you."

Afterward she stopped at a coffee shop to get hot water for the tea bags she'd taken to carrying in her purse. She was irritated that in trying to convince the woman of her own disinterest she'd also lied to herself. As she stood in line, a man in a business suit struck up a conversation. Vivienne ignored him at first, but he was cute in a Mediterranean way—wavy black hair, tan skin. He insisted on buying her a fancy latte and then flatly asked for her number. Flustered, Vivienne agreed.

The exchange didn't last two minutes, but, back in the car, Vivienne felt the old longings stirring. Who was he? And what could he be to her? Mostly, though, she missed sex. Stress usually made her forget about it, but now her body remembered. Yet there wasn't the same rush; somehow, the power she held over men wasn't intoxicating anymore.

Her phone beeped. *Was so nice to meet you. Dinner this week?*

The familiar thoughts kept coming: *Could he be the one? His suit looked expensive. What does he do? Should I sleep with him?* Her stomach growled. She pictured the fridge back at Blad's, stocked with condiments, peanut butter, white bread. This guy would buy her a nice dinner.

She responded: *What about tonight? Are you busy?*

No, how about 8?

She typed, *Let's do it*. Too sexual. She settled on: *Yes, where?*

They met at an Italian restaurant downtown, just the sort of place she'd imagined he took women. She'd been to places like it, with guys this guy probably worked with. Quiet, but not too quiet. Just casual enough to drink without feeling self-conscious. A long bar, and a bank of red booths. She chose the bar.

He remembered her name, but she'd forgotten his. He was Thisguy. Thisguy, ordering a plate of fried calamari and a bottle of red wine.

Thisguy was an analyst for a gas pipeline. He grew up in Dallas.

He maintained eye contact and dropped casual notes, like, "My new house," into the conversation. Vivienne understood that she was meant to be impressed. And she wore her loveliest impressed face. Thisguy, she learned, was actually pretty nice. But she was familiar with his routine. His eyes shone in that way that men of his milieu shone in her company. He was realizing how nicely she would fit into his life. How good she would look in that house.

"So why doesn't a girl like you have plans tonight?" he asked. "How'd I get so lucky?"

Because I was hungry. "I did have plans." She said. "But I canceled them." Tonight, she was flirty Vivienne.

Thisguy smiled. "Oh, really?"

"Maybe," she said.

"So what do you do?" He refilled her glass.

"I work in art." And then Charlie flashed before her eyes, painting in his mountain shed.

"Oh—at a gallery?"

"I'm actually looking for a gallery now," she said. "I worked for a private collector before."

"Are you into putting art in your house? Like, decorating with it? I'm looking for a decorator." He smiled. "I've got a lot of empty rooms."

She smiled back. "I can come take a look sometime."

He held up his glass. "I like how bold you are, just texting me like that. Most women wouldn't do that."

Vivienne amused herself with the thought that it was only her looks preventing Thisguy from seeing that her boldness rode the line of desperation. What he really meant was that most women who *looked like her* wouldn't do that. Thisguy was sweet but so buttered up on himself that he had no idea what was going on.

After dessert, they walked four blocks to his loft. He was packed for the move to his new house, but the bed was still set up. He poured more wine, which Vivienne sipped and then dumped down the bathroom sink. She didn't want to be drunk. She didn't know what she was doing, but she wanted to feel like she did.

They were standing in the kitchen, leaning against the black granite island when he took her waist and kissed her. His mouth was rough and sweet. In one motion, he tugged the tie on her wrap dress, and it fell open. Seeing her, he sort of growled and scooped her up. Vivienne felt herself drop onto the bed as he nosedived into her cleavage. She closed her eyes and tried to make it feel good. Mostly it felt ridiculous.

Thisguy stood, his erection pitched beneath his zipper, and grinned a victorious grin.

Now she was paying the price. She was supposed to do something with that erection.

She crawled under the covers. He joined her.

"Who are you?" he said dreamily.

"I'm not a decorator," she said.

He stopped unzipping his pants and gave her the blankest look she'd seen in a while.

"Earlier you said you have a big empty house you want to fill," she said. "You said it like you thought I was a decorator, but I'm not."

"Oh." He ticked an eyebrow at her. "Okay."

She was watching him roll on the condom, always a strange thing, when she realized absolutely that she didn't want him. She didn't want him at all. For the first time, she felt as if she was giving him something—she'd never felt this about her body—that she didn't want to give, something she should protect. But he was avid and ready and she'd given him every indication. . . . As he leaned over her, she pressed her hand to his sternum to hold him back.

"What is it?"

"I'm sorry, I can't," she said, feelings frogging up her throat.

He moved to her side.

"I didn't mean to lead you on," she said. "I thought I could."

"If you can't, you can't."

She didn't know how to read him. He was a stranger, after all. She noticed the sweat beading in his dark mat of chest hair, how he blinked at the ceiling. She wanted to go home to her air mattress.

"I'd like to see you again," he said.

She didn't want to see him again but kept it to herself. "That's kind of a condescending thing to say," she said.

"Why's that?"

"Because you're saying it like I'm lucky, like you don't usually want to see girls you pick up at coffee shops."

He rubbed his chin. "I didn't mean it that way."

"I figured you didn't," she said. "That's why I told you."

He hesitated. "Do you mind if I go to the bathroom and finish off?"

Afterward, he followed her to the door. His hair messy, his eyes heavy and soft, he looked nothing like the analyst-in-a-suit she'd met in line. She felt bad that she still didn't know his name. Driving away, she figured he might call or at least send a text. And she knew she wouldn't respond to him. Even though she felt a little sticky and unsatisfied, she was also relieved. He was nice, and she hoped he thought she was nice too. And that was it. There was really nothing else to feel but predictable emptiness at the fact that there was nothing else to feel. Goodbye, Thisguy. Her mind turned to Preston, the man for whom there was no predictable outcome.

She accelerated around the corner and hit a mean pothole. Within a few blocks the engine was clanking. She pulled over and tried restarting it, but it only hissed as if it hurt. She sat in the car, thinking that she could call Thisguy. He would probably come get her. If she handled things right, she could stay in his new house. She probably wouldn't even need a job. Things would be a lot easier. But she couldn't gauge what was easy anymore. What used to be objectively easy had become hard. She remembered Bracken's tumbler, still in the glove compartment, and threw it out the sunroof. It shattered in the dark street.

When she got back to Blad's, she found him on the couch, his computer in his lap, his feet propped up on her air-mattress pillow. The apartment was dark; only a corner reading lamp glowed over his head, dragging shadows down his face. He didn't look up or say hello. Vivienne wasn't in the mood to pep things up. She lugged in the suitcase of laundry she'd been storing in the trunk of her car and joined him.

"Do you have to put your feet on my pillow?" she said.

"Sorry," he said, and moved them.

She wrapped a fleece blanket over her shoulders. He was scrolling through a dating site. "See anyone promising?" She dropped her head onto his shoulder.

He clicked out of the window. "Nope."

"Maybe you'd like an older man?"

Blad put up his hand. "I don't want to talk about it."

"My car is dead," she said tiredly. "I barely made it home."

He pulled his shoulder away. "Your car died?"

"Yeah," she said. "I parked it outside. It won't restart. It just makes a horrible noise."

He crinkled up his face, as if he hadn't heard her right. "What are you going to do?"

"Walk, I guess," she said. "I hadn't thought about it."

"You're going to walk to find a job?" he said, his voice rising. "And walk to your job every day?"

"I'll get more exercise. I'll take the bus," she said. "I don't know, Blad."

He shook his head. "This is Houston, Texas. This is not Wiener Schnitzel, Switzerland. I realize that you don't follow the news, but we aren't exactly known for public transportation. I don't understand how you're going to find a job if you don't have a car."

Vivienne clamped the blanket over her body. "You're worried I'll be living here longer if I don't have a car," she said. "I would stay somewhere else if I could."

"Poor Vivienne." He rolled his eyes and went off to the kitchen.

She followed him, flicking on the overhead light. "Why are you being mean?"

He was glaring at the dirty dishes illuminated in their greasy sink soup. "It's like I'm supposed to have all this sympathy because normal life things are happening to you." He filled the kettle with water and lit the stove. "You've been here for five months."

"I'm trying," she said.

"You can't use my car," he said. "I can't be paying rent and lending you my car."

She wanted to remind him she'd never asked to use his car. But the whole thing was hard for them both, and it seemed wasteful to fight over who had it the hardest. Blad reached past her to grab his Davy Crockett YOU MAY ALL GO TO HELL, BUT I'M GOING TO TEXAS mug from the cupboard. He tore open his tea bag and poured the water over it. He could really be dismissive.

"I want to get out of here too," she said. "I don't love sleeping on the floor. There are little centipede bugs in the carpet."

"Would you prefer new wood floors?" Blad snapped. "And those are silverfish, and they're harmless, and there's only like a family of five of them in the whole apartment. Not my fault they like your area. Maybe you need to clean it better. But that's right—you've never had to clean anything in your life. You've spent your whole life taking advice from people who don't change their own lightbulbs. That's your problem."

Vivienne felt the heat of hurt feelings rise to her cheeks and spread to her palms. "I know it's hard for you, but it's hard for me too. And just because I'm getting used to"—she paused—"this kind of thing doesn't mean I deserve to have a hard time."

He bobbed the tea bag in the steaming water. His white T-shirt was pale yellow in the armpits; his faded black Thai fisherman pants sagged. He stood with his feet knotted together, one on top of the other.

"Blad?" Vivienne said.

He tossed the tea bag into the sink and hid behind his mug. They stood in silence awhile.

"I don't think you get it," he said finally, his eyes on the floor, his voice even. "This is what this life is. This is it. I hate lecturing you, but you have to think about consequences, and you have to think about other people. When you're rich you don't have to think about other people, but now you do—because you're officially poor, Vivienne. Do you get that? You can't keep living here like it's Vivienne-land, with your boxes and your suitcases everywhere, for as long as you want—"

"I'm not trying to stay here for as long I want."

He set his mug on the counter and rubbed his temples.

"I know I have to work," she said. "I get it."

"I don't think you get it. You have to *work*. My dad was a custodian at our high school for thirty-five years. He cleaned kid piss off the bathroom floor for thirty-five years."

Vivienne exhaled. "What are you trying to say? One minute you say you're supposed to be broke for something you love. Now you say you have to suffer and get by. Either way you lose."

"You have to do both," he said.

In the fidelity of his words, Vivienne felt terrified. She ached for consolation in Blad, but in his own way he was telling her there was none. Not the deep consolation she wanted. And there was no consolation for him in her.

Blad looked exhausted, pale bags beneath his eyes, his shoulders slanting. *This is what this life is.*

How many nights had he spent, drinking tea alone, after she'd complained for hours about something like not being able to afford a plane ticket to Cabo with Waverly? Vivienne was only now learning how it felt to be invisible; Blad had always known.

"What do you think Preston is doing?" she said. He felt such a long way off.

"Drinking coffee."

Vivienne nodded. "Probably."

"I know you miss him."

Vivienne nodded again. "I'll try harder, Blad."

She couldn't fall asleep. The street noise, her head swimming—the twitchy gallery owner, Thisguy popping a fried calamari into his mouth, her stack of unpaid parking tickets. Finally she sat up and opened Blad's laptop. Two new emails: an automatic notice from a temp agency that her résumé was received, and something from Timmy, subject line, *sorry.*

> *Hi viv,*
>
> *I know its been awhile. Ive been thinking a lot about everything I said back at your aunts funeral, and I wanted to apologize for showing up like I did and asking you to do those things. I feel really bad. Karlie is doing great. She's doing a big event at the bayou society tomorrow. Im proud of her. Shes not all bad. Im sorry again. Please dont tell anyone, please. Hope youre doing well.*

Vivienne went to the Bayou Society's website. There on the splash page was Karlie eating cherries from a ceramic bowl. She held one cherry between her teeth, her lips covered in a thick gloss. *Don't read any further,* Vivienne thought; *stop now.* But she couldn't stop:

> *The Bayou Society and* Houston Chic *magazine are pleased to invite you to the event of the season! Celebrate spring with Karlie Nettle of our favorite style blog, NettleBee. Karlie will take you on a photographic tour of her home and give you expert tips on*

how to create the space of your dreams with confidence and spunk! Let her teach you how to make your next dinner party shine with seasonal inspiration. Join us following the talk for a champagne reception in the azalea solarium, and meet Karlie!

In the morning, Blad came tapping on the wall. This was their way of pretending Vivienne had a door. She rolled over and blinked at him. He wagged her foot. "Wake up," he whispered.

She tried to sit up, but as usual she was stuck in the sunken air. "What is it?" she said.

He was wearing his striped pajamas, smiling. His whole face was a light. "I just got a call from the firm . . ." He paused, biting his lip.

"Okay?" Vivienne said.

"And they're taking me on full-time!" he cried. "Salary, benefits, everything! Full-time environmental consultant!"

It took a second for her to take it in, and when she did she yelped, instantly wide awake, and squirmed up to grab him. He shook his fists in the air and jumped on top of her. The impact popped the air mattress. They both screamed and exploded in laughter. "But, but, but, hold on—" Blad said, in a fit, slapping the pillow. "I can afford to buy a new one!" In that moment, there was nothing more plentiful or joyous in the world than Blad and his brand-new air mattress.

After Blad left for work, Vivienne decided her spirits were high enough to sit down and make a budget. But, counting it out, she found she only had one hundred three dollars to spare. That was not enough for a month of food, even if she only ate cheap food. Blad was right, she needed to work. She needed to work—now. She had to go back to the store. Financially it was her only option. She felt foolish for thinking she had the luxury not to return. She was prepared for the rude customers and the aching feet, maybe even the running into people she didn't want to see. She would hold her head high, and she would have enough money to buy groceries.

The bus ride was long and crossed parts of the city she'd never seen. She stared out the window—ghostly tracks of condemned apartments along feeder roads, a farmers' market in the parking lot of an abandoned big-box store, a woman in her car, resting her forehead on the steering wheel until the van behind her honked, the blue tarps of underpass shelters, snapping in the wake wind of big rigs. Gradually, the neighborhoods changed, becoming greener, until the bus turned onto Memorial Drive and the road opened into tree-lined, oil-money splendor. The bus stopped and several women got off, some holding the hands of their children. Her stop was next.

The speed and indifference with which the bus pulled away, leaving her there on the corner of Voss and San Felipe Boulevards, was astonishing. She knew this intersection in her bones, but she'd never seen it from this perspective. The streets struck her as wide and crowded, and loud in a scary way. She felt like a very small person in a world of mean cars.

The boutique was in the shopping center across the street. She stood waiting for the light to change, just looking at it. It was the same. Everything here was the same except for the flower beds. When she'd quit, there were yellow pansies, and now there were white periwinkles. She crossed the street and beneath the arcade and there she was, before the door marked in cursive: *Please ring bell.*

She pressed the bell and heard the chime she knew so well. A girl who looked like she could be her younger chestnut-haired sister came to the door, smiling.

"Hi," she said. "Welcome!" Her teeth shone white, her straight hair glistened, her whole being announced itself in pink cashmere and saltwater pearls. As Vivienne followed the girl inside, the smell hit her like a punch in her face. Her past had a very sweet odor.

"Are you a bridesmaid?"

"No, I'm Vivienne; I used to work here."

"Oh!" she said. "I'm Ainsley!"

"Hi, Ainsley," Vivienne said. "Is Maddie here?" Maddie—the store manager—was usually there in the mornings, preparing for the day's fittings, setting the work schedule, pinning plastic silver *Bride!* tags on rhinestone tiaras, the store's party favor with a wink: We know you wouldn't really wear anything this cheap, but isn't it fun to pretend?

Ainsley made a pouty face. "No, she's not here right now, I'm sorry."

Her voice tightened at the end of the sentence, so that "sorry" seemed to ooze from her nose.

It hadn't occurred to her that Maddie may not be there. "Do you know if y'all are hiring? I've been away—traveling—and I'm thinking about coming back. I worked here for three years."

"That's amazing. I just started two months ago. I love it. So fun."

Vivienne smiled.

"It's so fun to be a part of so many girls' special days."

Vivienne kept smiling.

"I don't think Maddie's hiring right now, but I'm sure for you it doesn't matter. And you know we always need help this season."

"Right," Vivienne said. "Lots of fittings for the summer weddings."

Ainsley's face got serious, conveying the toil and enormity of the coming summer season. "Totally," she said. "Let me just call Maddie and tell her you're here."

She went behind the counter. Vivienne caught a citrus note in the air as Ainsley swung her hair over her opposite shoulder. "You want something to drink?" Ainsley mouthed, the phone to her ear. "Hi, Maddie! It's Ainsley; how are you?"

Vivienne fiddled with the jade friendship bracelets in a wicker basket on the display case. They'd been moved to the other side of the counter. Vivienne had ordered these herself after reading that jade signified love, that it was said to bless everything it touched.

Ainsley said, "Well, guess who I'm here with?" There was a pause. "Vivienne!"

Another pause.

"Cally?" Ainsley whispered to Vivienne.

Vivienne nodded, picturing Maddie scrunching up her face, sitting in the bayou-view office of the condo she shared with her husband, who seemed as if he lived in New York. Ten years Vivienne's senior, Maddie had always been nice in the most professional way. She'd treated Vivienne with a pleasant degree of distance.

"Yeah, Vivienne Cally!" Ainsley said. "She says she's thinking about coming back! We need extra help for fittings, right—" Ainsley went quiet. She glanced at Vivienne and nodded. With every subtle alteration of Ainsley's face, Vivienne knew.

She hung up. The light in her bright green eyes—contact lenses, Vivienne thought—dimmed. "I'm sorry," she said. "Maddie says she has all the help she needs."

Vivienne felt the chill of Ainsley's voice like a north wind. Perhaps she'd never entirely trusted the warmth of the women she'd known because of the speed with which that warmth could turn.

"What did she say?"

"That we don't need any help." She squeezed up her voice again. "But thanks."

"I realize that," Vivienne said. "But I want to know what she said. I know that's not the reason."

"I'm sorry."

"Please tell me what she said."

Ainsley shifted her weight. "I don't know what to say."

"Just say what Maddie said."

She pouted her lips impatiently. "Maddie thinks it would be inappropriate."

"Inappropriate?" Vivienne calmly stared her down. Every dark thing in her wanted to destroy every precious, curated detail of this girl-woman behind the glass counter. Vivienne wanted terrible things to befall her so that these dresses would look to Ainsley as they did to her, like frilly, limp corpses. There was a part of Vivienne that even wanted to take Ainsley to the back room and pound the innocence right out of her, so that she would just answer truthfully, and without that nasal voice, because Vivienne knew that nasal well, and she knew that no woman really spoke like that.

She turned and left, walking out the back way. Ainsley called after her, "You can't go back there!"

She pushed the door open hard and ran behind the dumpster and threw up. The sun was shining hard. She had no car to hide in, nowhere to stand in the shade and close her eyes. She held her hair back and spit, then leaned against the brick wall. The panic ebbed. Now she just felt empty.

Ainsley peered outside and grimaced. "Are you okay?" she said, disgusted but sympathetic, not nasal at all.

Vivienne wiped her mouth on her forearm and stood upright. "I'm fine."

She made her way to the French café in the next shopping center. After washing her mouth and face in the bathroom, she ordered a hot water with lemon, and a miniature oatmeal cookie, and sat by the front window. The café was busy with women lunching. They were so engrossed in one another, laughing too loud, sharing quiche, listening empathetically to gossip. She'd spent many hours in this café, doing the same thing.

She took one sip of the hot water and let it go cold. The cookie was soft and bland—*like me*, she thought. She remembered Timmy's email, remembered Karlie eating cherries from a ceramic bowl. At once her self-pity hardened to anger, at all these oblivious, annoying women, at how invisible she felt, and at Karlie Nettle—for everything, for the whole sad, erratic mess of her life. Karlie Fucking Nettle. Who'd never had to account for a dime in her life. Who never worried about anything despite all her self-obsession, all her meanness. Well, not today. She checked the time and left.

THE BAYOU SOCIETY occupied a plantation-style mansion, bright white with black shutters, set deep in the jungle of Buffalo Bayou and, being a playground for garden clubs all over Texas, belted by expansive manicured grounds. A long pebbled driveway led to the entrance. Beside the guard station, a sign read *Welcome NettleBee*. The guards were unaccustomed to seeing anyone approach on foot. They asked Vivienne for her name and were delighted to inform her she was not on the list. With her most persuasive feminine charm—it came back to her in an instant—she replied that she was one of the organizers with *Houston Chic* magazine, that her car was parked in the staff lot, and that she had just gone out the back way to drop some things off. One guard made a call, but when no one answered they both gave up and let her pass.

Women were gathered on the front steps, wearing colorful spring dresses and chatting beside potted hibiscus trees. Waverly was there, laughing, bouncing baby Grace on her hip. Her hair was long and layered around her face. She was wearing a short white eyelet dress. Vivienne hung back and watched as the women filed inside, then followed a few minutes later.

The solarium was beautiful, a huge sun-drenched hexagon of glass overlooking the lush lawn, where peacocks grazed beside koi ponds. Pink azalea garlands hung from the vaulted ceiling; each white chair was draped in linen and tied around the back with a ribbon the same shade of pink as the azaleas. All of it reminded her of past days, when she took this kind of loveliness for granted, when she needed this loveliness. Now just the sun shooting a blade of pink light through the stained-glass ceiling dome onto the Mexican tile floor amazed her. It was like being inside an azalea bloom, except for the air-conditioning. It probably wasn't so cold inside an azalea.

She noticed Waverly talkng with Reis beside the champagne fountain. Waverly was mid-sentence when she saw Vivienne. For an instant she froze, her face darkened, and between them everyone else disappeared; then she turned back to her conversation, seeming to purposely direct Reis's attention away. Vivienne felt momentarily bloodless. She stared at Grace, a pudgy thing with Waverly's big eyes and Clay's hairline. She wanted to run, but anger held her still. The women, about eighty in all, took their seats, and a long-limbed woman in a polka-dot blouse introduced Karlie as their very own "belle of the blog." And then Karlie took the podium.

Seeing her, Vivienne realized she had almost forgotten what Karlie looked like. She'd forgotten, or maybe she'd never seen, what force Karlie possessed, what a presence she was before an audience. She was skinnier than Vivienne had ever seen her and wearing a floor-length teal prairie skirt with a starched white button-down shirt tied at the front. Her hair was stick-straight and deep red, and she wore a heavy turquoise necklace under her collar. She was striking, and yet—watching her take in the applause, brushing her hair behind her shoulders—Vivienne had to look away.

"First of all, I just want to say how incredibly happy I am to be here," Karlie said, signaling to an assistant, and the podium was carried off. She spoke into a little wireless microphone attached to her ear. "I remember coming to the azalea solarium with my mom for afternoon tea, and for cotillion in high school, as I'm sure we all do, so how fun is it to be here all grown up!" She laughed, and the women applauded. "I also want to thank y'all for reading my blog. It's definitely a labor of love, and I obviously couldn't do it without my amazing readers. I'm so excited to share my home with y'all. I really want to inspire other women as they jump into doing their own homes."

Long silk drapes were drawn across the windows, and for the next half hour Vivienne sat through a slide show of staged professional photographs, of Karlie's kitchen, master-bedroom suite, backyard pool, media room, personal office, and game room. After the slide show, in the light of the open glass, Karlie took questions. Vivienne could tell she was relishing it, sitting in her plush floral armchair, sipping champagne as she answered, as if soaking in a bubble bath. She paused deliciously over each question, pursing her lips over how hard it was to decide on carpet instead of wood for the bedroom floors. But glancing over the listening faces in the crowd, Vivienne realized that it wasn't all vanity on Karlie's part. She seemed to be answering a need. In the women's faces, she saw validation of their own hopes and efforts.

Cake was served, and Karlie vanished to a back room. Vivienne wanted to talk to Waverly alone. In trying to be casual and mingle as she waited to follow Waverly out, she noticed there were two groups of women—those who talked about their children, and those who talked about their work. The women who talked about their children seemed to know she was an imposter; they hardly opened their circles when she approached. Yet standing there awkwardly with her champagne, she felt foremost in their awareness, as if her exclusion was conscious and enjoyed. She slipped away.

The women who discussed work were friendlier. One woman kept saying, "That's not a very entrepreneurial choice for your site," to another, who replied defensively, "But I'm not trying to be an entrepreneur." This declaration, spoken loudly, silenced the circle and made every eye glance around and see Vivienne.

"What do you do?" they asked.

Vivienne didn't know what to say. She became very aware of her physical self, how unadorned it was by comparison, how plain she had become.

"Nothing right now . . . I'm between—I'm myself," she said. "I guess that's what I do right now."

The women just looked at her, waiting for her to explain.

Suddenly a finger was lifting her hair. "Is that hard to do? Being yourself?" A few women laughed.

It was Reis, accompanied by Waverly, holding baby Grace. Waverly wasn't laughing.

Reis cleared her throat. "Kar's coming out."

As the room burst into applause, Vivienne said to Waverly, "Can I talk to you?"

Waverly's eyes skimmed the room and stopped on Karlie, who was shaking hands and kissing cheeks. Karlie's painted eyes brushed over them both, and in the subtlest instant, Vivienne saw her surface disturbed. Timmy was close behind. They made eye contact—it felt like a flinch—and Timmy looked the other way. Vivienne knew, all of a sudden, that no matter what she said or did, it wouldn't make a difference. Timmy would always stand behind Karlie. And who would stand behind her? Who would care? Vivienne had no ammunition but her own injured heart and eyes that saw what no one here wanted to see. Even if Karlie lost Timmy, and the blog, and the money, Vivienne was still alone. And wouldn't she be more alone then—reduced to such a vengeful person? She wouldn't even have her heart anymore, just her injury.

"Follow me outside," Waverly said.

Waverly led Vivienne down a small gravel path, to the rose garden. The roses were beginning to bloom, dotting the flat green lawn with color. Vivienne could hear the bees. They sat on a bench hung from the bough of an old live oak. Waverly put Grace on her lap and gave the child a pacifier off her finger. She'd been wearing it like a ring. Vivienne watched

Waverly carefully, something inside her silently exploding. It had been months since they'd spoken. She looked older and less girlish. She was a mother.

"She's beautiful," Vivienne said, taking Grace's fat hand. The tiny fingers wrapped all the way around Vivienne's pointer finger. Grace gurgled at the appearance of a new thing to squeeze.

"I'm surprised you're here," Waverly said, only glancing at Vivienne.

"I knew you'd be here." In her determination, Vivienne had only wondered if seeing Waverly would be awkward. Instead, it was sad.

Waverly pushed off the grass and they swung gently. The chain creaked. Grace made a happy coo through her pacifier. "You look tired," she said. "Too skinny."

"I am tired," Vivienne said.

Waverly put her lips against Grace's head. "I'm tired too."

"Your dad—" Vivienne began.

"I'm not discussing my dad. I'm not discussing anything about that." But then she kept talking. "He didn't do anything wrong. People don't like him because he's successful and knows how to run a business. He's efficient. They want to take him down because he's efficient. He shouldn't be punished for being successful. He's worked hard his whole life. He deserves his success."

"I was just going to say I hope you're okay," Vivienne said.

"But you don't hope he's okay, right?" Waverly shook her head. "You probably think he's guilty."

Vivienne didn't answer.

"I feel like I should be mad at you," Waverly said, her eyes firmly on Grace. "But I'm not."

Vivienne knew that Waverly was wearing her bravest face. She did this when they were young, tried not to cry. Vivienne was the one who got to cry, never Waverly. She was too bright, too positive; she was the light others needed to keep from crying.

Vivienne wondered how she could manage to tell Waverly what she came to say.

Waverly said, "I left you messages. I was worried about you. I wanted to be with you at the funeral. I had a baby and you never called."

Without thinking, Vivienne grabbed Waverly's hand and held it. She recognized the way it felt as Waverly, soft and bony, a little bird. "I'm sorry," she said.

"I had a baby and you never called," Waverly repeated. She pressed her cheek against Grace's little head and broke, lifting her eyes to Vivienne for the first time. "I've needed you. It's been so hard to do this without you." She paused, wiping her eyes. "You don't need me like I need you."

This was the time to tell her everything, but the secrets she came to reveal—Karlie's secrets—struck her now as petty and ugly. It was a sudden and peculiar feeling, needing absolutely nothing from Karlie or the Bayou Society, wanting nothing of that life.

"I know I have to let you go," Waverly said. "You needed to leave us."

Grace blinked up at her mother. Vivienne was filled with a wordless ache, adrift in her own motherless world yet anchored to the love of her oldest friend. She had caught Waverly's hand as they drifted, this very meeting bringing them together, also pulling them apart on disparate currents.

Vivienne wrapped her arms around Waverly's shoulders. She couldn't talk without touching her. "I'm sorry I ignored you. I didn't know what to say."

"I miss you," Waverly said.

"I miss you too," Vivienne said.

"I pray for you every day."

"You do?"

Waverly nodded. "Always. I think you're the bravest woman I've ever met."

Vivienne closed her eyes to soak in the light of these words—*I think you're the bravest woman I've ever met*—and hugged Waverly tight, knowing she would never hug her like this again. Above them, the oak spread its limbs mightily. Something at the base of its trunk caught Vivienne's eye—a plant she recognized.

Growing in the gnarl of the roots was a young, frail edelweiss flower.

Vivienne went over and knelt near the flower. She almost picked it for Grace but thought better. How unusual for a Swiss mountain flower to be growing in Houston. A spindly white flower with yellow sunbursts in its center, not particularly pretty compared to the roses but very much itself.

Waverly knelt beside Vivienne, Grace on her shoulder. "What is it?" she asked.

Vivienne pulled up some grass and rained it over Grace's fuzzy head. "Edelweiss flower," she said. "It means noble purity."

ON HER WAY home, she got off the bus two stops early. Something about the sunset light was especially beautiful, like God's light. It gave her a warm, vivid feeling, and she wanted to walk in it. In the neighborhood, she recognized right away that she was close to the Menil. The museum would be closing now, but it was lit so nicely in the evenings. She would stroll awhile and see it.

She'd only gone a few blocks farther when she realized where she was really going, pulled by the same feeling that drew her off the bus. It was down this street that she had walked with Preston that spring day two years ago. The recollection stirred her old visions of the future. The woman who'd passed this way at Preston's side thought she'd be married by now. The changes that had brought her back here instead felt as subtle as the changes in the big trees arching against the pink sky. They looked no different to her eye, but the time had breathed through them as well.

His apartment was fully snuggled in ivy now. How strange to be here, returning home from her aborted mission to expose Karlie. She could see the lousiness of the idea through Preston's eyes. The knowledge that in her need to clear her own name she'd almost implicated his filled her with a deep shame, and a deeper gratitude that she had known better. She wanted something more after all, something good. Was it so terrible that he'd known this about her before she knew it about herself? That he'd tried to coax her into seeing it too? She could no more resent him for his mistakes than she could claim she hadn't made mistakes of her own. Hadn't they both tried their best? So what if their best wasn't very good.

Just then a light brightened the window. A moment later the door opened. Vivienne knew she should go—it would be awkward to be caught on the driveway like this—but her feet wouldn't move her away. It was Preston. He'd come back. And he was taking out the trash. The bag was too full—he held it out as if something was dripping and made his way down the stairs to the trash bins. Seeing him, her heart rested: For so long he'd been so *big* in her mind, so hurtful, but really he was just a nerdy, skinny man who took out the trash in crew socks, boxer shorts, and a T-shirt, someone's son.

He was back up the stairs before he paused and turned around. He squinted at the driveway.

"Vivienne?"

Without even knowing it, all this time she'd missed his voice. "Hi," she said.

He jogged down the stairs. When he got closer, he stopped. "I smelled you."

"You smelled me?"

"That's why I turned around," he said. "I didn't see you. I just thought it smelled like you suddenly."

"That's funny."

"It's a good smell." He was backlit by the window light, but she could see he was smiling. He looked just the same.

"I was walking by," Vivienne said. "My bus stops nearby—I didn't think you were here."

"Your bus?"

"I moved." She wanted to sound casual but couldn't. "You came back."

"Turns out I missed Texas," he said, with the same caution in his voice. He brushed his fingers over his hair, which was a mess, as if he'd just woken up, and then glanced down at himself. "I'm sorry about what I'm wearing. I would have put on pants if I'd known I was going to see you. I'm just really surprised to see you. How have you been?"

"Good," she said. "Fine. You?"

"Good, fine." He shifted his weight. "Do you want to come up for a minute?"

She could tell he was trying to be light. She answered quietly, "I'll miss the bus. Thanks, though."

"I could give you a ride home."

It would be so easy to say yes. *Yes*. Wasn't it the single word they'd each needed to say all along? It would be so good to trust him again, to tell him everything, to fall into his warm quilt, to land in the arms of his day. And still she couldn't say it. "I should go," she said.

"Okay," he said. "I feel like I'm saying the wrong thing—"

"It's okay; me too."

They stood in silence. The sky was getting dusky.

"Will you stay here?" she asked, after a moment. "In Houston, I mean."

"I don't know, depends on work," he said. "My firm from Paris has some connections in Seattle."

She cleared her throat. All the old crannies of her heart longed for his sanctuary, but she could not move closer. "I know you didn't mean to hurt me," she said.

Preston crossed one hand over his stomach, rested his free hand on his cheek. Up in the trees, the cicadas broke into song, breaking the quiet. "Thank you for knowing that," he said.

She saw his eyes on her only dimly but felt them distinctly. "Good luck," she said. "I know you'll do well wherever you end up."

"I know you will too." He opened his arms.

Vivienne nodded and let him enfold her. The word was yes, the word was love, the word was us. They held very still together. She let go first. "Take care," she said.

She walked away fast. Around the first shadowed corner, she buckled. Her bag slid off her shoulder; she braced her hands on her knees. The pain streamed through her heart. She let it hit her straight on.

The full moon was rising. For an hour she walked through the neighborhood, crossing Buffalo Bayou all the way to Washington Boulevard, the oldest street in Houston. Night had fallen. The convenience stores and parking lots were all lit up. She was turning toward Blad's when she noticed a white clapboard house set back from the street—a feed store. It was probably the only original house left on the street.

Taped inside the window was a handwritten sign: *Hiring! 'Cause, dear Lord, I'm retiring!* She cupped her hands against the glass. Inside, baskets hung from the wood-beamed ceiling, and feed bags were stacked alongside ramshackle antiques. A vision of breathtaking clarity came to her: handmade quilts, mobiles made from all kinds of unlikely objects hanging from the ceiling, and beautiful paintings—paintings by her friends Kitty and Charlie. The picture unfolded with such spontaneous harmony that she felt caught by it, alone on the doorstep, blinking at the treetops in benediction.

She went around to the back. There, behind the hurricane fence, she found ducks and chickens. In the moonlight, she could make out their round shapes resting in coops under the canopy of two enormous magnolia trees. The hens made curious peeps; a screech owl noted her appearance from some unseen branches; a duck honked. The land had an earthy tang to it, foreign to the big city—sweet magnolia blossom, damp mulch, guano, and mana. Vivienne smiled. *How wonderful.*

That was a memorable day
to me, for it made great changes
in me and in my fortunes.
But it is the same with
any life. Imagine one selected
day struck out of it, and think
how different its course would
have been. Pause, you who read
this, and think for a moment
of the long chain of iron or
gold, of thorns or flowers, that
would never have bound you,
but for the formation of the first
link on one memorable day.

—CHARLES DICKENS

I

BLAD INSISTED. HE WOULD CO-SIGN SO THAT SHE COULD get a lease and would loan her enough for two months on a place that didn't require a first- and last-month deposit.

He was her adviser. Never rent an apartment with high turnover. Ask questions. Avoid buildings with live-in landlords. A dated kitchen was one thing, but a hot plate was entirely another. If she wanted the place to feel like home, she needed a stove with an oven, even if the stove was from Montgomery Ward circa 1969. Try not to rent an apartment with a plastic tub, unless she wanted to spend her evenings relaxing in what was essentially a big plastic bin. In that line, a "vintage" place with details like tile, built-in bookshelves, and those 1950s bathroom heaters was always preferable to a new place with no character.

If she rented in a cheap landscaped development for young singles, with hollow granite countertops and walk-in closets and white cotton-ball carpet, she'd only be fulfilling the prophecy of some real estate developer's idea of his consumer, and soon her character would become as generic as the plaster walls. He accompanied her to meet landlords in case the landlord was a rapist. On the weekend, they drove around looking for FOR RENT signs, listening to Blad's Official Apartment-Hunt Playlist, while at night they both worked, Vivienne on applying for jobs, Blad on environmental-impact reports.

The apartment in the Heights, just a few miles from Blad's, was an upstairs studio at the corner of two neighborhood thoroughfares. The landlord insisted on a one-year lease and one month's security deposit, but he allowed Blad to co-sign. The building was beige stucco and bland, built sometime in the sixties, with old beige carpet and and gray linoleum in the bathroom, but it had a stove, and the tub was porcelain, and there was an interior courtyard. Two hundred fifty square feet, including the kitchen and bathroom, for five hundred twenty-five dollars a month.

She sold every shoe and every dress there was left to sell, painted her walls pale yellow, and lined the windowsill with grocery-store African violets. She stocked the cabinets with mix-and-match dishware from Goodwill. On the wall beside the front door, she hung Kitty's watercolor of Matagorda Bay, and in the bathroom, right next to the mirror, two small canvases of the Alps, sent by Charlie.

On her birthday, Blad took her shopping for cheap furniture. He was happy to do this, because he could afford cheap furniture now. He strode through the big store with a serenity about him, touching the smooth surfaces of things. He bought a table and chair set and a dresser and passed his old ones on to Vivienne. As a birthday present, he bought her a mattress from the as-is department so that she didn't have to sleep on an air mattress anymore. They set it up on the floor. Draped over it, her old floral duvet had the look of an expensive rug.

That night, they sat against the wall in the studio and shared a container of boxed champagne, passing it back and forth between them, drinking from the spout.

"Happy birthday," Blad said, handing her the box.

"Happy birthday to me," Vivienne sang.

"I'm proud of you," Blad said.

"I'm proud of you," she said.

"You've got your own apartment on your thirty-second birthday."

Vivienne smiled. "I've never had my own place before."

"Just don't forget to turn off the stove," Blad said. "And please don't leave your keys hanging in the lock."

"I love you, Blad," Vivienne said. "Thank you for everything."

"Love means never having to say thank you," he said extravagantly, and winked. "But you're welcome."

She slept in her old sheets. They'd been balled up and sealed in a box and still smelled like the room where she grew up. She made a nest of them and lay listening in the glow of the streetlights: cars thrumming by outside, louder than she'd imagined. Drunk people yelling. Muted thuds, muddled voices, a dog yapping. She thought she'd be more frightened than she was. Her heart was calm. The four thin walls felt, if not like home, like a home.

II

VIVIENNE GOT TO KNOW A FEW OF HER NEIGHBORS, AND they were mostly women. There was the old woman who'd lived in the building since the sixties, who had a hovering and mousy way of coming and going. Vivienne harbored quiet fears of becoming this woman, of thirty years from now possessing the same feeble, scurrying manner. There was also the happy woman, whose abundant positive energy seemed a compensation for that of the old lady. She hugged everyone, so much so that after the first few hugs, Vivienne didn't feel very special about it anymore.

For a month now she'd been nannying three days a week for her next-door neighbor, Audrey. They'd met a few days after Vivienne moved in, when Audrey knocked on Vivienne's door after Vivienne left her keys hanging in the lock. Audrey was a private caretaker who worked for elders in empty mansions in River Oaks. She and Vivienne discovered they were the same age. Audrey had a three-year-old son named Arthur, a sprightly kid with a pile of brown curls and matching gaps between his top and bottom teeth. Arthur stayed at day care or at his grandmother's during the day, but Audrey was taking extra shifts just to cover the day care and her mother lived across town. She asked Vivienne if she would help for nine dollars an hour cash.

Today she went to Audrey's at two. The scene there had become familiar: Audrey in pink scrubs, tooting around the one-bedroom apartment, dropping toys into piles and giving Vivienne random instructions. She kept her black hair back in a loose ponytail and wore white nurse shoes with a confidence reflected in her impressive posture.

"If he wakes up and starts going ballistic, you can let him watch a show, but only one show. Otherwise, draw or something. Or take a walk. And don't let him play with your phone. I made a casserole for dinner. He pooped right before he fell asleep, so you probably won't have to change anything atomic. I promise he'll be out of diapers soon. I'm giving myself till next week. It's nuts. He's not getting into his preschool if he's still in diapers. We're doing daytime pees now, but he's still scared to poop. I promise, any day now. Sing him the potty song if he pees in the potty."

She began conducting with her finger, singing to the melody of "Jingle Bells," "Artie pottied, Artie pottied, Artie is a big boy! Artie pottied, oh, yes, he did, what a big smart boy he is!"

Audrey was a tiny person whose energy belied her frame, with big blue eyes and a permanent tan, the legacy, she told Vivienne, of her Italian ancestors. She was the kind of girl who would have intimidated adolescent Vivienne and Waverly at the mall simply by being so forthright and brunette. When Vivienne had answered Audrey's knock, Audrey handed over the keys and said, "Good job." She was blunt with life details, revealing them with the same cavalier ease she did the childcare instructions. She'd dropped out of Sam Houston State in Huntsville because she thought the classes were too easy and she wanted to earn money, not sink into debt, so she moved back to Houston and got certified as a home health aide.

They stood over the crib in the bedroom Audrey and Arthur shared. Audrey shook her head. "It sucks," she said. "He doesn't have a dad. But the thing is," she said, leaning in, "I think I made it happen because I feared it so much. I think subconsciously I thought I only deserved to be a single mom."

Vivienne looked down at Arthur. He slept as hard as he played.

"Have you been to a lot of therapy?" Audrey asked.

"No," Vivienne said. "Have you?"

"Here and there. Girls from the west side don't go to therapy unless their parents send them, right? Like, their parents have to legitimize their problems before they help themselves?"

Sometimes Audrey said things Vivienne only somewhat understood. "I don't know," she said. "I was just thinking that I used to feel like I didn't deserve to be anything else but a rich guy's wife."

"Better to be a pretty girl in a crappy studio apartment," Audrey said. "You know how many women actually want the privilege of being bored?"

"Because it's a lot less stressful," Vivienne said.

"Well, if it counts for anything, I've done a great job making my life stressful."

"So have I," Vivienne said.

Arthur woke an hour later, wailing "MOMMY" in his usual ear-splitting way. Vivienne bargained with him—one video and then a walk. He watched *Thomas & Friends* as if he were a mental patient, his round eyes glassy, apple drool running down his chin. He was so blazed out on the screen that he didn't notice her staring. She loved how Arthur was basically openly insane. He said things that made no sense, had little control over impulses, danced at random, and often mumbled to himself. He was the most fun and sincere human she'd ever met, the first child she'd ever known. She liked his scruffiness. He was a no-nonsense guy.

Once Vivienne asked him if he minded going to day care, and he replied, "Mommy has work." Vivienne remembered her own fancy-pants day care and the over-air-conditioned concierge bus that dropped her off in the afternoon, to a house occupied by a silent housekeeper wiping down an already-spotless countertop. She and Arthur—they were both day-care kids.

He darted out of the bedroom, his black sneakers blinking red behind him, and flexed his biceps. "Rarrrrr!" he said. This meant he was ready to go.

She pushed him around the neighborhood, pointing at the flowers, asking him about the colors. He squealed, "Boo! Wed! Gween!" He was still getting the hang of yellow, orange, and purple. They stopped at a park on a quiet street of apartments, and Arthur ran it out while Vivienne jogged after him. He ran in circles, leapt like a clumsy gazelle, rolled around, and dug little holes in the grass where he claimed "the air-pwanes would land." So Vivienne got down on her knees and made her hand into an airplane that landed, much to Arthur's delight, in his shallow dirt hole. He ran to her to sip from his water bottle, flapping his arms like a pterodactyl.

"Let's go to de sweeping star," he said.

"What's the sweeping star?" Vivienne asked.

"It's ober dere," he said, pointing to a wisteria bush in wild bloom.

She wiped his nose as he wriggled away, then crawled after him through the opening in the branches into the hollow of the wisteria. It formed a delicate umbrella, like the secret underside of a waterfall, sunlight beaming through fractured branches.

"Dis is de sweeping star," he said, very serious.

"What does the sweeping star do? Should we sweep?" She sat cross-legged.

"No, sweeping!" he cried, stomping his foot and plopping down. "Like nighttime nap."

"Oh, sleeping?" Vivienne said. "The sleeping star?"

He nodded. His gapped teeth shone out from his mouth. "It's, it's, it's—" He sighed, and wiped the curls from his forehead with the back of his dirty hand. "It's de, it's, it's when de—" He furrowed his brow, then grinned. He'd found the word. "Magic! It's when dere's magic."

Vivienne gasped. "There's magic here?"

He nodded fast. "Yes, and de people, de people, dey come here, and dey get de magic!" He held his arms open wide and puffed his cheeks.

"Wait, wait," Vivienne said, closing her eyes. "I smell it, Artie. Do you smell the magic? Doesn't it smell good?"

Arthur sniffed. "And de people, dey get the magic because dey smell!"

"Yes, they smell it." Vivienne reached for a hanging purple blossom and held it under his nose. "This is purple," she said.

He giggled, without verifying whether he'd smelled anything.

Vivienne brought the flower to her nose—the sweet, magic scent of wisteria, a weightless purple blossom in her palm.

"Who aw we?" Arthur asked suddenly. He wanted to understand the game. The people came here to breathe magic in the flowers, but who were the people?

With a stick, Vivienne drew a circle around them in the dirt. "We're the people who live here," she said. "We protect the magic." She lifted some pollen from the ground with her fingertip and wiped it in two lines across Arthur's cheeks.

"We de good guys."

Vivienne smiled. "Yes we are." She dabbed the pollen onto her own cheeks.

Arthur clambered to his feet. "My gotta go peepee!" He pulled his pants and training diaper down to his ankles, stuck out his belly, and urinated at the base of the wisteria, his tiny, chub-pocked buttocks clenched with effort. When he finished, he pulled it all back up and turned around with big eyes. He was nearly out of breath.

Vivienne put her hands atop her head. "You know what this means?" she gasped.

He froze, then screamed. "My peepee in de potty!" To Arthur, anywhere other than his diaper was the potty.

Vivienne took a deep breath and opened her mouth, hanging there as Arthur looked on with a delirious smile. "Ohhhhhhh . . . Artie pottied! Artie pottied! Artie is a big boy! Artie pottied, oh, yes, he did, what a big smart boy he is!"

Beneath the shelter of wisteria, he danced and danced as she sang, and finally fell into her lap, limp with triumph.

III

"WELL, YOU'RE ALIVE," RANDAL SAID.

Vivienne stood in her doorway and crossed her arms. "How did you know I live here?"

He took off his black Cutter hat. "I called the post office and asked for your forwarding address."

"Is that legal?"

"Don't know. The mailman owed me a favor. Can I come in? Last time I saw you, you kept me outside in a hurricane."

He'd trimmed his beard so that it didn't connect to his chest hair anymore. The sheer size of his body made letting him inside her apartment, which was a mess, with the unmade bed in plain sight, impossible.

"Hang on." She grabbed the yogurt she'd been eating for breakfast. Barefoot, she stepped outside and shut the door behind her. "Want to sit in the courtyard?"

He glanced over the railing. Below them was the courtyard, a communal, treeless square spotted with puddles. "There?"

"Yep," Vivienne said, already on her way down the stairs.

"So you don't want me in your apartment," Randal said, taking a seat beside her on an iron bench. "You still know how to shoot them darts, Cally."

"It's a mess," Vivienne said.

"Well, this bench is a little damp," he said, "but that was some good rain last night. Clouds are moving fast."

Vivienne looked up. Low, gray clouds were streaming over from the Gulf. She ate a spoonful of yogurt. "So, what are you doing here?"

"I'm here simply as a messenger of friendly greetings," he said, lifting his hands. "Nothin' more."

"You came by to say hi to me?" Vivienne said.

"I tried calling," he said. "I got a cell phone. I'm not just a door knocker."

"I have spotty service," she said. "I don't always pay the bill on time."

"All right," he said. "I am here simply as a messenger of friendly greetings, and I have a pair o' box seats to George Strait tonight."

Vivienne laughed. "Nice ulterior motive. Whose box?"

"My box," he said. "No strings attached. I'm not gonna talk about trying to have dinner with you or any of that stuff you don't wanna hear about."

"It's not just that I don't want to hear about it," she said. "I don't want you to think about it."

"Harsh dart, Cally," he said. "You used to care what I thought."

"That's because I was scared of you."

"Well, a lot's changed," he said. "For one, I quit smokin' cigars."

"Randal, do you wear a doctor's coat with a cowboy hat when you see patients?"

He laughed. "You bet I do."

"Do the women still have a lot of spider veins?"

"You bet they do," he said. "You're feisty. I like this new, hardscrabble Cally." He slid his boots over the concrete. Someone had inscribed it in fingertip print: JIM 1968. "You think Jim is still around?"

"If he is, I hope he doesn't still live here," Vivienne said.

He squinted around at the building. "You doin' okay?"

She became aware of her hair, tied back in a messy bun, and her sweats, stained with Arthur's tempera paint.

She nodded. "I'm fine."

"You're not gonna tell me anything, because you think I'm gonna go screaming back and tell everyone what I find," he said.

It was clear he was joking, but she didn't find it funny, not because she cared but because she felt so distant from the person who did care, or had the energy to care. "So are you in the inner circle now?" she said. "It's not easy to get a box, especially for George."

She hadn't seen George Strait in many years, but there was a time in her life when she saw him every year when he came through for the Houston Livestock Show and Rodeo. The rodeo in all its bright, manure-stinking glory—she loved the livestock show most, especially the chubby auctioneers singing their mumble beside steers the size of compact cars. George Strait was always the biggest night; she and Waverly looked forward to it for weeks, hyperactively lip-synching in Bracken's Astrodome box, or down on the floor, in the first rows, swooning over George's butt.

Randal snickered and scratched his short beard. His hands, she noticed, were so milky and soft.

That was what gave him away every time. Randal couldn't play a good ol' boy with hands like that. Even Bucky, privileged city boy on a four-wheeler that he was, had rough spots on his hands.

"I had what you might call a revelation," he said.

"That it's lonely at the top?"

"Not exactly, but that's one to keep in your back pocket," he said. "Old Richard Cory."

"Who went home and put a bullet through his head," she said. "I remember studying that poem in college."

"Well, here I was at the gala for the grand opera," he began, "or maybe it was the ballet, but it was at the Wortham. Last Christmas. Place all decked out with the giant tree and all the lights and holiday crap. Real pretty. And I'm standin' there havin' a whiskey and thinkin' about when I first moved to Texas. People were sad back east, and it was cold. If you've ever been to Delaware you know what I mean. The sky is dark all winter, and where I grew up it's full of factories. Guys with lunch pails going home, and smokestacks. I wanted to move somewhere the sun shined. Somewhere big and not crowded in a bunch of other states. I chose dermatology because it's a way I can help people feel good. People laugh at dermatology, but acne is no small pickle. You've probably seen these pocks under my beard. I still don't want people to see 'em, but I know they do. Acne is a trauma. People with good skin take it for granted. They don't realize how hard it is to have something you don't want on your skin. I believe beauty's on the inside and all that, but bottom line is, wantin' to have nice skin isn't just superficial. I believe it helps people find the confidence to bring out their inner beauty and all that stuff."

He shot Vivienne a glance for emphasis.

"When I got out of med school and came here, I didn't know squat. I bought some old guy's practice and I put my face all over town, and then people started coming in. And everyone was nice to me. And they started to ask me for money, so I thought, why not, I'll give it to 'em. And the more you give, the nicer people are. That felt good. I realized there was an echelon where people were the nicest, so to speak. I decided I wanted to get there. And it was all to make things more beautiful. Skin, painting, museums, dance, symphony, culture, whatever."

As he spoke, his accent dipped in and out of Texas and Delaware.

"Whatever I can do with my money to make this city more beautiful, I'm gonna do it. I grew up surrounded by ugliness, and it's hard on the spirit. Houston needs it. We got a zoning problem. You know they're namin' a park after me in Conroe? I saved an arboretum."

Vivienne smiled. "That's nice."

"Anyway, so I'm standing there at this gala, and I realize I hit the top, because this isn't a small invitation. This isn't one of those things where they invite everyone with money so they can get more money; this is, like, they're not even asking for money, they're just invitin' you."

"Congratulations," Vivienne said.

"Don't sass it, Cally, I'm not finished," he said. "I'm in this kinda blissed-out moment of accomplishment, and I hear over my shoulder a woman say somethin' like, 'You have to talk to him; everyone knows he's desperate; he'll give anything to a woman; I'll come save you in five minutes.' Something like that. And I think to myself, it's a dog-eat-dog world. And then appears this gorgeous woman who starts talkin' to me about kids, school lunches, giving me her card, that kinda thing. It took me a minute to put it together, and then, sure enough, along comes the voice I heard, all charming, saying she had to introduce her to so-and-so."

"You realized they were talking about you," Vivienne said.

"I did," he said. "I admit it hurt like hell. Made me feel like a hurt kid again. Like everyone was in on the joke but me."

"You really didn't know people talk like that?" Vivienne said. "I've heard you talk like that."

He nodded. "I had a taste of my own cheese, and I didn't like it. It's strange seeing how other people see you and realizing it's a whole lot different from how you see yourself."

"Especially when you know you played a role in making them see you that way."

"Right," he said. "It's my doing too. But my opinion of me dudn't change just because they have some wrong ideas about me. Far as I'm concerned, I'm still top dog."

Vivienne dropped her head and cracked up. "Well, I'm still not interested."

He hooted. "You're different, but you're the same Cally. You know something? I'm not interested either. The funny thing is, even if I hadn't had my revelation, I still wouldn't be interested in you anymore."

"Good," she said.

"Now, let me get it clear," he said. "I'm not interested in you because I realized I didn't want to play the game anymore. I realized the game wudn't fun, and I wudn't makin' any real friends, and that my way with you was barkin' up the wrong tree. But if I was still climbin' the ladder with my nose in some Tomball gal's ass, well, then you really wouldn't do me any good now like you woulda in the past. Your stock's plunged."

"Thanks, Randal."

"You're welcome."

"So what are you going to do now?" she said. "Buy a house in the hill country and open a small-town practice?"

He balked. "Nah, I'm still in it. I'm just not buyin' into it. My pride is out of it. That was my mistake. I like the game better when I know how to participate. Now it's not so people'll like me, it's because I earned the money, and it makes me happy to do what I want with it."

Vivienne hesitated. "Did you know what Bracken was doing?"

"No," he said. "But I can't say I'm surprised. Raisin' thirty million for some condo project and bailin' himself out in the meantime."

"Bailing himself out?"

"Properties that lost money," he said. "Repayin' investors with funny money. Funneling cash through that art nonprofit. Boosting his lifestyle."

"Do you think he'll go to jail?"

Randal shrugged. "I guess we'll find out soon. He's tellin' everyone he didn't know anything about it. Says it was the people below him. He bought up a lot of land he's gotta get rid of now. Lots of opportunity."

Vivienne thought of that office, the hushed machinery of it, and the boisterous tenor Bracken cast over the whole operation. There was no way he wouldn't know something like that was going on. It was more likely that he was the only one who would know.

"You know, I can get rid of those blackheads for you," Randal said, tapping his nose but looking at hers. "No charge."

"Thanks," she said. "It's good to know you can see them from there."

"Do you need money?" Randal asked.

"No, I don't need money."

"You do probably need money," he said. "You're just not gonna—"

"Take it from you," she said. "I'm not going to take money from you."

"How does it feel living poor?"

Vivienne rubbed her forehead. "I try not to think of it that way."

"I bought a property off Bracken," he said. "You know the old feed store on Washington with the animals out back? He was gonna raze it and build more of those flashy condos, but he had to turn it over. He dudn't know it was me who bought it."

"That old house with the big magnolia trees? You own that place?"

Randal's eyes turned intricate and maybe a little misty. "Can't say exactly why I bought it. I felt called. I like Washington Boulevard. Full of history."

"What are you going to do with it?"

"Don't know either," he said. "Sit on it till I lay an egg."

"Are you going to run a feed store?"

"Why, you want to run a feed store?"

"I wouldn't know how," she laughed.

"Well, you could figure it out," he said.

"Maybe it could be something. There aren't a lot of places like that left in the city. It's beautiful."

"That's what I'm saying. Hell, I told the old guy who runs the business to keep it open. He's retiring, but I say keep the place alive. Last thing we need is more condos and another parking lot. We got enough of those. I like to take the long view."

"Maybe I could help."

Randal turned and looked at her square. "If I heard my ears right, then you and me should have a serious talk soon." And then his eyes widened. "Who's that?" It was Audrey, walking upstairs, a grocery bag in one arm and Arthur in the other.

"That's my neighbor," Vivienne said.

"You think she wants to go to the rodeo?" he said, a touch shy.

Vivienne lingered on him a moment. "Hey, Audrey," she called out. "Come down here for a sec."

Audrey put her groceries inside and came downstairs in her scrubs, Arthur on her hip. He tilted her slightly. She was spraying mosquito repellent on his legs. She glanced over Randal, then glanced over him again. "Are you that dermatologist guy on the commercials?"

He stood and held out his hand, clutching his hat to his middle. "Randal Stanley."

Audrey stood a full foot shorter than him. She raised her hand to shake his and opened her eyes toward Vivienne. "Do you know this man?"

Vivienne smiled. "Yes, sort of. Yes."

Randal cleared his throat. "My friend Vivienne is indifferent about accompanying me to see George Strait tonight. I was feelin' a little sorry for myself, but then I saw you walking there, and I realized that I don't even want to take my friend Vivienne—I want to take you. And I understand you're the neighbor."

Audrey turned bright red.

"You should go," Vivienne said.

Randal nodded. "I hear George is retiring soon."

Audrey cleared her throat. "Can you give us a minute?"

Randal patted Arthur on the head and removed himself to the street. "Who dat guy?" Arthur said, pointing after him.

Audrey whispered, "Is he for real?"

"That's just how he is," Vivienne said. "He's kind of slimy at first, but he's actually fun and funny."

"Slimy? How do you know him?"

Vivienne wasn't even quite sure how she knew Randal. What surprised her in answering the question was that she did feel as though she knew him. "He's an old friend," Vivienne said. "I can watch Arthur."

Later that afternoon, Vivienne and Arthur watched Randal and Audrey drive off to see George Strait together. Audrey agreed to go under the condition that she drive. From the sidewalk, Vivienne held Arthur's wrist and made him wave. She had to laugh—in a million years, she could not have imagined the sight of Randal Stanley's big black hat pressed against the roof of her neighbor Audrey's Camry.

IV

TWO MONTHS LATER

IT WAS JUST ANOTHER HOT DAY. AUGUST WAS ALMOST over. The clouds were big and blinding white, and at the horizon, things seemed to melt. Inside the expensive coffee shop where Preston sat impatiently checking the time, it was freezing. He was surrounded by ladies lunching, casting him snoopy glances. She would be there soon. For a guy who used to find it annoying when people spoke of the "universe" as though it was their personal Magic 8 Ball, he had come to receive its wild declarations as genuine. Today he awoke and he knew—call her and ask.

Since the night he let Vivienne walk away for the second time—though it had felt like the hundredth, like she'd always been walking away from him—he'd called himself a lot of names. He'd said all the wrong things, he'd blown his chance, he'd watched the gold slip through his fingers. She had landed on his driveway like an angel, and he'd let her fly away. He derided himself because the outcome hurt—their separation, his distance from knowing where she'd been in those months since Paris, what she'd done, what she'd felt. Details so precious and stricken from him.

He'd been working as much as possible, freelancing for a firm that couldn't afford to hire him. Once in a while he had a beer with Blad, but he never asked about Vivienne. It felt too too easy, like an invasion of something sacred. It wasn't what she wished, he knew that much.

Blad was absorbed in his job, busy and thriving, a last, tacit connection to her, someone they shared.

When he stopped berating himself, things clarified. Letting her go was right. He had broken his own heart, but he had followed through. Depending on how he looked at it, he was either cowardly or brave in letting her go, but, really, he was neither. He'd never had the power to change her or convince her of anything. He felt lucky just to know her and amazed that he'd gotten to kiss her. She was the woman who taught him how to love. He wanted her to be happy.

He checked the time again. Now she was five minutes late. The table wobbled under the weight of his elbows. He folded a napkin and slid it under its short leg; when he sat up she was coming through the door.

He immediately stood. "Hi; thanks for meeting me."

Waverly put one hand self-protectively to the small gold cross pendant on her chest. "Hope there wasn't too much traffic coming over here," she said, sitting down.

She seemed even more nervous than he was. It was weird being alone with her. He'd always felt he had nothing to talk to Waverly about; observing her discomfort now, she'd probably felt the same. She didn't want anything to drink, not even water. She'd just come from Starbucks.

They got through the usual pleasantries. She was less peppy than he'd imagined. Maybe she hated him, he didn't know. Her pink collared shirt looked professionally pressed, and she sat straighter than any woman he'd ever seen. She listened as he went on, asking her for Vivienne's new contact information. He was taking a job in Seattle next month, and he wanted to see her before he left. He didn't tell Waverly his more exact intention: If Vivienne asked him to stay, if she so much as smiled at him in a way that even suggested she'd want him to stay, he would stay.

"Do you think she'd want to see me?" he asked.

"I don't see her very often," Waverly said. "I don't know."

The way she said it, with reluctance, it occurred to Preston that actually they did share something: They both missed Vivienne. He remembered how severely he'd regarded Waverly, how he'd held her up as a symbol for why it could never work between Vivienne and him. Preston felt galled by his pretension on a daily basis lately. "I think I owe you an apology," he said. "If I was ever dismissive to you."

"I don't remember us ever talking much," Waverly said.

"But I was—I thought Vivienne shouldn't be friends with you." It came out harshly, but he was glad he aired it.

She didn't seem to mind at all. "I thought the same thing about you. Maybe I was mad at Vivienne for caring about you—I don't know, because I didn't get you. She never talked to me about you, but I always had this feeling you would take her away."

"I didn't," he said.

"No, you didn't," she said.

"I didn't get you either," he said.

"I still don't get you," she said. "But my husband likes you."

He laughed. "Fair enough."

"I do think she'd want to see you," she said. "She always liked seeing you."

She gave him Vivienne's new address and phone number. He drove straight there. It wasn't far from his own apartment, that graduate-school apartment from which his income had yet to graduate. He climbed the concrete stairs. It was hot, and the concrete made everything hotter. It was hard to reconcile her with such a bland apartment complex—she was so inextricably braided with beauty to him that anything less seemed tragic. But he had to stop himself here. She would hate that.

Still, as he knocked, the particleboard door light against his knuckles, he couldn't help trying to piece together the unlikely arc that had led her here and that led him here now. He knocked again, more eagerly. This time the force of his hand ticked the door open. It creaked, drifting on its hinges. Without entering, Preston looked inside.

A small, tidy room, lit through a single rectangular window. He beheld the picture of her little world—a pair of black slippers by the door, the leather shaped by her feet, a half-full glass of water on the counter in the kitchen corner, a child's drawing taped to the fridge, a trio of floral pillows lovingly arranged on the bed, a line of violets on the windowsill.

She couldn't even help it, infusing beauty into the dimmest of places. He felt quiet, near to her. The room smelled so much like her, that enchanting particular sweetness, that he could have grabbed the sweater hanging by the door and buried his face in it. He noticed the painting on the wall—a quiet Texas landscape—and remembered her words in the Rothko Chapel that day: *I believe happiness is more powerful than sadness.*

"What are you doing?"

He turned around and saw a woman, compact and displeased, a sweaty, adorable toddler on her hip and a casserole dish covered in foil in her free arm. "I'm looking for Vivienne," he said.

"You're letting her AC out." She brushed past him and went inside, sliding the casserole dish into Vivienne's fridge. Then she came back out of the apartment, and with one adept hand, closed and locked the door behind her. "Why are you poking around? Who are you?"

"I'm Preston. I'm a friend of Vivienne's."

Suddenly her face opened. "You're Preston," she said. "I've heard of you."

Preston didn't know what to make of this. He just tried to be as polite as possible. "Do you know where she is?"

She replied matter-of-factly, "At work."

"Bib-bee-in!" the toddler said.

"Can you tell me where she works?"

She narrowed her eyes. Maybe she would tell him, maybe not. Just then a large man appeared from the apartment next door. Preston was sure he recognized him—*no way*, it couldn't be—but as he approached, Preston felt certain. It was the guy in the bolo tie. And he was still wearing a bolo tie. He put his long arm around the woman and said, "You're the guy who's been looking for Vivienne?"

"I've never been here before."

The bolo-tie guy nodded. "Naw, you're him," he said. "We met a good while back, not formally, but I remember you. I knew you'd come around sooner or later. I'm Randal Stanley."

The woman smiled. "Audrey Navarro, and my son, Arthur."

"Mommy! Wandal! Awfur!" Arthur cheered.

"Nice to meet you all," Preston said. He felt very tentative and confused but also determined. "Can you tell me where she works?"

Audrey and Randal glanced at each other. Something passed unsaid between them. "Old Washington Boulevard," Randal declared. His voice had a resounding quality; it bellowed through the heat and against the walls. "The white house with the pretty trees in the back."

PRESTON FOLLOWED THE address. He parked on the street so that she wouldn't see him pull up and waited a moment in the car, staring at the house. He could tell it had good bones. To think he'd driven by it a thousand times, unconscious of its future meaning. He was still unconscious of its future meaning. He knew something was going to happen, but it was still *before*. He was sweating intensely.

He went up the walk and opened the door; some cowbells jingled. It was hot and sticky inside. Through the back window he saw a few men in painter's overalls, cleaning brushes and folding tarps beside a coop of large golden chickens. He wandered around, hardly noticing anything—he was only looking for Vivienne. To his great surprise, he found her in a back room, ripping out laminate flooring. He could have watched her all day. She must have sensed he was there, because it was only a moment before she looked up. She was wearing a dirty T-shirt and baggy cotton shorts, a red bandanna tied over her hair. She was as sweaty as he was. For an instant, Preston didn't recognize her.

She got to her feet. "Well, hi," she said. "Where did you come from?"

He didn't know how to answer that. "What are you doing?" he asked.

Her cheeks were flushed, her eyes bright. "New floors."

He could hardly believe it, but it felt as if they'd just talked yesterday. It was that easy with her. He began to peer around, out the back room and into the main space. The setting came into focus. The room was being cleared out and painted but also preserved. "A gallery," he said.

"I'm really only doing the floors and putting on fresh paint," she said. "But not on the ceiling. I love the old cedar." She paused. "I'm keeping the animals. I want it to be a little sanctuary."

Preston didn't know what to say. She had to know his silence said it all.

"I got a loan," she said. "Father Bennison helped me—my aunt's priest. Part of the profit will benefit the church ministries. There's more space upstairs, but it's just storage. Maybe one day it can be an arts camp for kids, I don't know, or I'll live in it—there will be air-conditioning." She smiled at him, the clearest, unpretending smile.

There it was.

Preston faced her. "Do you think you'll need an architect?"

Her eyes changed. In the faithful span of those seconds, she looked at him as though she'd always been waiting for that question.

"Yes," she said. "Do you know one?"

Preston nodded. "Yes."

Epilogue

Vivienne Cally Weds Preston Duffin

Miss Vivienne May Cally and Mr. Preston Thomas Duffin were united in marriage on May 5, on the banks of the Seine River in Paris, France. The ceremony was officiated by Kitty Crawford of Beaumont, Texas, and Paris, France. The wedding party included Mr. Randal Stanley and Mrs. Audrey Navarro-Stanley of Houston, Mr. and Mrs. Clay and Waverly Fitcherson of Houston, Charlie Reed of Austin, Texas, and Tom Jennings of Wengen, Switzerland. Serving as flower girl and ring bearer were Grace Fitcherson and Arthur Navarro-Stanley. Escorted by herself, and presented in marriage by herself, the bride wore her late mother's handmade wedding gown and sandals from Thailand given by the best man, City Councilman Bladimir Caro of Houston. Following the ceremony, the bride and groom hosted a picnic in Ms. Crawford's garden. After a honeymoon in the Swiss Alps, the couple will reside in Houston. The bride will keep her name.

Acknowledgments

I'm indebted to the great Edith Wharton—who wrote the beautiful story that inspired me to write this story. Heartfelt gratitude to Susan Golomb and Caroline Zancan—you both brought this novel to life. And to Kate Levin, Diane Brown, Andy Hall, Sidney Goldfarb, Lee Krauth, Aram Saroyan, Tony Barranda, Mitra Parineh, and Maggie Flynn—thank you for being such wise and generous first readers and believers. Thank you dearest Rita Williams—for being my champion and friend. Your guidance and reassurance meant everything, and made the difference.

To my family—Vanessa, Jeff, Lincoln, Oscar, the Seymour Nation, and my parents Michael and Suzette—thank you for so much joy and love and encouragement. During many uncertain years of writing, I knew your support was always certain. And to my sweet mom especially—thank you for listening to me every day, for teaching me kindness, patience, and resilience, for loving me into being. To my dad, thank you for telling me all about situational awareness, for teaching me to ask questions and see the world with a sharp, creative eye.

And to Toben, my steadfast North Star—we made it here. Thank you love.

Finally, deep gratitude to my grandparents and to my great-grandmother Suze van der Zee-Spruyt, who always wanted a writer in the family and whose faith in me I can feel.

About the Author

YVONNE GEORGINA PUIG was born and raised in Houston, Texas. She currently lives in Santa Monica, California, with her husband.